WINTER SHADOWS

TENTH OF THE PRAIRIE PREACHER SERIES

P J HOGE

iUniverse, Inc.
Bloomington

Winter Shadows
Tenth of the Prairie Preacher Series

iUniverse books may be ordered through booksellers or by contacting:

iUniverse
1663 Liberty Drive
Bloomington, IN 47403
www.iuniverse.com
1-800-Authors (1-800-288-4677)

ISBN: 978-1-4759-3576-9 (sc)
ISBN: 978-1-4759-3577-6 (ebk)

Library of Congress Control Number: 2012912180

Printed in the United States of America

iUniverse rev. date: 08/22/2012

With special thanks to Sarah and Mike H.

For more information, please check out:
www.PJHoge.com

At early dawn, a 1968 blue Monaco with a black hardtop plowed westward down the dirt road nearly obliterated by snowdrifts. The back window and one of the back doors consisted of duct taped plastic to keep out the blustery elements. The intoxicated driver's vision was nearly obscured by the ferocious ground drifting and the snow flurries. He had everything he could do to keep the vehicle on the road and moving. Finally, he approached a spot where the snow had blown clear of the road. The driver tromped down on the gas.

He gained speed as he came to the top of a hill, forgetting completely there was a turn just beyond. The car careened into a ravine, landed and rolled four times before coming to rest. For a brief minute, there was a lot of noise. The crunching of metal, breaking of glass and last vibrations of the engine before it went dead. The sounds of the machine obliterated the sound of bodies hitting the frozen earth.

Then there was a moaning, a child's whimper and then it was silent. The only sounds were the whistling of the winter wind across the prairie. It was if nature had won the battle over man and his machine, and now could return to control of the prairie.

1

The early morning wind whistled across the frozen North Dakota prairie to deem every loose snowflake airborne. When the sun finally tried to come out, it was nearly obliterated by the low gray clouds and light snow. While the wind made the buildings shudder, just looking out the window was enough to make a person's bones shiver.

It was nearing the end of February 1971. Everyone was ready for spring; everyone except Mother Nature. She was not about to relent early and seemed determined to give the central plains a second dose of winter.

The alarm rang and the lights came on in the old two-story farmhouse. The house was old but well cared for and in the last year, a large addition was built to the north and west. Elton and Nora Schroeder owned the farm.

The house had originally been the home of Engelmanns and later sold to Nora and Elton. The elderly couple lived in a small home nearby until Lloyd's Alzheimers progressed to the point that tiny Katherine, though spry, could not care for him alone. Lloyd was in his early eighties and although very thin, was quite tall. When he started wandering at night, they moved back in with Schroeders. Elton installed the 'Pa Alarm', which alerted everyone in the house when Grandpa decided to go outside alone. The Pa Alarm wouldn't stop him from going out, but would let the others know so they could go retrieve him.

The morning ritual at the Schroeder household began when that alarm went off. Everyone except Grandpa Lloyd dressed and gathered in the kitchen, coffee cup in hand and stared blankly at the coffee pot while it perked. There, they gradually regained consciousness. Coffee was the lifeblood of the group. If they were awake, there was probably a cup of coffee nearby.

Grandma was the first one in the kitchen that February morning in 1971. She started the coffee pot. She was about four eleven and was lucky if she weighed ninety pounds dripping wet. She had sparkling blue eyes, pure white hair and a big loving smile.

The next to come into the kitchen was Elton. He was in his mid-sixties. He loved Katherine and Lloyd Engelmann more than most folks did their real parents. His own family had been a mess, and he felt an extreme loyalty to these folks.

Elton mostly had a big smile and a happy nature. He gave Katherine a kiss on the cheek, took his cup and turned to stare at the coffee pot until it finished perking. The mechanic and farmer was about five seven and slightly built. However, he had a huge heart.

The door from the mudroom opened and his son, Kevin Schroeder shivered in. He was about five eleven, in his early thirties, and the family cut up. He came over from his home half a mile to the west every morning and evening to help with chores.

"Brrr! Got some coffee? I spilled mine coming up the steps," Kevin asked. "You guys need salt out here. Have you got some in the mudroom?"

"Yah, in that bag."

"Okay, I'll throw it out there so the steps can clear before we go out."

"Thanks Son, I appreciate that," Elton nodded. Then he kissed his wife who had joined them.

"My, it looks frightful out there," Nora said. Almost the same height as her husband, she was a slender, graceful lady in her mid-fifties. Her hair was soft auburn and her eyes were dark brown. "I'm hungry for something different for breakfast. Any suggestions?"

Grandma thought, "Hot oatmeal with canned peaches. We have some seedless grapes too. What do you think?"

Elton frowned, "No rolls or meat? Bacon, sausage? Why a guy could starve plum to death around here!"

Grandma grinned, "Oh don't worry. I'm sure we can dredge up some caramel rolls from the freezer."

"Now you're talking."

Kev came back in the house, rubbing his hands together to get warm, "I hope the weather breaks before you guys take off to South Dakota. When are you planning to leave again?"

"Sunday afternoon. If the weather isn't nicer, we'll put it off. Neither Byron nor I want to get our two wounded veterans stuck in a snow bank."

"Good thinking. It is four above, but the wind is howling at least forty miles per hour. The wind chill has to be well below zero. Andy and Horse wouldn't last ten minutes in this mess." Then Kev added, "There are miles of nothing between here and Pine Ridge."

"What about Pine Ridge?" Andy asked as he took down his coffee cup. He was Schroeder's youngest son who had just returned from Vietnam. He had lost both his knees to artillery fire and was now walking with a walker. He was becoming more accustomed to his artificial knees, but couldn't manage very far without his walker. He was improving but still struggled with his many leg injuries. "I could probably stand the weather, but Horse couldn't."

"Horse couldn't what?" the other young veteran asked as he came into the kitchen in his wheelchair. Jackson Fielding was Andy's Army buddy and lost his right foot in the same firefight that injured Andy. Because his family situation wasn't very good on the Pine Ridge Reservation, he was unable to go home to recover. Consequently, Schroeders invited him to their home. The trip to the Pine Ridge Reservation was to visit his family. "I can do as well as you, Spud."

Spud was Horse's nickname for Andy. The whole Army unit called him that. They called Jackson – Horse, short for Crazy Horse.

"Yah, yah," Andy laughed. "I can just see you hopping through the snow banks."

"I wonder what kind of tracks you'd leave with your walker?" Horse teased.

Kevin asserted, "The wind is blowing so hard there's nothing that even resembles a track!"

Elton groaned, "Don't care how either of you'd do. I don't want to be out in this weather any more than I have to."

Andy and Jackson had not been down to help with the chores yet because of their wounds, but they were beginning to get around much more. They would both be starting to work for the Schroeder family-owned service station in Merton. Elton and Kevin had set up a small engine shop

3

in the back of the family garage not far from the house. In a couple weeks, Andy and Jackson could work there doing small engine and appliance repair. It wouldn't be full time so they could set their own hours. It would give them something to do while they were healing.

"You think we won't go to Pine Ridge then?" Horse asked expectantly.

"We're sure going to try," Elton assured him. "But it won't do us any good to get stuck in a snow bank between here and there. Don't worry Jackson, we're sure going to try. I know you want to see your family."

The ring of the phone so early was startling. It was Jackson's Uncle Bear calling from Montana. Elton answered and said, "Jackson is up. I'll hand him the phone." Then he hesitated, "Sure, I can talk to you."

Jackson frowned with worry when it was obvious that Bear wanted to talk to Elton. The expression on Elton's face did not ease his concern.

Elton listened and then sat down while Bear continued to talk. Everyone in the kitchen was now spellbound in Elton's half of the conversation. Finally, he said, "Have you talked to Byron? Okay, you do that and I'll tell Jackson. I'm really sorry. We'll see you soon. Take care."

Elton hung up and turned to Jackson. "I need to talk to you alone. Let's go to your room, okay?"

Jackson lamely nodded and moved his motorized wheelchair toward his room. His doctors insisted that he keep his leg up, while the amputation of his foot and ankle was healing. He had been plagued with serious infection and there was worry he might lose more of his leg. Even though he could get around with his crutches, he needed to spend most of his time in the wheelchair with his leg up. It would be several months before he could get his prosthesis.

The two men went into the room and Elton sat down on the chair by his desk. "Uncle Bear heard from your Aunt Mabel this morning. There's some very bad news from Pine Ridge. He is talking to Byron now, and we'll be leaving as soon as we can for there."

"What happened?" the young man stammered.

"We don't know for certain yet. Your Mom, Clayton and two of the kids went out last night. They aren't home yet. It isn't unusual that your parents stay out all night, but the kids were both quite sick with bad coughs. I guess the other kids have it too, but not as bad. Apparently, your folks were going to Whiteclay, Nebraska to buy medicine for them."

When he said Whiteclay, Horse's head snapped in instant anger, "They don't sell medicine in Whiteclay! All that's in Whiteclay is four liquor stores! They went there to buy booze! The folks live near Three Moccasin Park southwest of Pine Ridge, so Whiteclay is only about two miles south of there. What time did they leave last night?"

"About eight, eight-thirty. Aunt Mabel expected them back in about an hour. She didn't know if that was the only place they were going to stop. So, they may have just gone to someone's home and stayed because of the bad weather."

"Don't try to sugar coat it. My check was deposited yesterday! Mom got some cash and they went to pick up booze. They might have had an idea to pick up some cough medicine too, but Clayton went to get booze. Which kids went along?"

Elton frowned, "I don't mean to pry, but don't Indians receive a monthly stipend from the government dependent on what percentage Indian they are?"

"Most folks think that, but it isn't true." Horse explained. "They only receive money if the tribe has a settled claim. Our tribe hasn't. Some tribes pay monthly amounts to enrolled members as a percentage of the tribal income; like for timber, land leases and such. So no."

"I guess like most things, we really don't know until we take the time to look into it."

"Yah, I know most white folks think that we get money, but we don't." Horse nodded. "Which kids were along?"

"The two youngest. Mabel called the police and they're looking for them now, but that's a double-edged sword. They stand a great risk of losing the custody of all the kids. Mabel is beside herself, so she called Bear. He's on his way out there now. He was going to call Byron and then leave for South Dakota. Mabel also called her son and he's going to pick her up. She isn't staying there any longer after your folks get home, no matter what. We'll be going there, too."

"In this weather? It's horrible! When I get ahold of my parents, I'll strangle them. What in hell do they think they're doing?"

"Look, they aren't thinking. Let's not borrow trouble. Okay?" Elton gave the young man a hug, "Let's go finish our coffee and wait for Byron to call before we get organized. Are you okay to go to the kitchen?"

Jackson nodded stoically, "There isn't anything else to do, is there?"

"No," Elton nodded sympathetically.

2

Byron drove in and gave a quick knock but came right in without waiting for an answer. "I just talked to Bear. I'm so sorry. We'll go down right away. I called Zach, too."

Byron took the coffee that Grandma had handed him, and said, "I called Pastor Adams. He's convinced the kids will be taken away. The social worker talked to them yesterday. The kids are all sick, malnourished and the house was cold again."

Now Jackson was furious, "I paid the fuel bill for the gas furnace! What happened this time?"

"Seems the whole tank went to a neighbor! The only heat the kids have is from the oven. Mabel said it has been running for two days straight."

"That does it! I can't afford to keep this up, no matter how many sketches I sell! The more I give, the more they blow! I need to just get back there. Sitting up here is stupid!"

"Jackson, you can't go back there." Kevin stated definitely. "The VA doctors won't let you go back. You'll do no one any good if you lose more of your leg, or worse. There's no bus service on the Reservation to get to your treatments at the VA. We'll figure out something. Just cool your jets."

"I know you guys believe that, but reality isn't like that! I keep thinking there has to be a way. Maybe it'd be better if the kids are placed in Foster Care." Jackson nodded, and then fought back the tears. "But they'd be split up. They are counting on me!"

Grandma gave him a hug, "I know. The plan to have Mabel stay there wasn't as successful as we'd hoped. When I heard that your Mom traded away the kid's winter coats, I could've gone down there myself! No wonder Aunt Mabel is about bonkers."

"Look, we've been trying to figure out a way to make this work," Nora said. "I'm going with you guys. I want to see how things are."

Horse studied her for a minute, "I don't know what to say. I'm mortified. Mom was a neat lady; but after my dad died and she turned to the bottle, she's changed. It's almost like her spirit died right along with him. I never knew Clayton when he wasn't drinking. He doesn't get physically abusive, but he sure has a horrible tongue when he's drunk. I know they love the kids, but you could never tell the way they treat them. It makes me sick. I really don't want anyone to see that."

"Jackson, I know how it is. Elton's father was a mean drunk, physically and emotionally. I had a brother that committed suicide when he was in his late twenties because of alcoholism. We know that it isn't your fault or the kids fault. We wouldn't think less of you at all."

"Thanks, but it's still grim."

"How old are the kids again?" Nora asked.

"Eight, seven, five, three and nineteen months. Why?"

"I have something percolating in my head, but I'm not sure yet." Nora hugged him, "I'm going to go change my clothes and throw our things in a bag."

There was another knock at the kitchen door. This time it was Zach Jeffries who came in. "What's up? I came as soon as Byron called."

Over a cup of coffee, Zach was filled in on the details of the morning. "I'll call the office and ask them to reschedule me. I'll take off until Wednesday. Let me go home and to get packed. We'll take my Suburban, so we have more room."

"I'm taking the station wagon, too." Elton said. "You coming, Andy?"

"Yes, I plan on it. Think I can, Zach?"

"That's part of the reason I'm coming. In case you and Jackson need something." Zach nodded, "And I want to see what's with this cough the kids have. We can take two cars. It might be a good idea to have two vehicles in this weather."

"I already talked to Marv, and he'll handle the church services on Sunday," Byron said. "He said to tell you he's praying for a good outcome."

As he went out the door, everyone dispersed. Some went to get the chores finished, some made breakfast, packed food and lunch baskets and clothes for the trip. Elton checked the oil and filled the cars with gas.

While Jackson was packing, the phone rang and it was Katie Ellison, Pastor Byron's daughter. They were sweet on each other and had a bond, but both acknowledged they were too young for a serious relationship. However, they were extremely close. He took the call in the sewing room.

"Hi Kate," he said. "Thank you for calling. I wanted to call you right away, but didn't want to wake you."

"I've been awake since Dad got the phone call from Uncle Bear this morning. How're you doing?"

"I'm worried sick and angry. I'd just like to shake my folks! What do they think they're doing, driving around in this weather with sick kids? Clayton's car barely runs as it is, and the last I saw it; the back window was just plastic and duct taped shut! I'm just sick. Kate, I just know there's something really wrong."

"Me, too. I'm praying for you. I really wish I could go down with you, but Mom says there will be too many to go along, and I can't miss school. I wish I could. Is there anything I can do to help you?"

"Yes, actually there is. I have some more sketches done for the clinic order and those three are finished for the gallery. Could you give them to Matt so he can deliver them? No one else will know what goes where. I'd really appreciate it."

"Of course, I'll talk to him today. I know where your calendar is and order list. Don't you worry about it."

"Thanks, I don't know what I'd do without you."

"You'd do fine."

"Kate," Jackson's tone became very serious, "I depend on you more than you know."

"Me, too," Kate answered softly. "Hey, whatever you need, I'll be here for you. If you get a chance, could you call me? I'm worried for your family."

"I'll call you. I promise. I wish you could come, but maybe it's best that you don't. Thanks for calling."

Soon, the group was assembling in the kitchen. Zach had picked up Byron and helped Andy get in the Suburban. Jackson got in the front seat of Elton's station wagon while Nora curled up in a blanket in the back seat. After waving goodbye, they pulled out onto the gravel road. It would be an eight-hour plus drive to Pine Ridge, depending on if the condition of the roads.

3

The roads were crumby and difficult but passable. The wind was unrelenting and punctuated with snow flurries. The three in Elton's car drank coffee from their trusty thermos and visited quietly on the drive.

"I can't believe that both Byron and Zach took off work to come down with us. Is there something that you haven't told me?" Jackson asked.

"Horse, you're part of our family. Of course they'd help. Zach knows what it's like when life takes an ugly turn. Since he is a pediatrician, he can take care of the kids—and you and Andy. Besides, they're going to take the kids away. We all know that it isn't good that those folks have been missing almost twelve hours in this weather. Or doesn't that worry you?"

"Yah, if Mom and Clayton were alone, I wouldn't worry. With the kids, I'm really worried."

"Besides Aunt Mabel is leaving today, regardless of your parents," Nora pointed out. "We need to get this taken care of, sooner rather than later."

"I have to just go back to the Reservation. I don't know what I was thinking; sitting up here," the nineteen-year-old berated himself.

Nora was lost in thought a bit and then asked, "I need to know if you've been happy staying with us, Jackson? I mean, do you think your life at the farm has been okay?"

"That's not hard to answer," Horse said genuinely. "I love it at the farm. I think anyone would consider himself fortunate to be part of your family. Honestly, that isn't why I want to go back. I need to take care of my family."

"I know. What do you call it,—your extended family?"

"Tiyospaye (*tea YO shpa yay*). Nora, I really do love those little kids. To a Sioux, family is the measure of your wealth."

9

"I understand that even though they're your step-siblings, they're still family." Nora smiled, "Jackson, why didn't your Mom put up a fuss when Byron signed on as your guardian until you reach the age of majority."

"As far as she is concerned, it was just more Army stuff. She thinks of me as an adult. So, it made no difference to her that the legal age is twenty on the Res. She didn't care."

"What are you thinking, Nora?" Elton asked.

"Oh, I don't know yet. I think we need to call Mr. Wolf when we stop for a bathroom break. What do you think Elton?"

Elton studied his wife briefly through the review mirror and then broke into a big grin. "You got it, Nora girl. I was thinking the same thing."

"You guys are spooky," Horse observed. "You don't even have to talk to each other! Have you ever been wrong when you read each other's mind?"

Elton chuckled, "Jackson, I can't believe you asked that! I've never been wrong! Well, except for a few minor things."

"Whatever," Jackson groaned.

The convoy stopped at a truck stop in Dickinson about an hour and a half later for refueling stop. Elton and Nora disappeared and made a phone call. They were on the phone about twenty minutes. Then they came back to where the group was having coffee.

"You guys look like the cats that swallowed the canary," Byron chuckled.

"Yah, guess we do," Elton chuckled. "So, have you drunk enough coffee to fill your bladders again? We'd better get on the road."

The small caravan drove on for six hours, making only one more pit stop. However, it was only eleven-thirty when they pulled into a gas station in Rapid City, South Dakota because of the time change.

"I think we should have lunch here and then go on to Pine Ridge. From what Jackson said, there aren't many places to stop on the reservation. I don't know about you guys, but I think better on a full stomach. Besides, the kids might need our picnic baskets," Elton pointed out.

"Is there a motel in Pine Ridge where we can stay?" Byron, the middle-aged Lutheran pastor, asked.

10

"No, nothing like that. Martin is about the closest and it's an hour east of there. Or you can go to Hot Springs, about an hour west. I think Martin is the best bet though. I'm staying at the house, but you guys won't want to," Horse stated.

"No, you can't stay there and probably neither can the kids. No heat? Are you wacky?" Zach stated. "Sometimes I think my pediatric patients are smarter than you and Andy! You give that infection in your leg a chance, and you'll be facing another amputation. You'll lose the whole darned thing, not just above the ankle. Settle down. You're staying in the motel!"

"Zach, it isn't the first time and it wouldn't be the only family without heat around here!"

"What is at your family's home?" Elton asked.

"We lived out on the road to Three Moccasin Park, in a three room house. There is no running water or plumbing. We have electricity and are lucky because we have a phone. Few folks do, but Uncle Bear insisted on that. The land belongs to Uncle Bear. Clayton pulled the house in from somewhere. There is a big kitchen and two other rooms. One is Mom and Clayton's and the other is the kids and Aunt Mabel."

"Oh my," Nora said, "I didn't realize that Aunt Mabel didn't have her own room."

"Nora, it's nothing like your home. We have an outdoor toilet."

Elton pointed out. "It hasn't been that many years that we've had indoor plumbing. Is the well good?"

"We don't have a well."

Andy frowned, "Then where do you get your water?"

"We carry it from the creek that's just west of the place," Horse answered and then busied himself looking out the window.

He was grateful when their food came, so the subject could be changed. The waitress brought the check, Zach picked it up and went to pay. Then he went to the telephone. He came back and announced that he had booked three double-rooms in Martin.

After lunch, the group headed south. A couple hours later, they arrived in Pine Ridge. It was a very small village only a couple miles north of the Nebraska border and a short ways to Wounded Knee. The Grey Hawks lived just southwest of Pine Ridge. The entire area was very run-down with little activity. There was no one around anywhere, but probably because of the pitiless cold.

11

They turned out of town on the road toward Three Moccasin. Near a ridge, Jackson pointed to a short dirt road, "Take this to the east. It's about a mile, just over the rise."

There it was. Jackson's home. It was a small, unpainted one-story shack set on railroad ties. The roof of the house was badly in need of repair. It was near the edge of a ridge that faced west, with badlands beyond. The area around it was prairie, now looking quite desolate with the winter wind blustering through piles of snow. To the north side of the weathered wooden house was an area nearly devoid of snow, where apparently the fuel tank had been. To the north was an outhouse.

The yard however was busy. There was a police car and another car there. Jackson looked at Elton in panic. "I just know this is going to be bad."

Certain that the wheelchair wouldn't make it through the door, Jackson insisted that he take his crutches to the house. Elton relented and came around to help Jackson out of the car.

Nora walked beside them. Her heart went out to Jackson. Being three quarter Sioux, he had black hair and brown eyes. He had a good, but thin build and about five ten. He was very good looking. He had a great smile, though they seldom saw it. He struggled with many physical problems after taking the artillery fire on his leg in Vietnam and having his foot amputated. When he was feeling better, he had a great sense of humor and a loving, outgoing nature.

As he got near the door, a young boy about seven peered out. The little guy spied Horse and made a beeline for him. Horse grabbed him in his arms as best he could while trying to maintain his balance. Elton helped steady him while they embraced.

"CJ, how's my guy?" Horse asked as he hugged the little kid with long black hair and his front teeth missing. One bottom tooth was growing back in.

"I told Clarence you'd come! I just knew it! I knew it! Clarence wasn't so sure, but I knew it!" the little fellow giggled through his tears.

"I would've been here sooner if I could have. Honest. Where is Clarence?"

"He's in the outhouse and won't come out! He's being mad at everybody. I came out to get him," the little boy answered. "I bet he'd come out if he knew you were here!"

"Okay, let's go get him. CJ, I want you to meet my great friends, Mr. and Mrs. Schroeder."

Elton knelt down to shake his hand. The little boy looked at him in doubt, "I thought you didn't have knees?"

"No," Elton smiled, "I have my knees. You're thinking of my son, Andy. He's in the other car. He is the guy Jackson calls Spud."

"Yah, that's him," CJ nodded. "I didn't know Spud had a dad."

"He does and this is his mom," Horse explained.

Nora shook the boy's hand, "Hello CJ."

"Hi Missus," he said and then took Jackson's hand. "Now can we go get Clarence?"

They all walked over to the outhouse. CJ knocked on the door and Clarence yelled, "Go away!"

"Aren't you going to come out and see me?" Jackson asked.

"Who said that?" a surprised small voice asked with suspicion.

"Me, Jackson."

"My brother, Jackson?"

"Yup. Come out and say hi."

The door creaked opened slowly until one eye peered around the side and then it flew the rest of the way open. Clarence grabbed onto Jackson so hard, they both toppled over, hugging on the ground.

"I knew you'd come!" Clarence cried, unable to control his emotion.

"CJ said you didn't think so," Jackson said as he held out his hand for Elton to help him get up. "He said you thought I wouldn't."

"Yah, I kinda hoped you would, or maybe not. You really don't have a foot, do you?"

"Nope. It's gone."

"Are you going to stay here with us now forever?"

"Not yet," Jackson said.

His joy instantly disappeared. Clarence backed away, "Then why did you come? If you don't stay, we won't be here anymore!"

Uncle Bear's pickup came into the yard. He got out and ran over to the boys. "I got here as soon as I could. I see Jackson made it."

Bear hugged the boys and then shook hands with the rest of the group from North Dakota. Then he said, "Let's go in and see what's going on."

"It isn't good, Uncle Bear. You don't want to go in there," Clarence warned gravely.

13

Uncle Bear knelt down to the young lad, "Clarence, we can't hide from things. Wowacintanka is courage. We must be brave and face things whether they're good or not. Okay? We'll be right here with you."

They opened the door to the house, and Jackson went in first. Aunt Mabel gave him a huge embrace, "I'm so sorry this happened, Jackson. Morrissey is here from the Reservation Police and he was just explaining things. Everyone, this is Mrs. Grey Hawk's son."

The lawman was a short man with short dark hair and a cowboy hat that had one feather protruding horizontally from the hat band. "Hello, you must be Jackson Fielding then?"

"Yes, I am. Did you find the rest of the family?"

"You might want to sit down."

"No, I can stand," Jackson said, looking around the crowded room with bare wood floors.

Five-year-old Clarissa came running over to him and hugged his legs, "Hi Jackson. I knew you wouldn't let them take us away."

Jackson patted her back, "Let me find out what is going on? Okay Clarissa?"

Uncle Bear pulled a bench over to the large, wooden table and motioned for Andy and Nora to sit down. He introduced everyone while Clarence brought a stool and folding chair for Zach and Elton. CJ pulled an old rocking chair over by the table. Zach insisted that Jackson take his chair.

The middle-aged Mabel introduced the folks who were there, Morrissey and the couple from Social Services, Wendy Thomas and George Thunder. While they were finding places for everyone to sit, Bear turned to Mabel and asked if there was some coffee. Mabel said she had some coffee, but no water. She sent CJ to go bring some water.

Elton offered to go with the seven-year-old. They went out of the house and picked up a pail out of the snow. Elton grabbed the other pail and CJ took his hand, "I can show you our short cut to the creek."

"It's a deal."

The two went down a steep slope about fifteen feet on a rocky path. At the bottom, they walked about twenty feet to the creek's edge. CJ picked up an axe with a cracked handle that leaned against a rock and started to chop the ice. Elton took it from him and he chopped the ice.

"I could have done it," CJ said. "I do it all the time."

"I know, but I can reach farther than you. Okay?"

CJ studied him a minute and then nodded. They dipped the buckets into the water and filled them. Then they clambered back up toward the house. They took the buckets into Aunt Mabel and she filled the coffee pot.

The house was a shambles. It was questionable if it was ever meant for human habitation. The walls had never been painted and there was no insulation or sheetrock. There were no beds, only mattresses on the floor. The bedding was strewn about the mattresses. Around the hand built table were several mismatched chairs to go with the mismatched cups. The kitchen had an enamel-chipped electric stove and a very old electric refrigerator that had a dent on the door. There was a sink with a pail under it, on a cluttered counter about six feet long which precariously stood on four two-by-fours. Over the sink was a single paned window and one in each of the bedrooms, each covered with old blanket pieces. There were no doors, only blankets hanging over the doors, held back on large nails.

The group made small talk about the weather until Mabel returned to the table. "Morrissey was just telling us where the folks were found."

Jackson was visibly relieved, "Oh thank God, you found them. I suppose they were holding up at someone's house, huh? How soon will they be home?"

"I'm sorry, Jackson. We found the car a few hours ago. They were on the road to Spotted Calf's place from the highway. The car went off the embankment and rolled over into the gully below. We only have preliminary reports now."

Jackson was dumbfounded, and went pale, "How are they?"

"The kids have been taken to Rapid City to the hospital. Frostbite, exposure and a few cuts and bruises, but they should survive. I'm sorry to say, your parents were both gone when we found them."

Jackson's expression froze, but he never said anything, or showed any reaction. Byron put his hand on his shoulder and asked, "How did they die?"

"It looked like Clayton's neck was broken when he was thrown out of the vehicle. His wife likely bled to death, but she had pulled the little ones under her before she died and covered them with her body. No doubt, that's what saved their lives. We'll know more after we get the coroner's report."

Nora took Jackson's hand. Uncle Bear and Aunt Mabel were embracing the little kids. Byron looked at Elton and they shook their heads. Then Byron asked, "What now?"

"You can claim the bodies at the morgue. This is the address. You need to make arrangements for burial and for the kids in the hospital. Someone needs to care for these kids. That's why Social Services is here. We understand that Miss Mabel is going back to her home today."

Mabel nodded, "Of course I'll stay until after the funeral. My son will be here later today, but he'll stay for their funeral too. The kids are fine until then."

The kids ran to Horse, and held on to him. "We'll be with you, right Jackson? You'll stay here with us, right?"

Jackson was unmoving, still trying to digest the news. Without thought, he caressed Clarissa's back, but he never said a word.

Pastor Byron said, "I'm Jackson's legal guardian. I can assure you that we'll make arrangements for the children."

"We have orders to remove them today unless a family member can take custody of them," Thunder explained. "I imagine that'd have to be Bear or Mabel."

"I can do that. I'll sign for their custody until we can make more permanent arrangements," Bear stated.

"I will, too," Aunt Mabel said. "Until after the burial."

"Okay, you take responsibility for them for now and then come in to our office Monday or Tuesday with a more permanent arrangement. We'll leave you to it then, and take care. Please accept our condolences. I hope that something can be worked out to avoid Foster Care. We'd likely be unable to place them together."

After some details were worked out, the social workers and Reservation police left. As they were driving out, Adam drove in to pick up his Mom. When he came in, Mabel told him what had happened. "I'll be staying for the funeral. I can't leave now."

"I know Mom, I'll stay too. I will call into work. We can go back after the funeral, but I can't stay any longer."

All this time, Jackson had not uttered one word and the children had not left his side. It was Uncle Bear who finally shook Jackson's shoulder.

He said, "Jackson, you must show your courage, Wowacintanka, now. We all need you to do your part."

"At least they died under the open sky," Jackson muttered quietly.

"Yes," Uncle Bear agreed. "I thought of that, too. And your mother saved the lives of the little ones."

Jackson nodded and his eyes filled with tears, but he never allowed himself to cry. He hugged the little kids and tried to pull himself together.

4

It took the group a short time to gather their wits. Nora had Elton go out to the car to bring in the picnic basket for those who hadn't eaten yet. While they ate, they figured out what needed to be done.

"We need to tell you something," Elton said over his coffee. "Nora and I spoke to our attorney Mr. Wolf in Bismarck this morning. He is looking into things for us already. Of course, it was before we knew about the accident. If we can, we'd like to take custody of the kids and move them to our place. They could be with Jackson and still be together. I know it isn't your home, but that is all we can do. What do you think, Jackson?"

Jackson stared at them, "Is that what you guys were talking about this morning?"

"Yes," Nora smiled. "Elton and I have talked about it before. We don't want your family to be split up. You know Jackson, we have plenty of room. We were going to ask your parents when we heard that the kids might be removed."

Uncle Bear watched them, "Jackson, are these folks for real?"

Jackson nodded, "Yes, Uncle Bear, they are, but they're nuts! That'd be six of us sponging off you."

"We don't look at it that way, Jackson." Elton was definite. "First of all, we want to do it. We have the room. They wouldn't be sponging; they'd be our family."

"Elton, there are five of them," Jackson reiterated.

"I know. We can count. Have you got a better idea, Einstein?"

Jackson dropped his head.

Andy piped in, "Look Jackson, Annie and I'll be there, too! We can all help out. Right, Zach?"

"Jackson, it would be a good solution," Zach stated.

18

"Byron, talk some sense into them," Jackson pleaded.

"Well, if they don't, Marly and I were going to take them," Byron explained. "We talked about it, too. Look, we can make it work. You're determined to cause trouble, aren't you?"

"I don't know," Jackson turned to his uncle. "What do you think Uncle Bear?"

Bear thought, "I think it'd be the best thing that could happen. What do you think Mabel?"

"I agree," she said. "That Grandma Katherine lives there too, right? I've talked to her over the phone a few times and I think she is kind person. You should be thankful."

"I know," Jackson said. "I truly am, but this is a major undertaking."

"Boy, I hope these kids aren't as much trouble as you," Elton said. "I guess you think we can only do little undertakings. Well, I see five little undertakings. Okay, that's the plan then."

"If there are any problems with the Tribal Council, I'll talk to them and tell them that I give you my complete support," Mabel stated.

"Me, too," Bear agreed. "And if I there is anything I can do, let me know. I don't know if I need to say something or sign something. Whatever I can do."

"Good to know," Elton nodded. "Horse, can you explain it to the kids? So they know where they will be and all."

"Kids, did you hear what Mr. Schroeder said?"

The kids had moved into their room and were sitting on their mattress trying to figure out how to run away. They weren't paying attention to the adult talk.

"What?" Clarence asked.

Jackson explained, "I cannot stay here with you. I'm not well enough. So I have to go back. But, Mr. and Mrs. Schroeder want you kids to come along. We can all be together at their house."

"Why can't we stay in our house?" Clarence frowned and stood up.

"Because Mom and Dad are no longer here. Auntie cannot stay and neither can Jack. You guys are too young to be here alone," Uncle Bear explained. "I have a job in Montana, so I can't be here with you."

"I can be here alone. I know how to do stuff. I can, I know I can!" Clarence decreed, with tears streaming down his cheeks.

Elton went over to him, "I know that you can. I took care of my brother when I was your age. That isn't it. There are rules, and the rules say that people have to be a certain age before they can live alone. So, we're stuck. You'll have to move. Either you can come live with us and Jackson all together, or you'll be split up and go to Foster Care. We cannot stop that."

Clarence turned on Jackson in fury, "I thought you were going to stay and be here with us! Instead you want to take us away too! I hate you Jackson! Why can't you be like you are supposed to be?"

Then the little boy ran outside. Elton was right behind him. He followed him as far as he could and then yelled, "Clarence, can you slow down? I can't keep up. You're too fast, Man!"

Clarence stopped and turned around to see the older man trying to keep up. Elton was huffing and trying to get his breath.

"Are you okay, Mister?"

"Yes, but can you hold up there? You know, I'm not a spring chicken anymore!"

"I suppose, but if you keep saying you're going to take me away, I'll just run off."

"Okay, I won't say it. Just find a good rock for us to sit on. Okay?"

"I s'pose," Clarence answered and looked around for a rock. He found a big one and asked, "This one okay?"

"Looks good," Elton wheezed as he caught up to the lad. "You're pretty fast."

"I'm a fast runner. I like to run, do you?"

"I used to, but I'm too old now." Elton said as he sat on the rock. "Let me rest a minute. This is a fine rock you found. We have a huge one out in our pasture that we call our thinking rock. Some of us go out there to think when we have problems. It's a pretty good rock. Do you have a thinking rock?"

"No. I usually go to the outhouse," Clarence said matter-of-factly, as he sat down next to the man.

"That's a good place, too. A lot of the world's best thinking is done there," Elton smiled. "But this is a good resting rock."

"It seems okay," Clarence shrugged. "Do you have cows in your pasture?"

"Yup and horses. We have hogs and chickens, too; but they aren't in the pasture. One of our best friends has goats. Do you have any goats?"

"No, we only have Cotton and Rags."

"Oh, what are they?"

"Cotton is a cat. We were going to name her Kitten, but Claudia couldn't say it. She called her Cotton. Since it is her favorite, we call her that."

"Is Cotton outside?"

"No, she's mostly indoors. She helps keep the mice down," Clarence explained.

"They do that. That Pastor Byron you just met in the house, he used to have two cats in his church to keep the mice down. Their names were Luther and Martin."

"What happened to them?"

"They died when they got really old. We had a cat at our house, but my daughter took her when she moved away."

"Don't you have any cats now?" Clarence asked.

"No, fresh out."

"Does that Pastor guy have any now?"

"No, his daughter is very allergic to them. She sneezes like crazy around them."

"Too bad. Bet he has a lot of mice, huh?"

"No. He's been lucky, so far," Elton said. "Is Rags a cat, too?"

"Rags is a dog. She's probably out chasing deer right now. She likes to do that?"

"I bet it would be fun if you were a dog, huh?"

"I guess." Clarence looked off to the horizon, "Mister, are they really going to take us away from here?"

"Yah Clarence, I'm afraid so. Don't think there's much way around it."

"This is my home, you know. I like it here," Clarence explained. "I don't want to live somewhere else. Can't you explain that to them?"

"I wish I could, but I don't think they'd listen. You know, those rules."

"Did I do something wrong so they want to take me away?"

"No," Elton put his arm around the lad, "Not at all. The grownups think they're helping you. They know you love your home. We all know that. It isn't your fault that things turned out this way. Your parents have died, and no one wanted that to happen. So, as much as you love your home, Clarence, it won't be the same."

"It would be if Jackson came back. He just doesn't want to be with us, that's all!"

21

"I can't let you say that because it isn't true." Elton got stern, but still kept his arm around the boy. "Jackson has been trying his very best to get back home to you ever since he came to our house. His leg isn't healing very fast, and the doctors say he has to be someplace where he can take care of it."

"I'd take care of him."

"Well, in that case, let's go tell them that. I'll have Zach leave his pain medication so you can give him his shots. Maybe he can show you how to do his chelation and physical therapy. You'll have time to figure out how to get him to his treatments in the VA, I guess."

Clarence frowned, "I don't know about that kind of stuff. I can carry water for him and fix peanut butter."

"That's good. Do you think if Nora, Mrs. Schroeder, showed you how to change the dressings on his leg, you could change it a couple times a day?"

Clarence looked down dolefully, "I know you're tricking me. I'm not a dumb little kid, Mister."

"I suppose you're right. I am kind of tricking you, but not really. I'm treating you like a grownup. See when you're a grownup, you have to think about all the details. So, you have to figure out what you can do and what you need help with. I know you won't believe me when I tell you that I do understand how you feel. Not completely exactly, but I have a pretty good idea. Problem is, there are some things that can't be changed. You can't make your folks be alive, or Jackson's foot to come back. And sadly, you can't change the rules so that you can live alone, no matter how capable you are. Those darned rules are just there. So, most of the time, a guy has to pick the second best solution."

Clarence thought for a while and then said, "They were going to take us away before Mom and Dad died. Did you know that?"

"Yes, I'd heard that. Rules again."

"So, what can I do?"

"Dunno. If Jackson comes back here, he'll lose more of his leg. Then he'll have to go to the hospital and you'll be alone anyway. Foster Care isn't that bad."

"Maybe we could be together. All us kids?"

"Sorry. I know they'd try to keep you together, but the lady said that they can't right now. So it looks like you'd be split up."

Clarence's eyes filled with tears but he didn't cry, "If I did go to your house, would Jackson and all of us be there?"

"Yup. Jackson is there. You kids would all be there too. Claudia and Clancy would be there as soon as they get out of the hospital."

"Would we have to stay there forever?"

"No. Only until the rules say that you could live on your own. Then you could move. I give you my word, we'd come back here to visit. Think you could see your way clear to make that deal?"

"I don't know. I might have to sleep on it. What if I don't like it at your house?"

"I guess you'd have to talk to me and we'd try to work something out. Just like if I don't like having you at my house; we'd have to talk about it. Because, you know, a deal is a deal. We can't be changing it willy-nilly."

"Willy-nilly? That's funny."

Elton looked at the boy and chuckled, "It really is, isn't it? Well, do you need to sleep on it before you decide?"

"Yah, I think I should talk it over with Jackson and Uncle Bear. Then I'll tell you, okay?"

Elton shook his hand, "Sounds very reasonable. We'll talk tomorrow. Shall we walk back in now, before I freeze my head and tail right off!"

Clarence sighed, "Okay."

5

The group decided Adam, Mabel and Zach would go to Rapid City to the hospital and check on those kids. They would stay overnight there and come back to the house in the morning. Nora and Andy were going to stay with the rest of the kids at the house while the men went into town to begin the funeral arrangements and get ready to stay overnight in Martin. That night, Uncle Bear would stay at the house with Clarence, who was determined not to leave his home until he slept on it.

The men went to make arrangements for the wake and funeral. Bear called Leonard White Feather, Laverne Grey Hawk's brother. In accordance with the Sioux custom not to leave a body unattended, Leonard would make certain vigil was kept for the deceased. He would meet with the men at the coroner's office. They made arrangements with the funeral home to pick up the bodies after they were ready and bring them to the hall in the town center where the wake would be held. The funeral home thought that would be late Saturday morning.

Elton talked to Mr. Wolf and Social Services. They thought they would be able to get things in order by Tuesday morning. Hopefully, they could take the children to their new home in North Dakota after the burial.

Nora gathered some clothes for the children for the night, while Andy read kids a story. It was a couple hours before the men returned. Nora set aside the soup from the lunch basket for Bear and Clarence to eat later. She worried about them staying in the house without heat, but Bear assured them they would be okay. "We'll just close off the bedrooms and leave the oven open. We'll sleep near the stove."

"If you're certain," Elton said. "You sure are welcome to come with us tonight."

"No," Clarence said. "You promised I could decide! Besides, Cotton and Rags are here."

"Yes, I did and you can. We'll be back in the morning early," Elton said. "You do need to do some thinking."

"Don't worry," Uncle Bear assured Elton. "If it gets too cold, I'll take him to some friends for the night. I'd like to help him think."

They all rode in Zach's suburban to Martin. Zach thought it would be better to have the veterans travel in that, while he took Elton's station wagon to Rapid City. He promised to call them in Martin that evening after he went to the hospital.

When they arrived and checked into their rooms, CJ became very quiet. "What's up, CJ?" Jackson asked.

"I miss everybody."

"We'll see them tomorrow morning. It'll be okay, you have my word," Jackson said.

CJ looked at him and said, "I don't like this. I'd rather be home."

"I know but we'll be brave and do it anyway, okay CJ?"

"Okay."

They split up into their rooms, Elton and Byron were going to share one room, Nora and Clarissa were going to share a room and then CJ could sleep with the boys, which made him feel pretty special. "You be good for Missus, Clarissa," the little boy told his sister. "I'll be watching out for Jackson tonight."

"I can watch out for Jackson, too," Clarissa offered, quite intimidated by the arrangement.

"Yes, but then who will take care of me?" Nora asked.

"Can't you take care of yourself?" the little girl scrunched up her face.

"It'd be more fun if you stayed with me. We could talk girl talk."

"What's girl talk?" Clarissa asked.

"Oh like talk about braids and stuff. Boys don't know too much about that. We might even have a bubble bath!"

"A bubble bath? Is that fun?' She stopped in the middle of a near smile, and looked at her brother, "I might want to see CJ."

"Well, guess what? All our rooms are next door to each other, so we can go visit them. How does that sound?"

As soon as they got in their room, the little five-year-old Clarissa became nervous. "Missus, can I go visit CJ now?"

"You can call me Nora, if you want. Okay? Let's have our bubble baths first and then we can go visiting."

"Okay, but we need to hurry. CJ is lonesome for me."

"He was going to take his shower. Then we'll visit. Cross my heart."

"Promise?"

"That's what cross you heart means, did you know that?" Nora smiled. "Let's see what we packed for you. I found the pajamas and bathrobe we sent you. You can wear that when we go visiting. I can rinse out these things so they'll be clean for tomorrow."

"I guess." Clarissa agreed uncertainly. "Are we going to do my braid first? One of Jackson's friends said she'd cut my hair. Do you know her?"

"Yes, I do. Her name is Kate. She is Pastor Byron's daughter."

"I didn't know that. How many kids does he have?"

"He has two boys and three girls at his house. Ken and Kate are big kids and the little kids are about your age. One girl is the same age as Clarence and her name is Ginger. Then there is Charlie who is CJ's age. The little girl is Miriam. She is about the same age as Claudia."

"Missus, do you think that Claudia and Clancy are lonesome?"

Nora pulled the little girl next to her as she sat on the bed, "I think they were, but now Aunt Mabel is with them. So they probably feel better."

"Yah," Clarissa nodded and cuddled next to Nora. "Are Mom and Dad lonesome?"

"No honey," Nora said. "When a person dies they aren't lonesome or sad anymore. They are never lonely."

"That's good, but I'm kind of lonely for them."

"I know honey, it's very sad. You know what? Their spirit is with us and they always will be. We get sad because we can't see them, but their spirit is with us."

"Oh," Clarissa nodded unimpressed, and thought a while. "What is a spirit?"

"That is the part of us that makes us who we are. It lives inside us. Everyone has one that is special just for them. Clarissa, it's okay to be lonely and sad. Folks are always sad when someone dies, because we can't see them anymore. I know, it's very hard to understand. Have you ever had a pet that died?"

"Clarence had a cat that died. It went flat, so we buried it."

"Well see, his spirit left when he went flat. But you remember him and you'll always remember him. So whenever you want to, you can remember him."

"He wasn't a nice cat, so I don't remember him. He bit me sometimes. He was a mean cat. That's why we got Cotton."

"Cotton is a nice name. Is that the kitty that is at your house now?"

"Yes. She likes Claudia the best, but sometimes she sleeps with me. She never bites."

"That's good. Cotton sounds like a nice cat." Nora smiled, "What do you say we go make a bathtub full of bubbles?"

"Okay."

Clarissa got more excited when Nora let her pour the pink bubble bath into the water and she watched the bubbles fill the tub. "Do the boys have bubbles too?"

"They can. Want to take off your clothes and get in the tub with them?"

"Are you going to?" Clarissa asked doubtfully.

"How about I'll take my bath later? That way, I can hand you the towel and stuff so you don't have to get out of the tub. Then you can watch the door while I take my bath. Is that a good idea?"

"Are you going to be here with me? A heart promise?"

"Yes, Clarissa, a heart promise."

By the time the bubble bath was over, the little girl was in a lot better mood. She put on her pajamas and robe and Nora braided her hair. Clarissa's hair was very long and even braided it came to her knees. Nora understood why she might want it cut.

They were pretty good friends by the time Clarissa had her pajamas on. Nora asked. "What do you say about us going visiting before I have my bath?"

"Okay."

Meanwhile, Jackson helped CJ with his shower and into his pajamas, then Andy took his shower. Then CJ became quite busy checking out the men's injuries and incisions. Andy opened the door to the knock and there was Nora and Clarissa.

"CJ, look who came to visit?" Andy grinned.

CJ ran to the door and smiled, "Hi. Clarissa! You smell like flowers."

"It is a bubble bath," Clarissa explained.

"A bubble bath?" CJ asked.

Then the two kids sat down and went into a deep discussion about bubbles. Nora sat on the edge of the bed, "How are you doing, Jackson?"

"Alright. Do you think it would be okay if I talked to Katie?"

"I think that's a great idea," Nora smiled. "We'll go over to visit the guys. That way, you can have some privacy. Come over there when you're done. Okay?"

"Okay."

Nora, Andy and the little ones went down the hall and knocked on the door. Pastor Byron answered and let them in. Elton was just hanging up the phone when they sat down.

"That was Bear. Morrissey talked to Spotted Calf. It seems the accident didn't happen very long before they were found or none of them would have survived in this bitter cold."

"When was it they were found?" Andy asked.

"About eight this morning. The deputy headed out to Spotted Calf's after they had talked to the guy at the liquor store in Whiteclay. The man said they were talking to Spotted Calf before they left. He overheard them say they were going to his place for cough syrup. Apparently, they followed him home. The deputy drove out toward Spotted Calf's and on the way, came upon the accident on the road. He radioed it in. It wasn't until later he got out to actually talk to Spotted Calf. I guess Clayton and Laverne went there, got the cough syrup and started drinking. They didn't leave for home until right after the sun came up. So they were found only a short time after it happened. That was lucky for the kids."

"Thank the Lord," Byron said. "I can't wait to hear from Zach."

6

The group visited for a while, but Andy took the kids to Nora's room to read them a story. After Andy left, Elton confided, "I'm really worried about Jackson. He's had almost no reaction to his Mom's death, but I'm afraid he is going to burst. Of course, the other kids didn't react much either."

"I think the little ones don't quite get it yet. They seem used to their folks being gone and besides, they're more worried about having to move away. I don't think it will set in with them for a bit yet." Nora said. "Jackson was going to call Katie now. That's why we came over here, to give him some privacy. I hope that he can talk some of it out."

"That's good," Byron said. "I know he's trying to be brave, but he had quite a time at the coroner's office. He worried that there would be no one with the bodies at the morgue, but the coroner assured him there would be someone there. They understand because they deal with a lot of Sioux and understand the custom of not leaving the dead unattended. Mostly, Jackson just stood and stared. All we can do is to be here for him when it finally hits him. I thought maybe it would happen when he saw them, but it didn't."

"What is required of this wake?" Nora asked.

"From what Bear said, it usually lasts about four days. Jackson thinks he'll stay there the whole time like families usually do, but I don't think his health will allow that. However, it has to be Bear that talks to him about that. The bodies lie in repose during that time, and folks can pay their respects, bring food, gifts and such. The food is shared with everyone there and none can be left behind. Mabel, Bear and Adam will take care of that. Afterward, there will give a short service and the burial in the nearby cemetery. The wake will begin when they are brought to the center."

29

The phone rang and Byron answered. It was Zach. "Hello," Byron said. "We're waiting to hear what you found out."

"The kids are doing okay, but Clancy has the worst hypothermia. We were close to losing him. They both have a roaring pneumonia. How are the kids there?"

"Their coughs seems better. Thanks for leaving the antibiotic with us. Clarissa and CJ are with us, but Clarence wanted to stay in his home. Bear is staying with him and has his medicine. Did you hear when the kids will be released from the hospital?"

"They are hoping by Wednesday. The doctors know that I'm from Bismarck; so if they have to, they'll transfer them to a hospital there. I'm hoping they can go home. Mabel is having a difficult time, but I'm glad she is here for the kids. They were very glad to see her."

"I bet," Byron said. "Do you think they know about their parents?"

"The doctor said he'd tell them tomorrow, but today they've been mostly out. I don't know how much they'll understand. Claudia is certainly a quiet little girl. She rarely says anything."

"Horse mentioned she's the thinker."

"The doctors are checking her hearing. It might be that she doesn't hear very well. We'll find out. How are the kids there?"

"Okay, but Clarence is very upset about having to leave his home. Poor kid. Gee Zach, they lived in abject poverty. I've rarely seen things this bad," Byron said. "However, it's still Clarence's home. Jackson is bottling everything up and has shown little emotion. I think I need to have talk with him."

"How are the vets doing?"

"Okay. Andy is reading to the kids and Jackson is talking to Katie. He thinks he is going to stay at the wake full-time for the whole four days."

"Absolutely not! He's pushing his luck as it is. He can go, but he can't be there non-stop. He'll end up in the hospital without a doubt."

"I know, I told him that. That made a quick trip between his ears."

"I can about imagine. Well, we're going to see the kids in the morning, talk to the doctor and heading to Pine Ridge. Okay?"

"Okay."

They visited for a while and Nora went to check on the kids. She was back in a minute. "They are all asleep, Andy and the kids. I didn't want to disturb them."

"I think they're all tuckered out," Byron said, grabbed the phone when it rang, "Hi Katie."—

"No, he isn't here. He called from the other room. How are you?"—

"Yes, we're trying to get things sorted out so that Elton and Nora can bring the kids to their house."—

"We were just talking about that. I'll go talk to him, Katie. Don't worry. We'll keep watch on him."—

"Oh, that would be nice, if Mom says it's okay."—

"Sleep tight, I love you," Byron hung up and told the couple, "I guess Matt and Diane might bring Katie and Grandma down for the day of the funeral if the weather is decent. Kate is worried about Jackson. I'm going to go talk to him."

Byron knocked on the door and it took a while, but finally Jackson opened the door. He was still stoic, but definitely upset. Byron came in and closed the door. Then he just put his arms around Jackson.

At first, Jackson started to pull away, but finally he broke down and cried. "Byron, my Mom is gone. I can't believe it. I was so damned mad at her and Clayton by the time we got down here! I was planning to tell them off! Here I was so furious, and she was dying! How could I do that?"

"You were reacting to the situation as you knew it, Jackson. Look, your parents were making some bad choices and you had every right to be angry. Just because you love someone doesn't mean that you agree with everything they do!"

Jackson was crying so hard that he had to sit down. "Byron, why didn't I come down here sooner? I knew how it was. I was being selfish. The kids are right about that. I let them down. They were counting on me. So was Mom. I let them all down!"

"No, you didn't. You were doing everything that you could think of to help. You wouldn't have been much help if you were sick or dead. Now don't do that!"

"Why does this stuff happen? I just don't understand."

"I don't either. We just have to make the best of what we can. Jackson, you have no reason to blame yourself. Hear me?"

Jackson nodded and began to cry again. He and Byron talked for over an hour before Jackson began to pull himself together. It was a painful time, but necessary. He finally quit blaming himself and put things in perspective. Eventually, he said he needed a cigarette so they decided to go see what Elton and Nora were doing.

Elton and Jackson were just about to go for a walk when there was a knock on the door. It was Andy. "The kids are asleep on the bed, but I decided to go have a smoke."

"I think I'll go take my shower," Nora said. "Just let CJ sleep in our room tonight, so we don't disturb them. If he wakes and wants to go to your room, I'll bring him over."

Nora kissed Elton good night and left.

"Well, what do you say we go for that walk? Coming along, Byron?"

"I'll catch up with you. I'm going to call Marly first."

The men went into the motel bar and sat down in a booth. After he lit his cigarette and sipped on his Coke, Jackson began to relax. "Do you think that Clarence is going to want to move?"

"No," Elton said. "But I think he will. This isn't what anyone wants, but I think it can work out. Jackson, we're going to count on you to help the kids adjust. Think you can?"

"I'll try, but they're pretty fed up with me now."

"They'll get over it. It has been a lot for them to absorb in a short time. I really think this will be the best for right now. What do you think?"

"Yah, it's a lot better than having them spread all over. Did you hear how the other kids are?" Jackson asked.

They visited for about an hour and before long, the day was catching up with them. They all went to their rooms to get some sleep. Tomorrow would be another long day.

7

Jackson slept very little and when he did, the young veteran was besieged with nightmares. The dreams were a conglomeration of terrors of war and his parents' deaths. He woke up swinging and screaming more than once. Andy would talk to him until he got settled again. Then the entire process would repeat.

Morning came early. The boys were already awake when Nora knocked on the door. CJ had awakened and was quite upset that he didn't get to sleep in the big boy's room. They told him that he could pick whichever bed he wanted to rest in while they got dressed for the day. The seven-year old took a running jump and landed in the middle of the bed closest to the door and tunneled down under the covers. Then Jackson and he had a tickle match while Andy got dressed. By the time they were ready for breakfast, CJ forgot all about the fact that he hadn't slept all night with them.

They all met in the motel coffee shop for breakfast. There was a small buffet, and CJ took a little bit of everything. Clarissa simply zeroed in on the pancakes and ate nothing else. The small girl scarfed down four large pancakes, smothered in butter and syrup. When she finally slowed down, she looked at Nora with a grimace. "I don't feel so good Missus. I think my butter is trying to get out!"

Nora asked her if she was going to throw up and she took her head no. "It's just running around in there."

"Okay, you just sit quietly and relax. You ate a lot of breakfast. Your tummy is overworking, but if you think you're going to be sick, let me know."

Clarissa leaned back in her chair, "I think if I sat on your lap, it would be quiet."

Nora smiled, "Okay, scoot onto my lap."

CJ asked, "Can I take those things in that basket for Clarence? They're pretty good and I think Clarence likes them."

"Certainly," Elton said. "Let me ask the waitress for a bag to carry them in. You think he will like the muffins?"

"Yah, and the butter."

"Okay, we'll get some to take along. That was very thoughtful of you to think about him."

CJ just shrugged and went back to eating the butter off his muffin.

Back in their room, Grandma called Nora. Grandma explained that Matt was checking the weather. If the forecast looked decent, they would come down on Tuesday. Carl, Matt's stepdad, had offered his brand new car for them to take down, because Matt's old car wasn't as trustworthy.

Grandma wondered what they should do for flowers for the service. Nora gave her the information and explained where the service would be, "But don't spend much on the flowers. If Social Services give their approval, we'll be bringing the whole family home. The kids need so many things. Katherine, they have very little. What we mailed before is almost all gone. I don't know for certain what happened to it all, but I didn't see a toothbrush or winter jacket anywhere. Remember all the jeans we had for them? I found only two pair. It is unbelievable. Our chicken coop has more insulation than their house does. I'm surprised they survived at all."

Grandma answered, "Okay, I'll let the others know. I don't think we'll get anything like clothes for them until they get here, except maybe coats. We want to get the rooms ready for them."

"I was thinking," Nora said, "We should keep the two bigger boys in one room, the girls in another and then the little guy can use the crib downstairs in the nursery. The kids used to sleep altogether on one mattress, so I don't think they'll want to be alone at first."

"You're right. Besides, everything will be strange for them. Well, I'd better get busy. Give Jackson my best, will you?"

"I will, Katherine."

While they were waiting to get in the car, Nora passed Katherine's message along to Jackson. He smiled, "I can't wait to see her again. I miss her."

"You guys are very close. She thinks the world of you." Nora said. "Say, I have a question. The kids call Elton and I 'Mister and Missus'. Is that an Indian thing?"

"No," Jackson explained. "That is my Mom. She insisted that we kids call most adults that; she said it was respectful. Does it bother you?"

"No, I was just curious. It's certainly okay. I was concerned we're missing something."

The weather was bright and sunny, but it was still very cold. Zero would be the high for the day. The kids were anxious to see Clarence again. They nearly bolted out of the car when it came to a stop in their front yard. Clarence met them midway to the house. All three were jabbering at once when they went into the house. They immediately went to their room and made a picnic of muffins on their mattress.

"You better be careful with that butter in there," Uncle Bear warned. He turned to his nephew, "You look horrible Jack, did you sleep at all?"

"You don't look so hot yourself!" Jackson answered. "I did get a little sleep. How did things go here?"

"Clarence and I talked a lot last night. I think he is coming around, but he's not quite there yet. I told him that I still have this place, so when he comes back to visit, he can be here. That made him feel better."

"A good well would be a great idea," Elton suggested. "That water from the creek can't be good. Do you know what all drains into it?"

Bear raised his eyebrows, "No, and I don't want to. With all the mining in the Black Hills, I shudder to think."

"I didn't know individuals could own reservation land?" Byron asked.

"It is jointly with the tribe, something like a lease. My idea always was to build a cabin out here. I might do that yet. They sell some of those modular log homes out in Montana. That'd be great. It'd be nice for the kids to come visit. Clarence is worried that he'll never get to come back and I assured him he would. I think he is beginning to believe it."

"I told him that too, but he doesn't know me from a hole in the ground," Elton pointed out. "He has no reason to believe me. Are there other concerns that you could tell us about?"

"He doesn't want to go to school at all; he hates it and he doesn't do very well in it. But if he has to go, he wants to be in his class here, where his friends are."

"I can understand that. He and CJ will probably have to change schools anyway. Being behind in school makes it hard."

"Dad," Andy interjected. "Maybe Jeannie could help tutor them, like she did with Ginger. She is a good friend of ours, and I'm sure she could help Clarence and CJ."

"Don't forget," Nora pointed out. "Diane lives at our house and she is a teacher, too."

"Maybe Diane could give the girls piano lessons!" Jackson smiled for the first time, "Matt's a teacher, too. I'm sure the kids will do well once those guys get a hold of them."

"I hope so." Bear said. "They're bright kids, but they missed so much school, they're falling behind. Clarence is just fed up with the whole business of having to move."

"I don't blame him. Are there other issues?"

"Yah, Cotton and Rags."

"I thought about that last night. We can bring Cotton, no problem. Of course, we'll bring Rags too, but I don't know how Elmer, our dog, will like it. All we can do is try. I figured they'd want their pets. Is Rags a male or female?"

"A female," Bear grinned. "And to answer your next question, she hasn't been fixed."

"Great. That'll be a trip to the vet," Elton raised his eyebrows. "We don't need a bunch of puppies."

"Yah, it's okay to take on five kids, but not a batch of puppies!" Jackson laughed, "I'll go have a talk with the kids, but I need someone to help me sit on the mattress."

Byron helped Jackson to the bedroom and once he got settled on the mattress, he left them to talk alone. When he went out, he closed the curtain, so they could talk in private.

As he sat down at the table, Byron asked Bear quietly, "I was hoping you could talk to Jackson. He wants to stay at the wake the whole time, but he can't. He is still on several medications for the infection and pain. He'll just get sick. He has to do his exercises, clean his injuries often, change the bandages and keep his leg up."

"He hardly slept at all last night. More like catnaps, and then wake up swinging or screaming. I was afraid we might get kicked out of the motel." Andy said, "We must have gone for fifty walks."

"I'll talk to him. Between his mom's family and so on, we'll have someone always there with the parents. We can't have him getting sick. The kids need him too much and with their coughs, they shouldn't be there all the time either."

"Zach called from the hospital. The kids are recovering, but have double pneumonia. They were going to stop in to see them this morning and then come down here for the day. He was hoping they'd be released from the hospital by Wednesday."

"I hope I can get to see them before I go back to Montana. You know, I think this will be hard on the kids at first; but in the long run, it might be the best for them. I don't want Jackson to move back here and vegetate. He had a heck of a time when Vienna committed suicide and almost gave in to the bottle. I was determined to get him out of it. His dad would have a fit if his kid ended up a drunk. I miss my brother. He would've never let things get like this. After he died, Laverne gave up. I hoped that Clayton would be good for her, but it turned out he drank worse than she did. It all went to hell."

"It didn't turn out very good. I want to thank you for being there for Jackson. You've been his anchor. I hope you know that," Byron assured him.

"I love that kid. He has been my anchor, too. You know when Vienna was gang raped, I was proud of how he supported her. It was admirable for a kid his age. But then, when she found out she was pregnant and committed suicide, he almost lost it. He quit school and stayed drunk for at least couple weeks or more. I tried to convince him it wasn't his fault, but he has always had a tendency to blame himself for everything. Finally, I just got mad at him and beat the hell out of him. It may not have been the thing to do, but I think it made him realize I wasn't messing around. He cleaned up his act."

"Well, it worked. I noticed that he was berating himself up yesterday over his parent's accident. He thought he should've been here."

"I'm glad he has you all to lean on. You folks have been good for him, and he is going to need support with all this. Taking the kids isn't going to be easy. They've lived like this all their lives and don't even know how other folks live. They've never had enough to eat or all the utilities working. Jackson had a good start. He was about ten when his dad died, so he knew another way of life. I hope these kids can get sorted out. I don't think Clayton ever left the Reservation. His eyes were too bad for the service, so he was just here. He quit school when he was thirteen or so, and missed most of it while he was going. I don't mean to be speaking ill of him, but that is the facts."

"We can only do what we can," Elton said. "But with everyone helping out, we can hope they'll do okay."

8

Around noon, the bodies arrived at the steel building that was the community center in Pine Ridge, and the family was there. There was heat in the building and bathrooms, for which Nora was grateful. Mabel, Adam and Zach arrived with doctor reports from that the children were improving, which brought a great deal of relief to everyone.

The flowers from the folks in North Dakota and Bear's employers were there, as well as some new quilts from Laverne's family, the White Feathers. Clayton's family had passed away, except for a brother who was in prison in Nebraska.

Jackson approached his mother's body with Byron. He was finally able to allow his tears to flow freely. He moved over to Clayton and just stood there. Byron put his arm on his shoulder, and said, "You're doing okay. You need not feel guilty, Jackson. It's okay."

The young man began to grieve. He was soon joined by Clarence, Uncle Bear, Auntie Mabel, Clarissa and CJ. The little ones took it quite hard when they saw their parents' bodies. Bear and Mabel had their hands full for a bit. The folks from North Dakota paid their respects and before long, left to go to the house. They wanted to begin to pack the things to take to North Dakota.

They were all very quiet when they arrived at the house. Elton and Zach went down to get a pail of water for coffee.

While they were chopping the ice to get the water, Zach said, "I can't believe that Jackson even thought he could come here to live. He wouldn't even be able to get water!"

"I know. You know there is hardly a box full of stuff to salvage from here. Most of the clothes and boots we'd sent before are gone." Elton looked up from his chopping, "Alcoholism is a demonic thing. I hope we can do the right thing by the kids."

"You'll have your hand's full. Elton, the doctors think that Claudia has severe hearing loss, likely from frequent infections. They were going to look into it more today, but it's enough to affect her speech."

"Will it come back?"

"No one knows yet, but we can stop her from losing any more. She needs to see a specialist when she gets over the pneumonia. I'll make arrangements when we get home, okay?"

"Yes, we better do that. The poor kid. Will the exposure to the cold have any effects on the kids?"

"So far, it looks like neither of them have severe frostbite, but they have some. They'll be very sensitive to hot and cold for some time, and chronic pain or tingling. It will be important to keep them both warm and dry."

"I figured. I was worried we might be looking at gangrene and such."

"I don't think that's the case. You know, neither of them had winter coats or mittens, but Mrs. Grey Hawk was wrapped in a blanket and pulled the kids under it with her. She only had a sweater. Clayton had a light summer jacket," Zach shook his head. "It was unreal."

"Jackson is having a hell of a time because he is blaming himself—he was so angry with those people. He was furious that they traded away the fuel tank and heater. He was going to cut them off. Then he learned they were dying while he was ranting about them! That's hard to take. Between you and me, I was ready to clobber them myself. There isn't a damned thing in that house. If it wasn't for the blankets on the wall, they wouldn't be able to survive inside. It makes me sick."

"Yah, we don't realize how lucky we are until we see how bad it can get."

They gathered the kids' clothes in a few garbage bags. Nora had spied a Laundromat in Pine Ridge, so she had the guys take her there. They all ate sandwiches from their picnic basket while they washed up the few clothes. At least what they had would be clean.

"I don't know how we're going to take Rags home. He isn't a house dog, and he sure isn't going to like being in the car for six hours. If Matt comes down, I'm thinking Rags should ride back in Carl's car," Elton smirked.

"Dad, you're awful! Carl has a brand new car! Matt would get in hot water for messing up his car," Andy pointed out.

"I guess, huh?" Elton nodded. "Okay, but I might call and see if Matt could borrow a crate for Rags to use. That'd be better."

"I think so," Nora said. "Honestly, sometimes Elton, I think you and that old Coot are one as bad as the other!"

Elton kissed her cheek, "I'm better looking."

Nora rolled her eyes and put the last of the clothes in a bag. "Do you think that Clarence and Bear will stay at the motel tonight? I sure hope so. Clarence needs a bath. I have no idea how those people could even wash up! Can you imagine having to carry the water up that hill?"

"The worst part is that you lose most of the water by the time you get to the top. CJ started with a full pail, and it was less than half-full by the time he got to the top. That's one steep path they have there," Elton explained.

Back at the house, Elton called Carl. "Could you ask Matt to bring a dog crate if he comes down? Seems we'll have a dog and a cat to bring back."

"How's Horse doing?" Coot asked.

"About as well as can be expected. The two kids in the hospital are better today, and the others are at the wake. Carl, you can't believe this place," Elton said.

"Sadly, I probably can. I have been on reservations before, and the Ritz they ain't. I've heard that Pine Ridge is one of the poorest, so I can about imagine," the former FBI agent said. "Magpie, how are the kids?"

"Okay, Zach said the doctors think that Claudia has a hearing loss and that's why she rarely talks. The baby and she both have double pneumonia, but avoided bad frostbite. You know—that so-called medicine they got for the kids was just plain old cough syrup! They never even saw a doctor. The other kids have bad coughs too, but they are responding to the antibiotic Zach brought. CJ and Clarissa are both chatterboxes and typical kids."

"Yea gads," Carl groaned. "Just what they need; to move in with you Magpie! The world will never be the same."

"Your mouth is always going more than your brain; so I wouldn't talk if I were you! Clarence is the oldest and so serious. He is a worrywart and keeps an eye on the other kids. He takes responsibility for all of them. This isn't going over well with him. He wants to just stay here and he's certain that he can take care of them. Between you and me, he probably could do as well as his folks did."

"Well, that's the facts. Don't worry, our clan will take care of them. Ian and I bought some cubicles for the wall in the playroom and painted them. We are waiting until you hear from Social Services before we put their names on them. I think I'm going to have to put more shovel holders in my tool shed. Elton, did you ever think that you'd be taking on a pile of little kids at your age?"

"No, but the situation didn't come up before. What would you do?"

"The same. I guess Ellison's were going to do it too, and I know for a fact, that Kevin and Darrell were trying to figure out how they could take them. You know this outfit. There isn't a person in the clan that would let those kids be split up."

"You're right about that. How is Grandpa Lloyd going to handle it when Grandma comes down here for the funeral?"

"All taken care of. Kevin and Carrie simply packed up baby Holly and moved over to the farmhouse. Lloyd is a little confused, but he's okay. You take care and good luck with the Social Services. If you need a reference, Mo and I'd be willing to lie for you. I know the kids would do well with Nora. And you aren't too bad if we keep a lid on you," Carl cackled.

"Very funny, Coot. You're a miserable old buzzard, you know."

When everyone returned to the wake, there were a lot more people there. They were introduced to numerous members of Laverne's family. Many offered to put in a word to the Tribal Council or Social Services. Laverne and Mabel had told them how well Jackson was doing, so they felt the kids would be fine.

Jackson was visiting with several friends and family members, but it was obvious that he was struggling with the pain. Zach went over to him and had a short talk with him. Between Zach and Bear's barrage of convincing lectures, they were able to get Jackson to leave. "Look, you're in pain and you're beginning to run a fever. If you don't watch it, you'll be in the hospital."

"But,—" Jackson started.

"No, Jack. You go get a hot meal and some rest. No more talk. I mean it," Bear's look penetrated the young man.

"What about you?"

"Mabel and Adam are going to stay here tonight. I thought Clarence and I might go to Rapid City with Zach if he doesn't mind. I want to see the kids and I know that Clarence would feel better. Could we do that?"

"That would be great. Clarence is too young to visit at the hospital, but in this case, the doctors may make an exception. I think it's a great idea," Zach said. "I have a motel there already, so no problem. Just grab your stuff."

Neither Jackson nor Clarence was happy about leaving, but when Clarence learned he would get to see other kids, he relented. He went over to Elton, "Mister?"

"Yes Clarence, what is it?"

"Could you and Missus take care of CJ and Clarissa tonight? I should go check on the other kids."

"We can do that. There are some clean clothes for you at the house. We fed Cotton and Rags before we came in. See you in the morning, Clarence. Get some sleep tonight, worrying will wear you out you know."

"Thanks Mister," Clarence said seriously. "I might tell the kids it'll be okay to stay at your house for a while, just until I get older."

"Sounds good, Clarence. Real good. I'd be proud to have you all stay at my place."

"Yah, me too."

Then the eight-year-old who shouldered the burdens of an adult, left with his uncle to look after his younger siblings.

Elton had to fight his tears. Byron saw it, and said, "I think that means you're okay, Mister."

Elton shrugged, "I hope so."

That night, the group had a nice dinner at the motel coffee shop. It was noticed that the basket of dinner rolls mysteriously emptied as it rested in front of CJ's plate. Jackson looked at the lad and asked, "CJ, did you see where the rolls went?"

CJ looked at him sheepishly, but didn't answer.

"Do you have them?"

Crestfallen, CJ nodded, "I put them in my pockets for Clarence. He likes them."

"How about we ask the waitress to bring us a bag to put them in? It'd have more room than crunching them into your pocket," Elton suggested.

"Can I take them to Clarence?"

"Sure. You can keep them so you don't forget them, and maybe add some more muffins to them in the morning. What do you think?"

"I can have them by my bed?"

"Yup, and you know what?" Elton assured him. "We might just order another basket of rolls to eat now and what is left, you can add to the bag."

CJ broke into a grin. "Okay."

Nora was concerned because Jackson was running a slight fever, as Zach thought. She sent him to bed and reminded him to take the sleeping pill that Zach had given him. "If you don't get some rest, you'll be sicker than a dog."

"I have so much to do," Jackson started.

"Do you want me to call Grandma?"

"No. Please don't. I can't believe how I told so many people how nice you are," Jackson groaned. "If they only really knew."

"That's what you get for lying," Nora smiled.

9

Sunday morning the group went first to the wake. The kids and Jackson stayed there, but Byron and Schroeder's went over to Pastor Adams church for the second service. Then they returned to the wake, and met Zach, Bear and Clarence.

Clarence felt better because he had seen the other kids. "Thank you Missus, for cleaning my jeans. Uncle Bear said my other ones could stand by themselves!"

Elton patted his shoulder, "That is okay, as long as they don't run off by themselves!"

Clarence gave Elton a big smile, "Remember, I'm a fast runner."

"That's right, you surely are."

"I told the little kids I decided we'd stay your place. They didn't cry, so I guess we'll try it out; as long as Rags and Cotton can be with."

"That they will. Cotton can live in the house. I really need a cat now. I think Rags and my dog, Elmer will get along."

"What if they have a dog fight?" Clarence worried.

"Then you and I will have to do some serious thinking, huh?"

Clarence studied him for a minute, "Maybe you could show me your thinking rock, huh?"

"That I could do," Elton put his arm around the young boy. "We'll do just fine."

"I should go talk to Auntie Mabel now. Okay?"

"Okay."

It was another long day. While the North Dakotans worked to get the house in shape to be left unattended, Zach shared the news that the kids

45

would be able to come back to North Dakota on Wednesday. They were all relieved about that.

Then they called North Dakota and Elton talked to Matt, "The forecast looks good, so as long as we don't get a freak storm or something, we're going to head out right after school on Monday. We'll be in Rapid City on Monday night. I talked to Zach and we'll stay at the same motel that he does. Then we'll head down to Pine Ridge after breakfast. I hear there is no place to stay there, huh?"

Elton said, "No, we're going to stay in Rapid City Tuesday night and then go the rest of the way home on Wednesday."

"That's our plan too. Diane and I got substitutes, and Katie has been working like a beaver to get her schoolwork made up ahead of time. Have you told Horse that we're coming?"

"No, we didn't want to get his hopes up and have them dashed. He is running a fever now, but he is still pushing himself."

"Such an awful mess. Oh, I borrowed a dog carrier and Megan is letting us use her cat carrier. What is her name?"

"Cotton."

"Cotton, cool name! And the dog?"

"Rags. She is medium sized with brown and white with shaggy, medium length fur and floppy ears. Her ears really do look like rags."

"Well, I'll see you Tuesday morning unless something unforeseen comes up. I hear the dress is rather informal for the wake and burial."

"Bear says it'll be mostly blue jeans. Talk to you later. I know it will mean a lot to Jackson when you guys show up."

Mabel and Nora had time for a good visit and Nora asked Mabel if she wanted to stay in Martin that night and get some sleep. "No, thank you. Traditionally we mourn for the full four days. By the time it is over, you're usually hoarse, worn out and ready to get some rest."

"I can imagine. Is it a very bad thing for Jackson to not be here full time?"

"He isn't well and the kids have so much to contend with, it's just fine. If he was well, it would be expected; but since things are the way they are, we're just happy that he has you folks to keep an eye out for him. Bear will be here tonight, so we're fine."

That evening before they left the house, the kids went on a scavenger hunt to find anything that they had stashed somewhere outside. The boys retrieved one very worn soft ball. The boys also brought in a Rag's favorite stick and wanted it to come along. Everything was packed; except for the few things that Bear would keep at the place, like the dishes, frying pan and table, to use when he came home.

It was the first night that Clarence stayed with Schroeders. The Grey Hawk boys decided to sleep in one bed in Nora's room, since the veterans had so much trouble sleeping. Then they went to the dining room.

Elton asked, "What do you kids want to eat?"

"Can we have anything?" Clarence squinted at the menu. "I don't get this writing stuff."

Andy helped him decide what he wanted and the other kids were going to have hamburgers.

When the waitress brought the food, CJ smiled, "Can I take the rolls back to my room tonight, Mister?"

"Well, Clarence is here so he can have some now if he wants," Elton explained.

CJ got a worried look on his face and Elton said, "But we can sure ask the waitress for a bag; just in case you want some later. How does that sound?"

"That'd be good," CJ seemed relieved. "I'll keep it by my bed."

"Okay," Elton smiled.

Before they ate, Byron said grace. Clarence studied the whole thing. After they said amen, Clarence commented, "Mr. Zach did that, too. Why do you guys do that?"

Jackson said, "To thank God for our food and what we have."

"Uncle Bear said God is like Wakan Tanka."

"It is much the same. Pastor Byron is like a holy man for the Lutheran church where we live. You know, like Pastor Adams is in Pine Ridge."

"Pastor Adams is a nice guy," Clarence nodded. "He stops by to check on us. We better tell him goodbye so he knows we aren't there anymore."

"We'll see him on Tuesday, so you can talk to him," Elton offered.

"Are you going to talk to those Rule people and tell them us kids decided to give you a chance?" Clarence asked Elton.

"Planning on that. Nora and I will meet with them in the morning," Elton explained. "I promise to tell you what we find out."

"I can tell them that's what us kids decided. Maybe that way, they'll let you take us to your house. Okay?"

"Well thank you, Clarence." Elton nodded. "Then they can talk to you kids, if they need to."

"They can talk to me," Clarence explained. "The other kids want me to do it for them."

"I understand."

Jackson slept better that night, but Andy had a couple nightmares. At breakfast, Byron shook his head, "You two are determined to get us kicked out of here, aren't you?"

"We do our best," Andy chuckled. "So, tonight will be the last night we stay here, right? Tuesday night we'll be in Rapid City?"

"That's the plan. Zach talked to the doctors. They were glad the patients would be there one more night. We'll have to pay a deposit on the pets, but they can stay in the room. So, Clarence," Elton said seriously, "You and CJ will have to make sure that Rags goes outside when she needs to. We don't want her to do her business in the room."

Clarence nodded, "Okay, she goes outside at home. Sometimes she sleeps with us. I hope she doesn't run off. If she sees a deer, she'll be gone."

"Oh, we better get her a collar and leash."

"She doesn't like collars. She wants to run," Clarence explained with a nod.

"I know, but she might get lost in Rapid City because there are a lot of cars and people there. We might lose her forever if she isn't on a leash."

"She doesn't like leashes," Clarence was definite.

"We don't want her to get run over," Elton explained.

"She won't like the leash."

"Clarence," Jackson said, "We have to have her on the leash when she goes outside on this trip. Then she can take it off. You hear?"

Clarence frowned but finally relented. "I'll talk to her, but she still isn't going to like it. You aren't going to make Cotton have a leash, are you? She'll bite you!"

"No, we won't do that!" Elton grinned. "I tried to put a cat on a leash once. I was bleeding before I got done and the cat had a fit. Dogs don't mind it so much."

Clarence gave Elton a determined stare, "Rags will mind it so much."

Clarissa had bacon and one scrambled egg with toast. When she looked at Andy's pancakes and shuddered.

Andy teased, "Wanna bite of mine?"

"No," she grimaced. "My tummy doesn't like them."

Andy laughed, "I think you ate too many. In a few days, you can try again, but only eat one. That might go better."

Clarissa looked at him. "You can have all of them."

Jackson, Andy and the kids went to the wake, while Byron and Schroeders went to the Social Services office to meet with George Thunder and Wendy Thomas. "We have things under control," George said. "The Tribal Council was pleased that the children would be with Jackson. I talked to Bear. Now I need you to sign for Jackson, Pastor Ellison. Bear and Jackson have promised to see to it that the kids learn about their culture and heritage. We were in contact with your attorney, Mr. Wolf and Pastor Adams.

"The only issue is your ages. Since the children are quite young, it would be better if they were with a younger family. However, most younger families cannot afford to take on five children. Wendy and I explained to them that you have a large extended family of all ages, that will be there for the kids too; so they won't be sitting around crocheting all day. In reality, and you didn't hear it from me, it is a storm in a teacup. I don't see a huge line of prospective families clamoring for them. After we pointed that out to the powers that be, they concurred.

"We got all the papers in order. I also talked to several relatives at the wake, so I feel very confident with this decision. Elton and Nora will be granted full, but still temporary, custody. We'll stop by to check on them in a month or so at your home. If there are no major issues, we can make it a more permanent arrangement. I don't know if you are planning eventually to adopt or what; but for now, you have custody. You can enroll them in school or whatever you need to do. Mr. Wolf looked into it and the kids will be covered under your medical insurance."

"That's a relief," Nora said. "We learned that Claudia has some hearing problems. We don't know yet what all that will entail."

"I'm sorry to hear that," Wendy said. "We've had their home situation on our radar for some time. The boys weren't in school very often, and I'm afraid have fallen way behind. They may have trouble in school."

Nora nodded, "We worried about that. We have a dear friend that teaches third grade in Merton Public. She has already volunteered to tutor the boys."

"That's good to know. Well, if you sign these papers now, we'll take it to the judge with our recommendation to approve. We expedited it because you will be leaving. You can pick up the custody papers after three this afternoon." George Thunder leaned back in his chair, "I hope you are aware this is going to be a major enterprise."

"Yes, we know that," Nora smiled. "But we also have a great support system, and a lot of folks that will help."

"How are the kids with all this?" George asked. "Clarence didn't seem very think very much of the idea."

"He and I had a talk. I told him to think it over. He thought about it, talked to Bear and Jackson and then told me yesterday that he would give us a chance, but only until he gets old enough to leave," Elton smiled. "I admire him. He has taken on the entire responsibility for the other kids and the pets. Hopefully, he'll become confident enough to relinquish some of that burden. For now, I think if he'll just share it with us, we should be satisfied."

George nodded thoughtfully, "Sounds very perceptive of you. Do either of you have any qualms about this?"

Nora shook her head no and then Elton broke into a grin, "To be honest, I have serious doubts about driving over 500 miles with a dog and a cat in the car! I don't suppose we could talk you into bringing them up."

"Not a chance!" George Thunder laughed. "Well, see you tomorrow."

Wendy asked, "How is Jackson doing? He didn't look very well yesterday."

"He isn't," Byron said. "He is running a fever and has been fighting the infection that took his foot since he got back from Vietnam. We're having a difficult time convincing him that he needs to take it easy. This has really thrown him for a loop. It'll be good for him to get home and back into a routine."

"Give him our best," Wendy smiled. "If you need anything, just keep in touch."

"We'll do that."

10

When the group returned to the wake, Elton took Clarence aside. "Could you go outside with me so we could talk?"

The two went outside and found a bench to sit on. "We just got back from the Social Services office. They're going to grant custody to Nora and I so you kids can come to our place. We promised them that we'll help you get a good education and grow up strong and sturdy. But Nora and I want something more than that."

Clarence frowned, "What do you want?"

"We want all that too, but we want you to be happy. We want you to enjoy life, have fine friends, learn about interesting things and enjoy the world Wakan Tanka created. Nora and I don't know much about Indian life, so Jackson and Bear will have to teach you what you need to know. It will be important for you to help with your brothers and sisters. Okay? We'll work it out so you can come back to Pine Ridge from time to time, preferably when it's summer. You can also keep in touch with Aunt Mabel and Uncle Bear."

"That'd be good."

"Now, the less fun part. The Rules say that you have to go to school. Can I have your word that you won't be a jackrabbit about that? Will you encourage your brothers and sisters to go? Cause if you say bad stuff about it, they'll hear it. Then they won't want to study either. Then the Rules people will get bent out of shape and put in you Foster Care."

"I really don't like school."

"Do you think the other kids might?"

"Doubt it."

Elton thought, "Do you know that for sure?"

"I know CJ doesn't, but maybe the other kids."

"How about if Nora and I get some really neat folks to help you out with it, can you promise to not grumble about it to the other kids and give it an honest try? If you do, I'll make you a promise. Whenever you want to grumble about any of it, or have any problems with it, you can come to me and we'll figure how to fix it. Sound like a plan?"

Clarence stared at the ground and shoved the snow around with his foot. "Can I tell you anything and you won't be mad?"

"You have my word. I don't get mad that often, except about two things. One: don't lie to me. I might not like the truth, but it is always better to know it. Two: if you give me your word, I want to be able to count on it. If you find out you can't do it, then tell me right away! You remember those things, and I'll be a happy camper. What would make you a happy camper?"

Clarence thought for a while, "I guess I'd like to go fishing. My dad was going to take me, but he never had time. I thought I saw some fish in the creek by our house, but we never got to go fish for them."

"I promise we can go fishing. But Clarence, let's not go ice fishing, okay? I'd rather go when the water isn't frozen. What do you say?"

Clarence giggled, "Okay. I know when people are old like you, they don't like the cold. We can go when it is warm out."

Elton frowned, "Well, thanks I think. That was almost nice. Speaking of cold, shall we go back in?"

The two started to head to the center when Clarence asked, "Have you told the other kids yet?"

"Not yet. Do you want me to, or do you want to?"

"I think I should. You know, they count on me."

Elton nodded, "I figured that. Oh, and Zach told us that Claudia and Clancy can leave the hospital Wednesday morning."

"Will we be gone by then? What is going to happen to them?" the little boy's face filled with worry.

"We're going to stay in Rapid City until they can come home with us. We won't leave them behind. We'd never do that."

"Good," the boy was relieved. Then he started walking again, "You might not be too bad."

"I won't have to worry about getting a big head around you, will I?"

"Huh?"

"Nothing Clarence, I just want you to know that I think you are a fine person."

Clarence stopped walking and studied Elton a second and then smiled a little. As they walked toward the center, he reached over and took his hand.

That evening after dinner, the group met in Byron's room. Byron got everyone's attention, "I thought we should have a talk about tomorrow. Things are going to be different, so I think you might want to understand what is going on. If you have any questions, we can talk about them now."

Everyone looked at him blankly, and he continued. "Tomorrow morning when we leave here, we must make certain that we pack all of our things. We won't be back here, so be sure to take everything along."

Clarissa's eyes got huge, "You mean, you don't live here? I thought we'd live here!"

"No, we live in a house," Nora explained. "We are just staying here because it is close to Pine Ridge. When we get to our house, you can unpack and know that you'll live there as long as you want."

"I thought the bubbles were at your house!"

"Not these, but guess what? We have bubbles up there too! So, you'll have bubbles."

Clarissa moved over and sat on Nora's lap.

Then CJ asked, "Will we have those baskets at your house?"

"What baskets do you mean, CJ?" Andy asked.

"The roll ones."

"We put them in a wooden bowl; but yes, we do. And guess what else? We have a cookie jar too!"

"A cookie jar?"

"Yah, Nora makes cookies and puts them in a big container."

"Can we keep them in a bag in our room?"

Elton smiled, "We might find you a better container than a bag to keep in your room. That way the mice won't get them. Okay?"

"I have to think about it. Will it be as big as a bag?"

"I think we can do that."

"Okay then."

Byron looked around to see that those questions were settled before he continued. "Now tomorrow, there will be a service at the center for your parents. Your spiritual leader and Pastor Adams will talk and then we will follow them while they take your parents' bodies to the cemetery. They will be buried there. Remember kids, they will always be with you in spirit and in your memories. It will be sad; so if you want to cry, you certainly can do that. Okay?"

Clarence thought, "Then what?"

"We'll pick up your things and load up Cotton and Rags. Then we'll drive to Rapid City and stay in a motel. The next morning, we'll pick up Claudia and Clancy and drive to Merton. We live outside of town in the country, so there will be a lot of room to run and play outside."

"Are we just going to leave mom and dad outside?" Clarence asked.

"No, we'll bury them and then put up a nice marker later with their names on them. It will be their bodies that are there, but not their spirits."

Jackson interjected, "Clarence, every Sioux has two spirits. One stays near their body, but the other will return to Wakan Tanka. We believe that the spirits of the Sioux live forever in the Black Hills (Paha Sapa)."

"I don't think we should just leave them in a hole. It's cold outside," Clarence became upset. "I bet you wouldn't leave your dad outside!"

"Clarence, my dad is buried not too far from where the folks will be buried. I'll show you his grave. That is what we have to do. Their dead bodies are no good anymore. Their spirits will be okay. You have my word."

"Will you show me where your dad is before we put my dad there? I want to see if it's okay."

"I'll do that, as soon as we get to Pine Ridge. Then you'll know where they are when we come to visit their graves," Jackson put his arm around his stepbrother. "Trust me, it'll be okay."

"I hope so." Clarence said uncertainly, "Are you sure they'll be happy? You know, my dad likes his whiskey. Will he have his whiskey there?"

"He'll have whatever he needs, Clarence," Pastor Byron answered.

"Okay. It seems kinda dumb to me. I might check with Uncle Bear before you bury them outside like that."

"That's a good idea, Clarence," Elton agreed.

"Oh and Mister, I need to tell Pastor Adams where we will be. I don't want him to come looking for us. He might worry we got lost or something."

"I'll remind you," Elton assured him. "Now if you guys have any more questions, be sure to ask one of us. We'll try to help you find the answer."

11

The next morning, everyone was rather quiet at breakfast. Clarissa seemed intrigued by Andy's waffle and did take a taste. She thought she might try one someday, but was still recuperating from the overdose of pancakes.

When they got back to their rooms, the kids started taking the blankets and pillows off the bed. "What are you doing with those?" Nora asked.

"Missus," Clarence explained. "You said we should take all our stuff."

"Oh, I'm sorry Clarence. We didn't explain very well. We did say that we should take all our stuff, but the bedding belongs to the motel. They let us use it."

"We better tell them pilamaya (*pe-LAH-mah-yeha*), huh?" Clarence suggested.

"That would be a nice thing to do," Nora smiled. "That was thoughtful of you."

Clarence smiled and was secretly pleased that Missus had said that. "Which stuff is ours?"

"I'll show you."

In a short time, they had everything packed. Nora and Clarence walked down to the desk to thank the clerk. "We wanted to thank you for the nice room and good service," Nora said.

"Pilamaya," Clarence said.

The clerk smiled, "It was a pleasure. Come again."

"Think we can, Missus?" Clarence asked.

"We might just do that."

Clarence took Nora's hand, looked at the clerk and said, "We might just do that."

When the family arrived in Pine Ridge, everyone got out at the cemetery. Elton helped Jackson walk with Clarence over to his father's grave. Nora and Byron followed with the other kids. When they got there, Clarence looked it all over. "Will Mom and Dad have a thing like that in front of where they are?"

"Yes, it's called a headstone. They will. Theirs isn't ready yet," Jackson answered. "It will be like my Dad's. Is that okay? See, your real Mom's grave is here, on the other side of where your Dad will be."

Clarence looked it all over and then shrugged, "Yah, I'll tell the other kids. Are all these stones for other dead people?"

"Yes," Byron said. "Sometimes families come and put flowers on the graves when they come to visit."

"Will we do that?" Clarence asked.

"We can," Jackson said. "Today, Auntie Mabel has a feather that each one of us can give to them when we say goodbye."

"Okay. Will the other kids get one too?"

"Yes, do you want me to tell them?" Jackson asked.

"No, I will. They won't feel as dumb asking me questions."

Byron knelt down next to the boy, "Listen Clarence, I want all you kids to know that you can ask any of us anything; and we won't think you're dumb. Okay? The only really dumb people are the ones that have a question and are afraid to ask."

"You mean we can ask anyone?"

"Yes. We are all part of your family now."

Jackson understood the doubt in Clarence's expression, "They are tiyospaye. All of these people here. If you wonder about who is our extended family, just ask any of us. Got it?"

Clarence looked desolate, "It was easier when I just thought in the outhouse."

Elton agreed, "I know the feeling. but it'll get easier. You've been very brave and have helped your brothers and sisters a lot. You're doing a great job; but if you need some help or a break, just ask any of us."

Clarence slowly nodded, "I want to forget about all of this stuff. I'm getting tired of it."

"I don't blame you a bit. I think everyone is. Two more days, and then you can relax. But if you need some help beforehand, don't be afraid to ask. Okay?"

When they parked near the community center, a car with North Dakota plates caught Jackson's attention immediately. While Byron helped him get out of the car and set up with his crutches, Jackson saw Grandma and started to cry right away.

"You came, Grandma! I didn't expect you'd come," he hugged her.

"I wouldn't let my boy face this alone if I could help it. What kind of a Grandma would I be?" she said as she returned his embrace.

"I missed you," Jackson smiled through his tears. "You knew how much I needed you!"

Then he looked up and noticed Matt and Diane right behind her. He hugged them. "Wopila tanka . . . . Er. I mean, many thanks. Thank you for coming and for bringing Grandma down for me. You guys are wonderful. You have to meet my brothers and sister!"

"Don't you want to say hi to everyone?" Diane asked.

Katie Ellison had stopped to hug her Dad and Schroeders. When she turned around, Jackson saw her and his mouth fell open, "Kate, my Katie."

She ran over to him and gave him a great embrace. He buried his face in her shoulder and cried. "I can't believe you came. I wanted to see you so much."

"I got here as soon as I could."

"What about school?"

Matt beamed, "She worked like a madwoman and got her work all made up before we left. We're here for you, Jackson. The rest would be too if they could. They all send you their love and prayers."

Byron patted his shoulder and pulled the wheelchair up beside him. "Young man, sit down before you keel over."

Jackson looked at him and said, "They all came for me. Isn't that something?"

"You would've done that for them, you know." Elton smiled. "Say, let's go see what Grandma has over at the car."

They all went over to Carl's car where Matt had the trunk open. Grandma was handing winter coats to the kids with hats and mittens. "You can't be freezing out here."

The kids looked at her in amazement. Jackson said, "What do you say, guys?"

"Pilamaya," they all said.

Clarissa caressed her pink coat, "It is so pretty, Jackson. Look how pretty it is!"

"It really is, Clarissa," Jackson smiled.

Katie pulled on her mittens that were gray with pink flowers on them. "There's a hat to match and Grandma has a scarf in there too. What do you think? Do you like it?"

Clarissa nodded while her hands kept stroking her coat and watching Kate in awe. "I really like it. What's your name?"

"I'm Katie," the sweet blonde, blue-eyed girl smiled. "I talked to you on the phone when you called Jackson one time. Do you remember?"

Clarissa felt like she had just met a fairy princess, "Yes. You are Jackson's friend."

"Yes," Jackson said as he took Kate's hand. "She is my very special friend."

Clarissa looked at Jackson and smiled, "I like her. She is pretty."

"I like you too, Clarissa," Kate said. "I better say hi to your brothers, okay?"

"I can show them to you, if you want, Miss."

"I would like it if you'd call me Katie. Okay? Can I call you Clarissa?"

"That'd be good." Clarissa said as she took Kate's hand and went over to where the boys were talking up a storm to Grandma and Matt. "Guys, this is Katie. You be nice to her because she is Jackson's special friend and she is really pretty."

Kate smiled. "Hi. You must be CJ and Clarence, right?"

"He is CJ." Clarence pointed to his younger brother. "Are you the one that went to the dance with Jackson?"

"Yes. We were all at the dance."

"He likes you," Clarence announced, and then added with a squint, "So I guess you're okay."

"Thank you, Clarence," Katie answered. "He likes you, so I guess you are okay too. I see you picked out some neat mittens. They will keep you warm. Did Grandma tell you that she made all the mittens, scarves and hats?"

"Miss Diane told us. She lives at Jackson's house. Do you?"

"No, I'm Pastor Byron's daughter, so I live at his house."

"So you won't sleep with us?" Clarissa asked with disappointment.

"Not unless we have a sleep-over. Do you think we should do that sometime?"

"I don't know," suddenly Clarissa became extremely shy.

"Clarissa, I think that would be a fine idea," Grandma said. "And I live at Jackson's house."

"Do you know where the—what was that thing?" CJ asked Andy.

Andy frowned, "I'm sorry, I don't understand."

"You know, that thing the rolls are in?"

"Oh, you mean the cookie jar?"

"Yah, do you know where the cookie jar is?" CJ asked the elderly lady.

"Why yes I do young man, and I also know how to open it! When we get to the house, you remind me and I'll show you how it works. Deal?"

"Okay," CJ cast a self-satisfied smile toward Jackson.

The back door of the hall opened and Aunt Mabel came out for a breath of fresh air. Nora went over to her. "You look so worn out, Mabel. Is there anything I can do for you?"

"No, I just needed to get some fresh air," the middle-aged Indian lady said, wearily. She had taken care of the children for a couple months, hoping to get her sister, Jackson's mom, back on track but to no avail. The whole winter had been a trial for her but she had done the best she could.

Grandma came over and reached out her hand, "Hello. You must be Mabel. I'm Katherine. I believe we chatted on the phone a few times. I'm so sorry for your loss. This must be a terrible time for you."

The short, round lady smiled and took Grandma's hand, "I was hoping I'd get to meet you. I see you brought coats for the kids. Thank you so much. The boxes of things you sent were mostly traded away. I was so upset." Then the lady sighed, "I guess I don't have to worry about that anymore."

"I hope you can come visit us often," Nora said. "I know how important you've been to the kids and Jackson. They would never have made it this long without your help. Please know that you're welcome to come visit whenever you can."

"I need your phone number, so maybe we can chat once in a while," Grandma smiled. "We'll need a lot of pointers with the kids."

"It will be difficult for them," Mabel acknowledged. "They have rarely been anywhere and know very little about the world. Their lives have been mostly at the house. It'll be quite a shock for them. I live in Eagle Butte, with my son and his family. He has a job there and his family doesn't live like this. Adam works for the Cheyenne River Reservation Council in Eagle Butte. He wasn't very happy about me coming down here and said this would come to no good if the folks didn't shape up. And they didn't."

"Do you live with him there?"

"Yes, he and his wife had twins and so I help her with the babies. They are a great joy. I have my own room there. I'll go back there now. I didn't want to leave these guys, but I just couldn't do it anymore. I knew that the kids would be taken away. I was unable to stop it."

"We know you did your best. Whenever you want, you can come visit them. I know they'll want to see you."

"That would be good. It was great to finally meet you," Mabel took Grandma's hand. "I better go back in. It's almost time."

Jackson called her, "Aunt Mabel? I want to introduce you to some of my friends. I see you met Grandma."

"I did. She's a fine lady," Mabel smiled as she pulled her coat tighter around herself.

"This is my friend, Matt Harrington. He helps me with my art stuff. This is Diane, his fiancée and the pianist. She and I talk in the middle of the night. And this is my Kate."

"Jackson has talked about all of you a lot. Thank you so much for being his good friends. That means a lot to his family here. And Kate, you are a pretty as he said! I'm so glad he found someone. He has a tender heart and needs someone to share it with. Do you live at the farm too?"

"No, I'm Pastor Byron's daughter and we live about a mile to the west. We're thankful that we got to know Jackson. I'd like you to know how much you helped Jackson. He was about frantic before you said you'd come down to care for his Steps."

Mabel smiled, "He has always called his stepbrothers and sisters that! Steps. Well, I had better get inside. They are about ready to begin the service."

The service was very moving. The little kids handled it pretty well, but Clarence and Jackson had a difficult time. Bear and Elton each took Clarence by a hand and stayed with him every second. Byron and Grandma stayed beside Jackson. CJ stayed with Matt and Diane, while Katie and Nora walked with Clarissa. She didn't want to put the feathers with her dad and mom, but wanted to keep them. Katie knelt down next to her and said, "We can get you one to keep for yourself, okay? To keep to remember them by. Would you like that?"

When their parents were carried to the gravesite, the group of mourners followed behind. It was only a short, frigid walk, and they gathered around the grave for the interment. The children watched wide-eyed as their way of life was put into the frozen earth.

Andy had ridden to the cemetery in the motorized wheelchair because Jackson was determined to walk. After the service, Andy traded places with Jackson, and Byron carried Horse's crutches back to the center.

Clarence didn't want to leave. No matter how many family members or friends tried to tell him it was time for him to go, he wouldn't budge from the grave site. Elton suggested to Bear that they go in and he'd stay with Clarence.

Elton sat down on the ground next to Clayton's grave. Clarence stood immobile for a while and then sat down next to Elton. Elton never said a word, but just put his arm around the lad.

Clarence watched as the bleak, wintery shadows grew across the frozen cemetery. Crying would not help him express the anguish and despair he felt. He leaned against Elton's arm.

They must have sat there for forty-five minutes without a word. The wind came up and began to whistle ice crystals around them.

Finally Clarence looked at Elton, "I suppose you're getting cold, huh Mister?"

"Yah, how 'bout you?"

"Yah a little, but you don't have to sit here with me. You shouldn't get so cold."

"I have to. I'll be with you no matter where you sit. You're my kid now."

Clarence looked at him in surprise, and then said very seriously, "Not really. Andy is your kid."

"He is, but so are you. Did you know that his Dad died when he was about Clarissa's age?"

"Really? Was he in a car accident?"

"No, a mining accident."

"So he is your kid the same as me, huh?"

"The very same."

"Clarence, how you feel about a person is more important than who is your real relative. So, you are my kid."

"Then you are like my new dad?"

"Yup."

Clarence thought a while and then said, "Okay, but I might not want to call you Dad. I called my Dad that."

"That's just fine, Clarence."

"We better go in, huh? I don't want you to get too cold."

"Very thoughtful Clarence," Elton answered as they got up and brushed the snow off their pants. "I promise you, we'll come back when it is nice out and you can visit your Dad and Mom here. Would you like that?"

"I think so. Jackson said we could put flowers on their graves. Can we?"

"We can do that. Or maybe, you would like to put a plant on their graves and then they can have flowers all the time," Elton suggested.

"I might like that. I'll have to talk to the other kids about it. Okay?"

"Okay."

"Mister, I'm going to miss them a lot."

"I know, Clarence. I really do know," Elton reminded the boy. "I was going to remind you to talk to Pastor Adams. Think we should do that now?"

"Yah, I guess I should."

12

That evening a very tired bunch gathered around the table at the motel dining room in Rapid City. Mabel and Adam had said their goodbyes at the house, because Adam had to get back to work. Bear was going to spend the night in Rapid City with the group so that he could see the little ones again before he went back to his job in Montana.

Zach met up with them at the motel dining room. "I'm sorry I didn't make it down to the service. Clancy was having a rough time this morning, and I didn't want to leave him."

"Thanks for being here for them. These guys needed someone, too," Bear said.

"Not a problem," Zach said as he picked up his menu. "I'm getting very fond of those little guys." Then he winked at the other kids, "I just haven't had a chance to get to know the rest of you yet."

"Do you live at our new house, too?" CJ asked.

"I used to. Now I live across the fence from there with my wife Suzy. We're so close you can come visit whenever you want."

"I can?" CJ exclaimed.

"You'll have to tell either Grandma or me, so someone knows where you are. But then you can," Nora answered.

"Or me?" Clarence asked.

"I guess he could tell you, but it'd be better if he told me," Nora replied.

Elton could see that Clarence didn't like that and interjected, "We all tell either Nora or Grandma where we are, because they run the kitchen. They have to know how many will be there to eat. If we don't tell them, we might not get fed next time."

"You do too?" Clarence was amazed.

"Yup. And Jackson and Andy. Everybody."

"I guess we want to get fed," Clarence nodded.

"I'll be sure to tell you!" CJ said. "I like to eat. Mister, can we get a bag for the rolls?"

"We sure can."

"I thought I'd come up to the hospital with you tonight, Zach, and see the kids. I want to take off early in the morning. I have a long way to drive tomorrow," Bear said.

"Certainly," Zach said. "I'm going up again after dinner. We can't pick them up until after eight tomorrow morning. I hope we have something warm for them to wear."

Grandma smiled, "Marly and I went shopping before we came down here and got Claudia a coat like Clarissa's and got a snowsuit for Clancy."

"Is hers pink too, like mine?" Clarissa asked.

"Hers is a pretty blue. Do you think she'll like that?"

"She likes blue. Mine is so beautifullest! I think pink is my mostest favorite ever."

CJ shook his head, "Your favorite is green!"

"It used to be; now it is pink."

Katie smiled, "You can have two favorite colors. I like several colors. Don't you, Diane?"

"Yes," Diane agreed, "I like most colors."

"You mean they're all your favorite?" Clarissa was amazed.

"No, just deep or dark colors. I don't like pale colors much."

"And pale colors are my favorite," Katie giggled. "Tink and I get along real well."

"Who is Tink?" Clarence frowned.

"Tink is my nickname," Diane explained. "Tink or Tinker. From Tinkerbell."

The kids looked at her blankly.

"Do you know who Tinkerbell is? How about Peter Pan?" Diane asked.

The kids still didn't understand.

Matt smiled, "When we get home, we can read you the book about Peter Pan. I bet you will really like it. Then you'll know all about the fairy named Tinkerbell."

Clarence made a face, "I won't like a book about fairies."

"You might like this one. There is the mean ship captain who has a hook for a hand and a crocodile! It is a very exciting book. You can start listening to it, and then if you don't like it, you and I can read something else. Is that okay, Clarence?" Matt asked.

Clarence thought about it and finally nodded, "I guess so. Do you have a lot of books?"

"Yes, I do. We all do, and if we can't find a good one that we have, we go to the library and borrow one. Do you have a library card yet?" Matt asked.

"No, I don't have any money," Clarence answered like an adult.

"You don't need money for a library card. The library has tons of books. I'll help you get a card. To get the card, you only have to promise to bring the book back when you are finished reading it and not wreck it. Then they let you take the book home to look at. Neat, huh? I'll tell you what. When you get settled at the farm, you and I will go to the library. You can scout it out, and then if you want, you can get a library card? What do you say?"

"Do you have a library card?" Clarence asked Jackson.

Jackson reached in his wallet and pulled out his library card. He handed it to Clarence who was greatly impressed. "When did you get one?"

"Not long ago," Jackson explained. "I went to Bismarck with Matt, Tink and Kate. I got a card."

Clarence turned to Matt, "Do I have to know how to read?"

"No, they have picture books. They really have all sorts of things there. We'll go one day and you can look it over."

"I might like to do that. It would be a good idea, right Mister?"

"It certainly would be."

"Do you have a library card?"

"Yes, right here."

Elton pulled out his wallet and got out his library card. It was rather tattered.

"Your card looks pretty beat up. Jackson's is shiny."

Elton explained, "Jackson's is brand new."

Clarence said, "Yours is old, huh? I bet you got it a long, long, long time ago when you were a kid."

Elton squinted at him, "You must really like skating on thin ice."

"I don't have skates, but CJ and I like to slide on ice. Once we fell in at the creek. We got wet and cold. Mom said we shouldn't do that anymore."

"She was right. I'll show you how to tell if the ice is thick enough to hold you. Then we can show you guys how to skate. But it is a good idea to have several people around when you skate, in case you fall in."

"You know," Andy said, "I think I'll go back to our room. The dog and cat are there and they might not be happy being left alone so long."

Nora gave her son a worried look, "You okay, Andy. You don't look well."

"I'm fine, just overtired, Mom. I need to get some rest."

Elton watched as his son got up from his chair, "We need to do some figuring. I think that the two vets should have room 102, so they can get some rest. It is the furthest from the front desk, so if they wake up with their nightmares, no one will hear them. Bear, you've hardly had any sleep. So you and Byron take room 104. Zach and Matt can take 106, it is near the back door. So will you take Rags and Cotton?"

"We'll take the boys, too," Matt offered. "I think the pets will be happier with the kids there. What do you say, guys?"

"That is a good idea, Mister. Rags would like to sleep with us," Clarence explained.

"Okay."

Grandma smiled, "I'll sleep with Katie, Diane and Clarissa. We can have that sleepover we talked about! Okay, Clarissa?"

"What about Missus?" Clarissa pointed out. "She will be lonesome."

"I'll take care of her," Elton smiled. "You girls take 103 and we'll take 105. Now, does everyone have a place?"

"That'd be a bad idea," Clarence sat back. "Mister, Cotton and Rags will fight if they're in the same room."

"I'm glad you mentioned that, Clarence. Nora and I will have Cotton sleep with us. The girls can't have Cotton in there, because it will make Katie sneeze her head off," Elton said.

"Oh, is she the girl you said gets the sneezes from kittens?" Clarence said. He turned to Jackson, and felt it necessary to emphasize the new information. "Did you know that? She sneezes from cats!"

Jackson grinned, "Yes Clarence, I know that."

Clarence could not fathom why that didn't disqualify her in Jackson's eyes. He just shook his head. Then he listed off his brothers and sisters on his fingers and then nodded. "We all have a place. We have to remember to pick up Claudia and Clancy tomorrow. We don't want them to get left."

"They won't be left behind," Elton assured him.

Zach said, "Never. Bear and I are going to check on them tonight and make plans to pick them up in the morning. They are definitely coming along."

"Can we go visiting tonight?" Clarissa asked. "To see my brother's room."

"Plan on it," Grandma giggled. "Right after our bubble baths."

Clarissa's mouth dropped open, "Missus, this Mrs. Grandma lady has bubble baths too!"

"I know honey, and so do the other girls! Isn't that neat? Clarissa, you can call her Grandma like we do, okay?"

Clarissa looked at Clarence for approval, and he looked at Jackson.

Jackson nodded, "I call her Grandma, because you know what kids? She is the world's best Grandma!"

Clarence thought a minute and then asked Elton, "Think that would be okay, Mister?"

"I think it would be. We all call her Grandma."

Then Clarence looked back to Clarissa. "You can call her Grandma, Clarissa. It's okay."

"Me, too?" CJ asked. "She knows where the jar of rolls is!"

"Yes, you too," Clarence shook his head, "Don't bug her about the jar."

"She's going to show me how to open it," CJ explained.

"I promised him I'd do that, Clarence. I can show you too, if you like," Grandma said.

When everyone began to leave the table, Jackson asked Kate if she would walk with him. She reached down, put her hand around his waist to help him to his feet and then gave him his crutches. "Do you want a cigarette?"

"Yes, I need to get my jacket. Okay?"

Once they got inside the door to his room, Jackson turned the lock. The nineteen-year-old pulled Kate into his arms and gave her a passionate kiss. She was surprised but then returned it. Then Jackson pulled back. "I have to sit down, my leg is giving out."

He unlocked the door and they went over to sit on the edge of the bed. Kate sat beside him, "I was worried that you weren't very happy I came."

"I was very glad, but I was afraid to show it. As it was, between the kids, Uncle Bear and everyone, if your Dad doesn't know how we feel about each other, he'd have to be nuts."

"Jackson," Kate took his hand and kissed his cheek, "He has known for some time."

"But I promised your Dad that I'd never give him a reason to doubt me and that I'd respect you. I'll never betray his trust."

Kate seemed surprised, "You haven't betrayed his trust."

"No, not yet." Jackson put his arm around her, "But if I'm alone with you too much, I'd be very tempted."

"I know," Kate nodded. "I'm responsible too; it isn't just you. Mom and I have had some serious talks about it. I know we have to behave. So, let's get your jacket, go outside for a bit and then find a public kind of place to sit. I want to have some time to talk to you alone. Okay? Did that make any sense to you?"

"It did," Jackson smiled. "Fifteen isn't that young, but you aren't even supposed to date until you are sixteen, let alone go steady with someone. Do you think we'll ever sit someday and wish we were younger?"

"Probably."

The young couple went down the hall and out onto the patio. Jackson smoked his cigarette and then went inside. The lobby had a big fireplace and the couple sat in front of the overstuffed sofa. There was even a hassock for Jackson to put his stub leg. Jackson had his arm around her and they talked about the events of the last week.

It was a little after nine, when Bear and Zach came back from the hospital and found them there. The men sat down and told them how the little kids were doing.

"We were getting ready to hit the hay ourselves," Jackson said. "I bet everyone is looking for us."

Zach smiled, "Oh, I bet they know where you are, but you really should get some rest. I'm not happy about the way you've been taking care of yourself. Doggone it, I'm your doctor and have to answer to the VA guys if you get sick."

Zach and Jackson became engrossed in their conversation about Jackson's health and headed down the hall. Bear smiled after them and held out his hand to Kate. She took it and they walked back together.

"I need to have a talk with that kid," Bear teased. "He shouldn't leave a pretty girl like you sitting alone."

"It's okay. He does need to take care of himself. I think he is running a fever again. He was so sick . . . ." Then she noticed Bear had been teasing. "Oh, you're teasing me."

"I'm so happy he found a sweetheart like you. Jackson told me how much you've done for him and how much he thinks of you. He is a good person, Kate. I think you are, too. I hope you two can take your time and build a wonderful relationship. You know life is long and can be a trial unless you have someone to share it with."

Kate smiled at Bear and gave him a quick hug. "You have always been so important in Jackson's life. He loves and respects you."

Zach and Jackson stopped and stared at them. Bear frowned at them, "Mind your own business. We're having a talk here. We didn't nose into your talk!"

Zach chuckled, "I don't know Jackson, I think you might want to keep a better eye on your girl!"

Jackson laughed, "Looks like it."

13

When the phone rang in the girl's room, Grandma sat up in bed and looked around. There, sleeping with Katie, was Clarissa. Sometime during the night, she had moved the chair over to the closet, taken down her pink coat and put it on. She was curled up beside Katie wearing her coat, hat and one mitten. The other mitten was beside her with her scarf.

Grandma poked Diane and then made the shush motion with her hand. Diane looked over and whispered, "I guess she was going to make certain it wasn't given away, huh?"

The girls got dressed and met the men in the dining room. Bear was just finishing his breakfast, "I'm glad you guys made it. I would've been sad to miss telling you goodbye."

He picked up Clarissa and gave her a hug, "You be a big girl for me, will you? And if you ever need to talk to me, they have my phone number. If I'm at work, you tell the machine. I can't talk to you until I get home; but I promise I'll call you right away!"

"A heart promise?" Clarissa asked as she gave him a hug.

Nora explained, "She means a cross-you-heart promise."

Bear looked at the little girl and kissed her cheek, "Yes, a big cross your heart promise."

"I'm going to be sad about it," Clarissa said.

"I know, but Grey Hawks are brave people. I know my girl is brave too. You be good and be happy. Hear?"

"I hear. Love you."

"Love you too, Sweetheart."

Then he gave Katie a big hug and a kiss on the cheek, "Keep Jackson on his toes, will you? It he goes all peculiar, let me know. I'll box his ears."

Katie smiled, "Thank you, Uncle Bear. I'll do that."

Nora gave him a hug, "Will you be able to come out to visit soon?"

"I hope so. This kinda shot any vacation time I was collecting, but I'll be out to see you as soon as I can. I have to replenish my supply of Grandma's caramel rolls."

Grandma kissed his cheek, "You are such a charmer."

Then he hugged CJ, shook Clarence's hand and gave Jackson a big embrace. "I love you, my boy. These folks are giving you a chance for a great start. Don't louse it up. Okay?"

"I won't, Uncle Bear. Drive carefully."

Everyone was quiet until the girls ordered their breakfast. Clarence surveyed the situation and said, "How soon do we get the other kids?"

"In about an hour," Zach replied. "All your colds seems to be a lot better. I want to warn you all, the other kids cannot get in the cold air for a couple months. They are still coughing like crazy, but they are no longer contagious."

"What's contagious?" Clarence asked.

"See, pneumonia is caused by tiny, tiny little bugs called germs. They make a nest in your lungs and that makes you sick. When you take medicine, like I gave you, it kills the bugs so you can't get sick from them. We call the bugs contagious when they can fly through the air and land on other folks. They get into their lungs, make a nest and make that person sick. But after the medicine, they can't do that anymore."

Clarence's eyes were as big as saucers, "Flying bugs! A guy should hide when somebody coughs on them, huh?"

"Yah," Zach said. "A person should always cover their mouths when they cough or sneeze, so their bug don't get into someone else."

Clarence could barely talk, "Are they all over?"

Zach began to think he might have overdone it a bit, "Yes, everyone has germs. We only need to be careful when we cough. So, we need to cover our mouths."

"Hear that everybody! Cover your mouth! Especially Jackson's friend, when you're around cats! If somebody coughs, duck!"

"Well, it isn't quite that dangerous." Byron said, "Good grief, I think you scared him half to death, Zacharias. We just need to be careful, Clarence."

Clarence was still thinking about it while they were checking out and loading the cars. He and Nora went to tell the lady at the front desk goodbye. Clarence told her, "Pilamaya."

Just then, she sneezed. Clarence hit the floor and covered his head like he was on a battlefield. Nora tried to keep from giggling, but helped him up. "It's okay, Clarence."

The lady apologized, but Clarence just wanted out of there! He ran off to find Zach like the devil was after him. "Mr. Zach, I need more of that medicine! Right away! They got on me! I just know it!"

"Why is that? You took your medicine this morning," Zach explained.

Nora caught up to him, "Well, Dr. Wizard, you terrified the little guy! The lady sneezed and I thought he was going to have a heart attack!"

"Mr. Zach, I could see 'em coming! Flying right at me! There must have been a hundred bugs! Now what can I do?"

"I'll show you," Zach grinned. "We'll go wash up. Soap and water are the best germ fighters in the world. Come, I'll help you."

Nora looked at Byron and said, "I can't wait until Zach has kids of his own! Poor Clarence, he probably picked up more germs going spread eagle on the floor than from the sneeze!"

At the hospital, Zach, Matt and Nora went to pick up the kids while Elton took care of the bill. Then he joined them. The kids had developed a trust in Zach, so were comfortable with him.

First, they picked up Claudia. Nora dressed her and put on her coat and hat. She could tell the little three-year-old liked the soft coat, almost as much as Clarissa liked hers. Then Matt took her in his arms and carried her. Claudia never said a word, but watched Zach to see if the situation seemed okay by him. After Matt carried her a ways, she began to relax.

Next they picked up little Clancy. He was nineteen months old, and even though he was obviously ill, he was a smiley kid. He held his arms out to Zach right away and Zach picked him up. Then Clancy and Claudia hugged each other. That was the first time Claudia smiled.

Nora got Clancy dressed in his snowsuit and Zach carried him. They headed toward the cars. They had decided that Jackson was going to ride with Matt, while Grandma was going to ride with Schroeders. Zach and Byron were going to ride in the Suburban with Rags and Cotton, who were none too happy about the trip. Clarence decided that he and CJ would ride with them to help with the pets; besides, no one in that car had a cough!

Clarissa wanted to be with Katie, so she and Katie sat in the backseat with Jackson. "Are you sure you don't need to keep your leg up?" Matt asked.

"I can't really anyway, and I'd like to sit in back with Katie for a while. Then maybe later we can change around," Jackson answered.

Katie explained, "He gets miserable if he is in one position too long."

Matt teased, "Personally, I thought he was miserable all the time!"

"I don't know why you're one of my best friends!" Jackson asked. "You're awful most of the time."

"Just lucky, I guess," Matt smiled and spoke directly to the tiny girl. "Claudia, can you sit by Diane?"

She looked worried for a minute and then Clarissa poked her and nodded with a big smile. "Okay. It's okay."

Claudia smiled back and nodded. Within a minute, she was cuddled up in Diane's lap. Matt had kept the heat on, so the car was warm. Diane patted the little girl's cheek and smiled, "Okay?"

Claudia watched her expression and then nodded back.

Nora held Clancy in the backseat of Schroeder's car. Andy sat in front so his legs could be straighter, and Grandma sat in back and helped with Clancy. Since Nora had been seriously injured by a malicious sow years before, she had lost a lot of her muscle in her one arm. Clancy was a bit heavy for her to carry, but he did snuggle up next to her in the car and fell asleep on her lap in minutes.

The group traveled in convoy, stopping only to eat in Dickinson and for various potty/gasoline stops along the way. It was well after noon when they finally stopped to eat at a restaurant in Dickinson. Elton chuckled while he and Byron took the dog for a walk, "At the rate this outfit is going, we should make it home by next week! Too bad we can't synchronize the pit stops"

"Yah, and Clarence was right. Rags sure doesn't like this leash."

"If we took it off, we'd never see her again. I don't think I'd want to explain that to Clarence."

"He is a very responsible kid."

"You know Byron," Elton said thoughtfully, "All I wanted is to have those kids in a good place so Jackson could heal up without all the worry.

But Clarence has really tugged at me. He reminds me so much of myself when I was a kid. I want him to be a happy kid and to learn to trust me, so he doesn't have to bear his burden alone."

Byron put his arm on his friend's shoulder, "I know and I truly believe that he will. You are a good guy. If the kid can't trust you, he is a tough nut to crack. It will take a while though."

"I know."

Matt came over to the men, "We've been noticing, when Clarissa talks to Claudia, she always touches her cheek first to get her attention. Those kids have been accommodating for Claudia's hearing loss all along."

"Has she talked at all?" Elton asked.

"No, she has smiled a few times. Hey, you guys go on inside and I'll walk with Rags. Should I just put her back in her crate when she does her business?"

"If you would," Byron answered. "It is plenty warm in the car and hopefully, we'll be on the road again soon."

It was dark when the convoy turned onto the gravel road toward Merton, the small prairie town in central North Dakota. Clarence and CJ began scoping out everything they saw. Zach and Byron were besieged with a million questions. The boys wanted to know where everyone lived, what they did, and most importantly, how many kids and pets they had.

When the cars stopped by the farmhouse, the kitchen door opened and folks started to file out to help bring things in. The Grey Hawk children were at their new home.

14

Elton stopped his car and went over to the Suburban. "How 'bout I ride to the barn with you guys and we can unload Rags and her crate?"

"You drive," Zach smiled. "I want to go carry Clancy in. He might get freaked in a strange place."

Elton drove up to the barn. "Here we are boys. My dog Elmer usually sleeps in the straw stacks, so I was thinking we could put Rags in the barn overnight. That way, she won't run away, but she'll be warm and safe. What do you think, Clarence? Would it be better for Elmer and Rags to meet in the daytime?"

"Yah, do you think they will fight?" Clarence worried.

"No, but we better be safe, huh?"

"Mister, will Rags cry in the barn?"

"No, there are other animals in the barn, so she'll have company. She'll have food, water and room to run around. I think she'll like it."

Clarence was doubtful, "How soon will I get to see her again?"

"Before breakfast, when we do chores. Have you boys ever milked cows?"

"No."

"Tomorrow you can think about if you want to learn, okay?"

"Okay," Clarence said. "Did your kids do it?"

"Yup."

"Is it hard?"

"Not a bit," Elton smiled as he and Byron moved the dog crate out of the back of the vehicle. "If it was, I wouldn't be doing it!"

Clarence watched him to see if he was serious, and then grinned. "I guess we can try, huh CJ?"

"Are we going to put Cotton in the barn too?" CJ asked.

"I think Cotton will go in the basement of the house until she gets comfortable there. If we put her out here, she'd run off. Cats go in and out of the barn all the time. Besides, there are barn cats down here."

"To keep the mice down," Clarence added, demonstrating his understanding.

Elton grinned, "Right on, Clarence."

That made Clarence feel good.

Inside the barn, the boys were impressed. They had never seen a barn so big or with so much stuff in it. There were four baby calves, living in the barn until the weather let up. Abner, Little Charlie's old horse, was inside because the cold and damp bothered his arthritis.

"How old is Charlie?" Clarence asked as he patted Abner's neck with Byron's help.

"He is six. He'll be seven soon. This is his horse," Byron explained. "You guys will meet him tonight because he's up at the house. I know he is anxious to meet you guys. There aren't too many boys his age around here. He is looking forward to having boys to play with."

"I don't have a lot of time to play, but CJ does. If he is an okay guy, CJ can play with him," Clarence answered matter-of-factly.

"But I don't have a horse!" CJ worried. "He might not want to play with me because I won't have a horse!"

"He doesn't play on his horse that often and besides, it is big enough for two. Charlie loves to dig and mess around," Byron smiled.

"I can mess around good, but I don't think I dig. Do I, Clarence?"

"We didn't have a shovel," Clarence rolled his eyes.

"We can fix that," Elton chuckled. "Besides, as long as you can mess around, that's all Charlie cares about!"

"Oh good!" CJ beamed at the prospect.

Clarence checked out the calf pen that Rags was in and made certain that she had her favorite stick, plenty of water and food. After he was sure she was okay, he patted her head. "Be good, Rags. I'll be back at sun up."

Then CJ hugged the dog and rolled with her on the fresh straw. "This is a good sleeping place, Rags. I will sleep with you tonight."

"Or," Elton suggested, "We can go to the house and have a big supper with some fresh rolls! Then you can sleep inside where it is warm. Which would you rather?"

CJ thought, "Can I take some rolls with me when I sleep where it's warm?"

"I think so."

"Bye-bye, Rags. I have to meet this Charlie guy," the young boy hugged his dog and took Elton's hand.

Zach took Clancy from the car while Nora helped Andy with his walker. "Before I go home tonight, I want to check over both you and Horse. This has been a lot of stress on you guys, and neither of you were in good shape to start with."

Andy nodded, "I'm just tired. Horse is running quite a fever and was coughing last night. He's really been pushing it with the wake and all that. His stub looked inflamed last night. He tried to tell me it was okay, but I know it better."

"It wasn't okay yesterday. The longer it takes to heal, the longer it will be before he can get his prosthesis. I'll check him out."

Zach carried the sleeping Clancy into the house. There a petite, pregnant, blonde girl met them at the door. She gave Zach a kiss and asked, "Can I come while you put him down so I can meet him?"

"Sure Suzy," Zach kissed his wife, "He is asleep now."

The nursery was on the main floor next to Nora and Elton's bedroom. Zach and Suzy took off Clancy's snowsuit. Suzy changed his diaper and got a warm sleeper out for him. It was made of fleece blanket material and had feet in it with a long zipper up the front. "That should keep him warm if he kicks off his blankets at night. Will his hands be warm enough?"

"Oh I think so. Schroeder's house is warm. He'll be fine. He is running a fever tonight again, but it's to be expected. I'll go get some water and give him his medication."

"Does he want to eat?" Suzy asked.

"His tummy was pretty messed up, so he has been on this high potency formula until he's feeling better. He doesn't like it very much."

Suzy dripped some from the bottle on her hand and licked it. She made a horrible face, "Yea gads! That's terrible! Have you tasted it?"

Zach shook his head with an expression of wonder, "Why would I taste it?"

"I don't know what they teach you pediatricians! You should taste it, so you know why a kid doesn't want to eat it? Here, taste it!"

He reluctantly licked the back of her hand, "Yuk! I wouldn't drink that either."

"See, now do you know why you should taste it?"

Zach hugged his wife, "I'll make it a point to do that before I send something home with some poor unsuspecting mom."

"Good, then my day hasn't been a total loss!" Suzy giggled. "So, what are we going to do with our little Clancy?"

"Hmm," Zach picked the toddler up, "Would you like to eat supper with us tonight?"

Clancy pushed the bottle away.

"No, you don't have to have that. I mean dinner?"

Clancy smiled.

"What are we going to do about the high potency stuff?" Suzy asked.

"I'll bring something else home tomorrow from work. What are we having for dinner?"

"Chicken and dumplings. Will that be okay for him?"

"I think so. Shall we give it a try, Clancy?"

The little boy nodded and hugged Zach.

Clarissa came into the house, holding Katie's hand. She was a bit taken back by the number of people there. Clarissa leaned against Kate, who started to take the little girl's coat off. She shook her head no, not taking her eyes off the people in the kitchen. Katie understood and suggested that she take off her mittens, cap, scarf and then unbutton her coat. Clarissa could live with that. "Let's go put them in your room, okay?"

Clarissa nodded, but paid no attention to what she was saying. Katie carried her things and held her hand while they walked through the kitchen. They passed by the huge dining room and up the stairs. Clarissa started to get nervous.

"It'll be okay, honest," Katie explained. "This will be the room for you and Claudia to share. Want to see it?"

Clarissa shrugged, very intimidated by it all. Katie opened the first door to the right at the top of the stairs. "This room is for Clarence and CJ. So, you and Claudia will be here, right next door."

"I can sleep with Clarence and CJ. They'll be scared by themselves." Clarissa said softly.

"I suppose you could. You have to talk to Aunt Nora about that. Okay? Let's just look at your room, okay?"

Clarissa hesitated and put her mittens, scarf and cap on the bed in the boy's room. Then she took Katie's hand and went with her. Katie opened the door. The room was painted a soft pink with a white ceiling and the carpet was green. The light fixture on the ceiling and the three lamps in the room looked like a flowers with pink translucent petal lampshades. The bedspreads and curtains were white with dainty pink flowers on them. The pillow shams had white and pink ruffles around them.

Clarissa gasped and her mouth came open. Her eyes were huge and she didn't even blink. "Oh, it is so beautifuler! Almost as beautifulest like my coat!"

"Like it?" Katie asked, mentally thanking her Mom. They had a long talk on the phone about how much Clarissa liked her coat, so Mom knew what to do with the room.

"Yes." Clarissa almost whispered. "Is this where you live?"

"No honey, this is your room. You and Claudia will share it, until you get older. Then maybe you would each like your own room."

"She wouldn't like that. I need to keep her from being scared."

"I know. Do you want to hang up your coat to keep it nice? You wouldn't like to spill on it, would you?"

"No," Clarissa pulled the coat tighter around her. "I better keep it on."

Katie nodded, "Okay. I have an idea. When we sit at the table, we can put it over the back of your chair. That way if you accidently spill, your coat will be okay. Will that work?"

"Can I sit on it?"

"Yes, you can. Let's get washed up for dinner, okay?"

Before they left the bedroom, Clarissa asked, "Katie, can I keep the light on? Otherwise, I won't find my room again. Maybe the boys will want to sleep in my room so they don't get scared."

"They might at that. I'll leave the door open. This door across the hall is Diane's room. So if you need something at night, you can knock on her door. Okay?"

"I'll just ask Clarence."

"That will work too."

Matt carried the sleeping Claudia into the house. Diane asked Nora, "Where do you want her tonight?"

"I think in the nursery. I'd worry that I couldn't hear her if she needed something during the night. Just put her on the daybed in there, please."

Matt carried Claudia down the hall and she started to wake up. Once in the nursery, Matt put her on the bed and Diane began to take off her coat. Matt kissed Diane's cheek, "I think I'll go help the guys take Cotton's crate downstairs."

"Okay," Diane answered and then noticed Claudia.

The little girl's eyes filled with tears and she dropped her head. Diane rubbed her cheek with her index finger. Claudia looked up, with tears quietly streaming down her cheeks.

"What is it, Claudia?" Diane asked as she sat next to her and pulled her on to her lap. "Why is my little girl sad?"

Claudia looked at Diane and then said softly, "Cotton."

Matt knelt down in front of the little girl and stroked her cheek. "You let Diane get your coat off and I'll take you downstairs to see Cotton. Okay?"

She watched his face and then touched his cheek, "Cotton?"

"Cotton," Matt nodded yes.

She smiled slightly.

Diane got her coat off while Matt got a washcloth to freshen her up. He tapped her cheek and he held out his arms, "Let's go see Cotton."

Claudia held out her arms to him.

They went through the kitchen but Claudia was oblivious to the folks there. Diane explained they were going to check out the cat and Matt took the little girl down the basement steps. Her grip tightened on his neck, but her eyes were searching every nook and cranny for her pet. When they approached the crate, Kevin looked up from putting the dish of cat food down. Matt explained, "We came to see Cotton. She is Claudia's friend."

Kevin smiled at the girl and said, "Hello, Claudia."

She never looked his way and Matt explained that Claudia couldn't hear very well. "The kids showed us what they do. We just touch her cheek and she'll look at you."

Kevin touched her cheek gently and smiled, "Hello Claudia. Shall I get Cotton for you?"

She nodded. Kevin carefully opened the cat crate and dodged the teeth of the snarling cat. "That's okay, kitty. You can settle down now. There's someone here to see you."

Kevin managed to grab the cat and put it in his arms sustaining only minor blood loss. Then he held the cat near Claudia. The little sweetheart giggled and hugged her kitty. The cat, miraculously, crawled right up into her arms and started to purr.

"Well, I guess they truly are best friends," Kev smiled to Matt. Kev sat on the rug by the crate.

Matt sat down on the floor across from Kevin and set Claudia between his legs. Cotton was curled up on Claudia's lap. The two hugged, purred and petted for quite a while until Elton came down the steps. "You guys okay down here?"

"We were just visiting while these two played. Dinner ready?"

"Yah, everyone is setting up to the table," Elton said watching the pair, "Isn't that something? The way that cat snarled and yowled on the trip home, I was half afraid to let her be around the little girl."

"Think we should leave the basement door open so she can come upstairs with Claudia?" Kev asked.

"Not yet. I'm afraid she might take off when the outside door opens. Let's wait until tonight after everyone has gone and then we'll open the door. It looks like Cotton might want to be with her friend, but I'd like her to make friends with her litter box before she runs around too much."

"Okay Dad," Kevin said as he put the kitten in the crate, but left the door unlatched so it would open with a small push.

Matt stood up, touched Claudia's cheek and held out his hands to take her. Then they raced to the steps before Cotton figured out she could get out of the crate. Claudia wasn't happy about leaving her kitten, but was happy to see Clarence. Her brother touched her cheek and asked, "You okay?"

She nodded.

"Come, eat now."

The family who called themselves the Engelmann Clan, used the immense dining room. It was built to accommodate their large, extended family for Sundays and holidays. At any rate, it was not the entire clan that met that evening in early 1971. Other than those who had gone to Pine Ridge; it was just Suzy Jeffries, Kevin Schroeder and his wife, Carrie, the rest of Pastor's family and Grandpa.

Grandpa Lloyd's Alzheimer's disease seemed to be better that evening and he wasn't too confused. He watched all the people gather at the table and all the little kids he had never seen before. He studied everyone, but never said a word. Somehow, he usually managed to conjure up a reason that he was related to someone he liked.

Andy and Jackson were given strict orders to stay in their wheelchairs after their energetic last week. Zack decreed that Jackson wasn't to use his crutches except for short minutes for at least a week, or he'd have his hide. The infection that had taken his foot was making a massive comeback above his now missing ankle and was causing inflammation up to just below the knee. "I'm not messing around, Jackson. If you don't take care of it, together with the cold you now have, you stand a good chance of losing more of your leg. I'll put you in the hospital."

Jackson didn't take the news very well, and it didn't help when Byron backed up Zach. "Jackson, we just got the kids here so they could be near you. If you don't take care of yourself, you'll be in Fargo at the VA!"

"I didn't want to get sick, Byron. I had to go to the funeral," Jackson started to tear up.

Byron hugged him, "I know Son, but I worry. You just try to rest until dinner is ready. Okay?"

Byron went out and closed the door. A few minutes later, there was a knock. "It's Katie. May I come in?"

"Kate, of course." Jackson wiped his tears with the back of his hand as he sat up on his bed.

Kate came in and closed the door behind her. She went over to his bed and gave him a hug, "Dad said you might need some company."

He put his arms around her, "I'm sorry. I bet you think I'm a big baby."

Kate smiled, "No, but you're so feverish. Are you getting pneumonia?"

"Zach said probably, and my stupid leg is all infected again! Kate, what am I going to do?"

She smiled, "I think you better follow the doctor's instructions or you won't only be sick, you'll get skinned too. You should've heard Uncle Elton a minute ago; when Zach reminded him he had to get back on those IV's for the Whipple's disease now that he was home!"

Jackson slightly smiled, "Oh yah, I bet he thought they had forgotten all about it, huh?"

"Zach never forgets," Kate giggled. "You just need to take a couple days of down time and recuperate. You did a lot while you were in Pine Ridge."

"Thank you so much for coming down," Jackson said.

"They'd have come anyway, but it was nice of Matt to drag me along."

Jackson chuckled, "You make it sound like he towed you behind the car with a rope!"

"Yah," Kate teased, "You should've seen how I had to beg to let me sit inside the car! Hey, Matt took those sketches sent in for you. He figured you'd be able to take a couple days off and still make the clinic order. Are you anxious to get back to your sketching?"

"Kate, I never even thought about it. I just didn't think. I don't think I thought since I heard about the car accident."

Kate kissed his cheek, "I know. So, how 'bout after I get your wheelchair over here, you and I go out to get some supper. Then if you want, I'll come back in and read a little before you go to sleep. Would you like that?"

"Yes, I really would. What about the kids?"

Kate looked straight into his eyes and said very clearly, "Listen to me. Schroeder's took the kids so you wouldn't be totally responsible for them. They want you to get well, and get a good start in life. They didn't bring the kids up here so you would drive yourself nuts about taking care of them! Got it?"

Jackson was taken by the conviction Kate said it with, "You really believe that?"

"Yes, I do," Kate put her hand on his cheek. "Everyone wants the best for all of you guys, especially me."

Jackson gave her a kiss, "We better get out there before they eat our dinner."

Kate agreed, "Jackson, will you promise me you'll take it easy?"

"You have my word, Kate."

Kate put her arm around his waist and helped him into his wheelchair. Then she flipped the platform for his bad leg, so it could lay straight.

Jackson took her hand, "Does it drive you crazy to have to help your boyfriend stand or sit?"

"Not as much as it bothers him."

Jackson grabbed her hand, "Kate, I hate it. I want to be able to dance with you and be the kind of guy you can depend on."

"You already are that, and once you get your foot, you'll be a dancing machine!"

"Think so?"

"Well, maybe with lots of lessons," Katie giggled.

The group began to set up to the table. Clancy was in a high chair between Zach and Suzy. Claudia sat between Matt and Diane on a high stool that had a back on it. Clarissa sat by Nora while Clarence sat next to Elton and CJ sat by Horse. There was a lot of sizing up going on at the table. The Ellison kids were watching the Grey Hawk kids.

Miriam Jeffries was three and lived with Ellisons, even though she was Zach's niece. She'd been severely neglected and abused by her parents, who were now deceased. Her early childhood had been a tragedy and she was under a psychiatrist's care. The psychiatrist felt it would be better for Miriam to be with other children, so that is why she lived with Ellisons. Since that summer it was her home, and no one wanted to move her. She was very small for her age partly because of years of malnutrition, although some might have been hereditary. She had black curly hair and sparkling large dark brown eyes. When she came to them nine months earlier, she was recuperating from a gunshot to her hip inflicted by her father. At the time, she rarely spoke, and was terrified of almost everything. She had come a long way, but was still not completely well.

She sat between Kevin whom she called 'Son' and his wife, Carrie. She loved them and they returned the favor. Kevin and Carrie had a baby only a couple months old, little Holly. Everyone was worried that Miriam, who always called herself Gopher, might be jealous of the new baby. Instead, Miriam thought that Holly was her baby, too. She even let her sleep with her stuffed toy, the beloved Mr. Bear.

Charlie Ellison sat on the other side of Matt. He and Matt were good friends, since they had a pact. The tow-headed, blue-eyed lad had an aversion to girl kisses, weddings and hated being a ring bearer at weddings. Matt had made him a solemn promise; he would not have to be in his wedding. Charlie had earned the nickname Lizzardhead by all the girls in his home, mostly because he was one.

Then there was Ginger. She sported mahogany colored hair, green eyes and freckles. She had been as much of a character as Charlie until she had attempted to remove her freckles with a mixture of spot remover and chlorine bleach. She almost died and still had effects from the mixture. She lost one of her little fingers and underwent several skin grafting surgeries. Her face was spared being badly scarred, but there were two little ones by her eye and she had a crooked little smile.

85

Everyone held hands and Pastor Byron said grace. Then they started passing food. Clarence frowned and asked Elton, "Mister, don't we have the papers?"

"I don't understand, Clarence. Which papers are they?"

"The ones that say the food on it."

"Oh, menus? They're called menus. No, when we are home, we eat what the ladies cook. They always do a good job. Is that okay?"

"Yah, I was just wondering," Clarence felt embarrassed.

"That was a good question though," Elton said. "I think if we had a lot of choices then we might have a menu."

"We did for Grandma's birthday party, remember Uncle Elton?" Katie said.

"That's right, we did."

Clarence was visibly relieved to hear that.

Then Byron said, "I'd like to introduce everyone, in case we missed somebody when we got home. Okay?"

After he listed everyone off, he asked, "Any questions?"

They all looked at him like he was daft. "I think we got it, Dad," Ken answered.

Clarence asked Ken, "Are you Mr. Pastor's boy?"

"I am. My name is Ken."

Clarence explained, "My Dad died in a car wreck. So Mister is going to be like my Dad until I get old enough."

"Uncle Elton is a good guy. You'll be lucky to have a dad like him."

"My real Dad was good, too." Clarence added.

Ken smiled, "I bet he was because he had a fine family."

Clarence nodded, but never said anything.

Then Grandpa Lloyd announced, "Well I'm glad you got here in time for supper. I was getting hungry. Wasn't I?"

Suzy smiled, "Yes you were, Grandpa."

"A guy shouldn't have to wait a long time to eat, should he?"

CJ perked right up, "No sir. I don't like to wait either."

"You're a fine man then. What's your name again?"

"CJ."

Grandpa shook his head, "It's too bad they ran out of names, but I guess letters are better than numbers, huh? CJ is pretty good."

CJ didn't know just how to take the comment, but it ended with 'pretty good,' so he was happy.

"I suppose your name is 1-2-3, huh?" Grandpa asked Clarence.

"No sir. It's Clarence."

"I knew a guy named Clarence once. He smoked a pipe. Do you smoke a pipe?"

"Not until I grow up," Clarence explained. "Then I can smoke the Ceremony Pipe."

"Never heard of that one," Lloyd said. "Saw one made out of Rhinoceros horn once."

Clarence watched the elderly man and then shrugged to Elton. Elton leaned down and whispered, "Grandpa's mind isn't so good anymore."

Clarence nodded and said to Grandpa, "I live at this house now."

"So do I," Grandpa grinned, "It is my house, you know."

"Oh, I like your house. It is big," Clarence said.

"He can live here if he wants, right Elton?"

"That's right Grandpa. This can be Clarence's home as long as he wants," Elton said.

"Then I guess we must be brothers, huh?" Grandpa looked at the lad.

"We can be if you want," Clarence said. "I never had a brother as old as you before."

"Well, you're the youngest brother I ever had."

Seven year old Ginger was just dying to talk, "My name is Ginger. I'll tell you my stuff. I know all about dirt, so if you guys want to know anything about dirt, just ask me."

Clarence shook his head and asked to Elton, "Doesn't her mind work good either?"

Elton chuckled, "It works just fine."

Ginger heard it and was not at all pleased. She crossed her arms, "I thought I was going to like you better than Johnny Freed, but I already don't! You are bad to say that. My mind is good!"

"Nobody talks about dirt. There is nothing to say about dirt," Clarence announced.

"I bet you don't know anything about dirt, do you?" Ginger was indignant. "I can show you jars of dirt in my room. I know all the names of it. I have lots of kinds of dirt I my collection."

"You keep dirt in your room?" Clarence squinted like she was from outer space. "In jars?"

"What do you keep in your room?"

"Not jars of dirt."

Ginger whined to her father, "Daddy, he is so mean."

"No Ginger, he isn't mean. He just isn't interested in dirt. I bet if you showed him your dirt collection, he'd be interested."

Clarence looked at Byron, "Not so much."

CJ offered, "I'll look at your dirt, Ginger. My name is CJ. I like dirt."

"Me, too," said Clarissa.

"Okay, when I'm not in school, I'll show you guys my dirt. We won't let Clarence see it."

"Ginger," her Dad reprimanded her. "Be nice."

She looked at him and nearly pouted, "I'm sorry, Daddy. I was so excited to have a new friend that I just got sad that he doesn't like my dirt."

"I'll be your friend," Clarence conceded. "I just don't want to think about dirt."

"Alright, we'll think about something else," Ginger offered. "You pick."

"I'll sleep on it and let you know tomorrow," Clarence answered.

Ginger indignantly flew into orbit, "What!?! Can't you just tell me?"

"Okay, we'll think about what we're going to think about!" Clarence rolled his eyes.

"That is just dumb," Ginger groaned. "Matt, can you tell him?"

"Don't get upset, Ginger. He is just a thinking kind of guy. That's a good thing."

"Well, I don't think, and I'm a good guy!" Charlie insisted.

"You're a good guy too," Matt suddenly felt the world closing in. He mumbled, "You both are."

Zach started to laugh, "Just try to explain about germs."

Clarence perked right up, "Ginger, we can talk about coughs and germs if you want!"

Ginger crossed her eyes, "I don't want to talk about germs. Yuk!"

"Did you know they come flying through the air?" Clarence was not about to quit. "They crawl in your mouth and make you cough!"

"Daddy, make him stop!"

"Clarence," Byron suggested, "Maybe we shouldn't talk about dirt, coughing or germs over supper. Okay?"

"Okay, sir."

Charlie asked CJ if he liked to dig and he answered, "I'll dig with you when I get a shovel. Okay? Mister told me you want a digger friend and I can do that, if Clarence says. I don't have a horse. Clarence doesn't play because he has to take care of us, but we can."

Clarence was licking his wounds over his last disaster and simply mumbled, "You can be his friend."

Charlie grinned, "Cool, CJ. Do you do Chicken Man Chores?"

"No."

"I can show you after school, if you want."

"Okay. That would be good." CJ took a bite of his dumpling, "Mister, can I take some of these wet breads in my bag?"

"I don't think that would be a good idea to put dumplings in your bag. Everything will get all mushy! Grandma will help you put them in the refrigerator though."

"I can show you where they are so if you need one, you can get it. Okay?" Grandma smiled.

"Okay and need to see the Roll Jar too," CJ said.

"We'll do that after supper."

Miriam had been quiet while the other kids ate and when they got quiet, she put down her spoon. She patted her chest, "Gopher. Mr. Bear."

Kevin translated, "She calls herself Gopher and this is her best friend, Mr. Bear."

"I have an Uncle Bear," Clarence said.

"Are you a Gopher?" CJ asked. "I'm a CJ."

She patted her chest, "Gopher, CJ."

"That's right. And she is Clarissa."

Miriam thought a minute and then repeated, "Issa."

Clarissa smiled, "She is Claudia. She doesn't talk. She likes Cotton, her kitten."

Miriam looked at Claudia, "Kitten?"

Claudia had been watching this exchange and smiled.

Miriam patted her chest, "Gopher."

Claudia watched and patted her chest, too.

Miriam nodded, "Kitten, Gopher."

After dinner, Clarence came over to where Ginger was sitting by herself and sat down. She had been very quiet throughout the rest of dinner. "Ginger, I'm sorry I made you sad."

Ginger shook her head, "That's okay. You don't have to like dirt. I guess it is kinda dumb to like it."

"I never thought about it. Maybe I will like it if you tell me." Clarence suggested, "Maybe we can find something else besides coughs and germs to do."

Zach overheard and sat down with them, "You know what? Next weekend when I'm home, I'll bring over my old microscope and some slides. I can show you kids some germs in dirt if you want."

"Will they make nests in us?" Clarence asked with concern.

"No, these are dead, so they can't do that anymore."

Ginger shuddered, "Gross."

"Really?" Clarence said, "That would be cool, don't you think Ginger?"

"Is it, Zach?"

"Yes Ginger, it is very cool. There are a lot of germs in dirt, too! Then we can look at dirt under the microscope. It'll be interesting to see that too!"

"Okay," Clarence said.

"Are we going to be friends then?" Ginger asked.

"I never had a girl for a friend before."

Zach said, "Listen, you can be great friends. Girls and boys both make good friends."

"All right. We'll try, okay Clarence?"

"Okay, Ginger."

Since it was a Wednesday night, everyone had school or work the next day. After dinner, Katie helped clear the table while Zach helped Jackson take his shower and redressed his wound. Then he gave him an injection of antibiotic and another for pain. "We're going to try to avoid you taking any meds by mouth because we know what your stomach does! Between Annie and me, we can do it. She'll be home tomorrow afternoon with her syringes!"

"Thanks," Jackson said. "I really feel tough tonight, but my stomach feels okay."

"Try to get some rest."

"Thanks Zach," Jackson said as he covered up.

A few minutes later, Katie knocked on his door, "It's me, Kate."

"Come in," Jackson answered. "I feel pretty silly. It's one thing for the kids to have someone read to them, but I can read myself."

"Okay, I'll just leave your water here," Kate said, a bit taken back.

"No, please. I didn't mean I didn't want you to read to me."

"Sometimes I don't know what you mean."

Jackson took her hand, "I've told you. I want to be with you all the time."

Kate felt his forehead, "Wow, you really are warm. Did Zach put some of the fever reducer stuff in your shot?"

"Yes, he told me to relax, so my stomach didn't get all wound up."

"Yah, that was no fun," Kate pulled her chair beside the hospital bed. She took the book and found the bookmark. She looked at him, stood up and gave him a kiss. Then she sat down and started to read.

Carrie and Diane gave the little girls a bath, while Matt and Kevin gave the boys a bath. Zach and Suzy had to leave right away because Zach had surgery at eight in the morning. Marly, Grandma and Nora did the dishes while the men wiped and put them away.

Ginger felt better because she and Miriam were allowed to help Clarissa and Claudia get ready for bed. The Ellison girls learned quickly to touch Claudia before they talked to her.

After the boys were ready for bed, Kevin and Carrie went home. Carrie worked at the bank in Merton and Kevin at the family gas station. Nora thanked them for staying at the farm while they were down in Pine Ridge.

The little kids all came into the kitchen to tell everyone good night and then wanted to tell Jackson goodnight.

"Come with me," Andy said. "I'm going to tell him goodnight and then I'm going to bed, too."

The crew went to the hall and knocked on Jackson's door, "We came to say goodnight," Andy said.

"Come in," Jackson said. "Hi there. You all look so clean and shiny. Ready for bed?"

"Is Katie reading to you?" Clarence was shocked.

"Yes, isn't that nice?" Jackson asked.

"I guess. Mr. Matt said he'd read to us after we tell you goodnight."

"That's very nice of him. What is he going to read?"

"I don't know. A book, I think," Clarence said.

"Well, good night. You guys be good and get some sleep. Okay?"

"We will, Jackson," Clarissa said. "Katie, tomorrow can you make my hair be like yours?"

"Do you mean short and curly?"

"No, I mean like sunshine color," Clarissa said. "I love that."

"I don't know about that. Your hair is a beautiful dark brown. I think that is gorgeous."

"I think I like sunshine better."

Jackson laughed, "Clarissa, yours looks like the moon dancing across a lake on a summer's night."

Andy added, "When it is shiny, it looks like there are fireflies are dancing in your hair."

"Ohhhh Andy," Clarissa sighed. "That is most beautifuller, huh?"

"We won't have time tomorrow night, but the next night we can see about getting it shorter. How does that sound?"

"That's good. Right, Clarence?"

"I guess. I think it is okay the way it is."

Clarissa asked, "What about Claudia?"

"We'll talk about that on Friday, too," Katie smiled. "She might not be well enough yet."

CJ and Clarissa gave Kate a big hug, and Clarence nodded from the doorway. Andy winked, "Good night you guys."

The door closed and Jackson smiled, "Your hair does look like sunshine."

"It's going to look like a tornado hit it, if I don't get some sleep! I imagine the folks are ready to go. We'd better say goodnight. How is your tummy?"

"Fine. Thanks Kate."

"Do you think that you can go to sleep or do you want to read to yourself?"

"I'll have a drink of water and then just go to sleep."

She handed him the water and he took a drink. Then he took her hand, "Kate, thanks for being you."

"You too, Jackson. Good night."

Matt had taken the big boys upstairs and started to read to them in their room. Then there was a problem. Claudia was going to sleep downstairs in the nursery with Clancy. Clarissa was not at all interested in sleeping in her room alone, even if it was a fairy castle. So, Diane took Clarissa in with the boys. Matt assured them that the book he was reading was for boys and girls. They started to listen to *Peter Pan*, while Diane took Claudia downstairs. She went into the nursery where Clancy was about asleep and read the little girl a story about a kitten. She doubted that Claudia could hear it, but she loved the pictures. Before long, the little girl was sound asleep. Diane covered her up and tiptoed out of the room.

She had a cup of coffee with Nora and Elton while Matt finished reading to the other kids.

"Byron and Katie both looked very tired when they left," Nora said.

"It's been long and tiring for everyone," Diane agreed. "I'm afraid our Horse is going to be horrible sick again. He isn't well at all."

"I know. The kids will be well before him." Nora pointed out. "How were Clancy and Claudia?"

"They both were sleeping soundly, but Jackson was starting to cough a lot."

"I'll give him some cough syrup before we go to bed," Nora suggested. "I hope it doesn't stir up his stomach. It has really torn him apart from time to time."

Matt came in the kitchen, "The kids are about asleep. I don't think that you're going to get Clarissa to sleep in that room alone. No way."

"Probably not."

"And just so you know, CJ isn't the only packrat. When I moved their clothes while they were taking their shower, I found bits of bread, crackers and even French fries stashed in Clarence's pockets."

"I found two slices of bread and celery sticks in Clarissa's coat pockets! Those poor kids probably never knew when they'd get their next meal," Diane added.

"It'll take them awhile. Grandma gave CJ a tour of the refrigerator and the pantry tonight. They were engrossed in a deep conversation about the cookie jar," Elton smiled. "I didn't ask, but I think it had something to do with whether it should be kept on a low shelf or a high shelf."

"I think I'll leave my door open and the light on in the hall tonight. Then the kids won't feel so alone," Diane suggested.

"I already left the hall and stair light on. I did convince Clarissa to turn off the lights in her room, since she was sleeping with the boys. They had their room lit up with every light bulb in the place. I couldn't talk them out of it," Matt explained.

"Yah, that room upstairs seems a long ways away to them. But Horse has to be down here." Elton added. "I'm thinking I better get some sleep. This could stack up to be a long night. Thanks for everything, Matt. It meant a lot to Jackson to have you come down."

"He is a good person," Matt said. "He must have thanked me four hundred times."

After Nora and Elton went to bed, it was just Matt and Diane in the kitchen. Matt took Diane in his arms and gave her a kiss. Diane hugged him, "You know I miss the cabin and our pets, but tonight I realized how much I love you. You are great with the kids and so patient."

"So are you." Then Matt chuckled, "I thought for a minute that Clarence and Ginger were going to require marriage counseling!"

"Yah, they didn't hit if off very well. Zach helped them bury the hatchet though. He is going to bring over his microscope so they can look at into it."

"Dear Lord, there really is no hope." Matt chuckled. Then he kissed her goodnight again, "I really have to get some rest. See you in the morning. I love you, Diane."

Matt reached over and opened the door to the basement. "Elton thought maybe Cotton would want to find Claudia."

15

About two-thirty, Nora got up to give the kids their medicine. She came back into the bedroom and woke Elton. He woke with a jump and immediately panicked, "What is it?"

Nora said gently, "Come quietly. You have to see this."

The two went down the hall and past the empty nursery. Elton frowned as he looked in the room but Nora just took his hand. She pushed the partially open door to Jackson's room. There on the floor, on the quilts given them at the wake, were the kids. They were all curled up by Jackson's bed with one little beige, shorthaired kitty. They were sound asleep. The little girls had their coats on and CJ's bag of food was nearby.

Elton put his arm around his wife, "I think we should just let them sleep there as long as they are warm enough. They need each other."

"I agree, but I have to give the little ones their medicine."

While they were giving the kids their medicine, Jackson woke up. "I'm sorry. I'll tell them to go to their own beds. They should sleep in their rooms."

"Jackson, unless it bothers you, I think they're just fine here."

"You sure?"

"Yup, how you doing?" Elton asked.

"Okay, I should go to the bathroom since I'm awake."

"I'll help you. I don't think you have room for your wheelchair to go around the kids."

"I'll get you some fresh water. Are you sure the kids don't bother you?" Nora asked.

"Not at all Nora. I kind of like having them here. You know, they are my family."

The family alarm awakened the sleeping household. Even Grandpa Lloyd slept through the night, which was a blessing because everyone was so tired. Jackson and Clancy were coughing like crazy and Jackson's fever was raging. Jackson was told to stay in bed, and he didn't even argue about it. Clancy took his cough syrup and went back to his crib and Claudia stayed with him in the nursery, looking at the kitten picture book.

Clarissa, CJ and Clarence came out to the kitchen in their pajamas. Elton teased, "Now just how are you going to help in the barn in your pajamas?"

"We didn't know where our clothes went," Clarence worried. "Mr. Matt took them when we had our showers. Maybe he needed to trade them for something."

There was a knock at the door and Kevin came bouncing in, "Good morning, everyone! Your morning cheer is here!"

Diane groaned at him, "How can you be so happy in the morning?"

"Cause he gets to see my dog," Clarence suggested. "Hey Mr. Kevin, do you know where our clothes went?"

"I think I can help you with that. Come with me to your room and I'll get you boys dressed. Are you young men drinking coffee or hot chocolate while we do chores?"

"We don't drink coffee," Clarence answered.

Elton nodded, "Hot chocolate it is."

"Who is going to help me?" Clarissa asked.

"I can," Nora answered.

"Or I can," Diane said. "I know right where your warm jeans are. You can help me at the barn this morning."

"Do you go to the barn?"

"Yes, Uncle Elton taught me how to milk cows. And Matt taught me how to milk goats, just like Heidi."

"Who is Heidi?" Clarissa asked as the two went off upstairs discussing the perils of Heidi.

Nora smiled, "I think they'll be reading Heidi next, huh?"

Grandma started pouring the coffee and Andy was thoughtful, "I will take some into Horse, okay?"

"Coffee wouldn't be so good, but I have the tea kettle on. You can take him some tea in a minute," Nora answered. "I'll fix a tray."

Andy watched his Mom, "I feel so bad for him. You know, I get on my pity pile a lot, but I have nothing to deal with compared to these guys.

I can never thank you enough for taking the kids. I want you to know I have the best parents in the whole wide world."

Elton hugged his son, "We know."

Andy shook his head, "And the most conceited."

"Is it conceit; if it's true?"

Zach came in then, and laughed, "Bragging about yourself again, Elton?"

"Well, if that don't beat all!" Elton groused.

"So is my guy is sick? I wonder if I should take him in with me to the hospital? His resistance is so low; he really shouldn't have gone to Pine Ridge. I know he had to, but it was too much for him."

"He would've crawled down there if we hadn't taken him," Elton said. "Guess where the Grey Hawks spent the night? Clarence gathered them all in Jackson's room. They slept on those quilts from the wake. They wanted to be together."

"Their ties to each other are about all they have left. I'd prefer they weren't on the floor, but I guess they used to sleep there all the time. They all need each other, even Jackson. It is easy to overlook, but he lost his Mom too."

"I know," Grandma said. "I was planning on having a long talk with my boy later today. We didn't get much time to chat down there. It breaks my heart to see him facing so much."

"I know," Nora said as she put her arm around Grandma. "He is lucky he has you."

"Well, I'm going in to see him and decide if I need to take him in," Zach smiled. "Then the little ones and then you, Andrew. Oh, I talked to Annie. She will be home around noon today and she will have your IV stuff with her, Elton."

"Yea gads," Elton rolled his eyes. "I have half a mind not to let you in the house anymore."

"Yah, yah, yah," Zach smirked. "You'd miss me."

Zach checked Jackson first and was very dismayed. "You've done yourself proud, guy. You now officially have double pneumonia and your leg is getting worse. I want to take you to the hospital with me and check you in for a few days."

"I can't, Zach," Jackson said emphatically. "The kids need me here. They slept in my room last night. This is all so new for them. I could maybe go to the hospital in a couple weeks."

"Oh, I'll schedule that then! Are you going to talk to your infections and get them to hold off?"

Jackson's eyes reddened. Zach put his arm around him, "Look, I understand. If you give me your word, I'll do everything I can to keep you home. Okay? You need to soak your leg at least six times a day, and stay in bed! Annie can handle the shots. How is the old gizzard?"

"Good. It has been good, really. Haven't even had a queasy stomach once."

"Okay, the only time I want you up, is when you are soaking your leg. If I was you, I'd time that around meal time for at least three of the times. Nora will redress it for you. The rest of the time, try to sleep. If the tummy goes wacky, I need to know right away. I'll talk to Nora about the kids sleeping in here, but you have to be able to rest, Jackson. I mean, they might feel bad if they can't sleep with you, but they'd miss you if you are dead, too."

"That's not very nice," Jackson said.

"No, but that's the choices we have. You're one sick puppy. I'm kinda partial to you, so I really don't want to lose you."

"Zach," Jackson took Zach's arm. "Would Schroeder's keep the kids if I died?"

Zach looked at the nineteen-year-old. "Certainly. Don't ever worry about that. They took the Steps for the long haul. If something would happen to them, there isn't a clanner that wouldn't keep the kids. They have a home now. Rest assured."

"Thanks," Jackson said. "I thought that. Please don't tell them that I asked. I think they would be hurt."

Zach patted his shoulder, "Your secret is safe with me. Now, I'm off to ruin Andy's day! He is having trouble with those poisons that he ingested in Vietnam, but I think it is because he hasn't had enough rest. I'm going to knock him out a lot today."

"You must enjoy your work," Jackson smiled.

"More than you'll ever know! Oh wow, did I get into trouble telling Clarence about germs! I waltzed right into that one!"

"I saw."

"Next weekend, I'm going to bring my microscope out and show Ginger and him stuff under it. That is, if I can keep them from killing each other!" Zach laughed.

"They are both so used to being the top dog, I was afraid they'd clash. It might be better to have them at odds than united. I doubt any of us are ready for that!"

"Good point."

Zach went in to check the little guys, and Nora was there getting them dressed for the day. "Little Clancy has his cough back again. Don't you?"

Clancy smiled.

"Nora is going to give you some different cough syrup. It should help you more."

Clancy shook his head no violently and made a face.

Zach grinned, "No Clancy, I won't make you drink that stuff in the blue bottle. This is the cough syrup. I tasted it and it is good. Okay? You can eat breakfast with everyone else. No more of that blue bottle stuff."

Clancy nodded, "No bubobble."

Then Zach checked out Claudia. He gave her a pill and then a drink of water. She smiled and put it in her mouth. He listened to her chest and checked her over.

"I think you're getting better," Zach smiled.

As he was checking her swollen glands, he moved her blue coat back. The pill he had just given her fell out of her cuff. He and Nora exchanged a glance.

Zach stroked her cheek, "Claudia, you must take your pill. Do not hide it."

She looked at him like she didn't have a clue what he was talking about. Then he placed the sticky pill in her hand, "You put it in your mouth and swallow it. Now."

She started to tear up. He stared her down, "Swallow it now."

She glared at him and then put it in her mouth, but she didn't swallow it. Then she smiled at him.

"Claudia, swallow it. Here! Drink this water."

She took the glass and a big drink of water. She smiled and handed him the glass back.

Zach stared at her, "Open your mouth."

There was the pill, tucked between her back teeth and her cheek.

Nora giggled, "I know what to do."

Zach explained to Claudia, "If you don't swallow it real fast, it will taste icky. You need to swallow it."

Claudia nodded but she still didn't swallow it.

Nora returned with a cookie. "Here you go. Eat some cookie and then some water."

Claudia took the pill out of her mouth, but Zach saw it. She frowned at him and then put it back in, making a horrible face. Then she took some cookie and drank the water. That time, when her mouth was checked, it was empty.

"You shouldn't be sneaky about your pills."

Claudia put her head down and seemed concerned Zach was upset.

"Okay," he smiled, "You take a little rest before breakfast. What is this fun book about a kitten you are looking at?"

Zach paged through the book and then Claudia relaxed. "This is nice book. You enjoy it, okay? I'll see you tonight. Have a good day."

In the hall, Zach assured Nora he would bring some liquid medication for Claudia home with him. "You know, these kids are used to squirreling everything away. Pills are probably not a good idea."

In the kitchen, the group was going through the coat bench to find some of the boy's coats from when they were little. The kids only had their new coats and Elton was worried they would get wrecked in the barn. The smallest they found was an old coat of Andy's that was a size eight.

Nora made the decision. "The boys can wear their new coats. If they get ruined, we'll get them some new ones for good. These are really warm and they need to be warm. We will doctor up Andy's for Clarissa and then get her another coat for every day. Okay?"

"Missus, I love my pink coat. Can't I wear that?"

"No Sweetheart, it will get all yukky and then you won't be able to wear it anymore," Nora explained. "It will get wrecked."

Clarissa hugged her pink coat on herself, and Diane knelt down by her. "Clarissa, I wear boy's coats at the barn and keep my soft stuff for good. Otherwise, the soft stuff won't be soft anymore and we don't want that to happen. If you wear Andy's coat, I'll let you wear my barn scarf. Would you like that?"

"You don't wear your pretty clothes to the barn?"

"No. Jeans and boys coats."

"Okay, if I can wear your scarf," Clarissa nodded.

Nora and Diane got her all fixed up and then Diane wrapped her long scarf around her head and neck. It was so long, there were still long tails. Clarissa loved it. When Elton took the thermos, he kissed his wife on the cheek, "We're off."

At the barn, CJ went with Kevin while Clarence went with Elton. The Ellison's didn't come over like they usually did, because they had been up late. Diane and Clarissa hung out together, but Elton gave Clarissa milking lessons.

Elton had Clarence milking on his own in no time. He was a natural and had good sense. While he was finishing Buttermilk, Elton showed Clarissa how to milk on Snowflake. She was a little timid and she had to have Diane help her. CJ and Kevin did their cows together, and while CJ didn't finish a cow on his own, he milked some on a couple. Clarence finished Buttermilk and only had to have Elton check to see if her bag was empty.

There were eight cows in the barn still milking. They rest were dried up awaiting the birth of their calves before long.

"When will the baby cows be born?" Clarissa asked.

"Baby cows are called calves. Some will be born next month. Won't that be exciting?" Diane asked.

"Can I pet the calves?"

"Yes," Elton smiled, "In fact, if Tink wants, you two can go feed the four baby calves that came early. Maybe you can decide what you want to name them. They are three little girls called heifers and a little bull. Tink has to feed them so you can go along, if you promise to mind."

"A heart promise?"

"Yes, a heart promise."

"I'll mind by a heart promise," she told Diane.

Elton showed Clarence how to run the cream separator while CJ and Kevin went to feed the horses. After they ran the whole milk from the cows through the separator they had skim milk and cream. Elton carried the skim milk to the pigs.

"I can take one of the pails, Mister," Clarence offered.

"I'd rather you opened the big barn door for me," Elton suggested.

The little boy pushed on the door with his whole body but got it open. Then he and Elton went over to the pigs. Elton poured the skim milk into the chute through the fence to the trough for the pigs. While he and Clarence measured out the ground feed for the pigs, Clarence asked, "Why don't you go inside the pen and dump the milk in the trough instead of outside into the trough?"

"Hogs can be very vicious," Elton explained. "When my little girl, Pepper was about Claudia's age, a mad momma sow attacked her. She still has a limp when she walks. Then Nora went to save Pepper, the sow attacked her. Nora almost died. She has scars on her arm and neck to this day from that. We all learned you can never be too careful around pigs. Don't ever let the kids go in the hog pen. Ever! Or you either. I don't go in unless there is some adult around to help me. Okay?"

"I bet I could do it."

"No. You cannot trust a pig. If they get angry, they can kill you. You have to promise me you'll listen and never go in the pen."

"If I had CJ watch, I—,"

"No. You cannot. If you don't believe me, ask Kevin, Jackson or Uncle Bear. Don't make me sorry I trust you. Okay?"

"How about if you are around?"

"Okay, only me though. Never just CJ. He is a cool guy, but a big hog would kill him in no time. I won't debate this with you. Have I got your word? Now you think about it, because once you give me your word—that means I can trust it. If you don't think you can keep your word, then tell me now."

Clarence thought, and then sat on the feed box, "Mister. I think I might have to go back to Pine Ridge."

Elton sat down next to him, and took out a cigarette, "Really? You decided so soon?"

"Well, I was never too sure."

"I remember that."

The two sat there for a while, and then Elton asked, "Is there a problem we can talk about, or have you decided?"

"We can talk about it, I guess, but I don't think I'll change my mind."

"How about the other kids? Should I tell Social Services that just you want to leave?"

"I don't know. I thought we'd have our own room."

"You do."

"I mean a room for all of us, together. Clarissa is scared to be in her room, and CJ got scared too. I was worried about the other kids and Jackson. That's why we all went to Jackson's room."

"I figured that happened. Can we think about it and maybe come up with a plan? Jackson is really sick and he has to stay in his hospital bed. Zach almost took him to the hospital this morning. If he doesn't get well, they might have to take more of his leg off."

Clarence's eyes got huge, "Really?"

"Yah, we're very worried about that. I know he loves having you guys in his room and he misses you so much when you're gone. It'd be nice if you could see your way clear to sticking around until he gets better; but I know how it is. If you have to go, then I guess you have to."

"I hate to have Jackson worry and lose his leg. Clancy still has a cough. Maybe I could see my way to staying until they get better. Then I'll go. Okay?"

"Sounds very thoughtful of you. Now, what are you going to do about giving me your word about the pig pen?"

"I guess I can do that, since I won't be around that long anyway. You have my word."

"Shake on it?"

"Yes, sir," and the two shook hands.

"Good to know I can count on you. What do you think we should do about your sleeping arrangements?"

"Can we sleep in Jackson's room, like last night?"

Elton thought, "Let's you and me talk to Nora about it. I think we can work something out. Claudia is probably well enough to sleep with you, but Clancy should be in his crib. He has problems sleeping with his bad cough. I think I'll ask Kevin to help me and we can set up the bed in the corner of Jackson's room for you other kids. If that's okay with Nora, do you think that would work?"

"I guess it would. What are all those pictures Jackson has in his room?"

"He draws them. He sells some of them in town. He does very good work, doesn't he?" Elton thought, "Oh my, you don't think the other kids will play with his sketches, do you?"

"I will tell them not to. If they don't listen, I'll sock them."

103

"That probably isn't a good idea to start socking. We have to puzzle on this one, okay? Let's think and then we can talk to Nora."

Elton started back to the barn and Clarence took his hand, "Mister, why is that Ginger so bossy?"

Elton grinned, "She really isn't. She is used to being the oldest of the little kids in her family, like you are. You know how it is when you have to worry about the other kids and keep track of them."

Clarence thought and then started nodding his head, "Yah. Am I the older one over her?"

"Oh no, you don't! You guys are both the oldest. You need to be a team instead of the boss of each other."

"I'd rather be the boss," Clarence stated.

"Yah, but I know it wouldn't be very easy to be the boss of Ginger! She really is a nice girl if you give her a chance."

"Mr. Zach said we could be great friends. I don't think so, but he said he's show us germs, so I'll try."

"That's all we can ask. So, how did Rags do last night?"

"She was fine. I think she liked it in the barn. Are we going to meet Elmer?"

"When I let the cows out, Elmer usually comes in then."

The girls got the giggles feeding calves but Clarissa decided she didn't like sticky calf kisses. The only names they could come up with were Slimy, Goopy, Yukky and Gross. They decided to think about names more later.

CJ and Kevin checked on the old horse Abner and decided his leg was getting better. Then the group had their break. The grownups had coffee and the kids had hot chocolate. They all sat on milking stools.

"I explained to Clarence and I want to tell you other kids, do not ever go inside the pigpen. It can be very dangerous. Okay? Pigs can be nice, but they can kill you. We don't want to take a chance. Have I got your word?"

Clarence looked at the kids, "He means it. That is how Missus got her arm messed up. You know how we talked about the marks on her arm. It was a pig that did it. So you mind, hear?"

"We hear, Clarence," the kids answered.

"Tell Mister, too. Give your word."

"I give you my word, Mister," CJ said.

"Me, too," Clarissa said.

"Good. If you ever need to go in the pigpen, be sure to talk to an adult," Elton smiled.

"Mister?" CJ asked. "Which word did I give you? Can I still use that word if you have it?"

Kev explained, "It doesn't mean that you gave him a word, it means that you made him a promise?"

"A heart promise?" Clarissa asked.

"Yes," Diane smiled. "A heart promise."

"Well, that's good. I was afraid I didn't know which word it was! What I needed it?" CJ asked, crossing his eyes.

"That would be a fright," Elton chuckled. "Okay Tink, can you and Clarissa take care of the chickens, and us boys will clean out the barn."

"Okay, come little one," Diane smiled. "Let's get the egg basket."

"Tink, did Heidi take care of chickens?"

"I don't know. Maybe we'll find out when we read our book."

Kevin looked at his Dad, and broke into a smile. "I love you, Dad."

"Well, I love you too, Son." Elton grinned, "But you still have to help clean the barn."

The men showed the boys how to handle a pitchfork, albeit short forks, and to help clean the barn. The little guys did a pretty good job, but decided they preferred pitching straw rather than manure.

"I agree," Kevin said. "You are very wise. Do you think that Grandma and Nora made a good breakfast for you?"

"I hope they did," CJ said. "I'm hungry."

When Elton opened the barn door and let the cows out, Elmer came in and headed right for the milk filter. That was his favorite thing. Elton poured some skim milk in a couple shallow pans for the barn cats and then Kev and Clarence brought Rags out.

Rags and Elmer looked at each other, drank some milk, smelled each other and walked around each other for a bit. Clarence was getting nervous, but Kevin told him to wait. After a bit, the two dogs finished drinking their milk and then went outside together. When the folks were walking to the house from the barn, they saw the two dogs running all around the yard.

"I think Elmer is showing Rags where everything is, huh?" Clarence asked.

Kevin nodded, "I believe so. If I were you, I'd still put her in the barn at night for a few more nights. Just in case."

"In case what?" Clarence asked.

"Oh, in case she gets lost in the dark or something."

"Good idea."

16

There was a mouth-watering aroma that met the milkers at the top of the steps after chores. Everyone hung up their coats in the mud room except Kevin who went home for breakfast. The kids all sat at the table.

"Oh, oh," Grandpa Lloyd made a face. "You gotta wash your hands before you eat breakfast. Who knows what you have on your hands!"

"We know." Clarence explained while looked his hands over, "They are okay."

Elton was just returning from the bathroom, after washing up, "You can't see germs, Clarence. That is why Zach is bringing his microscope. They are very tiny, but can make you sicker than a dog."

CJ's eyes sprung open, "Is your dog sick, Mister?"

"No, but—well, it is a good idea to wash up before you eat."

"Where would I get germs in the barn?" Clarence asked. "Everything looked pretty clean."

"Remember cleaning out the barn?"

CJ looked at his hands critically and then started to lick them.

"Yikes CJ, go wash up. Please!" Grandma grimaced.

"Yah, I guess. I'll go clean up," Clarence almost groaned. "Come on, CJ. Mister might be right."

"I didn't clean barn, so I don't have to," Clarissa stated.

Diane shook her head, "Remember how sticky those baby calves were?"

Clarissa made a face and nodded, "I forgot about that."

"It is usually a good idea to always wash your hands before you eat," Nora suggested. "That way you don't have to think about it."

"You sure have a lot of rules," Clarence frowned as he returned to the table. "Is Jackson here?"

107

"He might be sleeping," Nora explained. "Would you check for me? Ask him if he wants to have breakfast with us or if he'd like me to bring him something? But Clarence, if he's sleeping just let him sleep. Okay?"

Clarence got off his chair and headed toward the hall. He went into Jackson's room and went over to his bed. His older step-brother was sleeping restlessly and sweating profusely. Clarence stared at him for a bit and then looked around the room. On the floor were the quilts from the wake of his parents where he had slept the night before and his brother's drawings that he didn't understand leaning against the walls. Outside the window, he saw Rags running along with Elmer. He didn't move.

Suddenly the pressure of the whole last week closed in on him. The young boy couldn't take it anymore. The tears flooded his face, silently. He wanted desperately to be somewhere familiar with the things and people he knew. He crumbled onto the floor and cried.

Wondering what was up, Elton came to the door to check. There he saw the little kid crying in a heap on the floor while his hero was in a fevered sleep on a hospital bed. Elton sat down on the floor next to the boy and scooped him onto his lap. Clarence put his arms around this man he hardly knew, grasped his embrace and just cried.

Elton never said a word, but sat there and held him while he cried. After nearly five minutes of desperate tears, Clarence said hoarsely, "I hate it, Mister."

Elton tightened his embrace, "I know Clarence. You've had a lot to handle. You've done a mighty fine job. Remember before the wake when we talked about taking a day off? Maybe you'd like to do that today? A whole day where you don't have to think and can just have a nice time. What do you say?"

Clarence asked, "Who'll take care of the kids?"

"Nora, Grandma, Andy—there are a whole bunch of people. They can watch them for one day. Would you like to hang out with me? I can show you around my work at the family shop, since you are part of the family now!"

"The other kids are part, too?"

"Yup, them too. You know, Kevin works there. Then we could go to lunch at the Hen House Café and order from a menu, check out the little town, maybe go see Pastor Byron's church and I know, we could go visit the guy that has goats. He lives in the same yard as Matt does. Would that sound like fun?"

"Will the kids miss me?"

Elton thought, "Don't know. Remember, we're going to let the others keep an eye on them."

"Will they?"

"I give you my word and you know what else? We can call home every so often and check. If there's a problem, we'll come home right away! Okay?"

"I guess so. I miss everything so much," Clarence started to tear up again. "I even miss my outhouse."

"Well, there's the problem!" Elton smiled as he patted the boy's back, "You've been trying to think without your thinking spot! I can show you where our outhouse is, or we can go out to the thinking rock."

Clarence couldn't have heard anything better, "You mean, you have an outhouse?"

"We sure do. We haven't used it in a long time, but it's still there. Maybe we should check it out after breakfast. What do you say?"

"I'd like that."

"Then there you go. Let's go eat. The folks are probably waiting for us to say grace."

"Can't you guys eat without saying that?"

"Sure, but we don't want to. You know, we should be thanking God, or Wakan Tanka, all the time but it's easier to make a regular time. Otherwise, we forget. So, we do it before we eat and before we go to sleep. If we're smart, we'd do it throughout the day."

"Are we smart?"

"Not so much, Clarence. Not so much. Well, my butt is going numb on this hard floor. Do you think we should go eat?"

"You don't have to wait for me. You can go."

"No, I can't. It's you and me, kid."

Clarence studied this almost stranger and then nodded, "Okay, we better go eat."

The two joined the family at the table, but no one made mention of them being late. Clarence sat in the chair next to Elton while Elton led the family in grace. Then they started passing the food.

The kids all liked Grandma's sausage links, scrambled eggs and cheese sauce. Clancy didn't like the hash browns, but did lick all the wild plum jelly off his toast. Claudia's scrambled eggs disappeared within seconds and she even ate all her second helping.

Clarissa watched Diane and then asked, "Miss Diane? Can I help you get dressed? You said you are going to wear something soft to your job?"

"Yes, I think you can. If Nora has an idea what she'd like you to wear, I can help you get dressed too."

"That'd be nice, Tink, if you think you'll have time. She can choose which dress she wants. I think I'm going to take the girls shopping in Bismarck this weekend. Would you like to come along? They need some jeans, dresses and another jacket for chores."

"I'd like that," Diane winked at Clarissa. "Wouldn't that be fun? We could pick out some nice colors, huh?"

"Maybe pink," Clarissa suggested.

Sensing that Clarence was having a hard day, Andy made a suggestion. "I thought I'd check out my model ships. If we find a good one, could you help me put it together, CJ?"

CJ's eyes sparkled with interest, "I think so, if Clarence says."

Clarence looked at Elton who nodded slightly, "Sure. Andy is cool. You mind him, you hear?"

"I hear." CJ answered. "When does that Charlie get here?"

Nora answered, "The bus drops him off just before dark. Why do you ask?"

"He was going to show me that Chicken Man stuff."

"That's good," Andy grinned. "Are you going to be a Chicken Man?"

"No, Charlie says I have to be on this thing first."

"What thing?"

"A motion thing, I think."

Elton broke into a big grin, "Did he say promotion?"

"Yes! That's it!"

"He means probation," Andy explained. "That's what you are on when you are learning stuff."

"That's it!" CJ nodded. "Is it hard to do Chicken Man chores?"

Nora smiled, "Not now. The hens are older now, but soon we'll have baby chicks and they are a lot of work."

"You know, Nora," Elton grinned. "Maybe we should get some turkeys after all. Carl will have his hands full with the ducks. Now we have a Turkey Man, too!"

"Good idea," Andy grinned. "Carl was not too thrilled about having to deal with turkeys and ducks."

"If I learn my motion thing, then I can do it, if Clarence says."

Clarence was very quiet, "I'll sleep on it."

"Oh, everyone. Clarence and I are taking a vacation day. We're just going to hang loose and check things out. We might have lunch in Merton. Is there anything we need to do?"

"No. Annie will be home about ten. She wants to give you your IV, Elton," Nora said.

"Yah, I'll do that before chores. I promise. I'm sure glad I can do the antibiotic with the pills now. Zach said I can be more liberal with my IV's since I'm digesting my food better."

"Sure Dad, but don't push it. You and Horse both think you are Superman," Andy pointed out.

"Like you?" Diane teased.

"Tink, don't you have to go to school?" Andy frowned.

Clarence looked at her with new interest, "Do you still go to school?"

"I teach school," Diane smiled.

Clarence shook his head in wonder.

As they were clearing the table, Elton said to Nora, "Clarence and I would like to talk to you this afternoon about where the kids are going to sleep tonight. Can we do that while I have my IV?"

Nora nodded, "Certainly, I'll think about it, too. Anything you want me to know while I'm thinking, Clarence?"

"The little kids get pretty scared when they're alone. Mister explained that Jackson might lose more of his leg, so we don't want to make him sicker, but I think he gets worried when we don't sleep with him."

"Okay," Nora nodded. "I'll keep those things in mind when I think. Thank you, Clarence. The kids are very fortunate to have you watch for them. You're a good man."

Clarence tried to act like he didn't make him feel proud, but it did. "Mister said you guys will keep an eye on the kids today. We'll call to see if everything is okay. Is that alright?"

"That'll be fine." Nora kissed her husband's cheek, "Grandma and I are going to make a list of things the kids need. You men have a great day."

Clarence and Elton left for Merton and their vacation day.

CJ and Andy went to peek in on Horse before they went to check out Andy's model ships. He was sound asleep. On the way back to the kitchen, CJ asked, "Why do you call him Horse?"

"In the Army, most of us had nicknames. Mine was Spud, and we had a friend called Chicago. Jackson's was Horse because he was from where Crazy Horse came from. You know, he was that great Indian hero. Then, it just got shortened to Horse. Like you are CJ, that's short for Clifford. What is your middle name?"

CJ stopped walking and scrunched up his face in deep thought. Finally he answered, "Don't know."

Andy smiled, "I like CJ, so it doesn't matter."

"Mr. Andy, can I call you Spud like Horse does?"

"You certainly can, now let's go through that box of model ships. Mom said we can use the card table. She doesn't want us to get glue all over the dining room table."

"Why not? It would never fall down then!" CJ pointed out.

Grandma dressed Claudia in the only pair of slacks the little girl had and one of Ginger's old sweatshirts that had a puppy dog on it. They met Diane and Clarissa at the bottom of the steps. Clarissa had two dresses and one was dirty. So, she had to settle with one that she wasn't that happy with, but she did put her pink coat back on.

After Diane left for school, the little girls decided to help Grandma make brownies in the kitchen. Grandma worried that they would get their coats all messed up and began to put aprons over them. That is when she noticed.

The pockets of both their coats were leaking. An oily sediment was all around each pocket and spreading into an ever larger circle around it. Grandma investigated. She reached into Clarissa's pocket and pulled her hand back, covered in sausage grease, cheese sauce and scrambled egg.

She gestured to the other pocket, "This one too?"

Clarissa nodded and then started to tear up, as did Claudia.

Grandma looked at Claudia, "You, too?"

Claudia dropped her head.

Grandma shook her head and told the little girls to sit down at the table. Then she sat down with them, "Look ladies, I know how very much you love your coats."

Both little girls nodded.

"If you put scrambled eggs and cheese sauce in your pockets, you'll wreck your coats. I bet you didn't know that, did you?"

"No Missus Grandma. Are they wrecked forever?" Clarissa worried.

"I hope not. If we wash them now, we might get the grease out. Otherwise, they'll always have big oil spots on the front."

"That would be okay, wouldn't it?" Clarissa asked, hopefully.

"I wish, but what happens is the oil spot picks up all the dirt and your coats will get all dirty and won't be soft ever again."

Clarissa was crestfallen, "I love my coat."

"I know, honey," Grandma patted her hand. "Will you let me try to get them clean?"

"I s'pose."

"Okay, take your coats off and I'll clean out the pockets. Then we'll try to fix them."

Reluctantly, the little girls took off their beloved coats and handed them over to Grandma. She cleaned out their pockets. There was plenty of food in them, even remnants of chicken gravy from the chicken and dumplings. Grandma was looking over the oil-soaked material as Nora came back into the kitchen.

"Clancy is napping and Jackson is still asleep. What are you ladies doing?" Nora asked as she poured herself a cup of coffee.

Grandma explained the situation and Nora bit her lip. "Looks like a problem there. I have some great stuff to soak the oil out, but then the coats will have to be washed and dried right away. I'll go get it."

The ladies went to work and poured degreaser into two large bowls. The wide-eyed little girls watched while the pockets of their treasured coats were submerged in the degreaser. Both little girls were in near tears.

Grandma tried to interest them in stirring up the brownies. They were slightly interested, but they kept a keen eye on their coats at the other end of the table. After twenty minutes, and the brownies were in the oven,

Nora checked the coats. "I think if we throw them in the washer, we might be able to save them."

Like little lost puppies, the girls followed behind her, hand in hand, as she gathered the coats to the laundry room. Grandma followed behind with the degreaser. The little girls stood quietly while Nora turned on the washing machine and dumped the degreaser, detergent and coats into it. Then she turned the knob and they heard the big machine make loud noises. Nora smiled and said, "Okay then. Let's go clean up the house."

The girls looked at her in shock! She was going to walk away from their coats while they were lost in this noisy thing! They hugged and tried to console each other.

Nora knelt down to them, "It'll be okay, heart promise! The coats will be here and when the buzzer goes off, we'll check them. Okay?"

Clarissa couldn't have felt worse, "Missus, can we stay here until we see our coats again?"

"Hey, I'll bring a chair so you can both see them."

Nora pulled a chair over and the girls climbed up. Nora opened the lid to the washing machine. They looked in and saw their coats. Then she closed the lid again, so the washing cycle could continue.

"Okay?"

"They're all spoiled now! I'm going to wait right here for my coat. We want to stay here, Missus. We want our coats," Clarissa wiped her tears.

Nora patted her head, handed her a box of tissues and helped them down from the chair, "It will be okay girls. I promise. Can you trust me?"

"We trust you, but we'll wait," Clarissa said definitely.

"Okay, if you change your mind, you can join Grandma or me. If you need anything, we're right here."

The girls stood in the laundry in front of the automatic washer as if they were at the funeral wake! Every so often, there was renewed crying and fresh tears. Before long, Claudia started coughing.

Grandma brought the girls a quilt and put it in the corner with a pillow. They sat down and she gave them each some juice and Claudia her cough syrup. However, they were not dissuaded from their vigil.

While Grandma was there, the gears in the washer changed and it went into the spin cycle. "It almost finished girls. It won't be long now."

The girls didn't budge, but held each other while the washing machine continued. Grandma asked, "Is there anything I can do for you girls?"

They shook their heads as if all hope was futile and went back to their mourning.

Grandma and Nora had finished with the housework and returned to the laundry room as the buzzer went off. "Guess what girls? The washer is done. Let's look at the coats and see if they are clean, okay?"

The girls nodded eagerly and stood up. The ladies removed the coats from the washer and pulled the coats out to renewed wails of mourning! "Girls, girls! It will be okay! Promise. They're just wet."

"They are spoiled forever! Our coats are broken!" Clarissa cried.

Nora and Grandma just shared a brief glance and then looked over the pockets. Thankfully, the oil had washed out and they looked clean. They shared a sigh of relief, and quickly put the coats in the dryer.

The girls started to cry again, not that they had completely quit before. Nora took them in her arms, "They're clean and now we'll put them in the dryer. In about an hour, they will be as soft and pretty as new."

Clarissa looked at her doubtfully, "We'll wait."

Nora smiled, "Okay, but let's visit the bathroom before you sit back down."

Clarissa squinted, "You aren't going to throw them away while we're gone, are you?"

Grandma smiled, "Nope. We'll all go along. How is that?"

Apparently that was okay, because the four went to visit the bathroom. After that, the girls were determined to sit on their quilt and wait. Grandma put the coats in the dryer and turned it on. Once it started to go around, the girls started to cry again.

Back in the kitchen, Grandma whispered to Nora, "Don't know about you, but I'm about ready for a shot of whiskey! I hope they figured out not to put gravy and sauce in their pockets anymore."

Half an hour later, Marly and Miriam stopped over to visit. Marly had some clothes of Ginger's that she thought Clarissa might use. When they came in, Marly glanced over toward the laundry room and saw the two pitiful little girls whimpering on the quilt. Cotton had joined the group of mourners and they were all transfixed on the dryer.

Marly stifled a giggle, "Should I ask what you did to those sweet little girls?"

Miriam then noticed and took off in their direction. She went over to the girls and hugged them. "No, no cry."

Clarissa explained and Miriam hugged them again. Then she toddled back over to Nora, put her hands on her hips and demanded, "Nora coats, girls cry! No no, Nora."

"Gopher, their coats are in the dryer and they'll be okay. They will come out and be soft and pretty."

Gopher looked the situation over and then took Nora's hand. "See coats."

"That's a good idea, Miriam. Should I show the girls that their coats are almost dry?"

Miriam nodded, "Dry, okay?"

Nora opened the dryer and took out the coats. They were still quite damp, but the girls could see they were getting better. That is the first time that Clarissa smiled. "They are better! They won't be spoiled, will they?"

"No honey. I promised you, remember?" Nora said as she put them back in the dryer. "See, you worried for nothing."

As if she had witness a resurrection, Clarissa hugged her, Claudia and then Miriam. She ran and hugged Grandma and Marly. "They're okay! They're so soft!"

Then the little girls sat down in front of the dryer and played with Cotton, while the ladies had coffee. Nora confided, "You should've been here when we first put the coats in the washer! You'd have thought we were roasting their pet or something!"

"It's going to be a challenge, no doubt."

17

CJ and Andy went down the hall to Andy's room. On the way, they looked in on Horse, who was very restless and mumbling in his sleep about artillery shells. Andy knew he was having a nightmare and touched his arm, "It's okay, Horse. This is Spud. We are home."

Horse sat right up and opened his eyes, obviously disoriented. "Oh," he stammered as he began to get his bearings. "I must've had a bad dream."

Then he saw CJ and asked Andy quietly, "Did I scare CJ?"

"No," Andy smiled, "We're just going to find a model ship to put together. I wish you were feeling better so we could work on Columbus's ships."

"Yah, me too."

"Won't Columbus do his own ships?" CJ asked.

"No, he's been dead a long time. He's the guy who found America," Andy answered.

"Was it lost?" CJ asked innocently.

Jackson chuckled, "Only to the white man. Indians knew where it was all the time, right CJ?"

CJ shrugged.

"But you didn't know where we were, now did you?" Andy poked.

"We didn't care where you were!" Jackson poked back.

CJ frowned, "You guys are making fun, right?"

"Yah, man, we are. Hey, need anything; water, breakfast, help out of bed?" Andy asked his friend.

"Maybe help to the bathroom. I don't think I could eat now," Horse answered. "Man, I really feel rough."

Andy helped his friend with his crutches until he got back to bed. He brought him some fresh water and helped him get settled again. "Want me to have Mom come check on you?"

"No, I just need to sleep. Zach really knocked me to the ground."

CJ became defensive, "Do you want me to punch him? I'll punch that Mr. Zach for knocking you down!"

"Not necessary," Horse smiled weakly. "He didn't knock me down really; he just gave me some medicine that made me sleepy."

"Oh, so like you won't cough like you did all night?"

"Yah, like that. You have fun with Andy, okay?"

"I call him Spud like you do. He said it was okay. He is going to call me CJ. Jackson, what is my middle name?"

"It is Jadako. It means small, but mighty and strong," Jackson answered.

The little boy stood tall, "That's kinda cool, huh Spud?"

"It's real cool! Do you want to be called Clifford Jadako now?"

"Nah, I think I like CJ better."

"Me too."

"Me three," Jackson agreed. "Have fun building your ships."

The two went to Andy's closet and took out a large cardboard box. It was filled with smaller boxes of models. The one that caught CJ's eye was an aircraft carrier. Andy read the box and it said "10 on up." He read it to CJ and asked, "You ten yet?"

"No Spud, I just turned seven. Is that close enough?"

"Well, I'll tell you what. We'll do a seven first and if that goes well, we'll do this aircraft carrier!"

CJ sat back and pursed his lips. "That'll take forever."

Andy grinned. "If we get started, we'll get there sooner. If we think about it, it will take longer. Besides, the seven one should go real fast."

"Okay," CJ held the box for the aircraft carrier. "Why is this one for a ten?"

"Because it has a lot of stuff on it. We'll learn how to do all the stuff in the other box, so when we get there, it'll be no sweat!"

"Okay," the little boy looked longingly at the aircraft carrier. "Which one are we going to do?"

"Why don't you put the aircraft carrier on that shelf, so we know where it is when we are ready. Okay?"

CJ smiled at that and nodded as he put the box of the model ship on the shelf. Andy looked through the box and found only one for a seven-year-old. It was a rather plain ship, but he thought it would be a good starter. He handed it to CJ, who was more than a little disappointed. They started to put things back in the box.

"Spud?"

"Yah CJ," Andy answered as he stacked his old models back, "What is it?"

"Where are we going to put the ships after we get them done?"

"In your room. Would that be a good idea? I used to have mine on the shelves in my room."

"Did anyone ever mess with them?"

"No. See, what's in your room is your private stuff. Mom, Grandma and Dad can come in whenever. The rule is you have to knock on someone's door to go in their room . . . unless they gave you permission. It is a place for your things, as long as they won't spill or start a fire or something. Then you'd get into hot water."

CJ sat cross-legged and thought, "How hot is the water?"

Andy smiled, "It isn't really hot water, it just means you'll be in trouble."

"You mean like in a jam? Auntie always said we'd get in a jam."

"Yah, like that. You know what? I'm in a jam now. I got down here on the floor, but I can't get up without help from a tall person. Could you get a tall person to help me?"

"Grandpa was in his chair. Should I get him?"

"Nah, he was going to sleep. Could you go find Mom?"

"Okay, Spud."

CJ carried the model box and Andy brought his old fishing tackle box, which he had used for his model tools and went to the dining room. Nora had set up the card table by the window for the boys.

"I could have done that Mom," Andy smiled.

"I know, but it was easy for me to grab. I checked on Jackson and he seems to be sleeping calmly now. Having his bed higher seems to help his cough. Thanks for doing that Andy."

"No problem. Looks like Grandpa is sleeping in his chair. Will he be okay there?"

"Yes, he does that all the time. Enjoy, you boys."

Andy noticed that CJ's attention span was almost as long as Charlie's attention span, or that of an angleworm. The little boy listened quietly while Andy read the directions through paragraph one. By paragraph two, he was taking all the parts out of the box and by three, he started to unscrew the glue cap. All reading was suspended.

Andy put the lid back on the glue and explained to the little guy the they had to sand the bottom of the boat to make it smooth. CJ looked it over and nodded. He grabbed the sandpaper and started scraping it any old way.

Andy explained about going with the grain and CJ listened carefully. Then he did it the way he had been doing it. Andy showed the boy how to do it correctly. Then Andy quickly put together the stand and did the work that needed to be done with the knife tool to keep it out of CJ's hands. They both finished about the same time.

Andy pointed out the necessity for cleaning off the sanding dust so it wouldn't get in the glue or paint. CJ pulled the cuff of his sleeve down over his wrist, slid it across the table until it fell to the floor. Then he brushed the rest on his pants and gave Andy a big smile, "That's all done, Spud. I did good, huh?"

"I'd have to say, that it was quick!" Andy tried to be encouraging. "Next time, you might want to use a damp cloth and a wastebasket. Now we have to clean the floor when we are done."

CJ was undaunted, "Okay. Now what?"

Andy explained that they had to make certain that all the sanding was smooth. Then they had to sand the deck of the ship. Since that was hard to do, he would do it while CJ sorted the little cannons and deck pieces.

That seemed to interest CJ. Andy showed CJ how to sort the stuff and he started to resand the boat. He became engrossed in his task and didn't notice CJ until he heard a "Boom, boom, boom!"

Andy looked up and CJ had lined up the little crates and anchors in a stack and then shot it down with the noise of his cannon and the help of his hand. The little pieces flew all over the room.

Andy looked at him and made a face. "CJ, now we have to pick up all the pieces or we might lose them."

CJ grinned, "Okay. I can do it. Can I put the pieces back in the box when I pick them up?"

Andy nodded, "Sure, CJ. Throw them back in the box. We will sort them out as we use them."

It was time to begin painting the ship. Andy had CJ's complete attention now because it was everything that he was interested in: making a mess that smelled terrible! But mostly, the work was permanent!

Within an hour, Andy was considering a vasectomy. He knew his limits. He was definitely not father material. He was still fresh from a great meatball fiasco with Miriam and had no idea what possessed him to build a boat with CJ! He liked little kids, but was really not into doing things with them. He just couldn't imagine why people would actually go to school to be a teacher . . . . to purposely want to be around these little humans! Yikes.

CJ watched while Andy painted the deck because it was small and needed careful brush strokes. Andy learned about mid-ship that you cannot see through a little boys head. CJ's head found its way between Andy's chin, the boat and his hands!

After accepting his fate, he suggested that the little boy go to his side of the table and ready to paint the hull of ship. It did require a short explanation of what a hull was, but all seeming satisfactory to the youngster; Andy cleaned his brush.

Then he set the hull on the stand, upside down, so that CJ could paint it. He made a silly mistake of thinking that CJ might need some instruction, but soon found that the child had the whole thing under control. Finally, Andy just sat back and watched, trying to keep it from getting too bad.

At one point, he looked over and noticed that Grandpa was watching. The elderly man looked at Andy, shook his head in disbelief and went back to sleep.

After half of the tiny jar of paint was on either the ship, tabletop, CJ's sleeves or hair, Andy decided it was finished. CJ thought it needed another coat, but Andy told him that it had to dry thoroughly before they did another coat. He was thinking like forty years to be certain it was totally dry, but gave in to the child by saying maybe that afternoon. Then they started to clean up. They only tipped the ship over on the newspaper twice and got most of the newspaper unstuck from the side of the hull, deciding the rest would have to be sanded, but they managed to not get any paint on the floor. Then they set the card table aside. Andy took CJ by the hand to the kitchen with the can of paint remover.

When they got to the kitchen, they realized that Marly was there. One look told Nora all she needed to know about her youngest son's morning, "Had fun?"

"Oh Mom," Andy groaned.

"Yes Missus! It was the most fun ever! And Spud says I am a fast worker, didn't you Spud?" the little boy just bubbled with joy. "But I sorta got a little bit of paint on my shirt. That's okay, isn't it? You can get it out of my hair, right?"

"No problem," Nora grinned as she took him over to the sink.

Andy happened to notice the girls sitting in front of the dryer, "What's that about?"

"You, Grandma, me and a jug of wine! Then we'll talk about it!" Nora crossed her eyes.

Andy just burst out laughing and gave him Mom the biggest hug in the world. "I love you, Mom."

"Pour yourself some coffee and get some milk for CJ. I'll clean him up."

As they were enjoying their break and the girls were keeping vigil on the coats, a car drove in. A man and a woman in uniform came to the door, knocked briefly and then came in.

CJ's face fell as he grabbed on to Andy immediately. "Are they police? Are they going to take us kids away?"

"Oh no, CJ," Andy put his arms around the boy. "They aren't police. They are ambulance people. They help sick people."

"Who's sick?" CJ panicked. "Is it that Grandpa or Jackson?"

"No, Annie is my wife and Marty is my cousin who lives next door. They just got home from work. It's okay, CJ. No one is going to take you away. Alright?"

CJ sat down, but scooted his chair right next to Andy's just the same. Annie came over, gave Andy a kiss and then held out her hand to CJ. "Hello. I'm Annie. We are tiyospaye. This is my partner, Marty."

"Hello CJ," Marty reached out and shook the child's hand. "Are you having a nice day?"

CJ nodded shyly, "We did boats."

"Really? Who did?"

"Spud and me did a boat."

"After I have a cup of coffee, could you show it to me?"

"If Spud says."

"I think that'd be fine. Marty and I did some boats together when we were kids."

That sparked the little guy's interest, "Did you make boats that floated? Spud says ours would sink."

"We did a couple that floated, didn't we?" Marty asked as he took his cup of coffee.

"Spud, do you think we could build one that didn't sink?" CJ asked.

"Maybe, but we might need to have Marty help us. What do you think?"

CJ sized up the uniformed man, "As long as he isn't going to make me move away from here."

Marty smiled, "You have my word."

CJ grinned from ear to ear, "Okay. I gave Mister my word this morning. That is like an important promise, right?"

"Right." Marty took a brownie, "I'll look in my closet at home and see if I have a ship model that floats that we can all work on."

"That's cool, right Spud?"

Annie rejoined them in the kitchen in her blue jeans and a sweatshirt. She had let her hair fall loose instead of up in the bun like she wore it at work. CJ was visibly relieved.

She poured some coffee for herself as the buzzer went off on the dryer. "I can get it."

"Let me help you. We had a 'thing' about it," Grandma raised her eyebrow as she joined Annie in the laundry room.

Annie noticed the little girls, "Well hello, ladies. I see you have a nice kitty. What's its name?"

Clarissa said, "Her name is Cotton. My name is Clarissa and this is Claudia. This girl is called Gopher."

Annie smiled, "I know Gopher, don't I? We are good buddies."

Miriam nodded and patted her chest, "Annie Gopher buddies."

Grandma emptied the lint trap and then opened the door to the dryer. She retrieved the beautiful soft coats and shook them. "Here they are girls, but be careful. The buttons are still hot."

Clarissa patted Claudia's cheek and said clearly, "The buttons are hot."

Claudia nodded and then reached out for her coat. Each girl took their coat and then hugged Grandma. Gopher hugged Grandma too; just because. Claudia started to put her coat on, but Clarissa stopped her. "We should put them in our room, so they don't get wrecked."

Claudia squeezed her coat and then handed it to Clarissa.

Then she and Miriam went to the kitchen, while Clarissa and Grandma took the coats to upstairs. Annie looked at the kitten, "Well Cotton, guess no one wants to talk to us, huh?"

With that, the cat ran off to the basement door. Annie giggled, "I think I'll go back to work."

"Don't you dare," Andy said as he held out his hand to his wife. "Come sit by me."

The little girls got up the table on their stools and when Clarissa and Grandma returned to the table, Nora asked if they wanted any more brownies. "It is almost lunch time, so don't fill up. You can each have a little one."

"Will there be more for later?" Clarissa asked.

"Yes, we'll put the rest away."

"I don't think I'll put them in my pocket, because they might leak, huh Missus?"

"That is probably a good idea," Nora smiled and discreetly winked at Grandma. "So, what is our plan for Saturday? Tink is coming along on our shopping trip. We're going to get the kids some clothes, but Katie wanted us to decide what we're going to do about hair-dos."

"Gee, this is out of my league," Marty grinned. "I'll go give Grandpa his shower and then check on Horse. Thanks for the brownies, Aunt Nora."

Clarissa's eyes got huge, "Is she your Auntie?"

"Yes ma'am, she is," Marty smiled.

"You and me are tiyospaye?"

"I guess so, right Annie?"

"That means extended family; so yes, you are."

"We are cousins," Marty smiled. "Like Andy and I."

"And Gopher?"

Marty gave Miriam a hug, "Why of course. Miriam is my very own special gopher cousin."

Miriam just beamed and patted her chest. "Gopher cousin."

Clarissa studied Annie and then asked, "Are you 'TOH-kah'?"

"Yes, Clarissa. I'm Indian, too, but I'm not Sioux. I am part Mandan."

Clarissa frowned, "I have to ask Jackson what that is."

"We can talk to him about it when he feels better. What hair-dos are you guys talking about?"

"Clarissa wants her hair cut and to make it blonde like Katie's," Marly answered.

"Hm. Your hair would look nice cut, but I don't know if you want it blonde?"

"I don't want that blonde-stuff, Miss Annie. I want it to be the color of sunshine."

"I told you, your hair is beautiful," Andy said. "I think Annie's hair is beautiful and it's like yours."

"Don't you think Katie's hair is beautiful?" the little girl asked.

"Ah, well, ah . . . . yes I do. I think I'd better go see if Marty needs any help. Coming CJ?"

"Okay, Spud. I think girls should keep their hair the way it is, don't you?" CJ said as he took Andy's hand.

"You know what I really think? I think boys shouldn't say anything about girls hair except that it's beautiful. Otherwise, we could be in a jam."

CJ giggled as they went out of the room.

"The problem is, Clarissa," Annie explained. "If you color your hair and then you don't like it, you have to wait a long time to take the color out. You'd be stuck."

"I really think I want it," Clarissa explained. "Katie has her hair that color for a long time."

"I know what," Annie grinned, "I'll call Suzy and ask her to bring her wigs over! She has a couple different colors, so you can try them out. How would that be?"

"That's a good idea," Nora said. "Very good. I could see this becoming a bad situation."

Annie called the church and talked to Suzy, Zach's wife, who was the church secretary. When she came back to the table, she said, "She had a very good idea! Tonight, she would bring her wigs and her sisters over and we can try them on. We can all see how we look! Would that be fun?"

Grandma giggled, "I even have one, if you guys want to see how you look with white hair!"

"That would be fun. I can talk to my sisters and see what they have too. What do you say, Nora?" Marly asked.

"Sounds great. I think that would be a lot of fun. Now, Zach said that we should cut Claudia's hair. Her long, long hair doesn't dry very fast and it isn't good for her ears. But with her problems with ear infections, he doesn't want us to be doing anything like a permanent or coloring it. I agree. What do you guys think?"

Annie got up from the table and ran to her room and returned with a lady's magazine. "Here are some haircuts we can look at."

The women decided that they would either leave her hair alone or get it cut. Claudia looked at the pictures and then pointed to the pixie cut.

Nora touched her cheek, "Is that the one you want? The Pixie cut?"

Claudia smiled, "Pixie!"

"Okay," Annie suggested, "I can keep your hair and make you a dream catcher like Ginger's. Would you like that?"

"Me, too?" Clarissa asked.

"Sure Clarissa."

Claudia looked at Clarissa for understanding, and Clarissa explained it to her. The little girl nodded and got a big smile.

"Okay, then," Annie giggled. "That's what we'll do! May I come shopping too, or are you going to have enough room?"

"We'll take the station wagon, and have lots of room," Nora said. "I think I should make an appointment at a hair salon, okay?"

Gopher had been watching the whole thing with rapt interest. She finally had to say something, "Gopher Ginger too?"

Nora thought, "Why not? All of us ladies can get our hair done! Won't that be fun?"

"Well little one, we had better get over to Grandma Jessups before she starts lunch or that rice flour won't do her much good, will it?" Marly said as she started to put Miriam's coat on.

Miriam smiled and nodded, "Gramma Shessup."

Miriam hugged Clarissa and Claudia. When she hugged Claudia, she touched her cheek first and said, "Bye-bye, Kitten."

After they cleared the table, Grandma Katherine said, "I'm going to take a cat nap. If Claudia is ready for her medicine, I'll lay down with her on the day bed."

"That sounds good," Nora said as she got the cough syrup. "It always makes her sleepy. You know, Clancy has been awful quiet this morning. I hope he is getting some rest. He coughed almost all night."

They all went into the nursery and Clancy was awake. He was standing in the crib, looking out the window. "Hello," Annie said.

He smiled at her, decided that she was okay and held out his arms to her. She took checked his temperature, changed his pants and gave him his medicine. He wasn't very perky, so she took him into the living room to rock him.

Grandma broke into a big smile, "Guess what I remembered? I have some afghans that I made that might just be the ticket for these folks. Do you girls want to help me look?"

Clarissa was ready to look, but wasn't sure what a ticket was or an afghan, for that matter. Grandma opened her bottom bureau drawer and there were six afghans that she had crocheted. Nora smiled, "I forgot about them! They were made of that fuzzy soft yarn, right? I always loved these little blankets."

Grandma put them on the bed, "Okay girls. You can each pick out one for your very own, but I'll take this one to Annie for Clancy."

Grandma took one that was medium blue with white stripes to Annie. She covered Clancy with it while he was in Annie's arms and he instantly cuddled into it, pulling the edge of it up to his chin. Annie smiled at Grandma, "I think he likes it."

"It can be his," Grandma patted him on the back. "I hope the little guy gets better soon. At least his cough is better today."

She went back into her bedroom where the little girls were testing the softness of the afghans. Grandma asked, "Did you decide which one you want?"

Clarissa said. "They're so soft."

Nora touched Claudia's cheek, "Which one do you want?"

Claudia surprised them all when she picked the one that was shades of beige. "Is that the one you want?"

Claudia smiled, "Cotton."

Nora handed it to the little girl, "It is the same color as Cotton."

"So, which one do you want, Clarissa?" Grandma asked.

"I can't decide. I love them both. This one is so beautifuler with the pink and sunshine! I love it."

"Then why don't you choose that one?" Nora asked.

"What if I wreck it?"

Nora knelt down next to her, "You won't wreck it. If you take care, you'll keep it for a long time. If it gets dirty, we'll wash it."

Clarissa pulled back a bit, "But it's so beautifulest."

Grandma took the small afghan in her arms and handed it to Clarissa. "Honey, I'd love to have you enjoy it. That is what it's for; to enjoy. So, please take it as a gift from me to you."

Clarissa held the afghan and could hardly breathe. "It's so soft. Pilamaya Missus Grandma."

"You're very welcome, Honey. You can call me Grandma. You don't have to say Missus Grandma. Okay?"

Clarissa just stood in awe and Grandma took the afghan from her and wrapped her in it. "There you go. Enjoy it! Come little Kitten, let's go take a nap."

Claudia took her hand and followed her off to the nursery.

Nora smiled at Clarissa, "What would you like to do?"

"I don't know."

"I was thinking a short nap might be a good idea myself. What do you say? Want to join me?"

Clarissa's eyes sprung open, "You mean I could sleep with you?"

"Sure, then after a short snooze you can help me make lunch."

Clarissa took her hand, "Missus? What's a snooze?"

"It is another name for a short nap."

"I think that's a funny name."

"It kinda is, isn't it?"

The two lay down on Nora's bed and Clarissa covered up in her new afghan. Her little hands kept caressing it. After a few minutes Clarissa asked, "Missus, does my Mommy and Daddy know about my new blanket?"

"They might, Honey. Do you think they'd like it?"

"I think so. My Mommy liked soft stuff too. You know, I had two Mommies. My first Mommy died and then I got another one. But she died too."

"I know. That is very sad."

"Missus, are you going to die?"

"Honey, we all die someday, but I think it'll be a long time. Until then, do you want to be my little girl?"

Clarissa cuddled closer to her, "I think so."

"That'd be wonderful. I'd like that very much."

After a few minutes, Clarissa touched Nora's hand. "Missus? Will I have more beautifulest hands like yours someday?"

Nora smiled, "You already do, you silly rabbit. You're a beautiful little girl. Don't you know that?"

"I don't have sunshine hair."

"Clarissa, do you think that Diane is beautiful?"

"Oh yes!"

"She doesn't have sunshine hair. Hers is light brown. Did you think about that?"

Clarissa thought, "Only but Katie does and she is really beautifuler."

"Honey, Katie would feel very bad if you didn't think that you were beautiful because of her. She is beautiful, but not because of her sunshine hair. She has a warm heart, a big smile and is very kind. You're all those things too! You are beautiful, and I know that Katie thinks so."

"Really? Katie thinks I'm pretty?"

"Yup, and so does everybody! It doesn't matter what color your hair is."

A few minutes later, Clarissa turned over and fell asleep holding Nora's hand.

18

Clarence followed Elton down the steps and toward the garage. Elton pointed to the northwest of the house by the windrow of trees. "There's the outhouse. We should go into Merton and get you some overshoes first thing. Then we can go wade through the snow without getting your shoes all wet. Okay?"

Clarence looked at Elton and nodded. Then he reached up and took his hand while they walked to the garage. "Over there," Elton continued, "That is the turkey shed. While we're at the shop, we need to order the baby chicks and baby turkeys. Can you remind me?"

"How many are we going to get?"

"I think about three hundred chicks and maybe, what do you think, fifty turkeys? Will that be enough?"

"What are we going to do with them?"

"Well, we'll eat some and then sell the rest. Let's see, there are a lot of clanners. I guess we should get a hundred."

"What is a clanner?"

"That is what we call our tiyospaye. You have met a lot of them, but you will meet a few more. They are a good bunch. If you treat them right, they'll be there for you. No matter what."

"How do I treat them right?"

"Hmm, let's see. I guess you have to be nice to them, help them if they need help, be their friend and like that."

"Think I can do that?"

"I see no reason why not."

Clarence looked over to the turkey shed, "How many turkeys does the shed hold?"

"I guess about hundred and fifty. Why? Are you thinking we should just fill it up? It's probably better to have too many than not enough, huh?"

"I s'pose."

"Okay, hundred and fifty it is! Don't let me forget," Elton said as he opened the garage door.

Inside Clarence gasped, "Wow! Are these all your cars?"

"No, the kids and Grandpa have their cars in here too," Elton said. "Let me show you Grandpa's. It is very old and he can't drive it anymore because his mind is bad, but he loves it."

Elton showed him the restored '46 Ford four-door sedan. "It is sure shiny," Clarence said. "Does Grandpa shine it?"

"No, usually Matt does it for him because he can't anymore."

"What happened to his mind?"

"He got a sickness called Alzheimers. It makes him forget things and get confused, but he still loves us."

"He seems nice, but he gets mixed up."

"Yah, that happens. We have to watch out for him. He can't go outside by himself or he will get lost. Well Clarence, do you think we should take the station wagon, the car or the old pickup? Your choice."

Clarence looked them all over, and stopped at the blue '54 Chevy pickup, "I really like this pickup. It is really cool."

"Fine choice, young man. Hop in!"

Elton helped the little man into the cab and then got the pickup out of the garage. They headed off down the road toward town. "You know, I forgot that guy that has the goats, works at the cheese factory today. So, we can't go see him today. One day soon, okay?"

"Sure," Clarence said, sitting as tall as he could in the seat with his arm on the door like a grownup. "Is it far to his place?"

"Not really. I'll show you around if you want."

"If we have time after we fix the outhouse."

"Okay."

On the way past the church, Elton said, "There is Pastor's church. He lives in the house right next to it. Our family goes there on Sunday. You're welcome to come along if you want."

Clarence studied Elton, "Does Jackson go?"

"Yes, he does. Maybe you'd like to talk to him about it and then let me know."

"Do I have to?"

"You talk to Jackson about it, but no. You don't have to."

"Okay, I'll sleep on it."

Elton smiled and turned his attention to the sky, "Looks like it might just warm up one of these days. Are you ready for spring?"

Clarence nodded, "When it gets warm, we're going fishing, right?"

"Yes sir. We are doing that."

"Mister, do you think that Rags and Elmer will get along?"

"Most likely. They seemed to be having a good time this morning. I think if they were going to fight, they would've started already. Don't you?"

Clarence nodded.

The old pickup pulled up to the front of a service station and stopped. Clarence sat ahead and looked over the dash, "Is this the shop?"

There were two gas pumps out front and a small office next door to three car bays. In the back were two heavy equipment bays. Adjoining the station was the Farmer's Union Elevator that had a store and a grain elevator.

"Is that store in your shop too?"

"No, that's part of the Farmer's Union Elevator. We're going in there after I show you the shop, so we can get your overshoes and order the chicks."

"Don't forget the turkeys," Clarence reminded him.

Elton grinned, "Thanks for reminding me."

The lad followed the man into the back of the shop. There were two cars being worked on and one pickup up on a lift. Clarence's eyes widened trying to take it all in. There was the sound of air-powered tools and a small radio playing a country song in the background. He was utterly fascinated.

Then he noticed a man's feet sticking out from under a car and he wiggled Elton's hand and pointed.

"That's Kevin." Elton smiled, "Hey, Kev, we came to see you!"

Kevin came out from under the car on his creeper. "Hello! I thought you were going on vacation today?"

"We are, but we thought we'd check out the shop. Clarence hasn't seen it yet."

"Hi Clarence," Kev grinned. "Wanna see under a car? Grab a creeper and come under with me. I'll show you if you want."

Clarence couldn't have been more excited, "Can I, Mister?"

"Sure. Here," Elton moved a creeper over, "You can use this one."

As he and Kev started back under the car, Elton said, "I'm going to be in the office to sign that contract. Anything else you need me to do?"

"Nah, Harrington and I are cool," Kev said, "Okay, Clarence. Don't have busy hands, okay? You must be careful so we don't get hurt, but I will show you . . . ."

Elton went into the back office where Ian Harrington was doing paperwork. Harrington looked up and smiled, "Noticed you brought one of your new kids along. Which one is that?"

"That's Clarence, the oldest," Elton nodded. "He is having a hard time with so many changes. So we decided to take a vacation day."

Harrington nodded, "Poor kid probably needs one. When are they starting school?"

"Nora and I thought we'd register them on Monday. That will give them a couple days to acclimatize. From the way it sounds, the two that are school age have missed so much school that they aren't doing well in it at all. They might have a time."

"Well, if there is anything Ruthie and I can do, just give a yell. I'll give you your desk back and I'm going out to the front to get the credit receipts ready. Need anything?"

"No, I was about to ask you the same thing," Elton smiled as he sat in his chair. "I'm glad you aren't much taller than me, so we don't have to readjust the chair. Gee Kev used it one day and I almost had to remodel it!"

"That's a blasted fact," Harrington smiled his big dimpled smile. He looked a lot like his brother, Matt, except he was shorter and had bigger dimples. Harrington worked as the office manager for Schroeder's two garages, the Farmer's Union store and the Cheese Factory in town.

Elton did some paperwork, called Nora to check on the kids and then headed back out to shop area. Kevin and Clarence were giggling under the car about something. "Are you guys having fun without me?" Elton asked.

The two came out from under the car. "Clarence has a good idea. He thinks we should take a creeper home for cleaning under the beds!"

Elton chuckled, "You might get yourself a full time job then! Want to hang out here more, or go to the Elevator with me?"

"I guess I'll go with you. Can I come visit you again sometime, Mr. Kevin? Mister and I are going to fix up the outhouse today."

"Whenever you have time, just let me know. The outhouse you say? Yah, the needs some work," Kev looked at his Dad curiously.

"It's going to be Clarence's thinking spot," Dad explained.

Kev laughed, "Good idea, Clarence. That is a great place to think! Make sure you put a magazine rack in there for some comic books."

"I don't have any comic books."

"Maybe you'll get some," Kev grinned.

The two went through the shop to the Farmer's Union store the back way. On the way, Elton explained different things in the shop to the little boy who had a thousand questions. He was enthralled by everything there.

They walked up to the counter of the store and Elton smiled, "Hi Doug."

"Hi yourself," the middle-aged man smiled over the counter, "Who is this gentleman you have with you?"

"He's my boy, Clarence," Elton said with pride. "Clarence, this is Doug and he is a clanner."

Clarence looked at Elton, "Tiyospaye?"

"Yes," Elton answered and then explained to Doug, "That is Sioux for extended family."

"Yes sir, we are that," Doug agreed. "I have two boys, Rod who is sixteen and Little Bill who is ten. How old are you?"

"Eight."

"You guys will meet on Sunday. The kids all like to race cars after dinner on Sundays. Do you race much?"

"No, I never have. I'm too little to drive."

"Oh, these are toy cars," Doug explained. "Come, I'll show you some."

They all went over to the shelf that had several toy race cars on it. Clarence was amazed and had never seen anything like it before. "Wow! Do all the kids have some?"

"They share and got a whole shelf of them in the hallway closet at the house. I'll have Andy show them to you when we get home," Elton explained.

"I'll tell you what, would you like to pick out one for each of you kids? Then Andy can help you practice before Sunday, so you'll know what going on," Doug suggested. "It will be my welcome gift."

Clarence looked at Elton for permission and even though he nodded yes, the boy shrugged, "Maybe not. There are five of us. That's a bunch of cars."

"I know, maybe the little one can't have a race car. He might swallow some parts of it or something, but I have a dandy car here that he can play with. Let's pick them out. Okay?"

"Okay."

Doug helped the boy pick out a car for each of the bigger kids and a wooden car on a pull string for Clancy. While he was doing that, Elton began picking up the Carhartt's for all the kids. He got them all overalls and jackets, except for Clancy. Then he started to pick out overshoes.

After Doug put the cars on the counter, they went over to help Elton. "Know what you're doing?"

"Kind of. The kids have good jackets, but nothing for every day, the barn and stuff. Clancy has a snowsuit and after the trouble with the frostbite, he can't be out in the cold much this winter anymore. Nora said that we can pass the Carhartts down, so it'd be a good idea to get them for the other kids. That duck material wears like iron."

"They should too for what they charge for them. Overshoes can be passed down. They never go out of style."

"That's because they have no style!" Elton laughed. "Why I think my five buckle overshoes are the same as my dad had when I was a kid."

At the counter, Doug started ringing up the bill. "I told Clarence these cars are a welcome gift so they can practice before Sunday."

"Thanks, Doug."

"Pilamaya, Mister Doug."

'You're welcome, Clarence. You guys have a nice day."

"Mister! Don't forget the chicks and turkeys!"

"Thanks Clarence! I'd have plumb forgot! I need to order 200 Leghorns, 200 Wyandottes and 150 Bronze turkeys—all straight-run. Did I get them all, Clarence?"

Clarence shrugged, "Turkeys and chickens."

"Hey, Doug?" Elton asked while Doug filled out the order. "Did Carl order his ducks yet?"

Doug chuckled, "He did. Fifty each of three kinds. I guess the Gophers couldn't decide which kind they wanted. I don't know how the poor man does it, but he seems to like being with those kids all the time. How many Gophers stay at the Petunia Patch anyway?"

"Don't know. Two babies full time, and then about seven others that are there part-time."

Doug looked at Clarence, "Has Elton taken you to the Petunia Patch yet?"

"No, sir."

"You'll like it. Carl has the cubes for you kids painted already."

"Cubes?"

"Yah, like a cupboard to keep your stuff in when you visit."

"I keep my stuff at Mister's house."

"I know, I mean just like your jacket and things when you visit there. Have Elton take you over there and you'll see what I mean."

"Okay, I'll sleep on it."

19

They took their packages and headed back through the garage. Kev saw them and waved, "Dad, Harrington needs to see you before you go. Have a good day, Clarence!"

"Bye," Clarence smiled back.

At the front office, Harrington was standing behind the till. Clarence looked around the small room with big windows that faced the gas pumps out front. There was a rack with maps and another with batteries of all sizes. He listened while Elton and the man talked. Then Elton set down his packages and said, "Clarence, I have to go look something up in my office. Would you mind waiting a second with Harrington? Oh, I'm sorry. I never introduced you. Ian Harrington, this is my boy, Clarence. I'll be right back."

Elton scooted out of the room and left them standing there. The dark haired fellow with big blue eyes smiled at Clarence, "I'm Ian Harrington, but everyone calls me Harrington. So you can too."

Clarence nodded, "My name is Clarence Grey Hawk. I'm called Clarence."

"Ever been called Grey Hawk?"

"No. Everybody at our house was Grey Hawk, so we had to call everybody something different. Do you live by yourself?"

"No, but I call my wife Ruthie and she calls me Ian. You know, now that you mention it, when I lived at home with all my brothers and sisters, I was the only one called Harrington. They were all Harringtons! I wonder why?"

Clarence studied the man, "Maybe they didn't know how to say that other name."

"You might have a point there. You have met my little brother. Remember Matt?"

"Oh yah. He's a nice guy. I guess he kinda looks like you."

Harrington grinned, "Except I'm better looking."

Clarence smiled back. "Mister; er, I mean Harrington, can I ask you something?"

"Sure can."

"What happened to your arm? It doesn't move much."

"I used to be a detective with the police force and a crazy person shot me in the arm. It doesn't work so well anymore, but it's getting better. It used to just hang there, but now I can use it scratch my nose!"

Clarence giggled, "Did it hurt?"

"My nose?" Harrington teased. "Yah, my arm did when I first got shot. It wasn't much fun. What do you want to be when you grow up?"

Clarence shrugged, "Don't know."

"Do you want to be a policeman?"

"Don't think so. I might be a fisherman."

"That's a cool idea. Do you fish a lot?"

"Not yet. My Dad was too busy, but Mister said he'll take me when it's nice out."

"That's great. My Dad and I are going to go, too. Maybe we could give you a call and we could go together sometime. What do you think?"

"I'd have to ask Mister and then I'll sleep on it."

Harrington nodded, "Good idea. So what's your favorite subject in school?"

"I don't like school."

"None of it?"

"Nope. Mister says I shouldn't say anything in front of the other kids, because maybe they'll like it. I sure don't."

"What don't you like about it?"

"Don't see why I have to know all that stuff."

"I know a few reasons. Want to hear?"

"I s'pose."

"Well, you have to know how to read so that you don't go into the girl's bathroom by mistake! That would be gross!"

Clarence giggled.

"And you need to know how to read a map, or you might get lost."

"I just won't go anywhere that I don't know."

"How about if we hear about a neat fishing spot and don't know how to get there? We'd have to look on a map."

"Can you find fishing spots on a map?" Clarence's eyes widened at this new information.

"Certain maps you can."

"Cool. I'll learn that then."

"And you need to know math."

"To go fishing?"

"Yah, how many angleworms would you take along if you wanted to catch a dozen fish? How many sandwiches would you want to take so you and I can each have two? All that kind of stuff."

"Hm, but I could just ask you and you could tell me."

"You could, but what if I'm wrong?"

"I might be wrong too. I know! We can let Mister bring the worms and sandwiches."

Elton came back in the room with the paper and handed it to Harrington. "What am I bringing worm sandwiches to?"

Both Harrington and Clarence laughed, "Fishing!"

"Tell you what! You guys can eat the sandwiches and I'll feed my worms to the fish!"

They went to the pickup and Elton helped Clarence into the cab. He put the packages in a box in the back of the truck. "We're off. So you know, I talked to Nora and checked. She gave us a list of things to pick up. The kids are all okay. Let's go to the Five and Dime and see about some fixin's for the outhouse. Ready?"

"Ready," Clarence said with pride as he sat straight and tall on the seat. "Harrington is like his brother, right? Friendly. They are tiyospaye?"

"That they are," Elton agreed as they drove the block down the five block main street. He diagonally parked in front of the Five and Dime Store and helped Clarence out of the pickup. They went into the store hand in hand.

"What fixin's are we going to buy?" Clarence asked.

"We have a couple things to pick up for Nora and then we need to get a good battery lamp, a toilet paper holder, plastic container with a lid, toilet paper and a new latch. Can you think of anything else?"

Clarence seemed surprised that they needed that much, "Dunno."

"What about paint or curtains?" Elton winked.

"I like it plain."

"You're probably right. If you make it too fancy, then everyone will want to think there."

Clarence grinned at the joke, "That wouldn't be good."

They picked up the bathroom things and that is when Elton saw a blue toilet seat and cover on sale. He picked it up and looked it over, "What do you think?"

"It isn't a water toilet, is it?"

"No, but no point a guy can't be comfortable, is there?"

Clarence giggled, "I guess not."

"Glad you agree," Elton put it in their cart, "Let's see what Nora has on her list. Toothbrushes, toothpaste, shoelaces, lunch buckets, and a stuffed animal for Clancy. Think we can handle that?"

"Yah," Clarence said as he took Elton's hand and they went down the aisle.

They stopped at the toothbrushes and easily picked out five different colors and a couple tubes of toothpaste. The shoelaces were easy, but it took some time to decide on a stuffed animal for Clancy. It had to be washable and soft with no hard buttons or eyes on it. Clarence found a wolf that fit the bill. It wasn't too big, or too small, so Clancy could easily hold it. Then they went to find the lunch buckets.

There must have been ten different designs with television or comic book characters on them, but Clarence didn't seem to know who the characters were. "Why do CJ and I have to have these things?"

"So you can take a lunch to school," Elton explained.

"I don't think you should get them, because we might not ever go to school."

Elton knelt down in the aisle next to the kid, "You never know when you'll want to take a lunch someplace. I mean, like if you go fishing. Where are you going to keep your worm sandwiches? It's always good to have a lunch bucket."

Clarence wasn't too impressed but finally agreed he would get one like Elton had when he was a kid. Elton picked out two dome-topped buckets, without any pictures on them. One was gray and the other was black with matching thermoses, so they could tell them apart.

On their way to the check out, they passed some bookshelves. Elton stopped and got a picture book for Clancy. Then he found a sticker book with fairies, pixies and sprites on it for Clarissa and a sticker book of kittens for Claudia. Nora had told him that CJ and Andy were putting together a model ship, so Elton thought a book about ships would be fun for CJ. He asked Clarence if he wanted one, but he shook his head no.

Without saying a word, Elton took a copy of Fishing World. Next to the bookshelves was a magazine rack that attached to the wall. He bought that for the outhouse. At the checkout, he picked up a comic book.

The guys loaded their packages into the box in the back of the pickup and Elton helped Clarence into the pickup. "What do you say to a quick tour of Merton on the way to the Hen House for lunch?"

"Okay."

Elton drove by the school and playground, but Clarence showed no interest. He was more interested in the bank where Carrie, Kevin's wife, worked. "Would you like to stop in and say Hi to her?"

Clarence shrugged, "I don't think she knows who I am."

"I bet you a Coke that she does!"

The two went into the bank. There were two teller windows and a partially open office on the side. Carrie saw them through the window from her desk and came to meet them. "Hi Clarence! What a nice surprise. I'm so glad you came to visit me!"

Clarence beamed, "You did remember me!"

"Of course I did. You are part of my family! Why wouldn't I?"

Carrie kissed her father-in-law on the cheek, "Wanna come into my office for a cup of coffee?"

"I never turn down coffee."

The guys went into her office and sat at the two chairs across from her desk, while she got coffee. She brought Clarence a cup of water. When she set it down in front of him, opened her drawer and took out a spoon and small jar. "I have some nectar here with sugar in it. I just add that to the water, give it a stir and whallah! Something good! You do like cherry, don't you?"

Clarence shrugged and watched carefully while she stirred up the cherry nectar for him. He took a taste and it was very good. "I like it, Miss Carrie."

"Tell you what, you just call me Carrie and I'll call you Clarence. Otherwise, I'll have to call you Mister Clarence."

Clarence got a bit shy, "Okay Carrie. You're nice."

"So are you. Did you have Dad bring you here to make a big deposit in the bank?"

He shook his head no, "I don't know what that thing is that you said."

"A deposit? That is like if I have a bunch of money and I'm afraid I might lose it; I put it in the bank so they can take care of it for me. That's what we do here. We keep your money safe."

"I don't have any money," Clarence said. "If I did, I'd let you keep it!"

"I have an idea. Stay here you guys."

A couple minutes later, Carrie came back with a pile of foot square boxes. She tumbled them on the desk. "I brought some of our piggy banks. You can pick out one for each of you kids. Then when you get money, you can put it in the piggy bank and when it's full, you can have me put it in the bank to save for you. All you have to do is open a savings account."

Clarence's eyes were huge. He had rarely heard so much stuff he didn't understand in one sentence! "What is a piggy thing?"

Carrie opened one of the six boxes. "See the slot on the top? You put your coins in there."

She reached in her drawer and took her wallet out. She handed Clarence a penny. "Now slip it in the slot."

He did and then shrugged. "How do I get the money out?"

Elton showed him how to open the rubber stopper on the bottom to empty it. Clarence grinned. "I see. Then I can bring the big bag of money to you to keep in the bank. How will I remember how much money I gave you?"

"Good question. We'll give you a bankbook and write in it how much you gave us. When you want your money back, you bring the book to us, and we can give the money back to you. And you know the best part?"

Clarence shook his head no.

"We even pay you a little bit extra for letting us keep it for you!"

"Wow! Did you hear that? Mister, do you have a piggy bank?"

"I used to. Now I just write a check to put money in the bank. When you are older, you can have a checking account too. Horse has one."

"Oh, so he doesn't have a piggy bank."

"No, now he has a checking account and a savings account, like Carrie was telling you about."

"Cool. Mister, could I have one of those money pigs?"

"Sure, I bet Carrie has paperwork for you. Right?" The older man asked.

"I do. You and Dad pick out which piggy bank you want, and I will get it."

After Carrie left the office, Clarence grinned to Elton, "I never knew about this stuff before. It is way cool. Where am I going to get the coins?"

"From helping with chores. I'll give you an allowance and then you can put it in your piggy bank. You can divide it and have some to spend, some to save and some for church—if you decide to go. How does that sound?"

"You'll have to help me. Or maybe Jackson can?"

"Either of us, or Carrie can. She's really good at it."

They left the bank with five piggy banks. Clarence picked one that looked like a big fish, CJ had one that was like an owl, Clarissa's was a bunny, Claudia's was a kitten and Clancy's was a clown. Carrie decided to take the pink pig home for Holly. Clarence signed his own signature card and had Elton and Carrie sign with him. They signed the other kids for them. When Carrie handed him the bankbook with his name on the front and the card saying he was a customer of the bank, he was so pleased he almost glowed.

After Elton put the piggy banks in the car, he took Clarence's hand. "We are going back over to the dime store."

"Did you forget something?"

"No, but we have something we need."

Elton went over to the wallets and asked Clarence, "Which one do you want? It has to fit in your pocket. Leather is the best because it lasts. Let's see. There are a couple here. This one has horses on it and this one has an eagle. What suits your fancy?"

Clarence could hardly breathe he was so excited, "You mean I get my very own?"

"Yes, you need it for your bank card and when Matt takes you to get your library card, you can put that in, too. You have to take very good care of it. It isn't a toy."

"I will sir, I really will. Can I have the eagle one?"

"Fine choice," Elton said as he took it to the checkout counter, "Then lunch."

After ordering from the menu, they had a lunch of cheeseburgers and soda pop. Then they went back to the farm. In the garage, Clarence asked, "Are we going to the house now?"

"Not unless you want to. I thought we could get that outhouse taken care of. What do you think?"

"Oh yes!"

Elton opened the bag from Farmers Union and got out Clarence's Carhartt jacket and his overshoes. Then they filled the wheelbarrow and a red wagon with tools and the things from the dime store they needed for the outhouse, some shingles and a short ladder. After loading them all up, they headed off to the outhouse.

Elton and Clarence took turns shoveling the snow to make a path to the small wooden outhouse. There they opened the creaking wooden door and checked it out.

There was an obvious leak from the roof, but with the exception of some derelict cobwebs and a lot of dust, the building seemed sound. "Well, young man, looks like we have our work cut out for us. Let's take care of the roof first."

"Our house used to leak, but Dad said it was just wrecked. I didn't think we could fix it."

Elton nodded, "I think he meant he needed the shingles to fix it. We are lucky because we have extra shingles from when we did the chicken coop. Have you ever put on shingles before?"

"No."

"Well, this will be your first time."

The two worked diligently. Elton showed the young boy how to remove the old shingles on the 4X5 foot building. It was a perfect size for learning. He showed him how to measure, hammer, nail and trim the shingles. Elton allowed Clarence to do most of the work and he could see the pride grow in the little boy.

When they were finished with the roof, Elton grinned, "Now if we had our lunch box thermos, we could have a coffee break!"

Clarence giggled, "Do we have a lot more work to do?"

"Not too much."

Before long, they had swept out the inside, attached the blue toilet seat cover over the hole on the wooden bench, put up the toilet paper roll, the magazine rack and fixed the handle. It looked pretty neat when it was done.

"Wow Mister!" the boy beamed, "We did it!"

"Almost," Elton smiled. "I have a couple things to add. Here is the plastic covered wastebasket to keep your flashlight and the extra toilet paper in so it doesn't get dusty. And here; I think you know where to put these."

Clarence was puzzled as he opened the bag from the dime store. There was the comic book like Kevin had suggested. Clarence giggled and put it in the magazine rack. "I have to show Mr. Kevin and tell Jackson! Let's go!"

"Oh no. Hotshot! We aren't done yet."

Clarence looked around and frowned, "I think we are."

"Look, we have a hammer here, a screwdriver there, junk all over. We need to put the tools away where they belong and clean up around here."

Clarence thought and then started to pick things up. "Why can't we just leave the stuff here? We know where it is."

"Well, just say Kevin wants to use the hammer. How is he going to know where it? If we always put things in the same place, then we all know where to find it."

Clarence nodded, "That's a good idea."

After everything was put away, the two gathered the rest of their packages and headed to the house. "Think they will have coffee for us?"

"Yes Mister. I think they will. I bet they'll be surprised at all the stuff we did, huh? I liked our vacation day!"

"Me too, son. Me, too."

20

The guys brought all their packages into the kitchen and were met by an excited family. Marty had gone home, lunch was over and Jackson had even joined them at the table while he was soaking his 'foot'.

It was almost like Christmas, with all the jackets, overshoes, race cars and piggy banks. Andy labeled their overshoes on the inside with a marker. Nora gave each child a nickel to practice putting money in their bank, while Annie helped the kids put their banks away. Clarence discreetly showed Jackson his wallet and bankbook. Jackson was dutifully impressed.

After coffee, Annie told Elton he had to have his IV. He had contracted Whipple's disease while working in a feedlot earlier in the year. The doctor explained that it was a malabsorption disease which could cause malnutrition and early death. It required two years of antibiotic and supplemental fluids from time to time to keep his system in balance. He was now able to take the antibiotic orally and had the IV's only twice a week.

Annie had it all set up for him and he went to lie down. Andy was going to play chess with him, but Elton reminded Nora and Clarence they were going to talk about sleeping arrangements.

When the IV was about half way through, Nora and Clarence knocked and asked if they could talk. The guys said sure. Andy asked if it was private.

"What do you think, Clarence?" Nora asked. "Need to talk in private, or can we let Andy hear?"

"Sure. Probably Jackson, too," Clarence suggested.

"Good idea," Nora said. "I'll get him before he goes back to sleep."

A few minutes later, they all gathered around Elton's bed. "You're looking a little better, Jackson? Do you feel better?"

"Not coughing so much, but I still feel worn out. I just wish I could start getting better. I'm so tired of it." Jackson nodded, "I know. I'm lucky, but it does get tiresome."

"That it does. So, where are these guys going to nest for the night?"

Nora nodded, "Zach told us some of what we can't do. Jackson needs to have room to get to his wheelchair or crutches to go to the bathroom at night. Clancy isn't doing so well, and needs to be sleeping in the crib, and Claudia needs to sleep on a bed."

Jackson looked at Clarence, "We better not let the little guys sleep in my room, because we don't want them to get sicker. Right?"

Clarence was quiet for a bit, "Clancy sleeps mostly with that medicine, so he'd be okay sleeping in the crib. As long as he can see somebody he knows. If Claudia sleeps in there too, he'd be alright."

"Okay," Elton said, "Clancy in the crib in the nursery. Will Claudia be okay if she can see Clancy?"

Clarence made a face, "Not so much. She can help him if he cries, but who will help her?"

Nora made a suggestion, "Can Clarissa sleep with her? There is plenty of room on the day bed for both girls and they can watch out for each other."

"That'd be good, if you leave the door open and the hall light on."

"Then you guys can sleep in my room," Jackson suggested. "We can leave that door open too, so no one needs to be alone."

Andy grinned, "Hey, we have that cot from my room. That'd be big enough for you and CJ."

Nora nodded, "Okay, but Jackson, will it bother you?"

"No, I'm only afraid that when I wake up screaming or punching it might scare them."

"Do you understand why Jackson does that, Clarence?" Elton asked.

Clarence shrugged, "No sir. Because he is scared?"

"Kind of. I dream that I'm back in the war."

"Do you have a dream catcher?"

"I do, Clarence," Jackson answered, "And it helps, but these are horrible nightmares from the war. Lots of guys have them."

"I get them too, Clarence. When I wake up, I don't know where I am for a minute. Someone has to talk to me to get calmed down again," Andy confirmed.

"I can talk to you," the little boy offered. "I can watch out for you."

"The best thing would be for you to call Elton. I sometimes swing pretty hard and might hit you by accident."

"What if you hit Mister?"

Elton smiled, "You'd be there for me. See, if you call me right off, then there would be two of us! Okay?"

"You mean, you and me together?"

"Yup."

"Okay Jackson. That will be okay. I'll explain it to CJ. Andy, do you need help getting the cot? I can help you."

"That'd be great, and Annie will help too. I think Dad was beating me in chess anyway."

After the beds were made, Nora went up to get the girls coats to hang in the nursery closet. The little girls were sure they needed to have them where they could see them. CJ and Andy went to sand their boat again before the second coat of paint.

Clarence decided to talk to his big stepbrother about all the things he needed to sleep on before he made a decision. Clarence pulled the stool up to the side of Jackson's bed while the young man rested. "You feeling better?"

"Yes, a little. Did you have a nice vacation day with Elton?"

"It was good. I got to go under a car with Mr. Kevin and then we went to meet this other guy that gave us the racecars. Jackson, is it hard to race those cars?"

"No, why?"

"Mr. Doug said that Andy could show us how to do it, so we knew what was going on."

"That's a good idea. I guess the kids set up ramps, curves and stuff like that. It will be fun. Besides, it is always good to know what is going on. Huh?"

"I s'pose. What if I don't like racing cars?"

"Then don't do it. Nobody is going to make you. It is a good idea to see if you will like it first. Don't you think?"

"I s'pose. I met this Harrington guy at the shop. He and I talked about fishing. Do you know him?"

"I do. He is Matt's brother. I like him."

"Me, too. He said there are maps about fishing. Did you know that?"

"I did. I hear they are pretty good."

"Harrington said he'd show me how to read them. Think I should?"

"Yes, I do. It never hurts to learn something."

Clarence hesitated, "Do you think I should go to school?"

"Clarence, I really hate to tell you this, but you have to. If you refuse to go, then Mr. and Mrs. Schroeder won't be able to keep you here. If you don't do like the rules say, the Rules people will take you someplace where they will make you go to school. Did you know that?"

"No. You mean the Rules people would make me move away?"

"Yes. Sorry. Unless you really want to go somewhere else?"

"I told Mister I'd give him a chance. I think he's okay. You know, when he talks to me, he usually gets down so we are the same size. I like that. And he lets me say stupid stuff and never makes me feel stupid."

"I know. I like that about him, too. Most of the tiyospaye are like that. The clanners are good people, Clarence. We need to thank Wakan Tanka for finding them for us."

"You mean like saying that grace stuff? Do they do that every time they eat? Have you done that?"

"Not yet, but it is really nice. We should thank God for what He gives us."

"Maybe I should ask Mr. Kevin to help me say a grace. Think he would help me?"

"I'm sure of it. Kevin is a great guy."

"He is pretty cool. Mister said you go to Mister Pastor's church. I s'pose that is because Katie goes there."

"No. I went first with Spud."

"Mister said I didn't have to go. I told him I would sleep on it. What do you think? Should us kids go? CJ and Clarissa will want me to tell them."

"I know. I go. I think Wakan Tanka and God are the same, just different names. You should try it, anyway. If you totally hate it, then don't go. These guys won't get mad at you. It doesn't mean that we still can't believe what our grandfathers did too. Okay?"

"I might sleep on it, but I guess we can try it. Everybody goes, huh?"

"Grandpa doesn't very often, because he gets too confused. Or if you are sick or something, but otherwise we all go, come home and eat in the big dining room here. All the tiyospaye meet here and visit."

"I guess I'll tell the kids. Maybe Clancy can't cause of his cough. He will get germs all over everybody!"

"He might at that." Jackson sat up and took a drink of water. "I'm feeling kind of weird. Do you think that you could get Missus for me?"

"Did I make you sicker?"

"Not at all. You always make me feel better! It's just this darned pneumonia."

"Okay. I'll run get her. You hold on, okay?"

Clarence ran out and brought Nora back with him. When they came in, Jackson was trying to reach his wastebasket. Nora grabbed it for him just in time. When he started to get sick, Clarence dashed to the living room as quick as he could.

"What's the word, Clarence?" Spud asked as he and CJ moved the card table back to the corner.

Clarence made a face, "Jackson's upping it."

"Upping it?"

"Yah, you know," Clarence did an imitation of someone vomiting.

"Oh, I get it. Yah, he has trouble with that medicine. Want to hang out with CJ and I?"

"Yah, I think so. If I see upping, I up."

"I know," Andy patted his head. "Me, too."

Andy and CJ showed him the ship they were working on and then Clarence asked about the car races.

"I can show you tonight after dinner. I think the school bus is coming now, so little Charlie will be here. Okay?"

"Will you forget?"

"I hope not, but if I do, can you remind me?"

"Okay."

21

Right on time, little Charlie Ellison came in the door with a big grin and said, "I'm here! I bet you were all waiting for me, huh?"

Nora smiled, "Hello Charlie. Yes, we were. Where are your school books?"

"Ah," the little guy furrowed his brow, "Dunno."

His big sister Katie came in behind him, "I have them. You left them on the school bus, you Lizzardhead! Honestly Charlie, don't you use your head for anything besides a hat rack?"

"I don't use my head," the little guy retorted and then turned to Nora, "Katie has my books."

"I heard," Aunt Nora shook her head. "You really must be more careful."

"Sorry Ma'am. Is CJ ready for his Chicken Man lessons?"

"He is looking forward to them. He and Andy are putting their model ship away."

"A model ship? Wow! I bet they wished I could have helped them, huh? Maybe I can ask my Dad and he'll let me stay home from school to help them tomorrow?"

"I really doubt that, Charlie," Nora smiled. "Could I interest you in some cookies and hot chocolate?"

"That'd be good. I didn't get to eat all afternoon at school."

Nora frowned, "Do you usually?"

"No," Charlie said. "That's what I said."

"Well, pick up your coat off the floor and wash up."

"How did it get on the floor? I thought I threw it on the bench."

"It fell off, Charlie. You should have hung it up." Katie shook her head. "Where did Ginger get to? She was right behind us."

Andy came in the kitchen, "I just saw her running by the window and Rags was running behind her. She looked terrified."

Andy opened the door and a very flushed Ginger ran into the house in a panic, "Aunt Nora! There is a vicious dog out there that chased me all over the yard. I yelled but nobody helped me!"

"Really? A vicious dog?" Nora comforted the little girl. "Ginger, it isn't a vicious dog. It's the kids' dog from Pine Ridge. Rags was just running to tell you hello!"

"I don't think so, Aunt Nora! It was growling and showing its teeth! It was going to bite me!"

"Rags doesn't bite," Clarence explained. "She's a good dog. You're just a scaredy cat."

"Am not! Aunt Nora, tell him I'm not 'ascared' of his dumb ole dog! And it was so going to bite me!"

"Not it wasn't."

"Was!"

Aunt Nora raised her voice, "Shh! Kids! Knock it off! The dog wasn't going to attack you and you didn't know that. So you had every right to be frightened. Why do you kids squabble so?"

"It's him!" Ginger pointed.

"No, it is her! She's bossy!"

"You think you know everything! So, there!"

"Andy, tell her she is bossy."

Andy looked at them, "You're just too much alike! That's why you squabble."

They both snapped, "I'm not alike!"

Katie giggled, "Is Jackson awake?"

"He might be. He got sick a bit ago. Maybe he would like some hot tea now. Could you ask him?"

"I will, Aunt Nora." Katie turned to her brother and sister, "Can you guys try to behave?"

"I already am," Charlie said as he sat at the table waiting for his hot chocolate.

"I just know that dog was going to bite me!" Ginger folded her arms. "So there. You guys will all feel bad when that dog chews my whole arm off!"

"She won't," Clarence said in exasperation.

"Tell you what," Andy suggested. "If you can keep from killing each other, after the hot chocolate; I'll put my coat on and we can go outside. Maybe if you introduce Rags to Ginger nicely; you can all be friends."

Ginger glared at Andy, "You just want me to get bit."

"Now why would I ever want my favorite buddy to get bit?" Andy sat at the table, "So, today you start your new job as Chicken Man helper, huh?"

CJ nodded. "Charlie is going to teach me."

"Dad ordered the turkeys and the new chicks today, Charlie. He said if you teach CJ to be the Chicken Man, he might promote you to Turkey Man."

"Wow! Will you learn fast, CJ? Is there a lot to learn about turkeys?"

"Not too much. They are a lot dumber than chickens, so you have to be more careful with them."

"I'm pretty careful, aren't I, Aunt Nora?" Charlie asked.

"As long as you don't dig trenches in the pen, like you did with the chickens."

"Yah, that was a bad mistake. CJ, don't ever dig trenches in the chicken coop. They fall into them and get stuck. Okay?"

CJ nodded.

"See, Aunt Nora. CJ already learned it."

"Andy says I'm a fast worker," CJ said as he took a bite of his cookie.

Kate knocked on Jackson's door and he said, "Come in."

"Hi," the pretty teen smiled. "I hear you aren't feeling so good?"

"Just a little upset stomach. How was your day?" The young man tried to sit up.

Katie helped him and rolled the bed up. She got him situated and then felt his forehead. "Your fever seems better."

He took her hand and gave her a kiss on the cheek. "I was thinking about you."

"Ah that's just because you were upchucking," Katie giggled. "You know, that's what happens when you meet someone while you have the flu!"

"No, I miss you a lot. Clarence was talking to me about going to church. He thought I went to church because of you."

Katie smiled, "I don't know if he likes it that we like each other."

"He's okay. He is trying to figure out so much stuff. This is all so different for the kids. What are they doing now?"

"Charlie and CJ are having their hot chocolate before they go do the chicken chores. I wonder if someone should warn the poor chickens! And Ginger and Clarence are arguing."

"Good grief! Those two really don't like each other."

Katie giggled, "No, I think they really do like each other. That's why they get so upset."

"We don't argue."

"We're a lot older than them! I'd hope not! Aunt Nora wanted to know if you wanted some tea?"

"Sounds good. If you help me, I can come out to the kitchen."

By the time they got to the kitchen, Andy was ready to go outside with Ginger and Clarence, who were now involved in a tenuous truce. The phone rang and Nora answered it. "Why yes. CJ is here. I'll get him."

"For me? Someone wants to talk to me?" CJ was in shock as he took the phone, "Who are you?"

"Marty."

"Hello. This is CJ. Are you that Marty guy that was here?"

"I am. I called to tell you that I found a ship that floats. Could you let Andy know I'll bring it over tomorrow, if you guys have time?"

CJ's head was swirling, "Spud . . . that Marty guy . . . he wants to play with us!"

"When?"

"Tomorrow."

"Tell him that will be cool, if you want."

"Mr. Marty, Spud and I will play with you tomorrow. Should I ask Missus? She always wants to know how to cook."

"You can ask her."

"Missus, can Mr. Marty come play with Spud and me tomorrow?"

Nora smiled, "Tell him certainly."

"Missus said certainly. I think that means okay."

"Good," Marty chuckled. "See you about ten."

"Bye."

CJ was beaming so hard it looked like his face would break. "Spud, that is the coolest, huh?"

"It really is, CJ."

Little Charlie watched it all and then frowned, "Aunt Nora, are you sure Dad won't let me stay home from school to help?"

"Sorry Charlie. But you guys can maybe do some on the weekend. How would that be?"

"I guess. When is CJ going to school?"

"Next week."

Charlie nodded, "I can show him around, huh? Hey CJ, I can show you to the guys! Then we can mess around together, huh?"

CJ shrugged, "If Clarence says it's okay?"

Clarence grimaced, "I'll have to meet the guys and see if they're okay."

"I'll show you to them, too. Then we can all mess around."

"I don't have time to mess around," Clarence stated. "I have to think."

Ginger snorted, "That is so dumb! I can think and mess around at the same time! You are just a stick in the dirt!"

"You mean mud," Andy said. "That isn't a nice thing to say, Ginger."

Ginger rolled her eyes, "I'm sorry you're a stick, Clarence."

"Ginger?" Andy squinted at her disapprovingly.

"Okay," she sighed. "I'm sorry I said that. Let's go look at that old dog."

"Don't call her 'that old dog'! She has a name," Clarence frowned.

"Alright, Punch and Judy. Let's go outside," Andy said. Then he whispered to his Mom, "I'm looking forward to that drink!"

Little Charlie put on his coat and then got his Chicken Man hat. It was an old straw hat that was fifteen sizes too big for him that Grandpa had given him. It wouldn't stay on his head, so he tied it on with a purple piece of yarn. Somehow in his mind, he decided it was nigh on to impossible to gather eggs and feed chickens without it. He watched while CJ put on his jacket and reached for his stocking hat. "Aunt Nora! What are we going to do? CJ doesn't have a Chicken Man hat!"

Elton came into the kitchen to pour himself some coffee about then, and started to grin. "I have just the thing."

Elton left and returned in a few minutes with his Hawaiian hat that was like Charlie's. "He can use this one."

CJ cast a worried glance at this big stepbrother, "I don't know. I can wear this one Grandma made."

"You need a Chicken Man hat. It keeps the chicken poop off your head," Charlie announced.

CJ was even more worried now, "Will the chickens poop on my head?"

Jackson rolled his eyes, "Charlie, do you really mean that?"

"Well, the chickens probably won't, but you never know. If you keep your hat on, you'll be sure."

CJ made a face but nodded, "Okay Charlie. I want to get my motion thing."

"Promotion," Charlie corrected. "Aunt Nora, how can he keep it on his head? He needs a tie like I have."

Nora brought a long piece of yarn from the sewing room and weaved it through the hat band and over the top of the huge hat. Then she tied it under his chin, which squashed down the crown, like Charlie's. By now, CJ was even more concerned, but Jackson gave him the thumbs up, so he followed Charlie out the door.

"Yea gads," Elton said after they were out the door. "I hope nobody sees them."

Jackson laughed, "The kids might have been better off in Foster Care after all!"

Andy and the two kids got to the picnic table on the patio. "You might want to sit here, Ginger. Clarence can call Rags over."

The little girl sat down and then asked, "Andy, will you protect me?"

"Yes, honey. You know I'd never let anything happen to you."

"I hope so."

"Don't be a baby. Rags doesn't bite. I'll call her," Clarence grimaced and called the dog who was following the Chicken Men.

When he whistled, Rags came running over to him. Ginger shuddered. Andy realized she truly was terrified, so he held her hand. Rags ran up to Clarence who ruffled her ears and gave her a big hug. Rags wagged her tail and licked his face.

Then he knelt down and talked to her. "Rags, I want you to meet somebody, okay? She is kinda bossy and a scaredy cat, so be nice to her. I know you won't want to lick her, but let her pet you, okay?"

Ginger was glaring at Clarence, but was too intimidated to say anything. He brought Rags over to her and stood beside her. "Say hi."

Ginger whispered hello, but never moved a muscle. Rags looked at the girl and then licked Clarence.

Clarence turned to Andy, "I don't think that Rags likes her, so she probably doesn't want to talk to her anymore."

"Give them a minute, will you Clarence?"

Clarence shrugged and stood there petting his dog. Ginger was slowly regaining her courage. After a few minutes, she said, "Hello Rags."

Rags looked at her and then back at Clarence.

"Is that enough, Mr. Andy?"

"A little more time, okay?"

Clarence was not excited about it but stood there, still petting Rags.

Finally, Ginger reached out her hand, "Hello Rags."

Rags moved over to her and wagged her tail. Soon they were petting and playing together. Clarence stepped back in astonishment. "She is letting her pet her! Andy!"

"That's good, isn't it?"

"I was sure Rags wouldn't like her."

Then the worst happened! Rags licked Ginger's cheek! Ginger giggled and hugged Rags back! Clarence was devastated. He ran over to Andy almost in tears, "Why is she letting her pet her? Why does she like her?"

"Isn't that good, Clarence? Isn't that what you wanted?"

Clarence frowned, "I don't know if I like it. I want Rags to like me best."

"I'm sure she will always be your best friend. Clarence, there is always room for another friend. It is a very good thing if your friends are friends with each other."

Clarence stared at him, "I might have to sleep on that."

Matt and Diane drove in about then, much to Andy's relief. They got out of the car and came over to where they were. "Hi. Having a nice day?"

Andy crossed his eyes, "I learned I'm not cut out for fatherhood! We were just introducing Ginger to Rags."

Diane was petting Rags, "I think she likes Ginger, huh?"

Clarence's eyes got huge and Matt noticed, "Hey Clarence, I came to give Grandpa a ride in his old car. Want to come with me?"

Clarence looked over the situation with his dog and that girl, and shrugged. "What do you think, Andy?"

"I will tell Mom. You go ahead," Andy smiled.

"Ginger and I have to go in for her piano lessons anyway," Diane said, not that Clarence gave a darn about that. He just took Matt's hand and walked away.

22

Elton put on his coat and decided to check on the Chicken Man lessons. He passed Diane and Ginger on their way into the house.

"I see Rags liked you?" Elton smiled.

"She did," Ginger tattled, "But Clarence was pouting about it. He wanted her to bite me."

Elton frowned, "Do you really think so?"

"Well, maybe just growl at me. Uncle Elton, why are boys so weird?" the little redhead crossed her eyes. "They are just goofy!"

As Elton approached the coop, he heard Charlie explaining the chicken business to CJ. "See, we get them when they're fuzzy and little. That's how they come out of the egg. We have to keep a light on them because they are afraid of the dark. I'll show you how to call them with your beak like their momma does."

"I don't have a beak," CJ pointed out.

"I know. I mean the momma calls them with her beak, but we use our finger. I'll show you when they come. We have to make sure they are warm cause if they get cold, they stand on top of each other. I guess the guy on the top is the warmest, but the guy on the bottom gets squished. So we have to tell them to stay on the ground. That is very important!"

"Okay. Maybe they need something to stand on to be higher!" CJ suggested.

"Maybe. We could maybe build them ladders so they would all be higher. That's a good idea! We will figure that out when they come. Then we give them mash feed and water. Uncle Elton says nothing lives without water, but we can't get them wet. Okay? I think their fuzz melts. But, pretty soon they get feathers. Then they aren't so hard to take care of. They eat grown up food."

"Like in a day or so?"

"No, it takes over a week! Then when they get a little bit bigger, we divide the girls from the boys. Uncle Elton gets straight run. That means they just run straight in and pick up whatever they catch. So, we have to sort them out. You can't tell a baby boy from a baby girl, so we wait until they are a little bigger. Then we put the boys in one pen and when they get big, we chop their heads off. But we can't tell them that, because they'll get worried. We put the girls in here and make them lay eggs. When they get old, then we chop their heads off."

CJ frowned, "So we chop everybody's heads off? Why do we chop off their heads?"

"Because they won't stay in the frying pan if they have their heads on," Charlie explained seriously.

CJ nodded back and Charlie continued, "Sometimes when they lay eggs, their egg shells can get soft and gooshey if we don't give them oyster shells and grit because they don't have teeth. So they eat those and then they grow false teeth. We give them scratch."

"What is scratch?" a bewildered CJ asked.

"Grain. They scratch it with their feet and peck at it. I think it is because they don't have shoes," Charlie explained.

"Huh?"

"I'll show you. We have to make sure their light is on. If it isn't, we tell Aunt Nora and she will put in a new light bulb. Uncle Elton gives them some skim milk at night and then turns the light out so they go to sleep. Otherwise, they will crow all night and keep us awake."

CJ worried, "What if I forget all this stuff?"

"I'll remember it to you. You can call my house because Aunt Nora has my phone number."

"Good."

"How is it going, boys?" Uncle Elton asked as he came in the coop.

"Pretty good. I think CJ is really smart. Uncle Elton, do the chickens know they are going to get their head chopped off or is it a secret?"

Elton shook his head, "I guess it's a secret."

"Okay, we won't talk about it in front of them. Will we, CJ?"

"No."

"We fed and gave them water already. I'm just going to show him how to gather eggs and then we'll go in," Charlie explained.

"Okay, I'll let Diane know."

"I don't think I need to take my piano lessons today. CJ and I are busy."

"Diane thought that she might give CJ a lesson, too."

"Will I like that?" CJ asked.

Charlie crossed his eyes, "Probably not, but maybe she will teach you the Lone Ranger song. Hey, I can be the Lone Ranger and you can be Tonto!"

CJ looked at him, "I don't know who that is."

Charlie groaned, "Uncle Elton, will you let CJ watch the Lone Ranger on the TV set?"

"I can do that, if he wants."

CJ shrugged, "Does this Lone guy wear a Chicken Man hat?"

"No, he doesn't CJ," Elton assured him.

CJ looked quite relieved about that, "Okay."

"Will we have time to mess around after we gather eggs?" Charlie asked.

Elton nodded, "I guess you can play in the yard, but don't wander off."

"Cool," Charlie grinned. "Maybe Mom will bring Miriam for her lesson so we'll have more time to play. That would be cool, huh?"

CJ shrugged.

"Are things okay, then?" Elton asked.

"Of course, Uncle Elton. Don't worry!" Charlie announced.

Matt and Clarence walked to the garage together in silence. When they got to the old car, Clarence grinned. "I really like this car. Mister said you keep it shiny for Mr. Grandpa?"

"I do. Would you like to help me sometime?"

"I s'pose."

"Hey Clarence, you can call him Grandpa. You don't need to say Mr. in front of it."

Clarence looked down and nearly cried. Matt was at first taken back and knelt down. He pulled the boy toward him with a hug. "Clarence, I'm sorry. I didn't mean to upset you. You can call him that."

"I don't know how to do anything, where anything is or nothing! I wish I could go back home. I knew what to do there," the little boy bit his lip to hold the tears back. "I am just dumb."

"Clarence, you're doing very well. Do you know that whoever you are; if you go to a whole new place, you have to learn new stuff? When we were down in Pine Ridge, we didn't know where to get water. Did we?"

Clarence shook his head no.

"But you did. See, it just takes a while. You'll know all this stuff in no time."

"Think so?"

"I just know it and just remember; you know what you know! Nobody else knows everything that you do. No matter how smart they are!"

"For sure?"

"For sure. Shall we go give Grandpa his ride?"

"Okay. I like you, Mr. Matt."

"I like you too, Mr. Clarence," Matt smiled back. "Let's go get Grandpa."

In the house, Diane started giving Ginger her piano lesson. The first notes had no more than been played when Clarissa appeared. She had been looking at her fairy book, but this really captured her interest. She stood spellbound at the edge of the keyboard.

After Ginger's lesson, Diane smiled, "Would you like to learn too, Clarissa?"

Her mouth fell open and she could hardly breathe. "Really? Can I do that?"

"Yes, you can. Come sit down and I'll give you your first lesson. Ginger, will you let Katie know that she'll be after Clarissa?"

Clarissa watched Diane's every move and was so excited when she got to play the first note. She was a happy little girl when she played the scales with Diane. Katie and Jackson came out to watch and they both clapped when Clarissa finished. The little girl jumped off the piano bench and gave Jackson a big hug. "I am so happiest ever!"

"I'm glad, Clarissa. You're doing a very good job," her older stepbrother encouraged her.

Nora, Marly and Miriam came in and clapped too! "You are doing a great job," Nora said. "I'm so proud of you!"

"Kitten, too?" Miriam asked.

"Not yet, Gopher. She has to get her ears fixed first. Then she can. Won't that be nice?" Nora answered.

After the piano lessons, the Ellison's went home and the Schroeder's went out to do the milking. Kevin came over to help and Clarence shyly asked Kevin if he wanted to see his thinking spot.

"I'd like that," Kevin grinned. "And I got something in my coat for you. We can go up after milking, okay?"

"Okay," Clarence said. "Matt said that everybody knows something that everybody else doesn't know. Is that right?"

"I think it is, Clarence. Don't you agree?"

"I don't know. I don't know about much stuff here. I get everything wrong."

Kevin frowned at him, "No, you don't and I don't like you to say that! You have had a lot of new things thrown at you in a short time, so of course it is confusing."

"Nobody threw stuff at me."

"I know, that just means we've all been telling you a bunch of new stuff since you walked in the door."

Clarence nodded in agreement, "Yah."

"See? You're doing just fine," Kevin assured him. "Why, you know how to milk Buttermilk like a pro."

"What's a pro?"

"A guy that gets paid for it," Kevin chuckled.

On their way back to the house, Clarence and Kevin walked over to the old outhouse. Kevin gave a nod of approval on the quality of the roof repair and all the 'fixin's' they did. "It looks great! I have a present for you!"

He reached in his jacket and pulled out a brand new comic book. "This is for your magazine rack!"

Clarence forgot himself for a minute and gave Kevin a hug. Kevin hugged him on the back, "It is a fine thinking spot, Clarence."

"Mr. Kevin," Clarence asked shyly, "Could you help me do something?"

"Well I can try," Kev grinned. "What is it?"

"Could you help me do that grace stuff? Jackson says that is to thank Wakan Tanka for everything, but I don't know how to say it."

"Let me think. What do you want to thank Him for?"

Clarence shrugged, "I don't know."

Kev set Clarence on one side of the bench in the outhouse, while he sat on the other. "Then we are in the right place, huh? The thinking spot."

Clarence smiled, "I s'pose I don't need to say that grace stuff."

"No," Kevin disagreed. "If you want to, you should. First of all, all you need to do it hold hands like we do, and then talk to God or Wakan Tanka like if He was there. So, you can say thanks for this or that without getting fancy. Some folks think the fancier they talk, the more God listens. Between you and me, He hears us jabber all the time, so He doesn't care. So, just say it. Then when you are done, say Amen. That just means 'so be it', so that everyone knows you are done talking. Want to practice?"

"I s'pose."

They held hands and then Clarence said, "Hi God or whatever your name is. Thank you for all this stuff. Amen."

"Very good, Clarence."

"Is that okay? It doesn't sound like what you guys say though."

"God knows exactly what you mean and He'll appreciate it. That's very good."

"Will everybody laugh at me?"

"No one will. You have my word." Kevin assured him, "Do you want to do it tonight?"

"Are you going to eat here?"

"Not tonight. Carrie made supper at our house. Do you want me to be here for you?"

"Yah, that'd be good."

"How about tomorrow morning at breakfast? Will that be okay?"

Clarence smiled, "Okay."

"It's a deal then," Kevin shook his hand.

At dinner, everyone was pretty tired. After the table was cleared, Andy asked if they were ready to try the race cars. "I don't know, Andy," Elton answered. "I think everyone is pretty tuckered today. What do you say kids? Would you rather do it tomorrow?"

"Will we have time to learn before those kids come?" Clarence asked.

"Yes, you will," Jackson answered. "You've all had a busy day. Maybe tomorrow would be a better idea."

"What did Zach tell you tonight?" Nora asked Jackson.

"He said if I behave myself and take it easy, I can start sketching again tomorrow."

"I'm so glad, Jackson."

Annie and Diane went to help the girls while Nora gave Clancy his bath. Andy and Elton helped the bigger boys. When Clarence was done, he went out and sat on the sofa in the living room with his head in his hands. Elton was walking through the room and noticed him. He went over and sat next to him, "Long day, huh?"

Clarence nodded.

"Anything I can help you with?"

Clarence just shrugged and then instantly crawled up and cuddled up into Elton's arms. He just held on for a few minutes. Before long, Elton could feel his breathing change. The little guy had gone to sleep. Elton held him for a while before he carried him into his bed.

When he put him on the bed, he gave the boy a hug, "Sleep tight, my little friend. You've carried a huge burden a long time."

He turned and noticed Horse watching him. Elton walked over to him, "How you doing?"

"Good. Elton, I can never thank you enough for taking the kids," Jackson reached out to him.

"You don't have to," Elton hugged the young man. "I only hope things go well for them. Need some fresh water?"

"No thank you," Jackson nodded. "Is CJ about ready for bed?"

"Yah, he and Andy are having a conversation about the ship they are going to build. Then he'll be hitting the sack."

"Good night."

23

Elton felt someone patting his cheek and he opened his eyes. There was Clarence whispering, "Mister. I think Jackson is getting ready to hit somebody and Grandpa is trying to run away! You better come quick!"

Elton climbed out of bed and checked the clock. It was a little after two. He took Clarence's hand and said, "Thank you for getting me."

Together they went to Jackson's room where they found the young veteran thrashing in his bed. Elton patted his arm and spoke calmly to assure him, "It's okay, Jackson. You're home now. It is safe. You are having a bad dream. Everything is fine. Take a deep breath."

Jackson opened his eyes, looked at them and tried to focus.

"It's okay," Clarence said, mimicking Elton's consoling tone. "You're okay."

Jackson seemed to relax a little, "I'm okay now, really. Thanks guys. I had a terrible dream."

"Do you need some water?" Elton asked.

"Yes, please."

"I can get it for him, Mister."

Elton handed him the glass and Clarence ran to fill it. After he was gone, Jackson confided, "It wasn't about just the war. It was about Mom and Clayton, too."

Elton gave him a hug, "Your brain has a lot of sorting out to do. Do you want to talk about it?"

"No, I'm okay. Really. Thank you, Clarence," Jackson took the water. "And thank you for getting Elton."

"I did like you told me, didn't I?"

"Yes, you did. You're a good man, Clarence." Jackson lay back on his pillow, "I think I can go back to sleep now."

"That's good because Grandpa Lloyd is trying to run away. Mister and I have to go get him, right?"

Elton nodded, "Yes, let's go see what he is up to. Good night, Jackson."

The two arrived in the dark kitchen and heard rumbling in the pantry. Elton reached over and turned on the light. Clarence frowned, "Can Grandpa see in the dark?"

"I have wondered that myself sometimes. I know I can't. Can you?"

"A little bit, but not much."

"Me either. Let's see what he is up to."

Grandpa was dumping powdered sugar into a bowl in the pantry and had the salt container in his other hand when Elton opened the pantry door. "Whatcha cooking, Lloyd?"

Grandpa was a bit startled, but explained, "I'm cooking lunch. I have to get to the field and Katherine is typing for Byron. I have to make my own lunch because she's busy. You and this guy hungry too?"

"Just a bit. Come on out and I can fry you an egg?"

"What do you say, Guy? Will an egg be enough for you?" Grandpa asked.

"I am Clarence. I'm not very hungry."

"Hello Clarence. I have a brother named Clarence. He looks a lot like you, but his hair is shorter. He smokes a pipe. We will let Elton make breakfast, okay? Want some coffee?"

Elton interjected, "Lloyd, we can't have coffee after dark. You remember what Nora says."

"What can we have?"

"Milk or juice."

"I will have that. What about you, Clarence?"

"Okay."

"Let's go sit down so Elton can make our egg. Okay?"

"Okay, come sit by me," the little boy said and took Grandpa by the hand.

"Are we going to smoke our pipes?" Grandpa asked.

"I'm too little to smoke yet," Clarence answered.

"Me too. I don't want to stunt my growth," Grandpa agreed. "You either, Elton."

"Okay, Grandpa. Here's some juice," Elton set the juice on the table with three glasses and began to pour it.

After he drank his juice, the old man asked, "Why did you guys wake me up? Did you want to go somewhere? Should I get the team?"

Clarence looked at Elton trying to figure out how to answer him. Elton smiled, "No. We were just wondering how you are."

"I'm okay, but I'm awful tired. Can I go back to bed now?"

"Sure, let me help you," Elton helped the elderly man to his room.

When he returned, he found a bewildered Clarence still sitting at the table. "I thought he was hungry?"

"Oh, he gets confused Clarence. That is why we have to talk him into going back to bed. Do you want some more juice?"

"No. I only drank it because Grandpa wanted me to have it."

"Yah, me too. Let's clean up the mess in the pantry and get some sleep ourselves, okay?"

"Okay."

A few minutes later, Elton and Clarence went back down the hall to the bedrooms. "Thanks for helping me tonight, Clarence."

"We're a team, right?"

"We are at that. Good night now."

Elton no more than dosed off when he bolted out of bed to a blood-curdling scream! "What on earth?"

He and Nora both headed for the door. They could hear the little girls crying and doors opening all over the house. Then went into the nursery where the girls were crying hysterically.

There was a very self-satisfied Clancy, holding his wolf. When he saw the gathered residents, he let go with another very convincing wolf howl and the girls screamed again.

Elton thought it was funny, Nora consoled the girls and Annie who had entered the fray was trying to get Clancy quieted down. In the hall, Elton met Clarence, "I don't know Clarence, we should have got him a stuffed fish! They're quieter!"

When Nora returned to bed about half an hour later, Elton put his arms around her. "Honey, I think I want to remodel our bedroom door."

"What in the world are you talking about?"

"I think we should just put in a swinging door!" Elton laughed.

"Might be a good idea. Elton, what have we done? Have we lost our ever-lovin' minds?"

"Yah, but we did that a long time ago," he cuddled up to her. "It will be okay. This has only been one day."

"I know. Only one day! Yea gads."

24

The alarm announced morning and the family began to gather in the kitchen of the old farmhouse for the daily Coffee Pot Stare Down. It was Grandma who first broached the subject. "Is there a quiet sound that a wolf makes? You know, like a purr or something we could teach to Clancy?"

They all shrugged, except Clancy who let go with another wolf howl. For a little guy, he did a very professional job and it didn't even make him cough!

Kevin came bouncing in with his wife and baby. "Good morning everyone! Why so glum today? It looks like it will be sunny and warm. You should be happy!"

"Stifle it," Elton groaned. "We were surrounded by wolves last night, so we are tired today!"

After chores, everyone gathered around the kitchen table for breakfast. As preplanned, Kevin, Carrie and the baby joined them for breakfast. As they took each other's hands before grace, Kevin said, "Everyone, Clarence asked to say grace this morning."

Nora smiled, "That's wonderful, Clarence."

Kevin nodded at the boy and gave him a wink, "Go ahead, Man."

Clarence cleared his throat and looked up to the ceiling, "Hello Wakan Tanka, thanks for all the stuff we have and for breakfast. Kevin said I can talk to you about anything, so can You to make everybody sleep at night? Mister and me are tired. That's all. I mean, amen."

Everyone answered amen and Kevin patted him on the back. "You did a fine job."

"Yes, you did," Annie agreed. "I liked your prayer!"

"No, Miss Annie, it was a grace," Clarence explained.

"I liked your grace."

"I'm proud of you, Clarence. Fine work," Elton nodded. "I really hope that God can see His way fit to have everyone sleep!"

Grandpa shook his head, "Well why wouldn't he do a good job? He is my brother, you know! Right, Elton?"

"I think you might be right, Lloyd." Elton looked around the table, "So, what is everyone up to today?"

"Mr. Marty is coming over to play with Spud and me," CJ said. "We are going to build a boat that floats!"

"Yes," Andy said. "But first, we are all going to learn how to race cars!"

"Kitten is helping me go through my big box of yarn," Grandma said and then smiled at Claudia. "Right?"

Claudia smiled back at her. Clarence frowned, "Does she help or make a mess?"

"She is my good helper. She helps me roll the yarn into balls."

"That's good," Jackson smiled. "Today, I'm going back to my sketching. I better get caught up. I have that big order for the Clinic to get finished."

"Are you far behind?" Nora asked.

"No, with the way you showed me how to do that calendar, I was ahead. So I'm okay. I'm sure glad you showed me how to do that."

Diane sighed, "Well, today is the last day of peace until after the school play. Tomorrow we start with heavy rehearsals and then the show starts on Wednesday through Saturday! I hope you all have your tickets!"

Clarence's eyes got huge, "We guys don't, Miss Diane."

"You do," Diane winked. "Matt and I picked them up for you at school. So you are all set!"

"Oh. Do we have to go to school?" Clarence asked.

"It is at the school, but Nora and I are going," Elton explained. "I believe you guys are sitting with us. Will that be okay?"

"Okay."

"Well, we better get moving, Kevin," Carrie said as she started to clear the table.

Clarissa helped push the chairs back in, "Missus and I are going to-, what are we going to do?"

"We are going to make some apple pies."

171

"Pies. I think I like pies, huh?" Clarissa asked.

"Yes, you do."

"What am I going to do?" Clarence asked. "Are you going to be home, Mister?"

"I have to go to work today, but I'll tell you what. If you don't have anything to do this afternoon, I could bring you back to work with me. What do you say? I think you have to race cars this morning, right?"

"Okay."

The phone rang and it was for Annie. It was their neighbor and good friend, Darrell. "Hey, Slick has time this afternoon and is coming out. Since it'll be nice, would you like to go riding with us? We thought maybe Horse's Steps would like to come, too. What do you think?"

"It would be a good day to exercise the horses. I don't know about the kids," Annie said. "I'll ask them. Oh, Nora is waving. She wants to know if you and Father Bart would like to have lunch here?"

"Of course, we would! Why do you think I called so early?" Darrell chuckled. "Slick and I were hoping to swindle lunch out of Nora!"

"Darrell Jessup! You're awful! I don't know how Jeannie can put up with you! Or Father Bart for that matter!"

"She just appreciates how lucky she is! Let me know how many kids will be going and if I need to bring this junior saddle. I'm off to grind feed now, so call in about an hour. Okay?"

"I will let you know," Annie giggled. "I think we'll be fine for saddles. We can use Ellisons. I'll talk to Marly."

"See you later."

"Are you going to race cars with us, Horse?" Andy asked.

"Hm. I might. What do you think, kids?" Jackson asked his step-siblings.

They all thought it was a great idea, even Clancy, who had no clue what they were talking about, clapped and cheered.

The group moved into the long hallway and opened the closet door. There on the second shelf was the entire parking lot of race cars. There was a variety; some very small Matchbox cars to some large cars about six inches long. Some were battery operated and some 'human' operated. There were some Slot cars, which ran on a special track. The shelf below and the floor was neatly stacked with all sorts of race tracks, slot tracks, curves, ramps and jumps.

All the clan kids had put their cars in the closet and ownership was transferred the whole group. The only time anyone 'owned' a car, was the first day it was raced. After that, whoever called 'dibs' on it, got to use it for a race. That way, everyone had a chance to play with all of them. If a person wanted to own their car, they had to take it home to play with.

The adults helped the little kids put batteries in the cars, since Doug had given them all battery operated ones. Annie showed Clancy his pull along car, which he tried to eat. Then he toddled off to find his wolf.

The kids lined up the cars and turned them on. They all sped down the hallway and crashed into the wall at the end. Claudia looked at it and shrugged. She shook her head no and went to find Grandma.

"Interest is waning," Horse chuckled. "Who won this race?"

"The blue car and the red one crashed at the same time," CJ announced. "The green one ran into the door before then. I think we should do it again."

And they did. They raced a couple races and decided the cars were about even in speed. Then Andy introduced the jumps and curves. That was more exciting. Clarissa was by far the most expert racer, and she didn't even have to try.

"How do you do that, Clarissa?" Clarence asked. "I can't get mine to turn without falling off the rail?"

"Like this," she smiled, set the car down and pushed the button. "See."

"But you didn't do anything," CJ pointed out.

"It can do it by itself. If I push it, it will crash!"

The boys tried, and by George, she was right. Soon they were all maneuvering the curves and jumps with great expertise.

Then the grownups showed the kids how to use the other cars. Then they broke down into smaller two man races and had more than one going on at once. It was a lot of fun.

When they were done, Andy explained that they had to put everything back neatly. That required a bit of explanation since CJ figured that anywhere 'in the closet' constituted where he found it. Jackson had to step in. "You need to park all the cars in a row, like you found them. Otherwise stuff will get wrecked when you dig through it to find things."

CJ shrugged and Clarence explained.

"Mister told me that about tools too, CJ. He said it would be okay to leave them lay around if we were the only ones using them, but if other guys are going to use it, they have to be kept in the same spot."

"Okay," CJ said dejectedly. "I bet Charlie doesn't care."

"No," Andy agreed. "He probably doesn't, but he knows he has to do it, too!"

"He said that. He said people even get mad if you put chicken poop in the refrigerator! Can you believe that?"

Annie almost choked, "Did he do that?"

"I guess, right Jackson? He said that you even told him not to do it anymore. So we won't. But we think if we didn't get married, we can probably do it when we have our own house."

"If you think like that, you won't have to worry about getting married," Annie giggled.

"CJ, I did talk to Charlie about that. You can never, ever put any kind of poop in the fridge. It can make people sick!" Jackson said sternly.

"I know that is what Charlie said. But when we get our own house, we don't have to listen anymore," CJ missed the point completely.

"And no one will ever come visit you, either!" Andy stated. "Yuk!"

Clarence listened to the whole thing carefully, "You guys are weird! I will never eat rolls from your bag again."

"You will if you get hungry. I don't care anyway. Clarissa will."

Clarissa made a face, "Miss Annie, do sunshine girls eat that stuff!"

"Absolutely no way! Ever!"

Clarissa turned to her brother with her hands on her hips, "No way, ever."

The group had no more than got the cars all neatly 'parked' in the closet lot, when Marty arrived with his model ship. Everyone greeted him in the kitchen and Grandma poured him some coffee.

"So, what have you all been up to this morning?"

"Mr. Marty, we raced cars in the hallway! We had some big wrecks and crashes! It was fun," CJ bubbled.

"Sounds like you needed an ambulance, huh?"

"Miss Annie was there. She did pretend bandages on them," Clarissa smiled. "Jackson said she is real handy!"

Marty chuckled, "That's what I think and that's why she's my partner."

"Oh Marty," Nora asked. "I was wondering if you would have time to give Grandpa his haircut today?"

"I brought my scissors and stuff. I figured it was time."

"I don't know what we would do without you! I'm so glad you took barber training before you became an ambulance attendant," Grandma said. "You take such good care of Grandpa. I really appreciate it."

"He's a pretty good Grandpa," Marty answered. "Does any veteran need to get their hair trimmed as long as I'm here?"

"Yes, we both do," Andy smiled. "I will pay you."

"Yah, yah, I know. No problem. I just don't want to be seen in public with you when your hair is dragging on the floor!"

CJ's eyes got huge, "Do you want to be seen in that place with me? My hair is longer than his."

"That's up to you. Did you ever have your hair shorter? It is a lot easier to take care of when it is short. You don't have to worry about keeping your hair out of the paint and glue," Andy pointed out.

"I had it cut one time. I liked it. I think I could do it again if Clarence says it is okay?"

"I don't know. Missus said we had to cut Clancy's hair because he is always rubbing it in his eyes and sucking on it. What do you think, Jackson?"

"I think it would be a good idea, if CJ wants too. What about you?" Jackson asked his little brother.

"I don't suck on my hair and I don't let it hang in my eyes! I like my hair! It is like my Dad's! I want it this way! Do you have to change everything? Everybody's changing everything!" He left the table in tears and ran out the door.

Marty started to get up, "I'm sorry Aunt Nora, I never meant to upset him."

"We know, but I think I should go talk to him. Okay?" Nora said as she put her coat on.

Outside it was easy to find Clarence, because Rags was sitting outside the outhouse, patiently guarding her master while he thought. Nora went up to the outhouse and patted Rags on the head. Then she knocked on the door, "Clarence. This is Nora. May I talk to you?"

"I'm thinking."

175

"I know, and that's okay. I brought your jacket so you can think longer before you get cold."

Clarence opened the door a crack and reached out to grab his jacket. He swiped it back in and closed the door.

After a couple minutes, Nora knocked again, "Clarence, may I talk to you, please?"

"Why? You just want me to be different! Everything is different and I hate it. I want to be the same as it was!" he broke down into tears.

"Clarence, we really need to talk. Let me in."

The door opened slowly and Nora entered the outhouse, finding a little boy crying his eyes out. She gave him a hug while he cried. After a few minutes, she patted his back, "Clarence, no one will make you cut your hair. That's up to you. Promise. I know Marty never meant to upset you. He likes you."

"I know. He is nice. But Missus, nothing is the same! I don't get to see my Dad or my Mom! I can't go to the creek and look for the fish! We guys used to try to catch mice in the bedroom! There aren't even any mice in the bedroom here! Everything is all different!"

"I know. I'm sorry about that Clarence. But if it's okay with you, we won't put mice in the bedroom. Okay?"

Clarence smiled, "We'd try to catch them and throw them outside. We didn't want them in our bedroom either."

"I'm glad we agree on that," Nora nodded. "Now, how would you feel about you and I going down to the creek in the pasture to see if we can see some fish?"

"You and me?" Clarence was surprised. "Don't you have to be in the house?"

"I'll tell them we're going and we should put on our overshoes because some of the snow is deep. Hey, while we are out there, I can show our thinking rock. What do you say?"

"I guess." Clarence looked at his feet, "Missus, can't I just go back to Pine Ridge?"

"If you really want to go back to the Reservation, you can. Elton and I promised you that. But you won't be able to go back to your house. Your Mom and Dad are gone. So, you can't stay there alone and, besides it wouldn't be the same." She sat on the bench, "Our Mom died when Keith and Kevin were not much older than you. Then our Dad died a year later.

It was never the same. There is nothing that anyone can do about it. That is just the way it is. We can't make it be."

"I don't like that."

"No one does, but we can't stop living because of it. There are many things for us in this world. We need to know and do all sorts of things. But you are very right. We also have to remember who we really are inside. Do you think that you can do that, and still learn new stuff?"

"I don't know. It just feels like everything is all different."

"I know, and it probably will for a while yet. But very soon, I promise, things will stop feeling that way. Think you can hold on?"

"I s'pose."

"Clarence, if you want to keep your hair long, you sure can. We can even fix the sides with those leather strips, so your hair doesn't get in your way. I know Indian chiefs used to do that. And guess what? Annie knows how to do that. Isn't that handy?"

Clarence looked at her, "Is that why Jackson said she is handy?"

"One of the reasons. Are you okay with the other kids getting their hair changed?"

"That's okay. I know that Clancy chews his hair and about Claudia's ears. Jackson had to cut his hair when he went to the Army. Why is that?"

"Because it's easier to take care of. The Army doesn't want their soldiers to have to put their hair up in curlers every night!"

Clarence giggled. "Can we go see the creek, Missus?"

"Sure, let's go get our boots on and tell the folks in the house so they don't worry. I needed some fresh air today. This is a good idea."

25

Nora popped her head into the kitchen while Clarence put his boots on. "Clarence and I are going for a walk to the creek. If you like, you can start cutting hair. Maybe later, Annie, you could see about putting those little braids with leather strips to hold the hair back from Clarence's eyes. Think you could do that?"

"Sure," Annie said. "Not a problem. I don't think he will squirm around like Clancy!"

"I won't, Miss Annie," Clarence promised.

The lady and the boy walked down past the barn. "Do you go outside very often?" Clarence asked.

"Yes, why do you ask?"

"You never go to the barn to do chores."

Nora smiled, "I'm fixing dinner then, so you guys can eat when you're finished. Besides, after I had a run in with that momma pig, I lost a lot of muscle in my arm. I'm not as strong as I should be. Winter cold makes that arm hurt some."

"Mister told me about that. What happened?"

Nora explained how her three-year-old daughter tried to put a baby pig in the farrowing pen and it squealed. The momma sow heard it and attacked Pepper, clenching her strong jaws on her foot and ankle. Nora tried to pull the sow away from Pepper, but the sow caught Nora's arm and pulled her into the pen and mauled her. She lost most of the muscle from her upper arm, neck and chest on one side.

Clarence listened in silence, and then said, "The kids and me talked about your marks. We wondered how you got them. Did it hurt real bad?"

"Yes, it did. Mostly though, it's healed up now, but my muscles will never grow back. I bet you can carry more weight than I can. And Elton told me you are a very fast runner!"

"I am. Missus? If you need me to carry anything, I'll do it for you. Okay?"

"Well thank you, Clarence. That is a fine thing to say."

"Missus? I don't think the kids need me so much anymore. I used to take care of them all the time. Now they don't talk to me so much. Don't they care?"

"Oh," Nora knelt down by the boy, "Of course they care. They love you a lot. They are always looking to you for advice and to know what to do. But it's good for them to get used to other folks, too. Besides, it gives you more time to relax. You don't have to do it all. You have done it for a long time and you did an excellent job, but you need to do stuff for you too."

"What stuff?"

"Oh, I don't know. Is there something that you would like to do?"

"Go fishing. Mister and I are going when it gets warmer out, because he doesn't like to get cold."

"Did you like racing cars?"

"It was okay, but I don't have time for that. It is good for CJ and Clarissa to do that. They need to play."

"Don't you?"

They started walking again.

"Not so much. I don't know what to do. I mess around with Rags sometimes. I like to listen to the cedar flute. Jackson got me one once, but Dad needed to trade it because we needed the money. So, I never played it."

"I'll talk to Jackson and see if we can fix that."

Clarence looked at Nora trying to understand what she meant. Then he shrugged, "Anyway, I have to think about stuff."

"You know sometimes Clarence, it is easier to think with someone else than to do it all by yourself. Did you know that?"

"I guess, but nobody knows what I think about."

"Maybe if you told someone, they would. Then you wouldn't have to be so busy thinking. Think about it," Nora suggested.

Clarence giggled, "That is silly."

Nora laughed, "Think about thinking! It really is, isn't it? Well, here we are at the creek. Let's see if we can find any fish."

The two quietly watched for a while but saw no fish. They finally decided the fish must be sleeping under a rock or a pile snow drifted across the ice, so they moved on to the pasture. They walked until they got to the flat-topped rock known as the thinking rock.

Clarence was hardly tall enough to sit on it, but he did. Nora sat next to him and the looked out over the farm. Nora pointed out Kevin and Marty's houses, the church and the parsonage. Clarence noticed the church cemetery.

"Is that a place where dead people are?"

"Yes, it is. It is called a cemetery."

"I thought so cause it had those stone things like my Dad and Mom."

"Headstones."

"Missus, can we really go back to Pine Ridge to visit? It seems like I have been here a long time already. What if I start to forget? I almost forgot about how my Dad looked," the little boy tried to cover his tears.

Nora hugged him, "I know, Clarence. Yes, we promised we can go back to Pine Ridge to visit when it is nicer out. You know, you have only been here a couple days. You really haven't been here very long at all."

"Yah, but it seems like it."

"You know what? When we get to the house, I'll help you with a calendar. Do you have one?"

"No, what is it?"

"It marks off the days so we know what day it is. We'll mark it and then every day, you can cross off what day it is. Then you will always know how long you have been here. We can mark when we plan to go visit Pine Ridge. You can just look at the calendar and know how many days are left. What do you think?"

"I s'pose. Is it hard to do?"

"Not at all. Jackson has one. You can talk it over with him."

While they were sitting on the rock, the horses became curious and approached them. The first one to come up to them was Abner, Charlie's fat, old gray horse. Clarence knew him because he had been in the barn with his bad leg. Apparently, Abner remembered Clarence too, because he nudged him on his shoulder.

Clarence giggled and Nora said, "I think Abner came to say hello."

"He's a nice horse. Who do the other ones belong to?" Clarence patted his nose.

"Let's see, Duchess is Katie's horse. She is a nice one, and Dakota is Ginger's horse."

Clarence made a face, "I bet Ginger bosses him around too, huh?"

"No," Nora laughed. "She is a little intimidated by Dakota. You have to respect animals, or they can hurt you."

"Like that momma pig?"

"Yes, like that sow. I scared her because she thought I was hurting her baby. She didn't understand I was trying to help."

"Too bad they don't talk people talk, huh?"

"Sometimes you can say a lot without words," Nora said as she patted Moonbeam's nose. "This beauty is Marly's horse."

"Do you have a horse, Missus?"

"No. I don't have enough strength to lift a saddle. Although it would be fun to have one. Someone else would have to take care of it, so that wouldn't be very fair."

"If you want to have one, I'll take care of it for you. Maybe Kevin could show me how. Maybe he could learn me how to do it? Okay?"

"I think you mean teach you how. That is very thoughtful. I'll think about it. If I had one, we could share it. Would that be a fair deal?"

"I think so. I have to sleep on it."

26

They arrived back at the house and found Marty was just finishing CJ's haircut. CJ wanted his like Little Charlie's and Marty complied. He looked rather spiffy.

Grandma volunteered to sweep up the mess so the boys could go work on their ships. "Are you going to build on the ship, too?" she asked Clarence.

"No, I think I'm going to help Missus lift stuff. I can help you too, if you want. I have good muscles."

"I don't need anything lifted right now, thank you. But if I do, I'll be sure to call for you first thing."

"Was that all there was?" little boy asked as he looked at the hair trimmings. "I thought there would be more because CJ and Clancy had a lot of hair."

Annie answered, "They did, but I collected it to make dream catchers for them."

"You know how to do that?"

"I do. Would you like me to show you?"

"I guess that'd be okay. Let me tell Missus."

Annie showed the bags of hair to Clarence. Then she showed him the reeds that she would use for hoops for the dream catchers. He looked it all over carefully and then asked, "Do you think if Jackson had a dream catcher with us guys hair in it, that his bad dreams would go away?"

Annie thought, "You know Clarence, sometimes the dreams from a war are horrible. It just takes time for them to go away. But, we can always try, huh? How about we ask him? He has a dream catcher now, but I don't know if it's a special one."

"Okay," Clarence said as he took her hand.

They knocked on his door and he said, "Come in."

They found him sketching. "I hope we didn't interrupt your work," Annie said. "We wanted to ask you something?"

"Shoot," Jackson smiled. "I can talk and sketch at the same time."

"Is your dream catcher special?" Clarence asked.

"Like how? What do you mean?"

"We were thinking about making you one out of the Step's hair, but we didn't know if the one you had was special," Annie explained.

"It's one I had from the Reservation. I don't know where I got it," Jackson said. "That'd be nice if you guys did that! Are you going to help Annie?"

"Dunno. I have to sleep on it."

"I'd like your help," Annie smiled. "That would be so cool."

"Really?" Clarence's face lit up. "You'd like me to help?"

"I sure would!"

"Okay, but only if Jackson wants one."

"I'd just love that!" Jackson smiled. "Guess what I just did for you?"

Clarence shrugged.

"Nora told me that you wanted to remember how your mom and dad looked, so I started a sketch of them for you. Would you like to look at it?" Horse held the sketch of the boy's parents up for him, "What do you think?"

Clarence's mouth fell open and his eyes filled with tears, "It looks just like them! Is it for me?"

"Just for you," Jackson assured him. "Kate will put it in a frame for you and you can have it in your room! Then you won't forget how they looked."

Clarence hugged his stepbrother. Then he suddenly got quiet.

"What is it, Clarence?"

"The other kids will need it. They'll forget, too. I guess we can share it, huh?"

Jackson smiled, "You can do that. After I get my order finished for the clinic, I can make some for the other kids. Do you think they would like that?"

"I think they would. You're a good brother," Clarence hugged him again.

"You aren't so bad yourself. I know we have no photos of Mom and Dad, but maybe this will help, huh?"

Clarence nodded, "Yes. Is that why you make these things for people, so they can remember somebody?"

"Sometimes," Jackson explained. "But sometimes folks want the sketches for things that they would just like for fun."

"Can you make sketches for stuff that I wanted? I mean, like one of me and Dad fishing? That'd be so cool."

"I could do that. I'll tell you what, if you are patient and wait until I get these finished for my customers, I'll make you one like that. Where would you be fishing?"

"Pine Ridge, at our creek. I saw fish in there and Dad said we would go fishing when he had time. He just didn't have time," the little boy shrugged. "Before he died."

"Well, I'll tell you what. You help Annie make the dream catcher and I'll make you a special sketch of you and your Dad fishing. Does that sound like a good deal?"

Clarence just beamed, "I'll try to help her, but I don't know how."

"I'll show you. You and I better get started because guess what?"

"What?"

"Sunday at dinner, we're going to celebrate Ken and Ginger's birthdays! So I promised I would help with the birthday cakes!"

"Sunday is their birthday?"

"No, Ginger's was the second and Ken's will be the ninth. We're celebrating in between," Annie smiled.

"How old is Ginger going to be?" Clarence asked seriously.

"She'll be eight, why?" Annie asked.

"See! I'm older than her! She can't be the boss of me! I'll tell her to knock it off!" Clarence blustered.

"You better back off, buddy," Jackson warned. "Why don't you guys just be friends instead of trying to kill each other?"

"Because she bugs me."

Annie laughed, "And you bug her! I think you should smoke the peace pipe."

"I'm too little to smoke," Clarence stated as he and Annie went out of the room.

About noon, the family gathered around for lunch. Ian Harrington and Elton were home before Darrell and Father Bart arrived. Elton congratulated everyone on their neat haircuts and then asked who the other places were for at the table.

"Darrell and Slick are coming over for lunch and then they are taking the kids riding for a little while," Nora explained.

"So you won't be coming in to work with me this afternoon?" Elton asked Clarence.

"I can if you want."

"I think you might enjoy riding horse, what do you think?"

"Jackson said I should probably try."

Ian patted Clarence's shoulder, "Good for you! I think you'll like it! Hey, I got something to show you tonight when Ruthie and I come over. I guess the girls are going to put wigs on—so I thought we might look at this new fishing map book I got! What do you say?"

Clarence grinned, "I'd really like that. Do you think Mister would like to look at it too?"

"I think he might. In fact, my Dad and Mom are coming over tonight too, so we can show him, too! What do you say, Grey Hawk?"

Clarence giggled, "Okay, Harrington."

"Which horses are they riding?" Elton asked. "And which kids?"

"Clarence, CJ and Clarissa. Oh, Zach called and he got an appointment for Claudia with the ear guy next week," Nora said.

"Good," Elton smiled as he tickled the little girl's cheek. "Then we can get our little Kitten hearing soon."

"Is it reversible?" Ian asked.

"Zach said not likely. All we can do is keep it from getting worse." Nora explained. "But maybe we can get hearing aids for her so she can learn to talk."

There was a knock at the door and Elton opened it for Darrell and Father Bart. The men entered and were introduced to the little ones. There was a bit of confusion about what Father Bart's name really was, and finally Jackson explained, "His name is Father Bart Fedder, but his nickname is Slick. That is his name in the tiyospaye."

The kids nodded, "Okay, Slick."

Clarence was studying Darrell closely and finally asked, "Do you know Ginger?"

"Yes, I do. She's my niece. Her Mom is my sister. Why?"

"Cause you look like her," Clarence shrugged. "Are you bossy too?"

Everyone laughed. Jackson said, "No, Darrell isn't bossy. But neither is Ginger. You two have to knock it off!"

"I can't," Clarence said, dropped his head.

Elton frowned, "Why not?"

"Cause she won't," he sighed. "So we just have to fight."

Harrington laughed, "I think you two had better find a way, or you'll both get skinned."

CJ's eyes got huge, "I saw a coyote once that was skinned! It was gross! You don't want to be skinned, Clarence."

Clarence shrugged, "It'll probably happen because we won't ever get along."

Nora looked at the lad, "Well, if I was you, I'd be figuring out a way."

"Yes, Missus."

Father Bart had been listening carefully, "You know, sometimes when you think you don't like someone; if you think of something very nice to do for that person, you can start to be friends."

"Like what? I let her pet my dog."

After lunch, the adult riders went down to the barn to saddle the horses. "Who is going to ride which horse?" Bart asked.

Annie answered, "I talked to Marly, and she suggested that Moonbeam, Sergeant and Duchess need exercise. I'm pretty certain that Dakota does too, but there is no way we'd want Clarence to ride Ginger's horse!"

Darrell chuckled, "No. That wouldn't be good! Let's see, Sergeant is strong but well-behaved. I think he'd be okay for Clarence. I'll keep the lead on him. Moonbeam is gentle enough for CJ, if you don't let her start to run. Okay, Annie? Duchess is very gentle so I think she'd be good for Clarissa. Do you want to keep the lead, Slick?"

"Sounds good," Slick nodded, "I hope I can help Clarissa enough. I'm not that experienced."

"Duchess is a good horse. Clarissa could probably handle her by herself, but you keeping the lead is more for Clarissa than for Duchess."

Marty helped the little kids get into their saddles before he left for home. The kids were excited but nervous. Nora took some Polaroids. The kids wanted to mail some to Auntie and Uncle Bear. Spud watched from the sidewalk, while Horse, Kitten and Grandma watched from the window.

Clarissa was very excited to be riding on Katie's horse, but pretty worried too! She didn't know Slick or Darrell and thought about crying until Clarence told her that she had to be brave, no matter if she got bucked off! Then she was really frightened and thought she might want to go in the house. Finally, Slick put his arm around her. "Don't worry, Clarissa. I'll be right here beside you. If you get worried, just let me know. You can tell me anything at all, okay?"

Marty reminded her that Katie loved to go riding. She finally nodded.

The kids were given instructions on what to do, and they were ready to go. Darrell and Clarence moved forward and Clarence's eyes got huge. He grasped the saddle with a death clench and his eyes did not move from Darrell. After a few feet, Darrell stopped. "Clarence, you need to relax or you'll hate this. Okay, Man? Sergeant isn't going to do anything to hurt you or himself. He wants to have a nice walk today. Now, let go of the saddle with your hands. Just sit on it, like a chair. If you sit in the kitchen, you don't hold on to your chair do you?"

Clarence looked at him and finally smiled. He let go and began to sit more comfortably. Then Darrell winked, "Better?"

Clarence nodded and they started off again.

CJ jabbered nervously to Annie and Moonbeam non-stop. Annie suggested that maybe he might want to take a deep breath. CJ shook his head no. "Jackson said a guy should talk to his horse. But he didn't tell me what to say, so I'm just going to say everything."

Annie giggled, "Okay then. You're doing a good job of that."

Clarissa almost had a heart attack when Duchess took her first steps. Father Bart kept reassuring her and before long, she was feeling better. The riders were gone for about an hour and a half. By the time they returned to the house, Clarissa, Duchess and Bart had bonded. Clarissa loved it all! She still didn't think that Duchess ever needed to run, or even walk fast, but she really liked it when she walked. When they got back to the barn, Slick dismounted Flame and then helped the little girl get off her horse. When she got on the ground, she put her arms around him and gave him a big hug. "I love you a lot."

Bart smiled, "I love you, too."

Annie was amazed that CJ never quit talking the whole trip. He must have told Moonbeam every thought that ever went through his head, and there were many! She helped CJ get off his horse and then he sighed, "Miss Annie, that was fun, but my teeth hurt."

Annie frowned, "Why do you teeth hurt, CJ?"

"I think they want a nap."

Annie giggled, "I bet they do. You know CJ, I wonder if you need to talk the whole time that you ride. Maybe you can rest once in a while."

"I might have to ask Jackson, huh?"

"Yes, you should do that."

Darrell and Clarence had a few nervous spots, but for the most part, their ride was good. "You have a real knack, Clarence. With a little practice, you'll be a good rider."

Clarence smiled a little, but was very pleased. "Mr. Darrell, how old were you when you started to ride?"

"Oh, about three."

"Then I am old, huh?"

"No. Bart didn't start riding until a few months ago. You can start anytime. A lot of folks don't have a horse, so they can't ride."

"I don't have a horse."

"Not yet, but you borrowed one from a friend."

"Do you think Ken is my friend?"

"Well sure. What do you think he is?"

Clarence shrugged.

"Don't you like him?"

"Yah, he's nice. I just didn't think that he'd like me."

"You are a neat guy! What's not to like?"

Clarence shrugged, "Dunno."

"Then you just think that he does. Make sense?"

Clarence grinned, "Okay."

The adults showed the kids how to wipe down and curry their horses. While they were putting the saddles in the tack room, Clarence insisted that he carry the junior saddle that he used, even though it was a little heavy. He needed a little help to get it on the pole rack where it was kept.

Darrell patted his shoulder, "Good work." Then he looked at the saddle, "Hm, I think it needs to be oiled. Some of the leather is drying out."

"Where? I better fix it for Ken. Can you learn me how?"

"Sure, I can teach you. Why are you so interested?" Darrell asked.

"Missus and me might share a horse. Her arm isn't good, so I'll have to do the work. Could you show me how to do that?"

"I'd be more than happy to teach you. We don't have time today, but we can very soon. I'd love that."

"Really?"

"Really."

"Wow!"

Nora had treats ready when they got back to the house. CJ never uttered a word, but Clarissa told of her adventures in great detail. Clarence was proud to tell Nora that Darrell was going to teach him how to take care of a horse and saddle.

27

That evening after chores and dinner, the family got ready for company. The girls decided to take over the kitchen for their 'beauty makeovers' while the men wandered into the living room to relax.

Before long, Maureen and Carl Kincaid came over. When Elton went to answer the door, the little kids all gathered around to see who was there.

Effervescent Mo Kincaid bounced in and took one look. "Lordie above, Coot! Sure and begorrah! What a fine looking bunch of Leprachauns!"

The kids looked at each other, unsure of how to take this middle-aged, jovial lady. Then they saw Carl. He was tall and a bit gruff looking, but he smiled at them.

Mo came over to the kids, "Come and be telling me your names! If you aren't a fine looking lot! Have the old folks here been treating you good?"

Clarence was taken back and nodded shyly. Nora smiled and said, "Kids, I want you to meet Mo and Coot. They live across the road from us. Come and tell them hello."

Clancy toddled right over and handed his car to Mo. "Beep, beep!"

Mo looked the car over and nodded, while Coot picked it up. He made a Brmm! Brmm! noise and Clancy giggled. Then he shoved his wolf out to him and let go with one of his wolf howls.

Coot broke up in laughter, "You make a fine wolf there, little Laddie."

Clarence moved over beside Elton and took his hand to pull him down to him. Elton leaned down and said, "What is it?"

"Do you know what they are saying? I don't know their talk."

Elton grinned and assured him that he would, "They are just being friendly. You'll start to understand them."

Clarence was unconvinced and held on to Elton's hand.

Annie picked up Claudia and explained to the visitors how to get her attention. Mo told her hello and then gave her a little book they had brought for her about kitties.

Nora brought Clarissa over to her and Mo smiled, "Well, if you aren't a little doll! Hello sweetie. Is it true that you like fairies?"

Clarissa nodded shyly and Mo said, "Well, then here you go, little one. I have a book here about fairies if you think you might be liking it!"

Clarissa took and smiled, "Pilamaya. My name is Clarissa."

"You can call me Mo," Maureen smiled, "And this guy is Coot!"

Carl shook her hand and said, "Hello."

Clarissa looked them over and then said, "I might want to go look at my book now, okay?"

"That would be a grand idea," Mo giggled. "We can chat later."

"Okay," Clarissa said as she took Claudia's hand and they went to the living room to look at their books.

CJ was watching the whole thing with great interest. When the girls left, he said, "I am CJ. I'm Charlie's Chicken Man Helper."

Mo gave him a quick hug, "I can see that happening! I bet you're a hand to be dealt to, huh?"

CJ shrugged and then asked, "Is Mr. Coot a policeman? He looks like one. He looks like he might take me away."

Coot pretended to look around the kitchen, "No way Fella, this looks like it would be a good hangout for you. What do you say?"

"I think so."

"Well, then you don't need to worry. Besides this way, you are just across the road from the Petunia Patch where I live, so we can get together. So, you are learning chicken stuff now? How much do you know about ducks?"

CJ shuffled his feet, "Nothing."

"Neither do I," Coot chuckled. "Maybe you and Charlie can help me learn. What do you say?"

"If Clarence says it's okay."

"Where would this Clarence be? I've heard so much about him."

CJ pointed at his brother who was half way behind Elton's leg.

"So you're the leader of this troop, huh?" Coot smiled.

"I s'pose," Clarence muttered.

"Fine pack you have here. Are they hard to keep a lid on?"

Clarence shrugged, "Dunno."

"Well, it looks to me like you've done a fine job. I hear that you know how to put up shingles. Is that a fact?"

Clarence never took his eyes off the man, "Mister showed me."

"Good to know. Do you think I could hire you this spring when I set up my duck coop?"

"I'll have to talk it over with Mister and Jackson. I will sleep on it. I don't know if I know how to do it."

"Well young man, then we'll have to learn, huh?"

Clarence raised his eyebrows, "Do you have a guy to teach us?"

"No but we can look it up in a book. What do you say?"

Elton smiled, "I think Andy had a book like that when he was in 4H club. Maybe we could borrow it. Shall I ask him?"

Coot said, "That would be dandy, don't you agree Clarence?"

Clarence shrugged.

Coot said, "Nora, it looks like the boys and I are going into the dining room to look at directions for raising ducks. Are the writing things still in the same place?"

"Certainly, help yourselves. We'll bring your milk, coffee and cookies to the big table so you have room. Okay?"

"You're a blessing," Carl smiled as he gave her a hug.

"Yikes Coot," Elton poked. "You sound more like Mo every day!"

"You say that like it is a bad thing!" Mo poked.

"Not at all."

A few minutes later, Matt drove in and bounced into the kitchen. "Hi everybody! Getting ready for your beauty party?"

"We are," Nora hugged him. "I imagine you're here to pick up Diane for the rehearsal tonight, huh?"

"Yes, and then a big one tomorrow afternoon at two. Thank goodness we have Sunday off. I'm beginning to hate any bit of music from *West Side Story*. I see Dad is in the living room. Bet he is conning Elton into helping him with the ducks, right?"

"Of course, but he's also trying to rope the little boys into helping," Mo grinned.

"That'll be good. I'll give them my great insight."

"Yah, Coot was waiting for that!" Mo giggled.

"Here Matt," Nora handed him a cup of coffee, "Take your cup with you! The cookies are in there."

"Hi, miss me?" Matt asked as he came up to the table.

"Ugh!" Coot groaned. "You must want something, huh?"

Clarence watched the exchange with worry, and asked Elton, "Mister, is Mr. Coot mad at Mr. Matt?"

Elton patted Clarence's back, "Not at all. They are just teasing each other. He really likes him a lot. Coot is Harrington and Matt's Dad."

Clarence raised his eyebrows, "Do you like to go fishing?"

"Why yes I do," Coot replied. "I'll tell you a secret, I'm not too good at it. How about you? Do you go fishing a lot?"

"No." Clarence answered. "My Dad was too busy, but Mister said he'll take me. Harrington said you guys might want to come, too."

"That'd be a great idea, don't you think?"

Clarence leaned back, "I'll have to sleep on it."

Matt chuckled, "What do you say that you boys come to town with me tomorrow morning, Clarence? We can go check out the library. I have to pick up Diane and Katie from the beauty shop at eleven. We can catch a hamburger before we get home. I can drop you off here before we go to the rehearsal."

Clarence looked to Elton, "Mister, who would watch the kids?"

"The girls are going with Nora and it will just be Clancy at home. I can keep an eye on him. I think it'd be a great idea. You can get a library card."

"Charlie is coming over in the morning to help us build boats," CJ pointed out. "Mr. Marty's coming, too. Charlie had to go to school, so he didn't get to help before. So, I can't come with," CJ explained to Matt.

"You know Clarence, if you go with Matt you could look up some of the things about our ducks. That'd really help out," Carl suggested.

Clarence really wanted to go but was nervous about it, "I don't know. Mister might need me."

"I'll tell you what. If Matt promises to call me and check up on me, I think it would be a good idea. I'll be here with Grandpa."

Clarence frowned, "Can you do that, Mr. Matt?"

"I sure can. So, should I pick you up tomorrow morning?"

"Okay, but if Mister gets scared, I might have to stay with him."

"I'll be by after chores and see how things are," Matt smiled. "So what have you got to do for the ducks?"

Before long, Darrell and Jeannie, Ian and Ruthie and Kevin and Carrie arrived. The girls were getting all giggly in the kitchen and setting up their collection of wigs. Kevin, Ian and Darrell joined the men in the safety of the living room.

"Ah, the duck pen!" Darrell laughed. "Are you going to build that before or after expanding the tool shed?"

"Maybe at the same time," Carl smirked. "Depends on how many helpers I can drum up."

"What are you doing to the tool shed?" Elton asked.

"Putting in racks for the fishing poles," Matt explained. "He roped me into helping with that months ago!"

"Ah, yah. I believe it was after you volunteered me to help with an ice skating party for about a thousand kids!" Coot groused.

"And I have never heard the end of it," Matt laughed.

"In trouble, again?" Byron asked as he came in with his coffee. "I have to get out of the kitchen! The girls were dragging out the fingernail polish!"

The evening turned out to be a lot of fun. The ladies did each other's nails, played with some new makeup techniques and tried on the wigs. They all tried on the wigs and then decided which was the prettiest. There was a lot of giggling and teasing. Even though Clarissa was certain that she wanted her hair 'sunshine' color, she didn't like the blonde wigs when they were on her. She liked the darker colors much better. They all agreed that Claudia's choice of a pixie cut was perfect for her.

28

Saturday morning was bright and sunny. Clarence was still nervous about going to town with Matt alone, so he talked to his big stepbrother.

"Jackson," the little guy said as he sat next to the desk where Jackson was sketching. "I tried to sleep on it, but I couldn't."

"What's wrong, Clarence?" his brother set down his sketch to give him his full attention.

Clarence shrugged, "Dunno. Mr. Matt said he'd take me to town to the library. I think that you might be scared to be alone."

Jackson studied the young boy, "Hm. I know I'll be okay here with Elton and Andy. We're going to keep an eye on Clancy and Grandpa until the ladies get home. It'll be okay."

Clarence looked down to his feet. "Jackson? Do you ever want to go home?"

Jackson gave his little brother a hug, "Yes, I do sometimes. I miss Pine Ridge. Then I remember no one is there anymore. Mom, Dad, Auntie and Uncle Bear are all away from there. It wouldn't be the same. Look, you can be tell me, don't you like it here?"

"It's okay, but I don't fit."

"Why don't you fit? It looked to me last night like you had a lot of new friends."

"But they're all new. They talk about stuff that I don't know."

Jackson picked the little guy onto his lap, "Listen here, you know a lot of stuff. Did anyone tell you that you don't?"

"No, but they think it. I don't know how to oil saddles or take care of ducks. I don't even know how to go fishing!" Clarence fought back the tears.

Jackson put his arms around him, "They'll show you how. It makes them feel good to help you do things."

"Why would Harrington want to help me?"

"Cause that's the way they are."

Clarence frowned, "But what could I do for him?"

"Be his friend back."

"That's not much."

"Well, you know he has a bum arm. You could help him lift stuff."

Clarence smiled, "You think so?"

"Yes, I do. You and Matt have been friends since you met, right? Has he ever been bad to you?"

"No."

"Then, I think you should go with him. Mind your manners and have a good time. I'll tell you a secret. I was nervous when I went to town with him the first time. Now he's one of my best friends in the whole world."

"Better than me?"

"You're my brother; that's closer than friends. We'll always be brothers, forever. Remember, we can have all kinds of friends. Elton says there is always room for another friend."

"You mean I can be friends with Mr. Darrell, too? He said he would learn me how to take care of saddles if I want."

"You say, 'he will *teach* me how.' Do you want to do that? Then, of course! Know what else? Matt and Darrell are best friends!"

"I thought Darrell was friends with Slick."

"He is and so are Matt and Andy! We can all have more than one friend. That's makes things interesting. We can do all sorts of things with different folks. It's a good thing."

"My Dad just liked Spotted Calf. He only had one friend," Clarence pointed out.

"That was because they lived nearby. Your Dad had other friends. Look how many people were at the wake. They were all friends."

"Dad said he didn't trust them."

Jackson hugged him tight, "Maybe your Dad didn't know that he could have more than one friend at a time. I think that was it. Don't you?"

"Dunno. I might have to sleep on it. I don't know if I like CJ and Charlie being friends. I mean, it is okay and CJ needs to play. But he talks like he'd rather be with Charlie than me."

"You'll always be his brother. Don't ever forget that. Now think about it; if you have a kitten and you're afraid it'll go sit on somebody else's lap, do you grab it tight by the foot so it can't leave?"

Clarence chuckled, "No way!"

"Why not?"

"Because it'd get mad at me, probably bite me and then run off."

"People are like that. If you grab too tight, they'll feel trapped. If they can come and go when they want; they'll come back. You can be friends with Charlie, too. I've heard him ask you."

"I know, but those guys are lunkheads. I don't want to put poop in my fridge."

Jackson chuckled, "Me either. But I love both those guys, even with their crazy Chicken Man hats!"

Clarence crossed his eyes, "I wouldn't do that! I might hang out with them, but I'd never do that!"

"Me either, but it doesn't hurt anything and they seem to have fun."

Clarence hugged his brother for a bit and then said, "I should go to town with Matt, huh?"

"Only if you want."

"I really want a library card."

"Then go. Could you do me a favor? I'd like you and Matt to drop off some of my sketches at the clinic."

"Okay, if Mr. Matt says." Clarence hopped down and said, "I better go wash up. Jackson, why do these guys wash their hands all the time? I think my skin is going to wear out!"

"Because they have running water and because they don't want germs. I don't think that you do either, do you?"

"No way!"

After Clarence washed up and Annie braided the leather thongs into the side of his long hair to keep it back from his eyes, he went to the kitchen. "You look spiffy," Grandma said as she gave him a hug.

Clarence grinned. He wasn't sure what spiffy was, but he liked Grandma's hug. "I decided I'll go to town with Mr. Matt."

"Good decision. Would you like me to dial the phone, so you can tell him?"

"Yes, please."

Grandma dialed and handed the phone to Clarence. He was starting to get nervous when Matt said hello. "I was just thinking about you! I was in the shower and decided to call you when I got out to see if you were coming with me."

"You were going to call me?" Clarence was very pleased. "Grandma dialed so I could tell you that I was coming. Okay?"

"I'm so glad. I'll be over to pick you up as soon as I get dressed."

"Mr. Matt, Jackson wondered if we could take some of his sketch things to that place."

"I was planning on it. See you in a bit."

Clarence had no more than hung up the phone when it rang. Grandma answered and said, "He's right here. I'll let you talk to him."

When she handed the phone to Clarence, he didn't know what to think. "Who is it?"

"Answer the phone and find out," Grandma giggled.

Nervously, Clarence said, "Hi. I am Clarence Grey Hawk."

Darrell chuckled, "This is Darrell. I was wondering if you had time this afternoon to come to my house. We could work on the saddles if you want."

"Me? To your house?"

"If you want," Darrell repeated. "I'll have you home in time for supper. Ask Nora or Grandma if you want to come."

"Ah, just a minute," Clarence hung the phone up. "Grandma, it's that Darrell guy. He wants me to come to his house this afternoon to put oil on the saddles. Is it okay?"

"It'd be fine. I'll tell Nora, but Clarence, you hung up! Let me dial him back for you!"

Clarence giggled, "Pilamaya."

When Darrell answered, he chuckled, "I wasn't sure if you were going to call me back! I'm glad you called. What do you think?"

"Grandma says I can come with. Do I have to bring oil?"

"No, I have all the things we need, unless Grandma would have some old rags we could use?"

"I'll ask," Clarence said and hung up again.

Grandma laughed, "You goofy kid, why do you keep hanging up on Darrell?"

Clarence grimaced. "I don't know! He said he needs some old rags."

"I'll send some with you. Want me to dial again?"

"Yes, Ma'am."

Grandma dialed and Darrell was laughing when he answered, "Hi Clarence. What did she say?"

"She says she has rags for us! Isn't that good?"

"It really is," Darrell agreed. "I'll pick you up about two. Okay? Don't hang up!"

Clarence was giggling now, "Grandma, is two okay? I can't hang up."

"Two will be great," Grandma smiled.

"Two is great. Can I hang up now?"

"Yes, you can. See you later."

Clarence was so excited, "Grandma, Mr. Darrell wants to see me!"

"I heard," she smiled. "That's wonderful. Now, will you help me get the rags ready?"

"Sure. Are they real heavy?"

"A little bit. Think you need a bag of them?"

"Dunno."

"Well, a guy can never have too many rags, can he?"

"I s'pose. I can lift them for you."

Half an hour later, everyone was ready for the day. Marty had picked up Charlie on his way over to work on the boat. Andy and CJ were ready for their co-workers, although Marty and Andy were beginning to have second thoughts what possessed them to do it.

The ladies were all headed to the beauty shop. Matt and Clarence loaded Jackson's sketches in the car. Just before they left, Elton called Clarence aside. "Do you have your wallet?"

Clarence wrinkled his brow, "No, I forgot."

"You might need it. Best you go get it. Here are three dollars for it."

"Why do I need that?"

"You might find something that you want to buy. Or you could give it to Matt to help pay for lunch. That'd be the proper thing to do."

Clarence nodded, "Okay. Do you think I can remember that? I don't know how to use money."

"I'm sure Matt will help you." Elton gave him a hug after he made certain his wallet was safely in his pocket. "Have a good time and behave."

29

The ladies loaded into the family station wagon for their trip to the beauty shop. They all had appointments to get their hair cut, trimmed, or permed. It was going to be a fun experience. The Ellison ladies were going to meet them there. Everyone was excited.

They had all done their fingernails the night before. It was the first time that Claudia and Clarissa had fingernail polish on, and they were delighted. Claudia kept looking at her hands and smiling, and was very careful not to suck on her fingers.

Clarissa was more excited about getting her hair cut. She was very tired of her long, long hair which she said was too 'big'. It may have been, because it was about three feet long when it was unbraided. Clarissa was only a couple inches taller than her thick hair. Now that she didn't want it sunshine color anymore, she was content to just get it cut.

The Merton ladies were lucky to get all their appointments within half an hour of each other. Claudia became a little concerned when the girl put the cape around her and leaned her back to wash her hair. Diane stayed right by her and held her hand. When the girl took the first cut, Claudia got some tears, but Diane reassured her. Then Annie gathered her long hair into a bag so they could make the dream catcher, she started to smile.

The girl finished and turned the chair around so Claudia could see herself in the big mirror. She was at first worried and then started to smile. She took both her hands and ruffled her hair. "Pixie!" she giggled.

The beautician gave her a big smile and a lollipop. Diane put her in a chair nearby while she took her turn to get her hair trimmed.

Clarissa was more worried than Claudia, but wanted to show Ginger that she was a big girl. Nora stayed by her and held her hand. Clarissa whispered, "Will I be pretty, Missus?"

Nora hugged her, "You already are."

Katie overheard her, "Clarissa, I wish I had pretty hair like yours."

Clarissa's eyes opened real wide, "Missus, did you hear that?"

Nora whispered in her ear, "I told you."

After her shampoo and haircut, the girl asked her how she wanted it done. Clarissa shrugged, "Missus, you say."

"Would you like to try to have it curly? Or in ponytails?"

"Curls."

"Okay," the girl said, "You got it!"

When the time was up, Grandma had her new permanent, Clarissa and Claudia had haircuts, while the others all had a trims. Nora and Diane sat under the hair dryers on either side of Clarissa while they all looked at magazines. When Clarissa's curlers were combed out, she looked precious.

"You look like a fairy princess," Katie said. "Your hair is just perfect. It has a nice curl and I really think that it is sparkling, just like Andy said. What do you think?"

Clarissa looked in the mirror, "You mean like fireflies?"

The girl who fixed her hair smiled, "We can make them even easier to see. Let me put the magic spray on and they'll really shine!"

The lady sprayed and her hair shone. All the ladies agreed that the fireflies were surely dancing in her hair.

CJ and Charlie set about to make an interesting morning for Marty and Andy. Elton kept Clancy busy with some clay to keep him from helping them too, because it looked like that would've been more than the young men could have handled.

Both kids knew about sanding, their way. Andy thought they should just let them do it, but Marty couldn't stand it and had to explain. He carefully showed them how to sand with the grain.

"Boys, the pieces of wood have to fit together real tight, or the ship will sink. You don't want that, do you?"

"No," CJ said. "Maybe we could put more glue on it."

"That much glue won't be good."

"Why?"

"Er, it'll make it too heavy," Marty felt he had landed on an good reason.

"How 'bout we tie balloons on the ship to hold it up?" Charlie suggested.

Marty crossed his eyes to his cousin, "Why not, Andy?"

"Ah, because it might get too light and then float away!"

"That'd be so cool, right CJ?" Charlie grinned.

"Yah, we'd have a flying boat! We should take it outside!"

"Guys, we can't do that," Andy said. "We have to build a regular floating boat. Okay?"

"Why?" Charlie asked. "I think a flying boat would be more funner."

Elton was sitting across the room and came over, "Boys. Let me check the directions a minute. Okay?"

He picked up the directions and read them while they all four watched and waited for his pronouncement. "Afraid it won't work to be a flying boat. It says so right here. Sorry. I can hardly wait to see what a good job you'll do."

A few minutes later, Marty came out to the kitchen to refill his coffee cup. "Thanks Uncle Elton. It seemed to help. They think that you think they will to do a good job, so now they want to. How did you know that?"

"Everybody is that way," Elton grinned. "But if Clancy keeps trying to eat this clay, I might want to trade off with you!"

Clarence got into Matt's car and sat as still as he could in the front seat. He never said a word for a ways and then Matt asked, "How was your morning?"

"Mr. Darrell called me. He asked me to come to his place. He's gonna show me how to oil the saddles this afternoon. Do you know how to do that?"

"I just learned a couple months ago."

"Really? I thought grownups knew everything."

Matt chuckled, "I wish that was true. Most grownups don't know as much as they think they do. Did you know that?"

"No. I mostly only talked to my Dad and he knew everything! He knew how to put those wire washing things in the cracks in the floor to keep the mice out."

"Really, you mean like SOS pads?"

"Yah, that was the ones."

"So that works real well, huh?"

"It did. But the mice just came in the crack by the door. It was too big to fill with those things."

"Hm. Too bad. Sounds like he was a pretty smart fella. That is probably why you are?"

"Dunno. I don't know very much."

"Well, you're willing to learn. That's what really smart people do! People's brains don't have much in them when they are born, so they have to put stuff in it. When babies are little, others put it in. When you get older, you can put it in yourself. That is why we like to learn how to read. Then we can go to the library and read about stuff we don't know about."

Clarence listened to him. "I hate to read. I don't know how to figure those marks mean anything."

"You know who is the world's best helper with that? Jeannie, Darrell's wife. She could show you how to do that in no time. She's really good at it."

"Will she yell at me?"

"No. Jeannie doesn't yell. Would you like me to mention it to her? You know, she taught Ginger how to read. I know she would be happy to teach you."

"You mean Ginger didn't know how to read before?"

"She was like you. She hated it, but now she likes to read."

Clarence relished that morsel of information. He thought a bit and then asked, "Do you think Ginger is bossy?"

"I'll tell you a secret, if you promise to keep it just between you and me."

"I promise. Mister says to give your word."

"She is so afraid that you won't like her, that she is worried. So when she gets worried, she gets mad."

Clarence rode in silence, "I do that sometimes. I didn't know she was afraid I didn't like her. I would've if she hadn't been mad."

"Were you maybe a little worried, too? Is that possible?"

Clarence giggled, "Yah. How did you know that?"

"Cause people are that way. You guys need to patch things up and be friends. You'll have a lot more fun that way. Then neither of you will have to be worried."

Clarence squirmed a little, "Harrington said maybe we should take Ginger fishing. I don't think I want her along."

Matt said, "Maybe when you start getting along, you will. Did you like the fishing map that Ian brought over last night?"

"I didn't understand the marks on it."

"If you told Harrington, he'd be happy to help you with them. You know he had to learn them."

"Really?"

"Yup. Harrington loves fishing. He'd love to have a fishing pal. You could be that guy."

When they got to the Clinic, Matt asked Clarence to help him carry some of the smaller sketches. He explained that they were very important and to be careful. Together they went down the hall to the office. Mr. Larson met them. "I see you have a helper today?"

"Yes," Matt smiled. "He is my friend and Jackson's brother, Clarence."

"Well, hello Clarence," Mr. Larson smiled as he got the checkbook out of his desk drawer. "Do you sketch too?"

"Dunno. I mostly do thinking."

Larson gave him a grin, "We need a lot more men like you in this world! Keep up the good work."

He handed Matt the check and said, "So, how many more do we have to get yet?"

"I believe six."

"When you come next time, I'm sure we'll have another order. The sketches are very popular, especially the colored ones. Think he can do that?"

"I'll speak to Jackson about it."

After they left the Clinic, Clarence asked, "Is that deal he gave you one of those check things that Carrie told me about?"

"It is. Would you like me to show it to you?"

The boy nodded and Matt showed him the check. "Yes, and down here is the name of the guy who wrote the check. The check tells his bank to pay Jackson this amount from that man's money."

The little guy was fascinated. "Is that why they put Jackson's name there? Cool. Do you think someday I can get one of those checks?"

"I think you can."

"I could have Carrie put it in my savings account. She told me all about them. Did you know that I have a card that says I have one of them?"

"No, I didn't. That is really great, Clarence. You take good care of it."

"I have it in my wallet. Mister bought me one so I can put my library card in there, too."

Matt smiled, "Well, if that is the case, I think we should head to the library! What do you say?"

"Okay!"

As they got out at the library, Clarence took Matt's hand. The little boy asked with all sincerity, "Are you going to hold on to me, so you don't get lost?"

"Yes. We need to stick together. Now, when we get in there, you have to whisper. We're only allowed to talk very quietly."

"Why's that?"

"Because some folks are reading in there, and we don't want to mess up their thinking. Okay?"

"Okay," Clarence whispered.

They entered the door and Clarence was fascinated. He had never seen so many books in his life, rows and stacks of them! Matt took him over to some books for his age. They started to look at them. Then Clarence saw one on ducks! He wiggled Matt's hand and pointed. "I bet Mr. Coot would like that, huh?" he whispered.

Matt nodded and took the book down from the shelf. They went over to a table to set down and look through the book. It seemed to be what they were looking for. Matt asked, "Do you want to take this one home?"

"Could I?" Clarence's face lit up.

"Sure. You can take home two more books if you want. What do you think would be interesting?"

Clarence thought, "How about fish or saddles?"

"Okay," Matt nodded.

The two spent about half an hour there and found three good books. One was about how to build a duck pen, one about fish and another about caring for saddles. Then they went up to the librarian and Clarence got his library card. He was so excited he couldn't stop smiling. The librarian handed him the card and he promised her he would take the best care of those books ever. She smiled and said, "I'm sure you will, young man. Bring them back in three weeks, and you can take some more. See you again."

"Okay!" Clarence whispered.

In the car, they put the books in the back seat. Clarence checked them twice to make sure they were safe before he asked Matt, "If I read all the books in the library, then all that stuff would be in my head, right?"

"Pretty much."

"Too bad they didn't have one about reading fish maps, huh?"

"Oh they might, but I think that Ian can teach you that. Do you think that you might want to ask Jeannie to teach you how to read?"

"Yah, I think that would be a good idea. Then I could put all that stuff in my head."

"That you could."

"Did she read all the books in there?"

"No. Some wouldn't be interesting to her, but she's read a lot."

"I should tell CJ. But he is a lunkhead, so I don't know if it would help!" Clarence giggled.

"Might not, at that," Matt agreed. "Shall we go pick up the ladies?"

"Okay."

"Now, a word of warning. When a man goes into a beauty shop and a girl asks if he likes her hair, he always has to say something nice!"

"What if their hair isn't nice?"

"Say something nice anyway, or you'll have a problem on your hands! Girls work hard to look pretty. If you don't compliment them, they feel bad or mad!"

When they got to the beauty shop, the ladies were just getting ready to leave. Clarence grinned and told each one of them how nice they looked. He gave Claudia a big hug and just stared at Clarissa. "Why are you looking at me like that?" she asked.

"I never knew you were pretty before. I thought you were just regular."

Clarissa frowned at him and gave him a whack. "That makes me cry, Clarence!"

Matt stepped in, "He didn't mean it like that Clarissa. He meant that you were pretty before, but now you look very special. Right, Clarence?"

"Yah, that's it."

"Alright, but you better be nice," Clarissa warned.

Clarence looked at Matt trying to understand what happened. Matt knelt down, "That was a tricky one, huh?"

"I don't think I like to come in this place."

"Most guys don't."

30

Clarence watched while Matt held the car door open for Katie as she got in, so he held the door open for Diane. Diane smiled sweetly and said, "Thank you, Clarence. You're a fine gentleman."

That pleased Clarence and he was smiling while he got in the backseat with Katie. "Katie, don't sit on my library books. I promised the lady I'd take care of them."

"I'll be very careful. May I look at them?"

"I guess, but don't tear the pages out. Mr. Matt told me that Miss Jeannie might teach me how to read and then I can read every book in the whole library. Then I will know stuff!"

"You really would. These are nice books."

Matt pulled into the parking lot of the Log House. They got out and Clarence followed Matt's lead. If he held the door open, so did Clarence. However, when they sat in the booth, Clarence scooted in first. After he was seated, he saw that Matt had let Diane in first. By then Katie was already sitting down. He started to panic. How could he fix it?

He squirmed down under the table and crawled out beside the booth. Then he motioned for Katie to scoot over. She did and he got in. Then he looked at Matt nervously, and Matt nodded his approval.

The waitress brought water over, and Matt asked the ladies what they wanted. Clarence was at a loss. "Where are the papers?"

Katie explained, "They don't give us menus here. It's written on this chart by the speaker. We just turn on the speaker to the kitchen and tell them what we decided. Isn't that neat?"

Clarence shrugged, "Dunno. I can't see the chart."

"Would you like me to tell you what they have?"

"I s'pose," the little boy was beginning to feel out of his element.

"They have hamburgers, cheeseburgers, chicken and toasted cheese sandwiches."

"A hamburger."

"What would you like to drink?" Katie asked.

"I don't know," he bit his lip and started to panic.

Katie patted his arm, "I'd like to ask you a favor. Would you share a chocolate milk shake with me? A whole one is too big!"

"I don't know what they are."

"I think you'll like them, and if you don't, we can order you something else. Okay?" Matt suggested.

"I s'pose."

Diane called in the order and then turned to Clarence, "So you got some books today. Are they good?"

"I haven't read them yet," Clarence shrugged.

"What are they about?" she tried again.

Matt answered for him, "Building duck pens, fishing and the other one is about taking care of tack."

Clarence frowned, "I thought it was about saddles."

"Tack is another word for saddles," Matt explained.

Just like that, Clarence started to cry. Matt took his hand and said, "Come with me. Let's go wash up, okay?"

Clarence nodded and together they went to the rest room where Matt gave the boy a big hug while he cried. After he calmed down a bit, Matt asked, "What is it, Clarence? What's the trouble?"

"I just don't know what to do! I want to go home to my real home. I hate this."

Matt held him, "I think I understand. You know you can't go, don't you?"

"Yah," Clarence nodded. "But I really, really want to. I don't want to think so much!"

Matt held him, "Look Clarence, you're with us. We understand! Please don't worry so much. You can ask us if you don't know what we are talking about. Okay? Sometimes we just forget. If you want to talk about your stuff, do it. We'd like to hear about it. See, we don't know anything about that stuff either."

"Really? You wouldn't think I was being goofy?"

Matt smiled, "No. You've a lot of things to share with us."

"I have dollars. Mister said I should help you pay for lunch. He said that'd be the thing to do."

"That's fine, but we'd like to hear about some of the things you used to do. Are you ready to go back now? We don't want to let the girls eat our lunch, do we?" Matt winked.

"No," Clarence took Matt's hand.

Back in the booth, the girls never mentioned what had happened. The men sat down and Matt said, "Clarence and I took the sketches to the Clinic. They might want some more colored ones."

"Wow!" Katie said. "That's so neat. Do you like those sketches, Clarence?"

"They're okay, but my brother is making some for us kids. He is going to make one of Mom and Dad so we don't forget them."

"That is a great idea," Matt nodded.

"Yah. My brother said that some sketches can help you to remember, but some sketches are for fun. He's going to make me one of me and my Dad fishing by the creek. There were fish in there, but Dad was so busy we never went fishing. Then he died. So Jackson said that this way, I could look at it and think of how much fun we would've had."

Then he noticed Diane, who had tears in her eyes, "I'm sorry Miss Diane. See Mr. Matt, I shouldn't say stuff."

"Yes, you should. I think that's wonderful," Diane smiled. "I'm really very glad that you told me."

Clarence made a worried face, "Is she okay, Mr. Matt?"

"She is fine. She's just being a girl."

Diane gave him a playful whack and a dirty look. Matt winked at Clarence, "We both got in trouble today, huh?"

Matt and Clarence were both giggling when the waitress brought the food. Katie and Clarence split the milk shake and after a taste, he decided that it was really good. "I like that a lot!"

"Me, too!" Katie said. "I'm glad I have someone to share it with."

"I'll always share it with you!"

"Good deal," Katie shook his hand.

The rest of lunch was fun and Clarence was more relaxed. He tasted the onion rings and decided that he liked them, especially if they were dunked in a pile of catsup.

At the till, Clarence took out his wallet and gave Matt his money. Matt thanked him and put it with his cash to pay the bill. The ladies thanked both men for their lunch. Clarence liked that.

When they got to the house, Clarence and Diane came bouncing in. Clarence was very excited to show Elton his library card and his books. Diane took him up to his room to put his things away. He didn't need his wallet to go to Darrell's, so he put it away safely in his drawer.

After they left the kitchen, Matt and Elton had a brief talk. Matt smiled. "I just wanted you to know he really misses his Dad. He told me that he was the only guy he really talked to. Sadly, I think that's probably true. How did the ship building go?"

"Yea gads, Matt," Andy said as he came into the kitchen. "That poor ship has more glue than balsa wood! Those little tornadoes got glue on the hard wood floor! Mom will have their hide. Marty and I worked for an hour to get it off."

"Are the kids worried?"

"Good grief, no! Why would you think that?" Elton looked out the window, "In fact, they have been outside for half an hour. I'd better go check on them. Will you keep an eye on Clancy?"

"Sure, Dad," Andy grinned. "Have fun."

Elton had no idea where the boys were, but he followed the dogs. Elmer and Rags were sitting outside the brooder house, so it was easy to guess the boys were inside. Elton opened the door and the kids jumped about ten feet.

"Whatcha plottin'?" Elton grinned.

"Nothin'," Charlie answered right away.

"Oh, why do you have all this stuff out here?"

"We had an idea. See Uncle Elton, this is where the baby chicks will live until they get big, so we're going to make it special for them."

"What are you going to do?"

"We're thinking that they really like cold water to drink, right?"

Elton nodded.

"So, if we make the hose come from the well to the brooder house, we could glue the hose to a dish. Then we could let the cold water run into it all the time! That way, they'd never be out of water. They'd like that, huh?" Charlie explained.

Elton thought and then nodded, "Probably, but the dish would get full and run over. Or what it if leaks? The baby chicks can't get wet, because they will get sick. So it wouldn't be good to have too much water."

"We'd glue the leaks shut and can turn it down so it drips. Then it won't run over," CJ suggested.

"If they have a deep dish, they mighty fall into it and drown because they don't know how to swim," Elton pointed out.

CJ's face brightened up, "Charlie and me could learn them how!"

Elton grimaced, "They don't have their feathers yet. So, they couldn't swim if they wanted to."

"We could put feathers on them," Charlie suggested. "If we picked up the feathers from the old hens, we could paste them on the chicks."

"Glue would work better, Charlie! That stuff works great! It glued my hair real good!" CJ stated.

"No. The glue would make the chicks sick. I'm sorry guys, but we better just use the chick waterers, like they are."

"Sassafras!" Charlie frowned. "I'm pretty sure it would work."

"Are you so sure that you might make a baby chick sick by trying?"

"No sir," CJ said. "We just thought . . . ."

"That's good. Keep thinking, but give me your word that you'll talk to me about it before you do anything. Have I got your word?"

"I guess," Charlie shuffled his feet.

"Charles, do I have your word? I don't want to worry about it."

"Yes, Uncle Elton. Can you think of something that we could do that wouldn't make the chicks sick?"

"First, have I got your word, CJ?"

"Yes sir."

"Okay, let's think. Hmm. Well guess what? I do have something you could help me with! It has nothing to do with chicks, but wanna hear?" Elton said seriously.

"What is it?"

"There is a big snow drift over to the north of the garden. When it thaws, it is going to flood the garden. It'll take forever to dry off. How about if you boys move that big drift to the south of the barn? Then when it thaws, it will go into the creek where it belongs. Could you do that?"

"Would we carry each shovel all the way down there?" Charlie asked with concern.

"No, you could fill up the wagon and take that down. If you boys do that, I'll pay you each $2 when you're all finished. But, you have to do a good job. No sloppy work."

CJ frowned, "But Mister, I don't have a shovel."

"Well, I'll get you one. Until then, we can go to the shop and I'll lend you one of mine. Okay?"

"Okay, Uncle Elton. We'll do a good job," Charlie assured him.

"Now don't be jackrabbits about it. You have to be neat. Okay?"

The boys shook hands with him and followed him to the shop to get their supplies. "Now, when you're finished working every day, you need to put things away. Okay? Don't leave stuff all over the place or I'll have to skin you."

CJ's eye got huge and Charlie gasped, "We promise."

Darrell drove in a few minutes later to pick up Clarence and met Elton on his way back to the house. "Hi," the young dairyman grinned. "What are you up to?"

"Trying to find something to keep the Dynamic Duo occupied! Yikes, I thought Little Charlie was one of a kind. Boy, was I wrong about that!" Elton chuckled.

"CJ?"

"Yah, I thought CJ was quiet and a follower. Well, the only reason he is quiet is because his little brain is going so fast, his mouth could never keep up!"

"Matt and I had a short talk about Clarence. You and I had talked about Jeannie helping out, and she is on board. So is Harrington. We'll get him caught up with his grades in no time. He just needs a little time to adjust. It has only been a week since his folks died."

"I know. He's doing pretty well, all things considered. So, you're going to show him how to take care of tack? That's good. Nora said they might get a horse and share it. But he'll have to take care of the saddle for them. So, he has a goal."

"What about horses for the other kids?"

"I plan on talking to Jerald tomorrow and see if he knows where there are a few more decrepit hay burners. CJ needs an Abner, and the other three are even smaller. Why didn't you lock me in a closet when I had my big mouth flapping about taking in five little kids?"

"I tried, but you were too far away. You know, you love it!" Darrell clapped him on the back, "Besides, it's good for you. Hey, when should I bring him home? Before or after chores?"

"Hey, I got an idea. The ladies put a huge roast in the oven for dinner. Why don't you do chores and then come eat?"

"We won't say no! Will it be too long for Clarence?"

"He might get nervous, but if he does, just have him call home. Okay?"

"Okay."

The two men went in where Clarence was waiting with Andy. He was showing Andy the book that he had checked out on taking care of tack. Darrell looked at it and smiled, "Studying up on it, huh? Good idea. Do you want to bring the book along?"

"Will it get messed up? I promised the library lady I'd take care of it."

"We'll take good care of it. Maybe Elton has a bag for us?"

"Oh Mr. Darrell, Grandma got a big stack of rags for us. I can help you carry them because they're pretty heavy."

"That'd be good. How about we split the pile and each carry part?"

"Okay, if you're strong enough," Clarence said sincerely as he pulled out the basket of rags.

The young man with mahogany-colored hair smiled, "I think if we split them, we could take them in one trip."

They took the rags out to the car and came back in to get the rest of Clarence's things. Then they said goodbye and went to Darrell's place.

When they drove into the yard, Clarence was trying to take in everything. "Is that Mr. Matt's house?"

"Yes, we call it the cabin," Darrell nodded. "I'll introduce you to our dogs. My dog is the black one and his name is Ranger. Matt's is the gold one and her name is Skipper."

Clarence petted the dogs and let them lick him. "I think they like me, huh? I bet Rags would like them, too."

"Might at that. Well, let's go to the house and see Jeannie. We can take your book up there so it doesn't get messed up. Maybe we can look it over while we have some cookies. What do you think?"

"Okay," Clarence said. "I had lunch with Mr. Matt today. We went to a place; ah, some kind of a house."

"The Log House?" Darrell asked as they went up the walkway toward his house.

"How did you know?"

"We like that place, too. What did you have?"

"A hamburger and a shake thing I shared with Katie because her belly wasn't big enough."

Darrell grinned, "That was very nice of you. Let's go in."

In the mudroom, he and Clarence took off their overshoes and jackets.

Darrell opened the kitchen door and took Clarence's hand, "You might have met Jeannie before, but I'll introduce you again. Okay?"

Clarence nodded shyly, "This is a nice house."

"Thank you," Jeannie grinned, as she bent down to greet their guest. "I'm Jeannie and you're Clarence, correct?"

"No, Clarence Grey Hawk," the little boy said seriously.

"Grey Hawk is a neat last name. Ours is Jessup. That isn't nearly as much fun, is it?"

Clarence shrugged.

"Could I interest you in some cookies? I made two kinds and I'm not sure which is best. I'll let you guys decide, okay?"

Darrell poured himself a cup of coffee, "I think we can handle that. Would you like some milk?"

"Yes, please."

"You may sit on the side by the window, if you like," Jeannie said. "Here are the cookies. Try them and tell me what you think?"

They both tried the cookies. Clarence tasted and thought very somberly. Then Darrell asked, "Well Grey Hawk, what's your decision?"

Clarence giggled, "I like the one with those colored things in them."

"The M&M's?" Jeannie asked. "What do you think, Darrell?"

"I agree. The chocolate chips are good, but there's chocolate in the M&M's too. So, you get both in them. Right, Grey Hawk?"

Clarence nodded. "Right."

"Do you want to show Jeannie what you got from the library today?"

The little boy wiped his hands on his pants and then took the book out and handed it to her, "Be careful to not mess it up, okay?"

"Cross my heart, I'll be careful."

Clarence got a silly grin on his face and Jeannie asked why.

"That's what Missus says. Mister says we have to give our word."

"I guess it means about the same. Wow, this is a fantastic book! Shall we look at it while we have our snack?"

Clarence nodded and Darrell agreed.

After they paged through the book, they decided to go to the barn. Clarence had never seen anything like Darrell's barn, with all the in-line milking stations and machines.

"Mister milks his cows with his hands. He showed me how to do that," Clarence explained. "I bet this is hard to learn."

"Not at all. In fact, I could teach you in no time."

"Really? I don't know too much," Clarence warned.

"That's better than thinking you know more than you do!" Darrell chuckled.

They went into the tack room, where Darrell had all the saddles on racks and with the gear all neatly put away carefully. He pulled out a table and Jeannie reached for three stools. Clarence helped her put them around the table. They had brought the rags in, and Jeannie sorted through them to find a couple for each of them. Darrell brought over one of the saddles, and put it on the table. Then he motioned for Clarence to help him bring over brushes, leather cleaner and conditioner.

Jeannie explained what they needed to do and Darrell showed him how. They also used suggestions from Clarence's book. Before long, they were all three rubbing away on the leather saddle so make it clean, soft and pliable.

31

At first, the three worked very hard. After a little bit, Darrell said, "Jeannie, Grey Hawk went to the Log House for lunch today!"

"Wow!" the perky brunette smiled, "What did you have to eat?"

"I had a cheeseburger, fries and part of Katie's milk shake thing."

"What did you think of the place?" Jeannie asked. "I love their burgers."

"It was good and I liked the onion fries in that catsup. But the shake thing was my favorite," Clarence answered. "Do you like them?"

"I love them!" Jeannie answered. "Who did you go to town with?"

"Mr. Matt asked me to go to the library with him. We picked up Miss Diane and Katie at that hair place."

"Oh yes, he mentioned you wanted a library card. Did you get one?"

"Yes Miss Jeannie. Mr. Matt talked to this nice lady. She said I could take these books home, but I have to keep them nice so someone else can use them when I'm done."

"What were the other books about?" Darrell asked.

"One is about ducks and the other is about fishing. Mister and I are going fishing when it gets nice out."

"Harrington sounded like he wanted you to go fishing with him too," Darrell grinned. "Did you two make plans yet?"

Clarence shook his head, "Not yet. I need to sleep on it. Do you go fishing, Mr. Darrell?"

"Not often. My brothers do, Sammy and Joey. I'll introduce you to them. Would you like that?"

"I don't know. Maybe," Clarence rubbed the piece of leather he was working on. "My Dad said that a guy has to be careful of people. You can't trust most of them."

"I know it is only my word for it, but Sammy and Joey are trustworthy," Jeannie said. "And they are fun too."

Clarence studied her, "I'll think about it and talk it over with Jackson and Mister. Okay?"

"Sounds good," Darrell nodded. "Let me know."

"A guy has to think. I tried to think a lot about this one thing. Mr. Matt told me that I should ask you and I talked it over with Jackson. I tried to think about it, but it just made me worried."

"What's that, Clarence?" Jeannie asked.

"Well, Mr. Matt said you could help me figure out those marks in books. If I learn them, I can read the whole library and know stuff. Then I won't be dumb anymore. Can you do that, Miss Jeannie?" Clarence asked seriously.

"I would be happy to help you get a start reading well. Then you can read as much as you like," Jeannie said. "But Clarence, you aren't dumb. I already know that. We can start as soon as you want. I would love to do that. Deal?"

Clarence thought and then reluctantly shook her outstretched hand, "Okay, but I'm no good at it. Mr. Matt said you won't yell at me, will you?"

"No. We can do it without yelling," Jeannie grinned. "I don't yell that much."

Darrell chuckled, "Except if you forget to take your boots off at the door! I did it once and boy, did I get yelled at!"

Clarence giggled, "You are grown up."

Darrell pretended to scowl, "What's that got to do with it?"

"You're teasing, right?"

"Yup," Darrell nodded. "Well look it here, gang. We got this whole saddle done in short order! It looks pretty fine, don't you think?"

The other two looked it over and then they all congratulated themselves. As they put the saddle on the rack, Jeannie asked, "Are we going to do another one, or milk?"

Darrell looked at the time, "One more and then we should probably milk. Matt won't be here to help and I don't know when Joallyn will be home from work tonight."

Clarence got worried, "I need to go home, Mr. Darrell. Mister will need me."

"We'll call him right after we finish this saddle. Okay?"

After they put the second saddle away, they picked up their cleaning things.

"What do you say, shall we go to the house? Jeannie and I are invited over to Schroeder's for supper tonight. I would love it if you could help us do chores and then we can all go over to Schroeders. If you don't want to, I can take you home right away."

"I would help you, but Mister probably misses me."

"Shall we call him at the house?" Darrell asked. "We can check out how everything is going?"

"Okay. If he doesn't need me, I could help you. As long as it doesn't take too long."

"I promise it won't, but you check with Elton first," Jeannie said.

Darrell dialed the number and when he handed the phone to Clarence, he teased, "Now don't hang up until you are all finished! Then I need to talk to him."

Clarence giggled, "Okay, Mr. Darrell."

Elton assured the little boy that the ladies were home, the kids were fine and that he had plenty of help with chores. He also said he thought it was a fine thing for him to help out Jeannie and Darrell. Clarence nodded and then handed the phone to Darrell.

"Hi Elton."

"My boy getting nervous?"

"A little, I think. We'll be over as soon as we get chores done and washed up. If things seem to be concerning to anyone, we will return the package right away."

"Boy, you've been watching way too many spy shows on television!" Elton chuckled. "But thanks. I appreciate it."

"We did a great job today. Got two saddles all cleaned up and even repaired a stirrup. Clarence is a good worker! I might have to hire him from time to time."

"I'm sure appreciation and thanks would go a long way with him."

"I believe you're right. Well, see you in a bit."

After washing up, they had another cookie. "Will it take me a long time to learn reading, Miss Jeannie? There are a lot of books in the library, so I have to hurry," Clarence pointed out.

"Not long. I have some workbooks here you can take home with you today! And you are a lucky duck! Diane and Matt are both teachers, so they can help, too! And know what else? Ian's wife, Ruthie, used to teach school, too."

Clarence thought a minute, "How long did it take Ginger to learn?"

Jeannie grinned, "She sorta knew how like you, but she just hated it. It only took her a few weeks to get so she could sound out the words. She was reading a lot in no time."

"I bet I can do it quicker, huh? If I really think on it!"

"You might, but don't work on it so hard you get a headache. That will ruin it all," Jeanne advised.

Darrell injected, "Besides, I think Harrington is planning on teaching you math for fishing. You need to save part of your brain for that!"

"Yah," Clarence's face lit up with a smile, "I really want to learn that!"

"Well, what do you say we go down to the barn, and I show you how we do chores here?" Darrell asked. "Elton said that the ladies put a big roast in the oven for dinner, so I don't want to miss out."

"Grandma and Missus are good cookers. Auntie was too when Dad didn't have to trade away the food. Then she couldn't cook so good."

"What is your favorite food?"

"We kids like bread because it makes you full and it's easy to carry in your pocket," Clarence answered matter-of-factly. "Clancy could even eat it. Sometimes when he was little, CJ and I would mush it up in water so it was easier for him. He didn't like that as much. Boy, does he like the jelly that Grandma makes. He can lick it off anything!"

The little guy listened carefully to the instructions that Darrell and Jeannie gave him while at the barn. He did a good job and he loved the goats.

"Mr. Darrell, I like these goats. They are like short, cranky cows, aren't they?"

Darrell chuckled, "I always liked goats, too. My first goat was named Arnold."

"How old were you when you got your first goat?"

"About five."

Clarence stood petting one of the goats, "I wonder how old I will be when I get my first goat?"

"Well, I guess that would depend on how soon you want one. I know that Elton isn't set up to keep goats, but I bet he would let you keep a kid if you had one."

"I'm only a boy. I don't have kids yet. I need to smoke and get a wife first!"

"Smoke?"

"Yah, the ceremony pipe," Clarence responded.

"Oh good, you had me worried." Darrell chuckled, "No, a kid is a baby goat."

Clarence got a quizzical expression, and looked to Jeannie, "Is he funning me?"

"No. That's what they are called."

"Oh," Clarence continued to pet the goat. "Maybe if I save my money in my savings, I will have enough to buy a kid before I am old. Huh?"

"Most likely," Darrell smiled. "Or you could earn it. You could work for me sometimes and then I could write down your hours. When you get enough hours, you could pick out a kid. Of course, Elton would have to agree."

"Really? You would let me do that? I would love that, if the other kids would be okay. You know, I have to keep an eye on them."

"We heard that," Jeannie acknowledged. "Let's talk it over with Elton and Nora to see what they say. Besides, you will have to keep up your schoolwork."

"Miss Jeannie, can't you just learn me? I can help Mr. Darrell and not go to school. I pretty much hate that."

"Sadly, you can't, but I know a secret. Want to know what it is?"

"I s'pose."

"You will be in my class at school! I will be your teacher this year! So, it will be like you said, except we will do it there instead of at home. What do you say?"

Clarence thought, "Why do we have to do it there?"

"Because they got more books there, sports and besides there are a lot more kids around."

"What kind of sports?"

"Like basketball, football—all that stuff."

"I don't know about that basketball. I don't know how to play it," Clarence stated. "I tried to do it once at my school and made a mess of it."

"I know how to fix that," Darrell said. "You and I can go over to Harrington's. He has a basketball hoop and everything!"

Just like that, Clarence started to cry. Jeannie and Darrell were both dumbfounded. Jeannie went over to him and put her arms around him. "What is it, Clarence? What is wrong?"

"My Dad said he loved that stuff. We never had a hoop and he had to trade away our basketball. He didn't get his money for whiskey, so he traded it to Mr. War Cloud. It took the basketball and our bat. But my Dad said we would have just got hurt with it anyway."

"That is too bad, Clarence. I am pretty sure that Harrington will be careful and you won't get hurt. I bet your Dad would be glad if you got to play. I know it makes you sad, but you are supposed to enjoy your life even if your Dad is gone. Okay? There is nothing wrong with that. That is what God wants us to do."

"But Jackson says we need to help each other. That is one of our tribe's virtues."

"I know, but we can help folks and still have fun. You know what? Sometimes the most fun is when you help someone!" Darrell added.

"It's kind of fun helping you," Clarence nodded.

"Well, when you are finished with that goat, let's go feed the horses. I heard from Kevin that you are pretty good with a pitch fork."

"Yah," Clarence giggled. "Mr. Kevin showed me how. I like pitching straw better than manure."

Darrell nodded, "I agree with you there!"

32

After chores, they cleaned up and returned to Schroeder's. Clarence's feet barely touched the front steps as he flew into the house. He was so excited to get home that he never even left the door open for Jessups. He gave Elton a big hug. Elton looked at him and asked, "Where are Darrell and Jeannie?"

The child's eyes got huge, "Oh no! I forgot! I left them outside."

He quickly ran to the door and they were taking off their overshoes in the mudroom. "I ran so fast that I forgot!"

"Thanks a lot, you dirty bird!" Darrell laughed, "And you forgot to take off your overshoes. You may get yelled at!"

Clarence looked at Darrell and got the joke, "Yah, huh?"

"I don't know there buddy, I'm beginning to wonder if you like me!"

"Oh yes, Mr. Darrell, I really do! I even think I can trust you, but I get too excited! I didn't try to be mean."

Darrell messed up his hair, "That's fine Clarence. Not to worry, you weren't mean. But let's go in, okay?"

"Okay," Clarence opened the door and let Jeannie go in first. "Sorry Miss Jeannie."

"It's cool, Clarence."

Elton greeted them. "Hi. Did my boy behave?"

"He did. He is a neat guy," Darrell smiled.

"We enjoyed his company," Jeannie said. "Oh, I have the books here for him to study up on his reading and also, his library book is in there."

Nora took the books, "Thank you. Is there anything that he needs to do tonight?"

"No. I will give him some pages tomorrow."

"You better put them up in your room, Clarence."

"Yes, Missus."

Jeannie watched him gather his books carefully and leave the room. "When is he starting school?"

"We are going to register them on Monday, so I imagine they will start on Tuesday."

"Okay. I'm looking forward to having him in my class. That will work out very well for both him and me," Jeannie said. "He asked me today to help him with his reading. We'll have him caught up in no time. CJ will be in Denise's first grade class, same as Charlie."

Andy shook his head, "I think you should send her a jug of booze, Dad! I tell you, Marty and I had a day with those two!"

Darrell grinned, "Fun, huh?"

Elton could hardly contain himself, "Oh, that's just because you two thought people should follow directions!"

"Not really," Andy said. "I gave up on that yesterday, and Marty had within an hour. But they never quit or even slow down! I almost collapsed before they went outside to move the snowdrift. When I was a kid, I was never like that!"

Elton, Nora and Grandma just laughed. Andy grumbled and left the kitchen, "I don't care what you say, I know I wasn't that bad!"

"So, where are the beauty shop girls?" Jeannie giggled.

"They will be here in a minute. Annie is getting them all dressed up in their new dresses. Clarissa keeps bobbing her head back and forth and saying it is so light! I bet it is though. All her thick hair must have weighed a ton." Nora smiled, "And Kitten keeps fluffing her Pixie cut. She really likes it."

"I noticed that CJ had his hair cut, but not Clarence?" Jeannie asked.

"No," Nora said. "He was very upset even thinking about it. He said his Dad wore his hair long, so he was going to also. Poor kid; he's pretty lost."

"He talks about his Dad a lot. He was his idol," Jeannie said. "Even though some of the stuff he told made me want to bat the man around."

Nora nodded, "I know, but he was still his father. Clarence loved him and looked up to him. I want to thank you kids for taking so much time with him. That will help him a lot."

"No need to thank us," Darrell said as he swiped a crunchy piece of beef from the end of the roast. "He is a good kid. Oh, I need to talk to you guys about hiring him. He would like to have a goat kid and I told him that he could earn it. What do you say?"

"Would he really be helpful?" Elton frowned. "Neither he nor I would like you to just make up a job for him."

"No, I'm not. It would be nice to have him help with chores on Tuesday and Thursday night, the days I work in at the Cheese Factory. Matt and Jeannie have to do them alone most to the time. Joallyn rarely gets home before six. We have plenty of help in the mornings; it is just the evenings. We are going to start calving and kidding in a couple weeks. That is when we will really need help. I was wondering, if he is settled by then, if he could come home with Jeannie after she drops off Diane. We would bring him home after chores. He was a big help tonight."

"Or he could stay for supper and then he and I could work on his reading. Please think about it," Jeannie smiled. "Or a similar plan."

"Sounds like a good idea," Elton said. "What do you think, Nora?"

"Yes, I think it would be good. I also think it would be good for him to start getting a bit of a life of his own. CJ and Charlie are going to be getting things ready for the chicks about then. Say Jeannie, do you know anything about the Kindergarten that Maddie Lynn goes to?"

Jeannie burst into a big smile, "I was going to mention that to you. Mrs. Swenson does a great job and her students do well. It would be a great start for Clarissa. Is that what you were thinking?"

"Yes."

"I would recommend it. It would good for her to get into the swing of things. Also, we could find out if she has any difficulties we need to see to. She seems pretty adjusted."

"She is, but she has an inferiority complex. I think that is just because she is so unfamiliar with everything. CJ will need some help in school but he actually attended more school than Clarence. Clarence was the one that always stayed home to take care of the kids. Besides, for good or bad, CJ and Charlie have crawled into the same pea pod!"

"Just what we needed, another Charlie!"

Right before dinner was on the table, Diane and Matt came home from the rehearsal. Darrell asked, "How did rehearsal go?"

Matt nodded as Diane went upstairs to change into her jeans. "Good, I guess. I feel like the batboy in the major league playoff! Bart and Diane do the work. They know what they are doing. I think it looks pretty good."

"I hope so," Jeannie said. "We have our tickets for Friday night, so we are expecting great things!"

"What do you do at this hearse thing?" Clarence asked.

"Rehearsal. We practice the show that we are going to put on. You guys will get to see it. I think your tickets are for Friday night too. I hope you will like it. Do you like musicals?"

Clarence grimaced, "I don't know what that is, Mr. Matt. Do you think I will?"

"I think you might! Katie is in the show. She sings and dances."

"Like a pow-wow?"

"Not quite like that."

"I talked to Miss Jeannie and she is going to help me read the library. She said she won't yell. Isn't that cool?"

"It really is. Diane and I will help you as much as we can once we get finished with the show. What did you do today?"

"I went over to Mr. Darrell's and he showed me how to take care of some tack. Guess what? I might get a job. Mr. Darrell says I can earn a goat baby. I will let you pet it, okay?"

"Well thanks, Clarence. What kind of a job?"

"Mr. Darrell cooks cheese some days and wants me to help you and Miss Jeannie milk. He said it will be real busy when the nannies get their kids and the cows are . . . . What is it?"

"Calving," Darrell answered. "On Tuesday and Thursday, after school you can come to my house and then help do chores before you go home. Elton and Nora said we could work out the details. So, you will have a helper, Matt. Think that is a good idea?"

Matt put his arm around Clarence, "I think it is a fine idea. I was going to ask Elton if Clarence can be my official helper keeping Grandpa's car clean."

"Would you like that?" Elton asked the boy who was smiling like crazy.

"Oh yes, Mister! Mr. Matt and I talked about it this morning! I would like it a lot!"

"Then I think that you should, but you have to listen to Matt! No goofing off."

"I'm not as much of a lunk head as CJ," Clarence pointed out.

"Ah! But are you a lizard head?" Elton teased.

Clarence laughed, "Not so much."

That night, after his bath, Clarence had a long talk with his stepbrother. "Jackson, Mr. Darrell said his brothers are trusty. Do you know them?"

"Which ones? He has a large family. Was he talking about Sam and Joe?"

"Yah, that's them. He said they go fishing, and if I wanted he would show me to them to see if we could go together."

"They are the best fisherman I know. You would be a lucky fellow if they let you come along!"

"For sure?"

"Yup."

"Could a guy trust them?"

"Most definitely! I thought you were going fishing with Harrington and Elton?"

Clarence shrugged, "I guess lots of guys go fishing, huh? Will that make Mister sad?"

"Not at all. He wants you to have a lot of friends."

"Will it be okay with the kids? I should probably stay home with them. What if they need me and I am gone? I know how I felt when I needed you and you were at the war place. I don't want them to worry."

"Look Clarence," Jackson put his arm around his little brother, "I know Mom and Dad always told you to watch out for the kids, but you and I need to talk about that."

Clarence studied his brother's face, "Why?"

"Remember when Auntie came to stay at the house?"

Clarence nodded.

"Did you have to watch the kids so much when she was there?"

"No. She and I both did it."

"It is the same here. We all watch the kids. It is good for the kids and for you! CJ is doing things with Charlie and they are busy. Clarissa will be starting Kindergarten with Maddie Lynn. They will do stuff together then. Look, Claudia and Miriam play together!"

"But those guys don't watch out for them."

"Yes, they do some. If Claudia was bleeding or something, Miriam would get help. Right?"

"I s'pose."

"And if CJ got hurt . . . ."

Clarence started to giggle, "Charlie wouldn't be able to get him help, because he would be in trouble too! They are both pretty wacky!"

Jackson laughed, "You might be right about that, but you know what I mean."

Clarence thought quietly, "So, it is okay for me to earn a kid goat and help Mr. Matt, huh? You and me can make sure that the kids have someone with them to help them. Right?"

"Right. So, relax."

"What about taking care of our tiyospaye?"

"That is part of it. We need to make certain that they are safe and then let them learn to do things and make friends on their own. That is also one of our virtues . . . . woksape (*WOK-sah-peh*) or wisdom. It is good for you to learn to make your own life, too! We all have to. Otherwise, we can't grow up to be strong."

"I didn't know that. Do you think that Dad knew that?"

"I know he did. He would have probably had you start doing it pretty soon himself, because he knew you had to grow up."

"Oh, maybe he didn't because he died first, huh?"

"That might be, Clarence." Jackson hugged him, "Anyway, I'm very glad you had a nice day."

"I did Jackson. Ahh, should I go to Mr. Pastor's thing tomorrow? Are you going?"

"I plan to, if Zach says I'm well enough. Kevin is taking CJ, Clarissa and Claudia to Sunday School at nine. I'll go to church later. Which are you going to do?"

Clarence shrugged, "I'll go with you. Okay?"

"Okay. You better get some sleep now. Good night, Clarence. Hey Clarence? I love you a lot. I'm proud to be your brother."

Clarence looked at Jackson in surprise and gave him a huge hug, "Me too."

33

Grandpa only got up once during the night. Elton and Clarence both heard him at the same time and went to the kitchen. He wanted some cereal, so Elton fixed it for him. Clarence sat beside him at the table and drank some juice while the old man talked. "You must still be smoking that pipe, huh?" Grandpa asked. "You're still short. Probably you might want to quit that. Look at Elton. He didn't and he's still short. You want to be tall like me, don't you?"

"Yes sir."

"Isn't he the best guy, Elton?" Grandpa asked as Elton put the cereal box away.

"He is. He got a job now. Did you know that?"

"Really?" the old man grinned at the kid, "Does your boss know you are short?"

"Yes, he knows. It is Mr. Darrell. I am going to help him milk goats."

"Honest job. I always had cows, but goats are okay. Is he paying you a lot?"

"He is going to write down the hours that I work and when I get, what did he say Mister? How many hours?"

"After you work eighteen hours, you can pick out a baby goat. As soon as it quits drinking from its mom, then you can bring it home. Isn't that great, Lloyd? He will be a real business man and farmer!"

"And know what else, Grandpa? I have a saving account!" the little boy beamed.

"Why, you'll be buying this place soon, huh? I didn't know you were going to sell it, Elton. Where will I live when you buy it?"

"You can live with me," Clarence said.

"Hear that, Elton? I can still live here! He is a fine brother! Don't you think?" Grandpa asked.

"It sounds like it. Are you finished with your cereal now?"

Clarence cleared the table while Elton walked Lloyd to his room and put him back to bed. Then he came back into the kitchen, "Are you excited about your new job, Clarence?"

Clarence nodded, "Do lots of kids have jobs? I never knew anybody that had a job but Uncle Bear."

"Aunt Mabel's son has a job. Adam, I think is his name, right?"

"Oh yah. But my Dad said that he thought he was better than everybody else because of it. I kind of liked him, but Dad was usually right about that kind of stuff."

"I suppose. I liked him. You know Clarence, people sometimes decide they don't like someone before they know them very well. Maybe your Dad just didn't get the chance to know Adam very well."

"I guess. Dad mostly talked to Spotted Calf. He was the only one that he really liked. Did you know that Spotted Calf yelled at his wife something awful and then Dad would. Then they would both laugh and laugh. Dad yelled at both my Moms and Auntie. He said they were dumb. But I know that Missus and Grandma aren't dumb. You guys never yell at them."

"Clarence, if we yelled at these ladies, we would be picking buckshot out of our rears!" Elton laughed. "I think your Dad was wrong about that. I don't think that your moms were dumb either and I know Auntie isn't. A person should never yell at folks. It never makes them like you any better and besides, all you do is scare them. Nobody thinks good when they are scared. They make more mistakes."

Clarence thought, "I know I don't think good when I get scared. I hated it when I got yelled at for school stuff. You're right about that. I have to sleep on the rest."

"Okay, let's get some sleep. Pepper's alarm clock will be going off before long!"

"Mister, do you think the other kids will worry if I have a job?"

"No. We can talk to them about it though. Would you feel better about it then?"

"That's a good idea."

Clarence took Elton's hand and they walked down the hall together. When they got to Jackson's room, Clarence pulled Elton down and said, "I think you are doing good for a dad. I'm glad us kids gave you a chance."

Elton hugged the boy, "Well, so am I. I'm proud you are my son. Sleep tight."

The alarm rattled the roof at the Schroeder farmhouse, and soon all the residents gathered in the kitchen staring at the family coffee pot. Even little Clancy, who toddled out with his afghan that he got from Grandma and his stuffed wolf, stood there in his blanket sleeper staring blankly at the coffee pot. After a few boring minutes, the little guy sat down on his blanket and sucked his thumb while he watched the coffee pot.

Grandma was making hot chocolate and Nora was getting the thermoses ready for the milkers. When the pot quit perking, everyone was there holding out their cups while Andy filled them. Annie poured hot chocolate for the younger ones.

CJ took a drink of his chocolate and asked, "Mister, how old were you when you got to drink coffee?"

Elton blinked, "I never thought about it. I guess five."

CJ's eyes shot wide open, "Then me and Clarence should be drinking it too."

"And me too," Clarissa spouted in exasperation. "Why do you always forget me?"

"I didn't forget you! You don't make no difference!"

Clarissa threatened, "I should whack you a good one!"

"CJ, your sister matters a lot, so don't ever say that." Nora intervened. "Clarissa, it isn't a good idea to go around whacking people,"

"But Missus, he isn't a people; he's my brother!"

Andy laughed, "Boy, if she doesn't sound like Pepper!"

"Who is Pepper?"

"She is Andy's sister. She will be home in a couple weeks to meet you," Annie explained. "She lives in another town with her husband, Chris."

"Oh, so she's old like you," Clarissa nodded. "Will I like her?"

Annie giggled, "I think you will. She knows what it is like to have big brothers."

"Do you, Miss Annie?"

"Yes, I have two big brothers, Conrad and Travis."

"Sometime can I get to see them?"

"One day soon, probably when it is nicer out."

"Oh Clarence," Nora smiled. "I got that calendar and after chores, I can show you how it works. We can talk to Elton about when we are going to Pine Ridge? Okay?"

"Pilamaya. I almost forgot about it, I did so much stuff." Then he looked at her with an odd smile, "I did a really lot of stuff, didn't I?"

Nora gave him a quick hug, "You really did. Say, we need to try on your clothes we got you for school. CJ tried his on. You also got a suit for good. You can wear it for church. Did you decide if you are coming with us today?"

"If Mr. Zach says Jackson can go to church, I'll go with him."

"What about Sunday School? The little ones, except Clancy are going. You'd be in the same class as Ginger."

"No, I don't think that's a good idea," Clarence scrunched up his face. "Ginger and school? No way!"

Elton rescued the situation, "I'm thinking I need to get my milkers down to the barn, or none of us will make it to church."

Kevin didn't help with chores because he and Carrie were running late. Their little baby, Holly, fussed all night, so they didn't want to put her in the nursery at church. They were going to bring her to Schroeders while they taught Sunday School. They said they would pick up the other kids before they went and check them into their classes.

While the chores were going on, Zach stopped over. He said that Jackson could go to church, but thought it was wise to keep Clancy home yet another week. Grandma was going to stay home with him and baby Holly.

Clarence was very pleased with his calendar and Elton, Nora and he marked off the days since he had been there. They decided that for certain, they would go to Pine Ridge on Memorial Day.

"What is Memorial Day?" The little boy asked as he looked at his calendar.

"That is the day when we remember the soldiers who died in all the wars. It is also a day to remember those we love who have died before us," Nora said. "We fix up their graves and put flowers on them."

Clarence nodded emphatically, "That would be good. We can fix up Dad's grave too, huh? Jackson, will they have those stone things?"

"Yes, the headstones should be in place. We'll plan on taking care of my Mom and Dad's graves, and your Mom and Dad's too. We have to think on if we want a bush, or just plants. Maybe we just want to put flowers on them."

"My Mom liked those winter flowers. You know, there were some by the hill to the creek. They have a name like being dead." Clarence tried to explain.

"Hm. That hill had some prairie roses on it. Are those the ones?"

"No. I know what those are. These are the winter ones. You know, the ones that croaked!"

Nora giggled, "Do you mean crocuses, Clarence?"

"Yah, I think that what they are called."

"Oh yah, they were over by the big rock, huh?" Jackson said. "I like them too."

"Me, too." Nora smiled. "I'm glad you told me Clarence. I will order some bulbs so we can plant them on your Mom's grave. Would you like that?"

Clarence shrugged, "I know Mom will like it."

"Then that is what we will do."

Diane and Annie got the girls ready for Sunday School. They were excited that they could wear their new 'for good' dresses. Annie helped Kitten pick out her dress. She chose a dark green cotton one with ruffles on the long sleeves and the bottom of the skirt. Her anklets were white with a tiny green design on them and she had new patent leather shoes. She even brushed her own hair, with Annie's help.

The little girl giggled a lot while she got dressed and was having a lot of fun. Then she gave Annie a big hug and ran off to her stepbrother. She climbed up on his lap and hugged him so hard it almost hurt. Jackson couldn't have been more pleased. He gave Annie a kiss on the cheek. "You have no idea how happy this makes me!"

Annie smiled, "I think I do. Come on, Kitten. Let's go show Grandma."

Clarissa jabbered the whole time that Diane helped her get dressed. She picked a soft one. It was a dark blue velveteen with a white crocheted collar and cuffs. The three quarter sleeves were slightly full, while the skirt

233

was a soft pleat. She wore her white tights and new shiny black patent leather 'maryjane' shoes.

Diane brushed her curls and then they put a dark blue velvet bow in her hair. "You are beautiful, Clarissa. Aren't you excited?"

Clarissa sat on the edge of the bed, "Can you come with me, Miss Diane? What if I get sad for everybody?"

"I would love to come with you, if you like?" Nora said as she came in the room. "Diane goes to church with Matt. I would be very happy to go with you on your first day."

"Will the other kids have their mommies there too?"

"No. Usually only on the first day, but that doesn't matter. We want you to be okay while you are there."

"What about CJ?"

"Elton asked him, but he said he was going to be with Charlie. So he is cool. Claudia is going to be in the same class that Kevin and Carrie teach. I will go with you."

"Clarence would be mad at me if I'm a cry baby. We have to be brave. Will it be a long time?"

"An hour. That is as long as we did chores this morning," Diane explained. "Not long at all."

"Will Miss Carrie show me where to go?"

"She or Kevin can. I'll just come with you. Okay?"

"I think I can be okay. I'm a big girl, right? I won't cry."

"Will you be worried? Because we want you to have fun," Nora pulled Clarissa on her lap.

"Does Ginger go alone?"

"Yes," Diane said, "But she has gone many times. On her first time, she had someone with her."

"I will go alone. I'll try to not to be a scaredity cat. Grey Hawks can't be sooky calves."

Nora got up and set Clarissa on the bed, "You wait right here. I got just the thing for you."

A few minutes later, Nora returned with a single pearl necklace. "Here, Sweetheart. You wear my pearl necklace to remind you it will be okay. If you start to get worried, just feel it and remember that. Okay? If you get too scared, just go to the room where Carrie and Kevin are. No one will mind."

Clarissa held her breath while Nora put her necklace around her neck. "It is so beautifuler. I'll take good care of it, heart promise."

Diane kissed her cheek, "You know Clarissa, if I ever have a little girl, I'd like her to be just like you."

Clarissa giggled, "Why do you need a different one? You got me already!"

Diane laughed, "You're right about that!"

Elton helped CJ and Clarence get dressed. He explained to them that men wore their suits to church and Sunday School. They were cool with that until it came to the neckties. With Elton's help, Clarence finally got his tied. After several attempts, the three decided that CJ should wear the clip-on bowtie. It would be less upsetting for everyone.

When they came downstairs, Nora took a picture of all four kids in the Sunday School clothes. CJ's tie was already crooked. When Andy asked how it went, Elton just crossed his eyes. "It was like putting a corset on a gerbil!"

Jackson was so proud of his Steps. He told them all to be good, not worry and have fun. The girls nodded, but CJ frowned. "Jackson! It won't work! If I be good, I can't have fun."

Jackson shook his head, "Just be good. Okay, CJ?"

CJ grumped, "I wish I could have fun."

"You might accidentally," Jackson grinned. "Just don't try to."

Nora gave each kid a nickel for offering and Jackson explained it to them. Nora explained to Carrie and Kevin that girls' nickels were in their little handbags and about Clarissa's unease with the situation.

"I can go check on her from time to time." Carrie offered, "Will that be okay, Clarissa?"

Clarissa smiled, "Will the other kids think I'm being a sooky calf? I don't want them to think that!"

"They won't. No one will even notice," Kevin assured her. "Here is Holly's stuff and you guys get your coats on. Are you not coming, Clarence?"

"I'll help watch Holly. I'm a pretty good babysitter. I babysitted these guys. I know to hold her head so it doesn't fall over and I can make her burp. I know how to make her quit crying, too."

235

"How's that Clarence? I wish I knew how," Carrie asked as she held her fussy baby.

"I'll show you," Clarence said with confidence.

He sat down and held out his arms for the baby. Carrie put Holly in his arms and he adjusted her on his lap. Then he put his knuckle in her mouth and the little girl eagerly sucked on it. He started to sing a Sioux song softly. She closed her eyes and quit fussing almost immediately.

Carrie and Kevin looked at each other in amazement. Kev asked, "Hey, want to spend your nights at our house?"

"I can sometimes, but I have to help Mister with Jackson and Grandpa."

"I know, but you do a good job with Holly!"

Clarence held Holly for a bit until she was sleeping soundly and then Grandma put her in her crib. When they came back into the hall, Grandma asked, "How did you learn to do that?"

"I figured it out. It didn't work so good with Clarissa, but my fingers were littler then. Babies are like puppies and stuff. You just need to pat their butts and stick something in their mouth. I don't mind changing their pants, but I don't like it when they up it. If they up, I up it, too. Then it's just awful!"

After Sunday School, Kev and Carrie brought some very excited kids home. The kids were babbling with joy when they came in with their papers. Claudia had a great time. She thrust her papers at Jackson and then clambered on his lap to show him her work. Kev said that she sat next to Gopher and they had a good time pasting cotton balls on the colored paper to make baby lambs.

CJ was very excited that he met some guys Charlie showed to him. They said he could hang out with them at school, so that was even better! He told all about how they watched the hand puppets and then stuck their pieces of flannelgraph on the board.

Clarissa had colored a paper and told about the song that they had learned. She really liked the other kids and her teacher. She thought it was great but was going to tell Diane that it didn't take as long as doing chores. She said it went by really, really fast.

Then she whispered to Nora, "I took care of your necklace. Can you take it off now, so I don't break it?"

"I sure will. I was thinking, we should put it in a special place so you can wear it again for something important. In fact, I have a jewelry box that you could have for your very own to keep. Then you can put it in my jewelry drawer. Would you like that?"

"I would love it the mostest. It is the beautifuler neckace in the whole world, huh? We can share it. I'll be very careful, heart promise."

"Okay Sweetheart. Let's go put it away. I need you to promise you won't wear it unless you talk to Elton, Grandma or me about it first. Okay?"

"I won't Missus. I don't know how to hook it anyway."

Elton dropped Nora and Grandma off at the front of the church before he took the vets around to the side door. Annie had to leave for work, so she wasn't along. Andy and Jackson went in the side door and got seated. Clarence rode with Elton while he parked the car. While they were walking to the front door, Clarence said, "Will I feel dumb in there?"

"I don't think so. There'd be no reason for you to feel that way. We will just go in and sit down. We will show you what to do when you need to do something. Okay?"

Clarence reached up and took his hand, "Pilamaya Mister."

"For what?" Elton asked.

"Cause."

34

They met Nora and Grandma and walked in together. The place seemed huge to the little boy. He saw a few people he recognized and then he saw Pastor Byron in his clerical robe. He wiggled Elton's hand and pointed, "Mr. Pastor is wearing a night gown! Look, Mister."

Elton knelt down, "It's like his Holy Man robe. Pastor Marvin is wearing, one too. All the ministers do when they have a service. Want to tell him hello?

Clarence shook his head shyly, "No. I don't want him to see me."

"Why not? You look mighty fine to my notion."

But it was too late, Pastor Byron had seen him. He came over to where they were standing and leaned down by Clarence, "Hello. I'm glad that you came today. I was looking for you. I hope you enjoy it."

Clarence grimaced, "I guess I will. Jackson said if I don't like it, I don't need to come back."

"Sounds fair to me," Byron smiled and then motioned for Pastor Marvin to come over. "This is another tiyospaye. His name is Pastor Marvin. Marv, I would like you to meet Clarence Grey Hawk."

The younger dark-haired pastor shook Clarence's hand, "I've heard a lot about you. I'm glad to meet you."

"Who said stuff about me?" Clarence asked.

"I hear that you are going fishing with Harrington. His wife is my helper at the church. Have you met her? Ruthie?"

"No, not yet. Harrington said I will. She helps you? What does she do?"

"She types and answers the phone."

"I always hang up on Mr. Darrell by accident. I think I get too excited," Clarence explained.

"That can happen," Marv grinned. "I hope you enjoy church today and if you want, you can come by and visit me at the church someday. I would love to show you around more."

"Me? Why would you want to do that?"

Marv shrugged, "Why not?"

Clarence frowned and then smiled, "Okay, if Mister says. I have to sleep on it first."

"Good idea," Marv stood straight, "Well Byron, let's get this show on the road."

The family went down the aisle toward where Jackson and Andy were sitting. Katie had come to join them and was sitting next to Jackson. She gave Clarence a big smile, "Hi. How are you this morning?"

"Okay," Clarence said with a grin.

When they got settled, Clarence was sitting between Elton and Nora. He looked around for people he knew. He noticed when Darrell and Jeannie came in and waved excitedly at them. Darrell waved back and Jeannie winked. Then horror of horrors, Ginger came up beside them and sat between them!

Clarence couldn't take his eyes off the situation. He poked Elton's arm and whispered, "Ginger is sitting by Mr. Darrell and Miss Jeannie! Why is she doing that?"

Elton smiled, "Darrell is her uncle. She sits with them quite often."

Clarence couldn't hide his disappointment. "I thought she went to that school thing. I didn't know she was going to be here, too!"

"A lot of kids go to both Sunday School and Church. You guys can too after you get more used to it."

"I might not. I didn't know she would be here," Clarence scowled.

"Everyone is welcome in church, Clarence. God isn't as fussy as people are about that. He wants us all to come."

Clarence raised his eyebrow as if taking exception to that, when he saw Ken come in and sit by a girl. He poked Elton again, "Who is Ken sitting by?"

"Her name is Becky Oxenfelter. You will meet her at dinner after church."

"Is she tiyospaye?"

"Yes. Oh look, there is Harrington."

Clarence's head swiveled around and he watched as Harrington and a pretty short lady came in. Harrington saw him and waved. Then he brought the lady over and introduced him, "Ruthie, this is Grey Hawk. This is my wife, Ruthie."

"Hello Miss Ruthie. This is Mister Elton."

"Oh, I know him, Clarence. He is one of my best buddies," Ruthie giggled. "Mind if we sit behind you guys?"

"Is it okay, Mister?"

"I think it will be fine, as long as they don't cause trouble," Elton chuckled.

Most of the service, Clarence was wide-eyed and trying to take it all in. He must have poked Elton a million times, whispering questions to him. Elton answered them all quietly and when Pastor Marvin talked, he put his arm around him so Clarence could lean on him. Clarence liked that.

After church, Charlie came bouncing up, "Hi Clarence! I saw you but I had to sit with my Mom today. Some time, we can sit by side each other, huh?"

"I guess, if Mister says."

"Cool. I'm coming to your house for dinner now, as soon as my Mom gets her baked bean stuff. Do you like that?"

Clarence shrugged, "I guess."

"She puts brown sugar on it. That's the part I like. I leave the beans because they taste like vegetables!" Charlie crossed his eyes. "Come on Katie. We gotta go now."

Katie gave Jackson's hand a squeeze and then said, "See you all in a bit."

On the way out of the sanctuary, Pastor Byron and Pastor Marv shook hands with Clarence. Byron bent down and whispered, "What did you think? Was it okay? Think you will come again?"

Clarence shrugged, "It was okay. I can come again, I s'pose."

Pastor Marv gave him a big smile, "I'm so glad! We'll see you next week then! And don't forget to sleep on it about coming over so I can show you around."

"Okay, I will."

35

"Well Clarence, what did you think of church?" Jackson asked on the way home.

"The singing part was kinda alright, but I didn't know the words. Hey Jackson, I didn't know that God is a sheep?"

"Why do you think that?" Jackson frowned.

"Cause this Jesus guy is God's kid, right? They always call him a lamb; so then God must be a sheep huh?"

"Ah gee Clarence, maybe we should ask Pastor Byron," Jackson slithered out of having to give an answer.

Nora boldly stepped in, not fully recognizing the treachery, "I think it is because Jesus never sinned or made mistakes, like a baby sheep."

Clarence's eyes got huge, "You mean he knew all the answers! About everything? Wow! I bet he read the whole library, huh? I thought sheep are dumb! Only turkeys are dumber than sheep. I s'pose it's a good thing he isn't a turkey!"

"Good work, Mom," Andy snorted in hysterics while she gave him a scathing look.

Clarence was now on a roll. Obviously, the lad had paid attention to the talk about the Sermon on the Beatitudes. "That's probably why he said that the poor are rich and that stuff. Like everybody knows that if you are hungry, you don't get over it until you get some bread. He might have been a nice guy, but I don't think that he was real smart."

"I think you might want to talk to Byron or Marv about it after lunch today," Elton said.

"Besides, if everybody who is dead comes alive again, we shouldn't put them in the ground. We should keep an eye on them. Gee, what if Dad comes to life and can't get out of that hole! Boy, would he be mad about that!" Clarence rattled on, "I don't know. I think church was fun to see, but it seems pretty wacky."

Elton chuckled, "The way you described it, it certainly does! You better talk to the preachers."

"Is that Pastor Marv going to eat at our house today? Does he have kids? Did you see that Gopher girl sat with Mr. Coot? I thought you said that Harrington goes to a different church like Mr. Matt, but he was there too."

"He goes to both churches."

Clarence shook his head in bewilderment, "He sure must like it."

"Somebody must have put a nickel in you," his brother teased.

"No. I put my nickel in that dish the guy had, like Mister said."

The boys went in at the house, but Nora and Elton drove to the garage to put the car away. Neither said a word all the way to the garage. After parking the car and they got out, Nora burst into laughter! The two laughed until they had tears in their eyes. "Oh Elton, what have we done! Why didn't someone stop us before we plunged off this cliff?"

"I think they all wanted to watch us crash!" Elton put his arms around his wife and laughed some more. "You have to love it! I can't wait to hear the preachers explanations!"

"All I could think of was trying to explain Easter to these kids. There are lambs, chickens and baby ducks all over everything!" Nora giggled, "And dead people coming back to life!"

"I can't wait," he took his wife's hand as they walked to the house, "I know, let's let Charlie explain it to them!"

Everyone quickly changed their clothes and the rest of the clan started to arrive. The Steps were all in fine form, even Clancy. All of the kids knew some folks, and were quickly introduced to the others.

Clarence was very impressed to find out that Pastor Marv had a boy, Clark, who was a year older than him. He was also a friend of Charlie's. Clarissa had met Maddie Lynn, his daughter, in her class so she recognized her. The little girls took Claudia and went to play with some dolls.

Dinner was on the table by twelve-thirty and every one was just sitting down to eat when the St. Johns clergy arrived. Sister Abigail brought some scalloped potatoes and Father Landers had brought a treat for everyone.

He had made some of his famous parsley potatoes. Father Vicaro groused that they were terrible and he hoped they all got eaten, so they didn't have to take home leftovers. Father Landers just patted the old man on his shoulder and said, "Don't listen to Mr. Cheer, here. They are really very good. The only reason he is whining is because he got into them last night and ate a bunch while we were at a meeting."

Sister Abigail confirmed the situation, "Then he got all peculiar when I explained what would happen if there wasn't enough left for dinner today!"

"This woman banished me from my own refrigerator! Can you imagine that?" an indignant Vicaro howled.

Everyone cracked up, except Coot. Vicaro was his cohort in crime and they two were very sympathetic to the other's trials. "Hey," Coot asked, "Did you hear when your cast will be off?"

"Doc said in a couple weeks. I can't wait. Then I can get away from these conspirators. They have no respect for me!" the short, balding man groaned.

Bart looked at him, "You had better keep a lid on it until you get your cast off. It could become a long couple weeks!"

There weren't many rules about where a person sat in the big dining room, except that usually little kids did not sit next to each other. That had a tendency to lead to spilled food and goofing off. So, the kids regularly sat between grownups. That was more than fine with Clarence, except that when he went to sit down by Elton like he usually did, he found Little Bill beside him. On the other side was that Maddie Lynn girl. Then he went over to Jackson, but he was sitting at the end of a table and Katie was sitting next to him on the other side. He could feel himself begin to panic.

Harrington noticed and motioned for him to come sit between him and Ruthie. Clarence felt very uncomfortable and a little silly that Harrington had noticed that he had nowhere to sit. He was very quiet and determined to not make Harrington feel bad that he let him sit there.

Ruthie smiled, "Ian calls you Grey Hawk. Is that what you like to be called?"

"It's okay. I've never been called that before, but it is okay."

"Should I call you that?"

Clarence shrugged, "If you want."

"You can call me Ruthie."

"Okay, Miss Ruthie."

She giggled, "You don't have to call me Miss, just Ruthie is fine."

"Okay," Clarence mumbled.

He felt himself panicking more, like the day at that hamburger place. He looked up and noticed that Matt was watching him. Matt nodded and gave him a wink. That helped a little bit.

36

Pastor Byron said grace and then everyone started to pass the food. Clarence only took the food that he knew he liked and didn't want to try anything that he could make a mistake about. He was so nervous that he dropped his fork on the floor. When he bent down to get it, he got the corner of the lace tablecloth caught on the button his sleeve. It started to pull everything down towards him. Ian caught the cloth before it knocked everything off the table, but some of the things spilled. That was more than the kid could take. He darted out of the dining room and flew out of the kitchen. He made a beeline for the outhouse.

By the time he got there, he was crying. He decided he was never coming out until he went back to Pine Ridge. He hated everybody and everything. He wanted to go home.

In a couple minutes, there was a knock at the outhouse door, "Clarence, it's me. Could you let me in so we can talk?"

"No Mister. I'm never going back in the house. They all think I'm stupid. Harrington won't want to go fishing with me, Missus hates me cause I messed up her food. I just want to go home!" Then he cried.

Elton waited a few minutes and then said, "Clarence, either you open the door or I'll have to take it off the hinges to get in. Then you will have to fix it again before you can use it."

"You can fix it."

"No. If I have to break it because you won't let me in, I won't help you fix it."

Clarence quit crying and thought about that. Then he grumped, "Then you shouldn't break it!"

Elton laughed, "Just open the door, Hotshot. You might want this dinner roll I brought for you."

The door opened a crack, "A dinner roll? I love them."

"Open up then. I won't give it to you unless you let me in."

Clarence gave a pout, but opened the door so the man could come in.

Once inside, Elton dropped the lock on the door and sat down. "Glad you have the lid down on the hole, huh? A guy should always do that before you eat."

Clarence nodded, "You can go in and eat. I know you like your dinner."

"I thought you did, too," Elton pointed out. "Boy, are you a knot head! You shouldn't take off until after you fill your belly! It could be a long time before you get fed again!"

"You guys have food a lot. At my house, we didn't eat every day. Dad said it wasn't good to do that."

Suddenly a look of sadness overtook him. He put his arms around Elton and crawled up onto his lap. "Mister," he wept. "I just can't stand it. I mess everything up and everybody must think I'm a big dope. I hate it. Can't I just go home?"

"I will call Social Services as soon as we get to the house, if that is what you want. I promise. But I'm not so sure that is what you really want, is it? Let's think on it. First, you have your brothers and sisters here. Second, Rags and Cotton are here. Third, you have friends here."

"I don't have any friends! Nobody knows me. They all think I am dumb!"

"You tell me one person that said you were dumb," Elton insisted.

"Ah, well, you know."

"No, I don't know. Was it Matt, Andy, Harrington, Darrell? Just who did?"

Clarence stopped crying and thought. Then he broke into a smile, "I know who did! Ginger!"

"Yea gads, Man! I don't think that counts. You two were squabbling."

"But you said . . . ."

"I know. Look here, sometimes things happen. Sometimes stuff falls off the table. That happens to everybody. No one thinks anything of it, so relax. Will you? You know what happened to Ginger at the Christmas program?"

"What?"

"She was in front of the church, holding a big light on a stepladder that was supposed to be a star. She had a real big sneeze and dropped it. It smashed the baby Jesus' head to smithereens!"

246

Clarence's eyes sprung open, "Did she kill the baby?"

"No, it was a doll, but it broke it to bits. She said she was never coming down from the ladder, ever. But she did."

"It wasn't her fault, if she sneezed."

"Was it your fault the tablecloth got stuck on your clothes?"

"I didn't do it on purpose."

"Well then, there you have it. So, why are you sitting out here freezing while the dinner is in there? I don't get it."

"Cause I don't know what to do. I get so nervous. I wanted Harrington to think I was cool. Besides, I don't know those people and now they think I am stupid."

"Oh. Okay then. I guess you have to stay out here then, huh? Too bad, I think we are planning to have that birthday cake for Ginger and Ken after dinner."

"Oh yah, huh?"

"It will probably take the guys from Social Services until morning to get here to pick you up. You should have brought your coat. It could get mighty cold by morning out here."

Clarence's shoulders fell. "You know I won't stay here all night. I will go to the barn later."

"You're pretty sneaky. You know Clarence, Grandpa was very concerned when you ran off. I better go talk to him and tell him you are leaving. It would be nice if you could tell him goodbye so he doesn't worry. Hey, I have an idea. You can eat and then we will call Social Services. A guy shouldn't make a big decision on an empty stomach."

Clarence got off his lap, "Mister? Will I ever get over feeling like this?"

"Yes, you will. Before long, you'll be just fine. You have my word."

"Okay, I'll try again, if you think I should. After Missus saw the mess I made, she will want me to—."

Elton stopped him, "Absolutely wrong! I won't let you even start to think that. Nora and I want you to be with us. All the time, no matter what. You got that? You'll make me very angry if you think that we could ever send you away because of some old tablecloth. Do you understand?"

Clarence looked at him, "Yes sir."

"Good. The only thing that would make me want to send you away is if you eat my last piece of peach kuchen! Then we would have serious trouble."

Clarence giggled, "You're funny."

"Hey, I'm not the guy that ran out to the outhouse without his dinner roll!"

They two shared a happy hug and then Elton said, "Shall we give it another try?"

Clarence nodded, "Okay."

Elton took the boy's hand and said, "I sure hope we were gone long enough so they got it all cleaned up."

Everything was back in place as they sat down. Ruthie handed Clarence a new napkin and said, "I dished up your plate again. I hope I got what you wanted."

"It looks good, Mi—I mean, Ruthie. Pilamaya."

Matt smiled, "That means thank you in Sioux, right Clarence?"

"Yes, Mr. Matt."

Clarence was grateful the conversation turned to other subjects. Father Vicaro was talking about getting his cast off in a couple weeks. Matt was excited because he friend from the priesthood called. Jeff said that he got the job at the Mandan Industrial School as a counselor at North Dakota's reformatory. His new job started in May. Kincaid's had already offered him a place to stay at their house.

Andy said that one of their Army buddies would be coming for a visit in May. His name was Swede and he lived in Minnesota. He had lost an arm over in Vietnam. Jackson had received a letter from Sonny, Chicago's wife who said that all was going as well as could be expected there. His recovery was slowly progressing. He was injured in the same fire fight as the boys.

Ian asked Matt how his begonia was doing and Matt became defensive. "I told you that you are not allowed to discuss my begonia! You or Tink! You guys don't know what you are talking about. It will bloom again. I just know it."

"When was the last time that it bloomed, Matt?" Pastor Byron asked.

Matt nearly whispered, "Couple years ago."

Jeannie giggled, "It seems to have a long dormancy."

"Watch it, lady!" Matt warned. "Maybe you shouldn't discuss it either."

"I think if you want it to bloom, you might want to take it out of the laundry room and give it some sunshine," Diane pointed out. "And water."

"Yah," Matt groaned. "I will probably do that."

After dinner, the ladies cleared the table while the men had another cup of coffee and talked about politics. The kids went into the hall to get out the race cars. Clarence went with them, but before long felt out of place.

He wandered out to the living room and stood beside Elton for a little bit. Elton was visiting with Jerald and put his arm around Clarence. "Oh Jerald, Nora and I are in the market for some old nags. No rush, but by the time it gets nice out. We need an Abner type for CJ and some real gentle ones for the little girls. Clarence and Nora are going to share a horse."

Jerald Oxenfelter smiled at the young boy, "So, what kind do you like? Have you ridden a lot?"

"No, but Mr. Darrell said he would learn me how to take care of it. I promised Missus I would do the work because a pig ate her arm."

Jerald nodded, "Hm, I think Darrell was telling me that you helped him and Jeannie clean their saddles, huh? He said you do good work."

Clarence shrugged.

"I will see what I can find for you. Any preference? Tall, short, black or green?" the jovial cattle buyer teased.

Clarence giggled, "I think Missus should pick. I don't know very much about horses."

"I will speak to her then," Jerald patted his shoulder. "By the way Clarence, I haven't had the chance to welcome you to the family yet. It is good to have you here."

Clarence shrugged, "Pilamaya."

"Now that is thank you, huh?"

"Yes sir."

"Good to know."

Clarence wandered away from the table and saw Grandpa sitting in his rocking chair. He sat in the chair next to him and the old man smiled, "They are a nice bunch, don't you think?"

Clarence nodded.

"So you're buying a horse, huh? Be careful, you have to save your money. Farming costs a lot of money."

"I will, Grandpa."

Then Lloyd started talking about the war. Clarence listened and nodded a lot. The old man told him all about World War I, before he nodded off to sleep. When he was asleep, Clarence went to get Grandma. "I think Grandpa is taking his nap now."

"Thank you Clarence. It was very nice of you to visit with him. He really likes that."

Jeannie came over, "Hey Clarence, do you have time now to look at those books?"

"Okay."

"We can go to your room, okay?"

"I can show it to you."

Clarence and Jeannie went up to his room and she said, "Oh wow, Clarence! This is a cool room. Do you like it? Is the bed comfortable?"

"I don't sleep here. I have to sleep in Jackson's room so the kids don't get worried. We guys all sleeped in the same room at our house, so they don't like being far away from each other. And I help Mister with Jackson and Grandpa."

"That is very responsible of you."

Clarence frowned, "Is that a bad thing?"

"Not at all. It means you're careful and to be trusted."

Clarence smiled, "I like that word."

"So, shall we sit at your desk?"

The two got out the books and before long, Clarence could recognize all the 'A's, cursive and printed. Then Jeannie told him the sounds that it made. They looked through a few pages of a book and found a bunch of them. Clarence thought it was kind of fun.

"Okay, your assignment, or job, is to go through these three pages and circle all the A's that you find. Tomorrow, we will look them over and then I will help you figure out what sounds they might make. Okay?"

"This was kinda fun. I like A's. Should I do them now, Miss Jeannie?"

"You can or do them later. You maybe would rather visit with some of the folks downstairs."

"Miss Jeannie, I don't know about that. Those kids are okay, but they all talk about play stuff. CJ likes that, but I don't care about it. I know that everybody thinks I should, but I really don't," he bit his lip.

"Well, then find someone else to talk to! Lordie be Grey Hawk, there a tons of folks down there! You could talk to anyone you want. I know what you could do! Did you show Coot your library book about the ducks? I think he would love to see that. Have you read it yet?"

"I tried, but I just looked at the pictures."

"I can help you, if you want. Okay?"

The pair read the book and then Jeannie suggested they take it downstairs to show Coot. "Do you really think that he would like it?"

"Yes, I do. Let's go."

Clarence was nervous when he and Jeannie approached the retired FBI agent. He tapped on his arm and said, "Excuse me, Mister Coot. Jeannie said it might be okay if I showed you this book I got. I got it so I could find out about that duck pen you are going to make. Do you want to see it? You have to be very careful and not mess up the pages. The library lady says I have to keep it good."

Carl Kincaid took the book and nodded, "Well thank you Clarence. That was very nice of you to think of me when you went to the library. I will be very careful. Did you read it?"

"Miss Jeannie read it to me cause I'm not so good at that. She could read it to you too, if you ask her."

"I think we can figure it out. Will you help me look at it?"

Before long, there was a bevy of men gathered around the table talking about the ducks. Coot asked Clarence, "Could you bring me a pencil, young man?"

"I can Mister Coot, but we can't write on the pages."

"I won't, but maybe you could bring me some paper?"

Clarence ran off and returned shortly with the paper and pencil. The men figured out where to put the duck coops and how to build them. Clarence didn't say much, but was very pleased that his book was a great help. Now he was certain that he wanted to read the whole library.

37

Folks started going home and the Schroeder bunch headed down to do chores. Diane had gone over to Matt's and was going to help over there. When Elton and Clarence carried the skim milk to the pigs, Elton said, "Hey, could we sit a minute? I would like to talk to you."

Clarence made a face, "Did I do something wrong?"

"Not at all. When we talked at your thinking spot, you said you wanted me to call Social Services. Do you still want me to do that?"

Clarence sat down, "Not now. I think I am going to stay at least until Miss Jeannie can learn me to read good. I don't have a library card in Pine Ridge."

"Good thinking. Clarence, you know that tomorrow we are going to register you in school. You can't be running away from there when you get upset. So, let's talk about what you will do there, okay?"

"Will I get upset?"

"Probably, once in a while. I know I do sometimes. Now, if you get upset at school, it would be best if you would talk to Jeannie, Matt or Diane. They will all be there. If not them, then find another teacher. Okay? Can you do that for me?"

"I thought you said we could talk about it."

"I did and we can. But I won't be at school with you, so until you get home, you should talk to the those guys. If you need me, or Nora, just have them call us. One of us will be there right away, or Kevin. Will that work?"

"I guess. I don't understand why I can't learn to read at home? I learned the A's today. Miss Jeannie said I did real good."

"I know, and I was very proud of you. But school teaches all kinds of things that a guy can't learn at home. Beside, remember the rules? Oh, hey, would you like to call Uncle Bear and Auntie Mabel tonight after chores?"

Clarence beamed, "Can the other kids talk too? It would be good."

"We will do that then. So, what do you think about school?"

"If I get worried, I will talk to Miss Jeannie or those other guys, like you said. Then when I get home, we can talk about it. If it is real awful, I will ask someone to call you guys and you will come right away. Is that right?"

"Right." Elton patted his back, "You know Clarence, I am real proud of how well you are doing, but you can talk to Nora and me even if you don't do so good. That is what we are here for."

Clarence hugged him. "Did you tell CJ?"

"I did, but he said he will just talk to you if he had trouble."

"I figured." Then he got a huge grin, "That's what I am here for!"

It was a quiet evening. CJ and Andy were busy messing around with their boat and Claudia went to bed early. Clarissa and Nora were going through her dresses to figure out what she wanted to wear when she went to her Kindergarten class. Clarence went up to his room and worked in his workbook. When he was finished, he brought it downstairs. He found Elton watching television and visiting with Grandpa.

"Mister, could you look at my workbook and see if I did it right? I have to show it to Miss Jeannie tomorrow and I want to do it good."

"Sure, let's go out to the kitchen where the light is better."

Elton looked over the boy's work. He had done an excellent job and circled almost every A in the three pages. Elton showed him two that he missed and he got very quiet. Elton finished reading the page and then looked back to the boy. He had huge tears in his eyes.

"What on earth is wrong, Clarence? Why the tears?"

"I'm just dumb. Miss Jeannie will be mad that I missed those A's."

"That's nonsense. My goodness, there must have been a million A's on those pages. Look buddy, no one is perfect. I bet Miss Jeannie misses some, too. Don't do that to yourself. I'll be upset if you do. You do the best you can, and if someone has a problem with your best—tell them to go fly a kite. Hear me?"

"I don't have a kite. I don't know how to fly a kite."

"You don't have to give them the kite to fly. They have to get their own. But I will tell you what, if I get to the dime store, I'll find us some kites. Kevin is a great kite flyer and he can help us fly them. How would you like that?"

"Would the other kids be upset?"

"No. I will get them kites too."

"Should I change my A's in the book, so Miss Jeannie doesn't know I made a mistake?"

"No, that wouldn't be a good idea. She needs to know how much you know; so if you change it, you will mix her up. But what we can do, is circle those A's in a different color pencil. That way, she will know. How 'bout that?"

The night was thankfully quiet. However, when the morning alarm went off, so did Clarissa's mouth. The little girl just bubbled non-stop about her Kindergarten, Maddie Lynn and her dresses. She barely took a deep breath all through chores or breakfast.

Diane had promised to help her get dressed after breakfast and fix her hair. CJ and Clarence rolled their eyes a lot, but the grownups told them to be nice to her and not ruin her day. It was her first day of school ever! She had every right to be excited.

Nora went upstairs with her to help her comb her hair one last time. As they did, Nora asked, "Would you want to wear the necklace today?"

Clarissa looked at Nora in shock, "Aren't you coming with?"

"Of course, I am. I just wondered if you wanted the necklace too."

Clarissa was visibly relieved, "I only want to wear that when I might miss you. I won't miss you if you are with me. Missus? Did your little girl go to Kindergarten?"

"No, she didn't. We've only had it a couple of years out here. We are very lucky to have Mrs. Swenson."

"I'm a lucky girl, huh?"

"Yes, you really are," Nora smiled. "Well, we better go. Elton brought up the car for us, so we can just take off."

"Miss Diane told me to 'break a leg'. She said that is what the people in their play say for good luck," she squinted. "That is sorta wacky, but I didn't want to make her sad."

Nora giggled, "It is a little silly, isn't it? But she wanted you to have a good day."

"I know. She should have a kid, don't you think?"

"She had a little boy, but he died when he was a baby."

"Really? She never told me that. Maybe it makes her cry, huh? I don't want her to cry. Maybe we should give Clancy to her. Would she like that?"

"It works just fine this way. Besides, she thinks you are pretty special."

"Are you going to give me to her?" Clarissa worried.

"Gee Clarissa, we don't go giving people away! We all hang out together. Remember, we are all tiyospaye."

"But you gave me a heart promise that you will be my Mommy until you die. Right?"

Nora hugged the little girl, "I sure did and you can count on it. I will be your Mommy. Cross my heart."

"Good, cause I worry."

"You don't need to worry about that, ever!"

Mrs. Swenson was a tall blonde lady with a very pretty smile. She opened the door and invited Nora and Clarissa in. She took them downstairs to the Kindergarten room in her basement. It was a cheerful place. The walls were light blue and there was dark blue carpet on the floor. On one side of the wall was a huge rainbow and Clarissa was sure there were sparkles on it. There were also bunnies, baby deer and flowers. Nora told her they were from a book called Bambi. She told her they would read it to her if she wanted. She wanted.

"I fixed up a spot at the table for just you, Clarissa. That is such a wonderful name. I really like it."

"I do to. I use it all the time," Clarissa answered matter-of-factly. "Where is Missus going to sit?"

"She will sit beside you this morning. Is that okay?"

"It's a good idea. She might get worried for me."

"We wouldn't want that to happen, would we?" the teacher smiled. "The other children will be coming soon, so do you have any questions?"

"I understand that school starts at eight and is over at noon," Nora said. "Is that correct?"

"Yes and we follow the regular school schedule. If the public school has the day off, so do we. Who will be picking her up?"

"Either Elton or I. If someone else is going to, we will call you."

"Right. I don't want the children going to the wrong place. If she isn't well, I'd prefer she stay home. I don't want everyone to get sick. I see from this Social Service chart you gave me that we don't know if she had the regular childhood diseases, huh?"

"No idea. Jackson said he thought some of them had chicken pox and Aunt Mabel said they all had measles, but I don't know if they were German or red. It is all very sketchy. They had little exposure to the outside world and were mostly at their home."

"I was glad we had that talk yesterday. I will try to keep that in mind. So, I heard that you went to Sunday School yesterday, Clarissa. Did you like it?"

"It was the most funnest ever! We did pasting and coloring. Then we sang a song. It was very short. We had to quit before we even got our clothes wrinkled."

Mrs. Swenson giggled, "Oh my. Well this will be longer, I promise. So, you know Maddie Lynn Olson already?"

"She is a girl with bouncy curls! Do you know her?"

"I do. She is in this class. Isn't that nice?"

"She told me that, but I wasn't for sure. She and I both are learning that piano stuff from Miss Diane. She started before me, but Miss Diane says I am doing good. Didn't she, Missus?"

"Yes, she did."

Clarissa didn't quit talking until the other kids came in, but hardly said a word throughout class. She was happy to see Maddie Lynn, She watched everything and participated. She seemed to be having a good time. Only once, did she scoot over onto Nora's lap for a bit. After a few minutes, she went back to her chair.

After class, the kids all went home and Mrs. Swenson asked Clarissa what she thought of it.

"It was good. I think I might come back if Clarence says it is okay. He will have to sleep on it. I can tell you tomorrow."

"That sounds good. What was your favorite part?"

"The songs, and the coloring and the cutting with a scissors and . . ."

"So there were a lot of things. What didn't you like?"

"When you guys were talking about stuff I didn't know. Like that Mouse thing. It made me feel lonely for my home."

"Is that why you sat on my lap?" Nora asked. "When they were talking about the Mickey Mouse club?"

She nodded.

"Well, guess what? We get that on our television set and we can turn it on and watch it together. Would you like that?"

"I guess so."

"Good, we'll do that then. Come Clarissa, we need to go home now. The men will be looking for their dinner."

"Why? Isn't it in the kitchen? I think Grandma puts it in the kitchen."

All the way home and all through lunch, Clarissa talked a blue streak. She told everyone the whole thing; every detail. Finally, Clarence said, "Clarissa, give your mouth a nap!"

"You just can't wait to get to your school! You are mad cause I got to go first!"

"No, I'm not. I just have an earache."

38

Clarence walked reluctantly with Elton while Nora walked with CJ to the car. They began lagging back and finally Elton knelt down, "Clarence, you better check your boots."

Clarence frowned as he lifted one foot, "Why?"

"I think you stepped in some cement, huh? If you go much slower, I'll have to carry you."

Clarence gave him a dirty look, "I can walk. I really, really, really don't want to go. I told you that. I hate, hate, hate it."

"Well, I guess you can stay here until the Social Services people come to visit. Then they will take you to a different home where you might like to go to school. I thought that you liked Diane, Matt and Jeannie, but maybe you will like some other teachers somewhere else better."

Clarence was fighting back the tears and hugged Elton, "I like them alright. I just don't want to go. I hate it."

"Look Clarence, it's up to you. I can't make it be any different. I wish I could, but I can't. It's a real bearcat. I think maybe we might want to talk to Wakan Tanka or God about it. What do you say?"

Clarence shrugged. Elton stood up and yelled to Nora, "Could you and CJ bring up the car? Clarence and I have to make a quick stop at his thinking spot."

"Okay, we'll wait for you in front of the house."

Elton took Clarence's hand and walked briskly to the outhouse. Clarence wondered if he was going to get a spanking, but he didn't think that Elton said that.

They went into the outhouse and sat on either side of the hole. Then Elton took his hands and said, "Okay. Now why don't you just tell Wakan

Tanka whatever you think about this mess. And you can ask him to help you be brave and do what needs to be done."

Clarence looked at him blankly, "That is dumb. He doesn't care about that."

"Then you can tell that Jesus guy. I know for a fact that He cares. So you just tell Him about it."

The kid pulled back and crinkled one eye, "Why would He care about me?"

"Don't know, but He cares about me. My guess is that He thinks you are just as good."

Clarence giggled, "What if He is a sheep?"

"Why would you mind telling a sheep how you feel?"

Clarence rolled his eyes and started, "Hey Jesus guy, Mister said I should talk to You about this school stuff, but I don't know why. He said that You will help me, but everybody knows that sheep don't go to school. I hate school and I still hate it, but Miss Jeannie said she wants me to me come. So, if You want, I'd like it if You could make it so my dinner didn't come up and I don't want to cry there. If You can do that, I'll think it over about sheep being dumb. I really don't want to be dumb anymore. That's all."

"Amen," Elton said. "Good work. Now, Jesus can worry about it while you go to school. You don't have to worry and can have as good of a time as possible. Deal?"

Clarence shrugged, "I sure wish I wasn't born dumb. Then I wouldn't have to put all that school stuff in my head."

"That would be a good idea, huh? Well, ready to face it?"

"Yah, I s'pose."

Elton grinned, "Come on! I wonder if they know they better order some more books for their library, because you're going to read them all!"

Clarence shook his head, but took Elton's hand after they closed the door to the outhouse. "Mister, I hope you don't be sad but sometimes I think you are a little wacky."

Elton chuckled, "I've heard that all my life, my boy. Hey, if it doesn't take very long at the school, we might want to stop by the church on the way home. Pastor Marv can give you and CJ a tour of the church and then we can go over to Byron's for a treat. Marly usually has good stuff in her kitchen."

"Think it will be okay at the school?"

"You told Jesus to worry about it, so you don't have to. Remember?"

"Oh yah, I forgot."

"And it will be fine, for certain."

The family went to the school office and talked to the lady at the desk there. "We are the Schroeder's and we are here to see Mr. Palmer."

"Oh yes, he mentioned you'd be in. And these will be the new students?"

"Yes, Clarence and CJ."

"Hi boys. Let me tell Mr. Palmer that you are here."

Within minutes, they were ushered into Mr. Palmer's office. He was a pleasant looking man with a friendly way about him. He had every one sit down and then he sat at his desk. "I have been looking over the files from the Social Services. They sent up their grades and things from Pine Ridge. I have talked to Mrs. Frandsen and Mrs. Jessup. They understand the situation and are eager to help. I think the boys will be in good hands."

"We know both Jeannie and Denise and they are fine people," Elton said. "The boys both know Jeannie."

"I understand that. I hear that you know Mrs. Waggoner and Mr. Harrington, too. Is that right?"

The boys looked at each other in shock and made a face, "I don't think we know them," Clarence answered. "I met a guy named Harrington. He is going to take me fishing."

"Diane's whole name is Diane Waggoner and Matt is Mr. Harrington." Nora explained, "Diane lives with us, so we don't call her Mrs. Waggoner."

"No, I suppose not." Mr. Palmer nodded. "Boys, could you do me a favor?"

"I s'pose."

"At school, could you call them by their whole name? It might make the other kids feel left out if you call them Diane, Matt and Jeannie."

CJ answered, "Sure, Charlie already told me that. He said we can't ride to school with them either, but if we did the other kids watch us come from the parking lot."

"Charlie Ellison?" Mr. Palmer chuckled, "I heard about that! So he is your pal?"

"Yah, and he is teaching me to be his Chicken Man helper," CJ offered with pride.

"That's good. So, Charlie takes care of chickens?"

"Yes, and after I get learned to do it, he'll take care of the turkeys. Then I will be the Chicken Man."

"That sounds like a good plan. What about you, Clarence? Are you going to take care of the turkeys too?"

"No. I have a job for Mr. Darrell. He wants me to help Jeannie and Matt milk on the days when he cooks cheese. Otherwise, I help Mister at our barn."

"Boy, you fellas are really busy, huh?"

"Nah, we hang around a lot too," CJ offered. "I helped make some boats with Spud. Have you ever made a floating boat?"

"Not recently. Oh, one problem we have, there are no immunization records for the children."

"We know. Dr. Zach Jeffries is their pediatrician and he said he will start their shots tonight. Is that okay?"

"It is fine. Well fellas, would you be interested in going to see your rooms?"

Clarence looked at Elton and Elton nodded, "Yes, they would."

They went down the hall and Mr. Palmer knocked on Mrs. Frandsen's door. She answered it and smiled at the group. "Welcome. The class has been waiting to meet you. Come in."

Mr. Palmer introduced CJ to Mrs. Frandsen and she took his hand. She took him to the front of the room and said, "Class, this is our new classmate. His name is CJ Grey Hawk. Can you tell him hello?"

Everyone mumbled hello except Charlie who waved so hard he almost fell out of his desk. "Hi CJ! Teacher said you can sit over on my side of the room."

"Charlie, calm down. Yes, I did say that. You can sit one row over from Charlie. Let me show you your desk."

She took the boy over to his desk and he sat in it. He was impressed. It was the nicest desk he had ever seen. She showed him how to lift the top to open it. "Here is where you can keep your things like paper and pencils."

"Do I share it with anybody? At my old school, we shared."

"Not your desk or the things in it. There are other things that we will share. I'll give Mrs. Schroeder the list of things that you need to bring. You may sit here for a bit and see how it fits."

The teacher went over to Schroeder's and handed them the list of school supplies. "I have your phone number, but I think that it'll only take a while for him to get adjusted. And this is Clarence? Hello, Clarence. I hear that you are going to be in Mrs. Jessup's room."

"Well, we need to take Clarence to his room," Mr. Palmer said. "Do you want to stay or come with us, CJ?"

"I'll come along. I want to see where Clarence will be in case I need him."

"Good plan." Mrs. Frandsen smiled. "So will you be starting tomorrow morning?"

"Yes. They will be on the bus."

"Charlie said I can ride with him so he will show me where to go," CJ explained.

"That is good to know. I'm glad to have met you and we will see you tomorrow. Everyone, let's tell CJ goodbye."

The whole class waved goodbye and they went out into the hall. Mr. Palmer walked down the hallway a couple doors, before he knocked. "Here we are."

Jeannie opened the door and welcomed them in. "Here is our new classmate, everyone. This is Clarence Grey Hawk. What do we want to tell him?"

"Welcome," the class recited.

Then Clark raised his hand, "Teacher, can I show Clarence where his desk is?"

"Certainly. I think he would like that, right Clarence?"

Unimpressed, Clarence shrugged even though Clark was a good enough guy. He followed him to his desk that was right across from Clark. "You sit here and I sit in the next row. Teacher said we can sit like this if we don't goof off. I won't cause my Dad would skin me. What about you?"

"I don't goof off."

Clarence looked around and almost collapsed when he noticed Ginger sitting the next row over and one up from him! Thankfully, she didn't look at him. He opened the desk and there was a big card for him that the class had made. He looked at it and said, "Is this for me?"

"Why yes it is. The class made it for you. Do you like it?"

"It is pretty good. Pilamaya."

The kids all looked bewildered and Jeannie explained, "We are very lucky children because Clarence knows some of the Sioux Indian language. He just told us thank you in Sioux. Right?"

Clarence nodded and the kids still looked a bit lost. Jeannie said, "Can we all try to say that? Won't that be fun? It is pilamaya."

The whole class repeated it and decided it was fun. Then Mr. Palmer said, "We must move along for now. Come Clarence. He will be with you all tomorrow morning."

"How do you say goodbye in that talk?" a little boy asked.

Clarence looked a little silly and waved. They all giggled and waved back. Ginger never looked up from her desk.

In the hall, they headed back toward the office. Jeannie came out the door and ran to catch up with them. "I forgot to give you a list of your school supplies."

Then she looked around and gave Clarence a quick hug. Then she ran off to her room. Clarence looked at Elton and got a little grin.

On the way back to his office, Mr. Palmer showed the boys the lunchroom and the playground. Then he said, "I have a surprise, come with me."

He knocked on another classroom door. The door opened and there was Diane. "Well hello there! What a nice surprise. Can I introduce you to my class?"

They all stepped into the room, and she said, "Everyone, this is my Dad, Mom and my little brothers, Clarence and CJ. This is my English literature class."

There were a lot of hellos and then Mr. Palmer said, "We only have a minute and wanted to say hello. So hello. Bye now."

Then they went out into the hall again. "Now, one more surprise and I will let you folks go."

They walked up some stairs and knocked at another door. Matt opened the door and got a huge grin, "Come on in. We were just conjugating verbs, but I think we can take a little break. Huh, kids?"

The class was in full agreement. Then Matt said, "I'd like you kids to meet some of my best friends, Mr. and Mrs. Schroeder and Clarence and CJ. The boys are going to start school here tomorrow."

The kids all said hello and Clarence whispered to Matt, "Are these all your class kids?"

"Yes, they are one of my Latin classes. I have some math classes, too."

Clarence's eyes got huge, "You know math too! I didn't know that."

"Now you do. We can talk about it later, okay?"

"Okay, Mr. Matt—Harrington," he grimaced as he looked at Mr. Palmer, who just smiled.

"Well, we will leave you at it, then." Mr. Palmer said. "We wouldn't want those verbs to go unconjugated."

The class moaned and Matt grinned. "Thanks for stopping by."

In the hall Elton said, "I enjoyed that. I knew these guys taught school, but it looks different when you see it. They have big classes."

"Yes. The elementary teachers have just the kids in their rooms, but Diane and Matt have several classes. Altogether throughout the day, they each have about 120 students."

"Wow! No wonder they are so dingy at home," Elton grinned.

Mr. Palmer raised his eyebrows and chuckled, "That can happen. These folks are some of my best teachers. They are a good bunch."

In the car, Nora asked to look at the lists of school supplies. "Looks like we need a trip to the dime store, Mr. Schroeder. We need to pick up a few things. What did you think of the school, boys?"

"It was okay," CJ said. "I think I will like my desk close by Charlie. I saw some of the kids in my Sunday School class. What do you think, Clarence?"

"It is alright. That Clark is okay. It was nice of him to sit beside me. I bet he knows all his reading stuff, huh?"

"He knows up to his grade, Clarence. Now I want you guys to listen to me. There'll always be someone that doesn't know as much as you do, but there will always be someone that knows more than you do! Don't forget that," Nora said.

CJ piped up, "I saw Ginger at her desk! Didn't you see her, Clarence? I said hi to her. Why didn't you? I bet you didn't see her, huh?"

"I saw her."

"Oh. You must have forgot to say hi then. She said hi to me."

Clarence shook his head and looked out the window of the car.

After the family bought the school supplies and Elton picked up a shovel for CJ like he had promised, bought kites for everyone and then they piled back into the car. They turned in at the church and went into the office. The boys were relieved because they knew everybody there; Pastor Byron, Pastor Marvin, Suzy and Ruthie.

"Well, how was the trip to the school?" Byron asked. "Did you survive?"

"Yes sir. I get to sit near to Charlie. And guess what? Clarence sits right beside Clark and near Ginger," CJ couldn't wait to transfer the information.

Byron winked at Elton, "So what do you think about it, Clarence?"

"It will be okay. Clark seems cool. He said that his Dad said that he and I can't goof off or he'll get skinned."

"I did say that!" Pastor Marv said. "Did Elton tell you that?"

Clarence thought, "No. He said I have to behave and if I think I am going to up it, have that sheep worry."

"Sheep?" Marv looked to Elton for clarification.

"Ah, yah. Can we talk for a minute, you, Clarence and I?"

"Sure, come into my office. Fill your coffee cup and Clarence, do you want something?"

"No thank you. I don't want to up it."

Marv chuckled and said, "Come into my office."

Byron smiled, "While they are doing that, I think that Suzy might have some Koolaid for the rest of us."

In Marv's office, Clarence sat down very seriously and waited until Marv got in his chair. Elton looked at him, "Go ahead and ask him."

"See, Mister told me to ask you about some stuff from church that I can't figure out. He said you could tell me."

"Okay, I can try. What is bothering you?"

"Well, that Jesus guy is a sheep baby, huh? What is the word, Mister?"

"A lamb."

"Yah. So then, God is a sheep. Our tribe thinks about buffalo because they are strong and stuff, but why do you talk to a dumb old sheep? I don't get it. Mister told me to let that Jesus guy worry about school for me, but I don't know if a sheep is very trusty."

Marv looked at Elton, "Thanks, Elton. You owe me one."

Elton smirked, "I know."

"Well Clarence, we don't think that God is a sheep. He is a spirit. Do you know what that is?"

"Yah, kinda. It is like an us but without our skin," Clarence shrugged, totally unimpressed. "A Sioux has two spirits. When they die, one stays by their skin until it goes to Bear Butte in the Black Hills. The other one goes to Wakan Tanka cause he just let us borrow it."

"Yes, like that. You got it. Jesus is God's son, but He was a human, like us."

"Then why do you say He is a Lamb?"

"Because He didn't do any bad stuff, like a baby lamb wouldn't tell a lie or do bad things. He is gentle and kind," Marv answered. "So we say He was innocent like a lamb."

"How do you know that? Do you talk sheep talk?"

"No, we believe that He didn't do anything bad, ever. We go by what we read in the Bible. This is the book that tells about it." Marv reached behind him and got a new Bible off the shelf behind him. "Here, you can have this one for your very own."

"Miss Jeannie hasn't learned me how to read yet, so I can't."

"Keep it until you do. I'll put your name it, okay? Then if you have any questions, we can talk about them. Will that help?"

"I guess."

"Did I answer your questions?"

"Kind of. So you just call Him a lamb like a nickname; like we call Claudia Kitten. Is that it?"

"I guess it is. So you asked Jesus to worry for you? How did that work out?"

"Okay I guess. I didn't up it at school, so I guess He did good. I'm sure glad He isn't a sheep."

"I am, too. I can see why you were worried. I've known some sheep that weren't very bright," Marv chuckled. "But they aren't as bad as turkeys!"

Clarence's face lit up, "You know about turkeys too?"

"Yes, I do. They are pretty dumb."

"How do you know that?"

"I used to take care of turkeys when I was a boy on the farm. I hear you are going to take care of turkeys too, huh?"

"No Charlie is going to. CJ is going to take care of the chickens. I am going to milk goats and cows for Mr. Darrell."

"Good work, Clarence. Well, are you ready for your tour of the church?"

"I guess so."

39

After the tour and treats in Marly's kitchen, the family went home. They got there just in time for the school bus to drop Charlie off. CJ and Charlie ran to meet each other and both were talking a blue streak. Clarence shook his head, "Those two lunkheads are going to get into trouble in two days! I just can tell."

Elton chuckled, "You might be right. I hope not. I worry about them being in the same class."

Clarence teased, "You better tell the sheep to worry!"

Elton gave him a surprised look, picked up a handful of snow and lobbed it at him. Before they got to the house, they were both covered in handfuls of snow. Nora shook her head and quietly went inside.

"I see the mob came home," Andy grinned. "How did it go?"

"As Lloyd would say, pretty wobbly to my notion!"

"You sound surprised," Grandma giggled.

"How are things here?"

"My little sister never shut up except for the two minute nap she took with Grandma," Jackson said. "That is the happiest I have ever seen her in my life."

"Yah, she told us about her Kindergarten so much that I feel like I was there myself," Andy added. "Oh, Zach called. He was leaving town and has the kids first immunizations in his bag. He also said that he got an appointment for Claudia tomorrow at two. I hope that is okay. I said it was."

"It will be fine," Nora smiled. "Dinner smells good. What's cooking?"

"I drafted everyone, even the little girls, and we made dinner. The girls are washing up now. They managed to get flour all over themselves, so they had to change clothes."

"I really think it is just because they have clothes they haven't worn yet," Horse smiled. "You guys, I can never thank you enough for all you have done for these guys. I didn't even know that they could be so happy."

"They're great kids. Speaking of which, where is Clancy?"

"Come see, Mom. Shh. Don't wake them," Andy took her arm and walked with her to the door to the living room.

There was Clancy squished into the rocker next to Grandpa. They were both asleep. Nora smiled, "How long have they been sleeping?"

"About half an hour. They sat and rocked a long time. Lloyd talked about his wars and then Clancy would listen and babble. Apparently they were enjoying it," Grandma said.

"That's sweet."

A few minutes later, Jeannie, Matt and Diane turned into the yard. They were surrounded by the kids the minute the car turned off. Then the whole troop came inside.

"Wow! What a bunch of noisy folks you are," Grandma laughed.

"Is someone sleeping?" Jeannie asked.

Then Clancy came out with his blanket and wolf. He let go with a wolf howl and Grandma giggled, "Not anymore!"

Jeannie went with Clarence to look over his workbook, while Diane got ready for her piano lessons. Matt gave Grandpa a quick ride in his old Ford and the Dynamic Duo went out to do chores.

Grandma looked at Elton as he came out after he had changed clothes. "What?" he asked.

"I just want you to know how proud I am of you. You are a good person."

Elton grinned, "You ain't half bad yourself, Miss Katherine!"

Zach came in the door, "Hello. Am I interrupting something?"

"Would that stop you from coming in?"

"Nope."

"Didn't think so."

Suddenly the house echoed with shrieks from upstairs. Everyone took off to the top of the stairs. There they were met with a stream of water coming out of the bathroom. Elton and Zach rushed into the room, while Nora and Grandma retreated to get some rags and a bucket.

In the bathroom, they found two soaked little girls trying to get the toilet to quit running. Elton plucked Claudia out of the way and reached behind the toilet to turn off the water.

When he was done, he backed out and asked, "What happened?"

Claudia had crawled up into Zach's arms and was holding on for dear life while Clarissa cowered in the corner. She shrugged.

"Clarissa, can you tell me what happened?"

"You gonna whack me?"

"No. What happened? Did something get stuck in the toilet?"

"Well, a towel sort of fell in there. Me and Kitten thought it would go down, but it just stayed there. I pushed that flusher some more, but then all the water came out. So I put a big towel in there to catch it. Oh Mister, it was just awful. Are you going to send me away?"

"Oh come here, little one," Elton took the little girl in his arms. "I'm not going to send you anywhere. This is your home. But we need to get the water mopped up, huh?"

"Are you mad at me?"

"No. Clarissa, I'm not mad. The next time that it starts to run; don't flush it anymore. Come and get someone right away to turn off the water. Okay?"

By now she was crying, not only from the scare but from relief that she didn't get into trouble. "I'm sorry, Mister. I didn't mean to make a mess."

"I know you didn't. That happens to the best of us. No worries, okay? Is your smile still under those tears? Let's see if we can find them."

She tried to smile and then Elton said, "I think it's still there. You go to Diane now and she can put you in some dry clothes. Okay?"

"Okay. Mister, I didn't mean to make a mess."

"I know, honey."

Zach had handed Claudia to Grandma and she went to get her dried off. The rest of them cleaned up the water. When it was just the two men alone, Elton asked Zach quietly, "Do you think that Clayton was mean to them?"

"Wouldn't be surprised. Booze will do that. But maybe she was just scared. At any rate, it's okay now, and you got your floor scrubbed!"

"I beg your pardon, Zacharias," Nora reprimanded him. "Are you insinuating my floor was dirty?"

"Not at all," he winced. "You have the cleanest house in the county!"

Nora laughed, "Yah, don't say that in front of Suzy!"

Zach frowned, "How come I'm always in trouble?"

Elton just looked at him and laughed.

After the water was cleaned up, Zach said he would come back after supper to give the kids their shots. He didn't want to do it when they were so upset.

"So, let me get this straight. You are going to wait for them to get happy again before you can make them cry? I don't get it," Elton chortled.

"Keep it up and they won't be the only ones that get a shot!"

While the kids were getting ready for bed, Zach and Suzy stopped over. Jackson met them in the kitchen and said, "I explained to them what is going to happen. I told them that the shots would make it so some germs couldn't grow inside them and then Clarence was on board. The other kids aren't too thrilled, but they'll be good."

"Thanks, Jackson. Should we do it in your room?"

"Okay."

The Grey Hawk children all gathered in Jackson's room with long faces; even Clancy who had no idea what was going on, had a pout. Zach looked them over, "I'm sorry to have to give you a shot, but it is better than getting sick, right?"

They all shrugged. Clarence piped up, "Jackson said it will make it so the germs can't live in us, huh?"

"Yes. Isn't that neat?"

"No germs at all?" "Clarissa asked.

"Well, these will just make it so some kinds of germs won't grow. There are other kinds that will, so you still have to wash your hands."

"I'm not ever going to wash up again," Clarissa stated. "I don't want another floody thing."

"Oh, that was just an accident. So, who is going first?"

"I will," Clarence said. "I have to show them how brave Grey Hawks can be."

"Fine man, Clarence."

Zach gave Clarence his injection. The little guy got a couple tears, but he did not let them fall. He was indeed brave. Jackson congratulated him on his bravery, "Strong wowacintanka."

Then he held out his arms so the boy could get a hug. Then CJ was next. He wasn't quite as brave, but he did pretty well. Jackson congratulated him too, and then he ran to Andy and crawled up on his lap. There, he cried a little.

Next, Nora held Clarissa's hand while Zach gave her the shot. She bit on her lip so that she didn't cry from the shot, but from her bit lip. After the shot was over, Nora took her to the kitchen to put an ice cube on her lip.

"Missus, am I going to look like a goony bird at Kindergarten tomorrow? My lip is all big."

"No, it will be okay in the morning. You were very brave too. I was very proud of you."

"Even if I made a floody mess?"

"Will you stop worrying about that? I have done that, you know."

Clarissa giggled, and then got worried. "Did Mister whack you? I bet he was real mad at you, huh?"

"He wasn't happy that it happened, but he wasn't mad. He knows that folks have accidents and it is no big deal. All you can do is clean up the mess."

Clarissa hugged her, "I like you, Missus."

"Well, I like you."

Claudia and Clancy were like old pros with their shots, having had so many with their pneumonia. They were neither happy about it, but they fared better than the others. However, Elton and Suzy made a big fuss over how brave they were.

When the family was finally all tucked in that night, Nora snuggled up beside Elton, "I guess today went pretty well, huh?"

"It did. Tomorrow will be the big test. What time is Claudia's appointment tomorrow?" he said as he kissed her neck.

"Two. Elton, in case I forgot to tell you, I love you with all my heart."

"No, you didn't forget, but I like to hear it. You know that you are what makes my life worth living. Think I should lock the door for a bit?"

"Might be a good idea."

40

About four, Nora woke to find Elton gone. She put on her robe and went into the living room. There she found Elton and Clarence asleep in the rocking chair. The little boy was curled up in Elton's lap. Nora gently touched Elton's shoulder and he woke.

"You guys better get some rest."

Elton looked down and nodded. He picked up the little fella, carried him into Horse's room and put him in bed. Then he took Nora's hand and they went back to their room. Once back in bed, Elton said, "He is really having a hard time with this school business. It's amazing, because he handled the car accident better than this. I certainly hope it goes well."

"Me, too. Did you have a long talk?"

"Yah, but most of the time we just rocked. I can't really promise him that he will like it or that it will be okay. We both know that it won't be a slam dunk."

When the alarm went off, the bedraggled family gathered in the kitchen. Clarence was more than glum, Clarissa was worried that her lip was swollen and CJ couldn't wait to 'meet the guys.' Jackson tried his best to encourage Clarence but before long, he called him into his room.

Jackson looked at his brother sternly, "Look, I know you don't want to go. Everybody certainly knows that by now! You're being a big baby about it!"

Clarence's eyes filled with tears, "Are you mad at me?"

"Not yet, but getting close. Either you come clean about what's aching you, or shape up!"

Clarence backed away from his brother, "I don't like you! You don't understand. You never got made fun at because you were dumb! I hate that. Kids made jokes about me. Then Dad would make fun of me, too! I bet nobody ever made jokes about you!"

Jackson grabbed his hand and brought him over beside him, "Now just how do you know that? Did you ask me?"

"Well, no. But I didn't think so."

"Don't think that you have a corner on the market! I have been made fun of. In fact, most people have been some. Folks are always willing to make fun of you for something. You and I both know that. You even do it sometimes. But this family has not and will not. These folks will help you as best they can, unless you don't do your part. You need to quit being a sooky calf and do what is expected . . . no matter if someone makes fun of you. Don't listen to them. If they don't know you, they couldn't possibly know what they are talking about. Hear me?"

Clarence thought, blinked and then finally said, "I could just whack them!"

"Don't you dare! You are not to fight! Hear me? If you whack someone, you will be in deep trouble. Social services will have a fit, Elton and Nora will get in trouble and mostly, so will you. If you think you have trouble now, just start whacking. You'll find out how bad things can be. We are Indians. There are some people who hate Indians, and they won't be afraid to clobber you if you start whacking. You will get into trouble quicker than anything! That I won't tolerate! Hear me?" Jackson pulled the boy on his lap, "Look Clarence, I don't want to be mean, but you're a big boy. I've been so proud of you most of the time; don't let me down on this. Everyone is giving you a chance. Show them what you are made of!"

"I'm made of just like you."

"Well, then be brave and wise. Quit whining and do what is expected. We'll talk about it tonight."

Clarence put his arms around his brother and they hugged, "I'll try."

"I know you will. I'm counting on you. If things get horrid, you can ask to talk to Matt. Okay?"

"Okay," then Clarence hugged his brother again. "But I really, really don't want to go."

"I know."

They heard the phone ring and went out to join the family. When they arrived in the kitchen, CJ was talking on the phone. He was saying, "Wow! Oh, okay. Yah. You're right! Yah, you are right. Me either!"

Elton shook his head, "Charlie had to call him this morning. Guess he lost a tooth and wanted to tell CJ."

When Nora hung up the phone, they asked CJ what Charlie had to say. "He just told me that his tooth fell out, so I'd know how to look for him on the bus. He said he'd wave, so I'd know who he is."

Elton smiled, "That is good, but I think that you recognize him. So, he lost a tooth huh?"

"Yah and now we figured it out."

"Figured what out?" Andy asked.

"Charlie said that he brushed his teeth so much that it wore out his tooth. So, he and me aren't going to brush our teeth anymore. We want to keep them."

"Oh no, you don't!" Nora said. "You're going to brush your teeth. You don't want to get cavities. You get cavities from NOT brushing your teeth."

"But Charlie said that old people have to wear pretend teeth because they wore out their real ones."

Nora raised her eyebrows, "I don't care what Charlie says, I'm certain his parents will explain it to him. You are brushing your teeth."

"You better listen to Mom, CJ. She is right. It keeps your teeth strong and healthy," Andy said.

"I was just lucky that I had some extra ones in my mouth when the first ones wore out. Next time, I might have to glue rocks in my mouth. But if you want me to be a rock face, I guess I will," CJ grouched. "When Charlie and I get our own house, we won't brush your teeth."

Diane cracked up, "You probably won't need teeth with all the chicken poop in your fridge."

"Miss Diane, Charlie and I aren't going to let you come to our house!"

"Just fine with me," Diane giggled.

"Jackson! Can you make her be nice?"

Jackson shook his head, "I think you better get ready to help with chores, or you'll be late for the school bus."

Clancy let go with a wolf howl and scared Cotton, who ran down stairs. Claudia whimpered because her cat had run off.

Grandma looked at Nora, "Where's our bottle?"

Nora giggled.

Elton walked to the bus stop with the two boys. Both had their small school bags stuffed with paper and pencils. Clarence left his library books at home because Horse assured him there would be books at school. CJ was worried that he wouldn't recognize Charlie.

Diane helped Clarissa choose to wear a pink, blue and yellow plaid dress for school. She was very proud of her school bag that was pink.

She hugged and kissed everyone goodbye. She was excited to get in the car so Nora could take her to Kindergarten. When they arrived at Swenson's, she was much more subdued.

"Do you want me to stay today?" Nora asked.

"That's okay. We forgetted the neck thing, huh? Will Maddie Lynn be here?"

"Oh, we did forget the necklace. You can wear it tomorrow. I will wait until Maddie Lynn arrives," Nora smiled. "She should be here any minute. Let me take you in and I want to make sure that Mrs. Swenson has our phone numbers. If you get too worried, ask her to call me. I'll come right over. Deal?"

"Okay. Does my lip look goony?"

"No, it looks just fine."

The morning was long and worrisome for all concerned. The only ones who didn't worry how everyone was doing were Grandpa and Clancy. They were busy playing with some wooden blocks. Grandpa would stack them up and Clancy would knock them down.

Claudia was a little lost soul. She followed the ladies around with a long face. She really missed her sister. About ten, Marly brought Miriam over so they could play. Things improved a lot then.

The ladies talked over Charlie's pronouncement on the cause of tooth loss. Marly said that Ken and Byron had a big talk with Charlie about it, but both felt it had fallen on deaf ears. Marly shook her head, "You know, he really is a lizard head! I feel so sorry for Denise Frandsen! I can't imagine what it would be like to have those two in the same class! And Ginger! What did Clarence say about her sitting near him? Ginger had a fit when she got home. She wants nothing to do with him! She decreed that she won't talk to him or let anybody know that she knows him. She threatened Charlie's life if he told anyone they knew each other."

"I know. Clarence didn't say that, but it was obvious that he ignored her today. Those two better work it out, or I will have to have to lower the boom."

Grandma laughed, "You girls. First you complain that CJ and Charlie get along too well and then whine because Ginger and Clarence don't."

"I just wish they'd come to a happy medium."

Before Kindergarten was over, Nora parked outside Swenson's house. She stood by the back door with the other parents, waiting for their children. Glenda Olson, Pastor Marv's wife, came up to her and smiled, "Was Clarissa excited about school today?"

"Yes, she was. I'm very glad that Maddie Lynn is in this class. That gives her someone she knows."

"Maddie likes it, too. She asked me this morning if Clarissa is a Gopher, because then she could go to the Petunia Patch."

"They haven't been over there yet. Coot and Mo have been at our house, but since the little ones were sick, we didn't want to go out any more than necessary. I know Coot had their cubes finished before we got back from Pine Ridge."

"Yes, I saw them. So how were the boys this morning? Clark said that he sits beside Clarence. Clark said Clarence doesn't talk much; but then few folks talk as much as Charlie and CJ." Then the pretty blonde giggled, "Except maybe Chatterbox!"

The door opened and the little ones came out to meet their parents. There were smiles, waves and then Maddie Lynn hugged Clarissa. "Bye, bye."

"I can see her tomorrow, right Missus?"

"That's right, Clarissa."

On the way home, Clarissa was looking over her papers and telling Nora every second of her class. "We singed a song that I just love the most in the world! I loved it the bestest."

"What was the name of it?"

"I don't know. It was about Sunshine!"

Nora smiled, "There are a lot of songs about sunshine. Could you sing some of it for me?"

The little girl sang the Lesley Gore song, *Sunshine, Lollipops and Rainbows* in perfect tune, although the words were mixed up.

Nora smiled, "You have a very good voice, Clarissa. You need a little help with the words, but you did a great job. Very nice. I think that we might buy the record. Then you can play it at home and learn it. Would you like that?"

"Oh yes!" the little girl grinned, and then frowned, "What's a record?"

"Well, remind me when I get home to show you. Okay? So, how was school?"

"I just love it the mostest! Mrs. Swenson is the smartest girl in the whole big world, but maybe for Miss Diane. Maybe I will be a teacher girl when I grow up. Do you think I could be, Missus?"

"I do think that you could, if that is what you want to do."

"I might want to be a singer girl too. I know Clarence won't ever want to be a teacher guy. He always worries about school. Sometimes he even ups it. He'd go to school and be dumb. The school guy would tell Daddy. Then Daddy would whop him and tell him he was stupid. Will our new Daddy whop him?"

"No, Clarissa. We don't whop people for not understanding their school work."

"I hope not. Clarence will sit in his thinking spot if he does. CJ and me thinked he was hiding from Daddy, but he said he had to think."

After a minute, Clarissa asked, "Missus? You said you could be my new Mommy, but Mister never said he could be my new Daddy. He says that Clarence is his boy, though, huh?"

"Well, he may not have said it, but I know that he thinks you're his girl. I think that you and he should have a talk about it."

"It's okay. He's nice to us kids. Clarence says we should just be quiet about it. So, I better."

Ian Harrington and Elton had just come home for lunch and were washing up when they came into the kitchen. Clarissa couldn't wait to show everyone her papers from school. She was so happy. The she said, "I learned a song too. I can sing it for you?"

"That would be real nice."

Clarissa sang her song and they all clapped. The little girl beamed. Then Nora took her to change her dress before lunch, while Elton taped her papers on the refrigerator door.

After lunch, while Elton was changing to get ready to go to Claudia's appointment, Nora told him about the conversation.

Elton frowned as he got his clean socks out of the drawer, "I wondered if there was more to the school business. That is probably why he has such a big thing about being dumb. You know, I'd like to slap that Clayton upside the head."

"Well, I know Jackson loved his Mom, but I have to say, I'm not impressed by some of her actions. Oh, Clarissa asked me today if you are going to be her new Daddy, because you never said. She said you call the guys your boys, but not her."

Elton plunked down on the edge of the bed, "Damn. I did the same thing with Pep when she was little! Why do I keep making that mistake? Here I was thinking I was better than Clayton. Guess I had better mind my own, huh?"

Nora sat down next to him, "Elton, we've all been so busy with the kids! I have spent a lot more time with the girls and Clancy, but hardly any with the big boys. Don't beat yourself up about it."

"Thanks, but I know that Pepper was hurt about it when she was little. I'm glad you told me. I am going to try to spend some time with the girls, too."

"Then I will try to spend some time with the boys; although I really doubt that CJ would rather be with me than Charlie!"

"At least we haven't had a phone call from the school yet about the Dynamic Duo."

Nora, Elton and Claudia arrived at the clinic with time to spare. Elton had carried Claudia in, but the minute she saw Zach, she held out her arms to him. He took her and smirked to Elton, "Eat your heart out."

Elton squinted, "You're so lucky I'm in a good mood."

"It was nice of you to come with us to the appointment. I hope it isn't a problem with your patients," Nora said.

"No, this would have been my lunch break anyway," Zach said as he tickled the little girl. "I want to see what is up with Kitten here!"

After some hearing tests which Claudia thought was a game, the doctor talked to them. "It is doubtful that we can do much to repair the hearing loss, but there is a lot of research going on. My guess is that in a few years, there may be more options available to us. For now, I think we need to get little Claudia some hearing aids. If it is okay, I'll order them and we can have them in about a week."

"Yes, please do." Nora smiled, "Will it be hard to get her used to them?"

"Depends on the child, but most of them like to be able to hear and are not frightened by it. She is young enough so that she should be able to catch up with her speech in no time. So, come back in on the 16th and the aids should be here. We can get them fitted and see how it goes. Okay?" The doctor winked at the little girl.

She smiled at him and then went back to taking everything out of Zach's coat pocket. The doctor continued, "I can tell you a lot more once we get the aids and see how she does."

On their way through Merton, Nora asked Elton to stop at the dime store. "I want to get Clarissa a little record player and a copy of that Lesley Gore song. You know the one she was singing."

"She has a really good voice. I wonder if little one here does too? I noticed at church that Clarence does. Of course, nobody can do a wolf howl better than our Clancy!"

Nora looked at Elton and frowned, "How soon do you think he will get over that?"

Elton laughed as he parked the car, "About when he starts chasing women!"

Nora's eyes became huge, "Oh no! I forgot about that! They're going to be teenagers, aren't they? Oh my Elton. What did we do?"

41

When they arrived home, Claudia went to play with the new baby doll they bought for her at the dime store. Nora gave Clarissa the record player. It was in a pink suitcase type box, which she loved. She loved the case so much; she didn't even think to open it.

When Elton asked if she wanted him to show her how to use it and she nodded shyly. While Nora went to change clothes, Elton took the little girl by the hand into the dining room. He gave her a talk about electrical outlets.

"These can be dangerous, so only plug it in when a grown up is around. Never stick something in it, ever! You will soon learn how to plug things in properly. Promise?"

"Why?"

Elton smiled, "Because there is electricity in there and if you don't plug it in the correct way, it can give you a shock or burn you. You don't want that to happen."

Clarissa frowned, "Maybe we should just use the record player without putting that electric stuff in it."

"That'd be a good idea, except that it won't work without it."

"Can I just make it go around with my finger?"

"No, you can't make it go around at the right speed. It'll be safe enough. Just make sure you have an adult plug it in for you."

"Okay, cross my heart."

"That's my girl," Elton grinned as he opened the suitcase box.

She stopped breathing and looked at him, "You think I'm your girl?"

"Of course. I might not have said so, but I thought you were already. You and Kitten. Would you gals like that?"

"I am so happiest! I know that Kitten will, too! You know my Daddy died in a car wreck and both my Mommies died. Missus said she plans on not dying for a long time. Do you?"

"I sure hope not. I have to take care of my little girls."

"Mister," Clarissa got real worried, "Will you whop Clarence for being dumb?"

"No. First off, he isn't one bit dumb and second, I don't like to whop folks. If you kids don't lie to me and honor your word, we'll do just fine."

"How do we do that honor stuff?" Clarissa studied his face.

"If you give me a heart promise, then you have to do it. If you can't, you have to tell me as soon as you can so I know if I can count on you. If you ignore it, I'll be upset. Those are the only two things that I will skin you for."

Clarissa's eyes enlarged, "Like take our skin off! Oh Mister, could you whop me instead?"

"I'm not going to do any of it. How is that?"

Clarissa bit her lip, "More gooder."

"You know what Honey, you better quit biting your lip. You'll have to have a bandage on it and that would be awful!"

"Okay," she put her hands over her mouth as he opened the phonograph player. "It is so—! It is like a real grownup thing! How do I make it go around?"

Elton showed the little girl how to pick out the adapter for the record and put it on, placed the record on the machine and pushed the button. Clarissa was in awe as the arm moved itself over the revolving record, dropped gently onto the record and began to play. When the first music started, she was so excited that she clapped, giggled and then hugged him. Then she ran to get everyone to come and listen to her record player as it played *Sunshine, Lollipops and Rainbows.*

Everyone raved, except Claudia who thought it was just something that was going around. Clancy however, was mesmerized. Nora noticed and said, "You know Clarissa, it might be a good idea to make sure that it is always out of High Pocket's reach! I'm afraid he would love to get a hold of it."

Jackson nodded, "After you use it, be sure you put it back in your room. It is a special gift and you must take good care of it."

"Oh I will, cross my heart! And Mister told me to keep the record in this paper, what did you call it?"

"The sleeve."

"In the sleeve. Then it won't get scratched up because it will make it sound bad."

Then Elton pushed the button and the arm went back to rest. Clarissa frowned, "Did you break it?"

"No, I have a surprise for you."

He turned it over and played the flip side. She was so excited that she could hardly stand it. She got up and bounced around the room to the music. "I am so happiest ever in the whole world."

The veterans stayed in the dining room with her while she practiced playing it. Claudia's doll had already been stripped of all its clothes except the diaper, which she was busy trying to figure out how to change.

About four o'clock, the school bus stopped at the Schroeder turn. Elton was there to meet the boys as they got off the bus. Charlie and CJ descended jabbering away like two magpies. They both waved nonchalantly to Elton and took the mud puddle trail to the house for treats. It was a minute before Clarence came down the steps. Elton searched the boy's face for a sign of how it went.

The little guy looked at him deadpan and then broke into a smile. He jumped off the last step and turned to wave to Clark, who waved back through the window. Then he took Elton's hand.

"Well, how did it go?" Elton asked. "I was thinking about you all day!"

"I didn't get yelled at one time! Not once! Mrs. Jessup is really nice and helped me a lot. She whispered that she was going to stop by today when Mr. Matt gives Grandpa his ride."

"How about the other kids? Did you meet a lot of kids?"

"Some, but mostly I just hung around. A guy has to think it over before he decides who is trusty, you know."

"Did you play at recess?"

"Mr. Matt got me to play catch with some other guys. That was okay, but I would rather have just played with him."

"I supposed he had to work and keep an eye on all the children."

"Yah, that's what he said. He told me that Harrington is planning on having me visit him pretty soon, so we can hang out. I told him I'd sleep on it. Do you think that would be okay?"

"I think it would be. We'll talk about it when he calls. So, did you make any new friends?"

"I saw that Little Bill guy. He was talking to some other guys, but he waved at me. Clark showed me to some guys that he messes around with."

"Did you like them?"

Clarence shrugged, "They were okay, but I wanted to think, mostly."

"I'm dying to know, how did you like it?" Elton stopped walking and knelt down to the lad.

"It was okay. I brought some papers home to show you and Jackson. I had a couple more, but there were mistakes on them so I threw them away."

"You don't need to do that, Clarence. We'd like to see all your papers."

"I don't want you to see the mistakes, in case you have to get mad."

"No, I won't. If you don't show me the mistakes, how are we going to know how to help you? Did you think of that?"

Clarence shuffled the snow with his foot, "Will you think I am stupid?"

"You need to tell us your mistakes so we can help you with them! That is why we'd like to see them. Understand?"

Clarence studied his face, "Okay. But if you get mad, I won't do it no more."

"Deal," Elton held out his hand to shake it.

Clarence shook his hand.

"So, think you can handle it tomorrow?"

"Yah, I think so. Mister, I really think that Charlie and CJ are knuckleheads. Those guys talk so much, they don't even think!"

Elton looked up and watched the two charging all over the yard, "I believe you are right about that!"

The plans were set for Harrington to pick Clarence up on Saturday afternoon, so they could work on their fishing gear and get it ready for their fishing trip. Elton told Clarence that he had a pole he could take along to show to Harrington.

CJ and Clarence had almost moved the entire snowdrift and were now making plans on how to spend their money. Their dreams were shattered when Andy told them they didn't have enough money to buy a life-sized airplane. Downfallen, they decided on comic books.

Clarissa watched the Mickey Mouse club in the afternoon and loved it. Claudia finally gave up on fixing her dolls diaper and just carried her around naked with a blanket. Clancy squished into the corner of Grandpa's recliner and the two talked about the wars. Zach had called to confirm he would be over Saturday morning with his microscope so that Clarence and Ginger could look at germs in dirt. Those two had not acknowledged each other in school at all, but both seemed more than content that way.

The next morning, things were perking along. The boys were happy with their lunch buckets because Grandma had put a brownie in each one. Clarissa knew most of the words to the Mickey Mouse club theme and couldn't wait to get to Kindergarten to show Maddie Lynn.

The family was invited over to Kincaid's place called the Petunia Patch for dinner. It would be the first time that the kids would get to see their cubes. It was a fun morning.

Clarence decided to take his library book about the duck pens along to school to read at recess. He wanted to do it before he talked to Kincaid that evening. Nora put it in his school bag and reminded him to take care of it.

"I will Missus. I gave that library lady my word. If I mess this one up, I won't get any more books!"

42

Clarence had a great morning. He smiled more that morning than the whole week! He was so happy he almost said hello to Ginger, but decided not to wreck a good day.

At morning recess time, he reached into his desk and pulled out his library book. He carried it carefully to the playground and sat on a quiet spot on a concrete ledge. He had just found the page that had the pictures of the inside of a duck pen and was looking it over.

It was sunny and warm, only a bit of wind. He took his stocking hat off and stuffed it in his pocket. His long hair blew a bit in the breeze. Mr. Matt wasn't watching at this recess. He watched in the afternoon. Mrs. Jessup wasn't out either, but Mrs. Frandsen and her class were outside. They were on the other side of the playground.

The paved area had thawed off, so some of the girls were jumping rope and some were playing hopscotch. There were some boys were playing marbles or bouncing the basketball. The kids from the high school were mostly on the other side, sitting around the picnic tables. They didn't hang around the little kids much.

A shadow came across Clarence's book and he looked up. There were three bigger boys, about fourteen or so. A really fat kid mocked sarcastically, "Lookie here. A Redskin that thinks he can read!"

The other boys laughed scornfully and Clarence just looked back at his book and tried to ignore them. The fat boy jeered at him and grabbed at his book, "What are you looking at, Chief?"

Clarence clutched his book as tight as he could, but a skinny boy swiped it from the other side. Clarence frowned, "Give me my book back!"

"I bet you stole it!" the other kid taunted, "You're all thieving Indians! Whatcha gonna do? Scalp us?"

Clarence wanted to whop them so much, but he remembered what Jackson said. He looked around for a teacher, but could only see one and he was helping some kid that had fallen down. Clarence yelled, "Leave my book alone! Give it back!"

The three boys started throwing it back and forth to each other to keep it away from Clarence. He lunged for it and missed. One of the boys dropped the book and another one stepped on it. Clarence dove toward it, and the fat kid tripped and kicked him. He fell on his face but landed on his book. He gathered it under him, but the skinny boy was trying to grab it from him.

Ginger had been jumping rope and saw what happened. Once Clarence fell down, she let out a yell and bolted toward them. She headed into those three bigger boys like a Kamikaze fighter. She bit, kicked and swung. The middle-sized kid kicked her down and smashed her face on the cold pavement.

Clarence saw it happen and then let loose. He was kicking and swinging at them all, "Leave her alone! Don't you kick her!"

Mrs. Frandsen and Joe Taylor, the high school football coach, arrived at the fray in seconds. Mr. Taylor grabbed a couple of the big boys by the nape of the neck and marched them into Mr. Palmer's office. Denise Frandsen tended to the little ones.

Before a minute had gone by, there were a couple more teachers there. Matt saw the fight from his classroom window and tore out to the playground. He ran over to the kids. Denise had Ginger in her arms and was consoling her. Clarence was still lying on the pavement. His head was bleeding from the back where he had been slammed against the concrete curb. Denise had wrapped her winter scarf around his head to stop the bleeding. The boy was barely awake. Matt picked the little guy up in his arms and carried him in to the school nurse.

Denise carried Ginger into the nurse's room. Her face was badly bruised and cut from being smashed into the pavement. She was covered in blood and dirt.

Matt was right by Clarence when he opened his eyes. Matt tried to assure him he'd be okay, but the young lad cried and shook his head no. Matt said calmly, "You'll be okay now, I promise."

"Mr. Matt. My book is wrecked! That library girl will never give me another one!"

Matt figured out what was bothering him and assured him, "I will get it and explain to her what happened. She will let us replace it. Okay? Then you can borrow some more. Don't you worry one bit about that. I'll go get it right now."

"Are you sure, Mr. Matt?"

"I'm positive."

Matt went out to the playground and found the book, pages blowing gently in the breeze, cast on the dirty mud by the curb. He picked it up and brushed off most the dirt. It was wrecked, a few pages were torn and back cover was destroyed. Matt was sure that few books had ever been protected with such fervor as that one.

The phone rang at the shop and Harrington answered it, "One minute, I'll get him."

He called Elton to the phone and he answered. After he listened but a second he said, "I'll be right there!"

"What is it, Dad?" Kevin asked.

"The school. There's been trouble. I have to go right away!"

"CJ?"

"They didn't say but that would be my guess. Could you call Nora for me? I'm going right over."

As Elton was walking as fast as he could down the hall, he saw Byron come in. "You, too?"

"Yah, must be Charlie and CJ."

The two went to the office and the secretary ushered them into Mr. Palmer's office. Both men could have fallen over when they saw the little kids sitting in the chairs, holding towels on their heads. Byron stopped short and said, "Did you guys fight with each other?"

"Not with each other," Mr. Palmer explained, "But they were in a fight. It seems that three of the high school boys came over and stole Clarence's library book. When he tried to get it back, they kicked him down. Wonder Woman came out of nowhere and took those big kids on. I have to tell you, if I'm ever in a jam I hope she's on my side."

"Ginger, why did you do that? You know you aren't supposed to fight," Byron said as he knelt down by his little tomboy and took her into his arms.

"Daddy, I just had to! Those big guys pushed Clarence down and were kicking him. He didn't even fight back. He was only trying to get his book. So, I did. I think I got them, too! I bit that big fat kid! Do you think I will get sick now?"

Byron picked her up and grinned, "No, I doubt it. Honey, you look like a boxer."

"I know. My face is wrecked. First I burned it off and now my eye is falling out. My cheek skin is still outside in the dirt."

"Oh, my little girl."

Elton had gone over to Clarence who looked up at him in fear. Elton pulled him onto his lap and when the boy realized he wasn't going to get in trouble, he started to cry. All he could do is babble about his book. "I'll never get another book and the library girl will be so mad, I won't be able to read the library! I will always be stupid."

"Calm down. What happened, my little man?"

"Those guys took my book and wrecked it. I didn't fight, honest Mister. I didn't cause Jackson said that would be big trouble. I got knocked over and then Ginger came flying. They smashed her face in, Mister! That made me so mad, I didn't care if I was in big trouble. They shouldn't have kicked her!"

Elton and Byron both sat there holding their wounded warriors, "Now what?" Byron asked the principal.

Mr. Palmer shook his head, "Please accept my apologies. This wasn't their fault. Those boys have been in trouble before for picking on someone. However, your children aren't in trouble. We patched them up as best we could, but you may want to take them in to get stitches. The nurse had to cut some of his hair to try to see what was going on. I hope that is okay. Please, feel free to take them home or whatever you deem necessary."

"Could you let our other kids know that they should go on home like usual?" Byron asked.

"Of course," Mr. Palmer started to say, when Jeannie came to the door with tears in her eyes.

"I'm so sorry, you guys. I wish I'd been outside," Jeanne hugged Ginger and then put her arm around Clarence, "Matt has your book and he promised he'll take care of it at the library. You don't need to worry about it. Okay? Are you guys taking them to see Zach?"

Byron nodded as Matt came up beside them. He said, "Good, because Clarence was almost knocked out. I'll call Nora, Marly and Zach if you want. I have a free period now."

"That'd be great," Elton nodded, "Oh, could you let the guys at the shop know?"

"We'll tell your kids and bring Kate, Charlie and CJ home with us tonight," Jeannie said, as she hugged the kids. "I'm so sorry, you guys. I'll see you later."

As the men started down the hall carrying their battered children, a large man approached them. He was accompanied by the fat teenager and confronted Elton, "That's what you get for dragging a 'Skin' in here!"

Elton looked at him and answered coldly, "Are you proud of what you drug in here, Sir?"

The man was taken back and then he sneered at Byron, "You should keep that witch on a leash. My boy told me that she bit him twice! She attacked him!"

"The next time your boy wants to pick a fight, have him give me a call. I'd be more than happy to oblige," Byron said sternly.

"That's no way for a preacher to talk."

"This time, he gets a pass. Next time, I'm a dad; not a preacher."

The man stood there dumbfounded while the men passed him on their way out of the school. They put the kids in Elton's car and headed off to town and to St. Anne's Emergency room.

Zach met them at the door and looked his little friends over. "Clarence, you'll need quite a few stitches. The nurse did a good temporary job, but the tape won't hold very well. Problem is I'll have to cut you hair."

Clarence shrugged dejectedly, "Will it come back?"

"Yes, it will."

"Okay."

Zach looked at Ginger's face, "My favorite little Buddy, what have you got against your pretty face? I'm always patching it up for you!"

"I know, but that fat guy was kicking Clarence! You would've bit him too!"

"I might have at that!" Zach chuckled. "I think we can get away with only two stitches by your mouth. It should heal up so there are no scars."

"That's okay, it won't make no difference. But Smitty—," she started.

Zach stopped, "You haven't called me that in a long, long time. Since you had your face burned!"

"I know, huh? It just popped out! I had almost forgot it!"

"Me too, I liked hearing it again. Now, what were you asking?"

"I'm really worried. Will Clarence and I get that sickness like Old Yeller did? You know, from biting those bad boys?"

Zach chuckled, "No. You won't. There were bad, but I doubt they had rabies!"

"Good, I was really worried. I don't want Daddy to have to shoot me!"

Zach shook his head, "Not today, anyway."

After the kids were all bandaged up, the four headed home. This entire time, Clarence and Ginger had not said one word to each other. In fact, they barely acknowledged each other's presence. "If you guys are interested, I'm willing to stop at the Log House. What do you say?" Elton asked.

"Okay, can we share a milk shake thing?" Clarence asked.

"I was thinking I wanted a coke," Elton answered. "But maybe someone else would like a milkshake."

"I was looking forward to a cup of coffee," Byron said. "Ginger, you love milk shakes. Will you share with Clarence?"

Holding her head, she groaned, "Do I have to?"

"You don't have to!" Clarence grumped. "I'll drink water. Maybe I don't want to share one with you!"

"Daddy," Ginger whined, "He said he won't share with me! I was going to, even if I don't like him. He could share just because I helped him."

"I didn't ask you to help! I was doing okay," Clarence announced. "I would have got up."

Ginger rolled her eyes, "You would not! You looked like you were deader than anything! That is why I had to bite them. It makes my tummy curl up think I tasted their skin! Ugh!"

"Don't you up it!" Clarence gasped, "Mister, I think she is going to up it!"

"Yea gads, you two," Byron reprimanded both of them. "Now hear this! We are going in, we will order and you two will do as you are told. End of story! We don't care if you dislike each other. Got it?"

"Yes, sir," Ginger pouted.

"Okay, Mister Pastor."

Ginger opened her mouth to give him a bad time about calling him Mister Pastor but Byron gave her a dirty look. She rolled her eyes and looked out the window.

In the front seat, the two men looked at each other and stifled their grins. On the way home, the little pugilists fell asleep before they were ten miles down the road.

Byron checked them in the back seat and then turned back to his friend, "I can't believe this! Of all the things we have done together, this is the furthest out!"

"And we aren't done yet! I have to say, I was sure it would be CJ and Charlie. You could've knocked me over with a feather when I saw these two."

"I know Ginger is a hot-head, but she never gets into trouble at school. But if someone she cares about is getting hurt, I doesn't surprise me a bit that she would come a-flying!"

"The way they carry on, you wouldn't think she and Clarence could stand each other," Elton chuckled. "The shop teacher said that Clarence didn't start punching until that kid kicked her. I think they like each other better than they would have us know. What a pair!"

Elton dropped Byron and Ginger off at their car and headed home. He arrived just about the same time as the teachers. They all came in for coffee and talked over the excitement of day. Clarence was reluctant to go in. "Mister, Jackson said he'd give me hell if I got into a fight at school. He told me no fighting. No way!"

"I think he'll understand what happened. This wasn't a regular fighting situation. You did nothing wrong. Hear me?"

"Will he whop me?"

"No. He won't."

"Will those Rules people take me away?"

"No. They won't. Mr. Palmer said it was not your fault."

"I hope so," then he started to cry.

Elton picked him up, "Look, you aren't in trouble."

"Yah, but the library lady won't let me have no more books, and then I will be dumb forever!"

Elton got stern, "Listen, Matt said he will talk to the library lady, and I will pay for a new book. It'll be okay. You have my word. And you are not dumb. I don't want to hear you say that ever again. That's an order."

Clarence hugged him, "Okay."

Inside, the whole thing was hashed over again. Jackson took his brother on his lap and said he was proud of him. Diane suggested that she would be happy to trim his hair around the places where it had been shaved so his scalp could be stitched.

"Maybe you should give him a crew cut," Jackson suggested. "Would you like an Army haircut?"

Clarence looked at him as if he was daft, "No."

"I will trim it so that it is all short, but not Army short. Okay?"

"Okay, Miss Diane. I don't want to look like Rags!"

"You could cut it like Kitten's pixie," Clarissa suggested.

"Boys don't wear pixie's," Clarence grumped. "I have sort of a head hurt, Mister."

"Yes, I suppose you do. Tonight I don't want you to help with chores. You stay in and we'll see how you feel tomorrow morning. Okay? Nora, did you let Kincaids know?"

"Yes. I thought we could still go over for dinner, but they know that Punch and Judy are all banged up. They'll take it cool. Mo had everything in the oven; so, I didn't want to cancel. Unless you don't feel good enough, Clarence. I can stay home with you."

"I can," Grandma said. "Lloyd and I can stay home."

"I can. He is my brother," Jackson said.

"No one is going to. He'll be fine. He just needs to take it easy," Elton said. "He can take a rest if he thinks he need to, right Clarence?"

"Right."

43

Clarence went to his room upstairs and tried to sleep. He had a difficult time sleeping on his back because it hurt his head. He turned over on his stomach and cried into his pillow. He hated today so much.

Mister and the teachers had all been nice; even old Ginger was nice to him. But he was worried that the library wouldn't let him take any more books.

While he was crying into his pillow, he fell asleep. Nora came up to check on him and found him resting. She covered him up with the afghan that Grandma had given him and pulled the door shut so he could rest.

After chores, the family cleaned up and headed over to Kincaid's house called the Petunia Patch. They were greeted at the door by Carl and Mo, who gave them a huge welcome.

"We are so glad the little Leprechauns finally got well enough to go visiting. We were getting worried you'd never make it over! Come, old Coot made you little ones a cube apiece. I bet you want to be seeing them!"

Clarence looked at Elton and shrugged; he still didn't understand her talk. The whole bunch walked into a huge room off the dining room where one wall was filled with brightly colored boxes on the wall. They were all painted different bright colors.

Coot proudly pointed to one near the floor, "This is for Clancy, down here where he can reach. It is next to Baby Matthew's cube. Come Clancy, look inside!"

Nora helped the little boy crawl up to the cube and peek in. There was a hook for his jacket, which Nora used to hang his coat. Then there as a picture book about wolves and a wooden duck on a string that quacked when it was pulled. Clancy looked around at the bright red cube and then to Mo and Coot who were grinning expectantly. He shyly took the book, sat down next to his cube and started to turn the pages. Then he grinned.

"Good," Coot beamed. "I guess that means he likes it."

"I'm sure he does, Carl. That was very nice of you to put some toys in it for him. You didn't have to do that," Nora smiled.

"Yes, I did. Otherwise, he might want to play with someone else's stuff, and then we'd have a disaster."

Mo took Claudia by the hand and over to a pale blue cube with a kitten on the front. "This is your cube, Kitten," Mo explained.

Then Mo helped her open it, hang her coat in the cube and then handed her the little set of plastic dishes. Claudia's eyes got huge and she took it to Grandma to show her.

Next, Mo said, "Now Clarissa, which one do you think is for you?"

Clarissa covered her mouth and giggled, "For me? The pink one?"

"Why I do believe you are right. Look here, this hot pink one even says Clarissa on it right next to the fairy princess on the door!"

"Pilamaya Mrs. Mo. This is the bestest cube I ever had in my whole wide life!"

"Did you have one before?" Mo asked.

"Not till now," the little girl hugged her.

She reached inside and found a book with a fairy princess on the cover. Nora showed her it was a paper doll book, and Andy volunteered to show her how to use it. She was fascinated.

Coot had taken CJ to the dark green cube. "This is yours, young man. You can tell it is yours, because it has a chicken on the front of the door, right above your name."

CJ nodded and opened the door. He took off his jacket and hung it up. Then he found a bat, ball and catcher's mitt. CJ was breathless, "Look Mister, now I have a real good ball and bat. I think the glove might fit, huh? Pilamaya."

Then Mo motioned for Clarence, "Come, this is your cube. Here it is, the teal blue one! It has a fisherman on the front above your name. Come, look it over."

Clarence hesitantly opened the cube and looked inside. There was the hook for his jacket and a box the size of a large shoebox.

"Take it out and open it carefully," Coot encouraged him. "Over at the table would be best."

Clarence followed the instructions and opened the box. It contained a tackle box with his name on it. Clarence didn't know what to do. "Wow! This is cool! Do you think Harrington has one like this?"

"Yes, in fact, he helped me put the stuff in it. He gave you the bobbers, hooks and stuff. Best keep it up away from the little tikes cause they might get into problems with the hooks. You can use it when you go fishing, though," Kincaid said.

"Pilamaya Mr. Coot. Look Mister, look what Coot and Harrington got for me."

"I see that, Clarence. That is fantastic!"

While the ladies put dinner on the table, the men took the kids outside to see the remains of the igloo. "I think a few more warm days, and I'll have to knock it down before it caves in," Carl explained. "Danny said he will come down and haul the snow away from the house so we don't have a flood. Next year, I think we are going to put the igloo over by the garage."

Jackson grinned, "Oh, you are having one again next year?"

"Well of course," Coot answered. "We just figured out how to do it this year. Next year, I think it should be a bit bigger. This was cramped when we had Bart's birthday party."

Andy patted him on the shoulder, "You are a little nutsy, huh?"

"Learned it from your old man," Coot took it as a compliment. "There are few nutsier than old Magpie!"

Then Carl showed them the tool shed and explained the plans that he and Matt had for expanding it and adding everyone's fishing gear. Elton shook his head. "I thought you were building duck pens!"

"Oh, I am, but over here. We will have three coops that open into the same fenced in yard. Danny told me what duck poop is like, so I don't want them all over the yard. Especially with the little ones toddling around. I talked to Darrell and he is going to help me put a pond inside the fence for them, when he comes over to plow."

"What are you plowing?"

"Oh, we got lots of planting to do. Mo wants to plant a huge flower garden because she left hers out East, you know. We need a vegetable garden and an orchard. I also my field."

"Your field?" Elton asked. "What is that?"

"Never you mind, Magpie. You'll find out soon enough. I'm pretty anxious for it to get nice out so we can start the projects. You know, this summer we're hoping to have more Gophers."

"More Gophers?" Jackson asked. "I thought you babysat the same kids all the time."

"We do, but with school out, some of the older ones will be here more often. We are hoping some of the Grey Hawk Gophers will come over from time to time."

Over dinner, Mo shared their news. "We'll have some more residents this summer. My granddaughter, Rain is coming out when school is out. She got her grades and sent them to Darrell. He said he would hire her for the summer. She'll be living with us."

"She was your bridesmaid, right?" Nora asked.

"Yes, she's the one."

"Very pretty girl," Nora nodded. "You said residents. Who else?"

"Jeff Wilson, Matt's buddy from out east. He got the job in Mandan at the reformatory. He called and said he will be starting May first; but his job there is over in early April, so he is coming up right after Easter. That way, he will be settled before his job starts and he will help me with my projects."

"I wonder if the poor devil has any idea what you have in store for him!" Elton chuckled.

"Well, it's not as bad as it would have been. I'm glad that you saw fit to take the turkeys. I hear you and Charlie are the poultry men, huh CJ?"

"Yes, sir. Charlie is learning me about chickens until I'm over promotion and then he'll be the Turkey man."

"I heard about that. Big responsibility you're taking on, CJ. You know those little baby chicks are going to be counting on you to take care of them."

"I know. Mister told me about that. He said we can't glue feathers on them."

"I bet they're glad you know that." Then Carl turned to Clarence, "And I hear you'll be working on my farm."

"No sir, I'm helping Mr. Darrell."

"Darrell and I are partners, so you'll be helping me too! That is just great! I heard you're a good man. I'll be proud to have you working for us."

"I hope so."

"What do you mean, you hope so? I heard you are responsible and diligent."

"I don't know what that dilly thing is," Clarence said.

"It means you stick to it and are a hard worker."

"I try to. I promised the library lady I would be responsible for the library book, but it got all wrecked. She'll be mad at me."

Coot leaned back, "Most likely not. Matt told me what happened. Sounds to me like those big boys are the ones that should pay for the library book! A clear case of malicious assault and destruction of property. They are fodder for the Reformatory, that's what they are!"

Clarence frowned at the man, "What were those words? I don't know them."

"I just meant they were the trouble makers and had better be changing their ways before they end up in bigger trouble. I'm glad that none of my Gophers act like that."

CJ asked, "Who are your Gophers?"

"Well, you guys, the Ellison bunch and all the clan kids. Our own grandchildren are too!"

"You mean we're Gophers too?" Clarissa asked. "Like Miriam and Maddie Lynn?"

"Yes ma'am. You are."

"Wow! Missus, did you hear that?"

After dinner, the men went into the living room while the kids went to play in the playroom. Grandpa promptly fell asleep in the recliner. Clarence looked at his tackle box again and came to sit down next to Elton. He fell asleep in no time, curled up beside him.

Elton looked down, "The poor kid had a hell of a day."

"I wish my legs were better, I'd love to do a little pounding on those hoodlums," Andy groaned.

"Nah, you don't want to get into hot water over the likes of them," Coot answered. "But it sure wasn't what the lad needed. Matt thought he was most upset about Ginger."

Jackson added. "That's when he started fighting."

"One would've never thought those two would go to the bricks for each other, huh? Have they buried the hatchet now?"

"No way," Elton rolled his eyes. "They still get along like cat and a dog!"

After the ladies finished the dishes, they came into the living room. "You know, we had better get this outfit home. It has been a long day and tomorrow night is the West Side Story," Nora said.

"Lordie above, and it will be grand when Mattie, Bart and Diane can be done with it. They're wearing themselves to a frazzle!" Mo giggled. "We are going tomorrow night, too. We have to cheer and clap like the Devil lost his pitchfork, so those three will be proud!"

44

Clarence didn't sleep well all night. He had a headache and his face was swelling and turning more bruised than before. Zach stopped by in the morning and suggested that he stay home from school for the day.

"But Mr. Zach, that West thing is tonight and Miss Diane wants us to see it. I said I would go. Mrs. Mo said we need to clap for them."

"I'll tell you what. If you rest all day, you should be able to go tonight. Okay? You can go back to school on Monday like usual. You shouldn't be at school when your head hurts so bad. Right?"

"I s'pose."

"Good, you take the day off. I'm on my way over to visit with Ginger. I guess her eyes are both black and blue this morning. Marly said her lip is so swollen, she can hardly talk. She'll probably stay home today too."

Clarence started to cry, and Zach questioned him, "What is it?"

"She got hurt because of me. I don't like her, but I didn't want her to be hurt. It was nice of her to help me, but kinda dumb."

"She was worried about you. Did you thank her for helping you?"

"No."

"Why not?"

"Because she just bugs me. Every time I think I'm going to be nice, I see her and she makes me mad all over again." Clarence grumped.

"You should tell her that you appreciate that she helped you. That would be the proper think to do," Elton said.

"Yah, but I won't say that I like her."

"You guys have to quit going at each other all the time," Nora said. "After the other kids go to school, maybe you can call her and just tell her thanks."

"I suppose."

"We'll talk about it later, Clarence."

After Nora got the beds made, she came into Clarence's room where he was looking at his book.

"Clarence, I want to talk to you about this Ginger business." Nora sat down next to the boy, "Folks understand that every person won't like everyone the same amount or maybe even at all. That happens and we can't control it. What we can control is how we act about it. You don't need to tell everyone how you feel. You certainly don't need to make faces, roll your eyes and that sort of thing. Please, I'm asking you nicely, knock it off. She isn't going away. She is a part of our family too! Some of us happen to think she is a real sweetheart. I don't want her feelings to be hurt or for her to be sad. Now, do we understand each other?"

"You mean you like her better than me? Cause I am new. I should just go—."

"Stop right there! You're my boy, for always! I don't like her better than you. I like both of you! You must stop saying you're going to leave every time you can't do what you want. I'm not happy about that. Okay?"

"Are you mad at me?"

Nora hugged him, "No. You're my boy. I just don't like it when you do this. Okay? Listen, do you love CJ?"

"Yah, I s'pose."

"Do you get unhappy with him when he acts like a lunk head?"

Clarence grinned, "I wish he wouldn't do that."

"But you still love him?"

"I know Missus. I promise to be nicer to Ginger. It is just that when I start, stuff happens. She says weird things and it makes me crazy!"

Nora giggled, "Yah, she thinks that is what you do. Tomorrow, Zach is bringing his microscope out to do something nice for you guys. I'd feel very bad if you two squabbled the whole time. That wouldn't be very fair to him, now would it?"

"No, I s'pose not. I guess I could be nicer. I'll try, Missus."

Nora gave him a kiss on his forehead, "That's all that I ask. Let me know when you feel like calling her. It is nice to thank those that help you."

"I know. Jackson said that. Missus, Mrs. Frandsen wrapped her pretty scarf around my head and it got all wrecked by my blood. I should tell her thank you, too."

"Oh yes. Hey, what about we talk to Grandma and see if she has a spare scarf to give to her. I can help you wrap it for Mrs. Frandsen. Would you like that?"

Clarence frowned, "But that's like Grandma thanking her."

"What about asking Grandma what she would like in trade for a scarf? Then, you paid for it and it will be just from you. Is that a good idea?"

Clarence nodded. Nora took his hand, "Let's go see what Grandma and Kitten are up to, okay? Then you can ask her."

They found the two sorting some laundry to wash. Actually, Grandma was sorting while Kitten was unsorting. "Hi, Clarence and I were wondering what you are up to?"

"Just getting ready to wash some clothes," Grandma smiled as she put a pair of blue jeans back on the pile that Kitten had just taken off.

"Grandma, Missus said I should ask you about something."

"What's that?"

"Mrs. Frandsen wrapped her scarf around my head that day and it got all bloody and wrecked. Missus said you might have a new scarf for her, but I want to trade you something."

"Sounds like a good deal. Could you go collect all the dirty clothes from everyone's room and bring it here? Then we can go pick out a scarf for Mrs. Frandsen."

The boy broke into a huge grin, "I can do that."

"I'll go with you to show you where everyone puts their dirty clothes!" Nora said. "Some of these folks around here have secret hiding places for their dirty socks!"

After the clothes were all sorted, Grandma took Clarence to her room and showed him the collection of hats, scarves and mittens she had made and stored in her trunk. He looked them all over, but he couldn't make up his mind.

Grandma said, "Let me help you. What color was the scarf that was wrecked?"

"It was like her hat; white with pink flowers on it."

"I'd choose this pink one or the white one. Hey, I know, I can add some pink crocheted flowers on this white one. Would that be nice?"

Clarence thought and then smiled. "I think she'd like that."

"I will put the flowers on this afternoon, okay?"

"Okay Grandma." He patted the white scarf, "You are nice."

"So are you."

He went down the hall to see Jackson. He was working on his sketches. Jackson looked up and smiled at him, "What you up to?"

"Grandma is going to trade me for a scarf for Mrs. Frandsen. Hers got all bloody from my head."

"That is nice. What did you trade?"

"I did a job for her."

"Good. That makes me proud of you. How is your head?"

"It's getting sore again and I'm sleepy, but I can't find a good way to put my head without making it hurt. I want to be awake tonight for the West Story."

"I'm looking forward to it, too." Jackson smiled, "Kate is going to be in it. She sings and dances. I can't wait. She is so nervous."

"Why would she be nervous? She does stuff right all the time."

"Clarence, what did I tell you? Everyone gets nervous. She wants to do a good job."

"Oh." The boy sat quietly watching her brother before he said quietly, "Missus got kinda mad at me this morning."

"Really? About what?"

"About me not liking Ginger. She said I have to get over it. I said I would, but I don't know if I can."

His big brother smiled, "I'm sure you can. You guys might someday actually enjoy each other."

"Doubt it. Missus said that she will be around and so will I; so, we might as well behave."

"She is right. You know, Kate is very special to me and Ginger is her sister. You are my brother, so you will probably see each other for a long time."

"You gonna get Katie to be your wife?"

"I don't know yet. We're still too young to get married, but I would like it if she would be someday. What do you think?"

Clarence thought, "I think it'd be okay. She is nice. She and I share milk shakes."

"I heard about that. What do you think of this sketch?" Jackson held up the sketch he was working on.

"It is pretty good. I think that baby calf should have a white spot on its nose, like the one down in the barn."

"Good idea."

Clarence went up to his room to look over his workbook from Jeannie. Before long, he stretched out on his bed and tried to sleep. He had just about fallen asleep when Nora knocked, "Sorry to disturb you, Clarence. We have company. I thought you might want to come downstairs if you feel well enough."

"Who is here?"

"Marly came over with Miriam and Ginger. She has to go to a meeting at the church and the little girls are going to play together. I thought that maybe you would like to tell Ginger what we talked about."

"I'd rather do it on the phone," Clarence said.

Nora smiled, "You can't call her. She is here."

"Okay, but don't know if it will work."

"Good man."

Gopher and Kitten were already in the living room playing with their baby dolls. They had all the clothes off their dolls and were trying to jam Cotton into a doll dress. The cat was not happy about the situation. The poor animal finally hissed and ran off.

Clarence shook his head, "They're knuckleheads, too!"

The two came into the kitchen where Marly and Ginger were sitting at the table with the veterans and the Grandparents. Clarence was not prepared for seeing Ginger. She was a pretty little girl with mahogany curls, green eyes and freckles.

Today, she looked horrible. Her eyes were both swollen and bruised. One eye hardly opened. It was the eye above the cheek that had lost all its skin. The other cheek only had a few scratches but her nose and upper lip were badly bruised.

Clarence's mouth fell open and without thinking, he went over to her and put his arm on her shoulder, "Ginger, does it hurt really bad? It looks terrible. I'm feel sad you got hurt for helping me. You should've let them hit me. I'd have been okay and you wouldn't have got hurt."

She looked at him in shock, "I thought they killed you! You were flat on the ground and that fat kid was kicking at you! It made me so mad, I just did it. Do you hurt?"

"Yah, my tummy is black and blue like your eyes, from the kicking. Can you see out of your eyes?"

"Sorta. Sorry you had to have your hair cut. I know you wanted it to be like your Dad, but it will grow back. I had my hair cut really short when I got my face burned off. It came back."

"Thank you for helping me, even if I wasn't dead."

"I'm glad you aren't dead."

Clarence grinned, "Me too."

Ginger giggled and then winced, "You going to that thing tonight?"

"I guess. Miss Diane is excited about it."

"Yah, I know. I don't want to go because I look like a monster, but Katie wants me to come watch her. I guess I have to."

"If Mister says, maybe you can sit by me and we can both look like monsters. Nobody will know who looks awfuller!"

Ginger giggled and then winced again, "Stop making me laugh, Clarence. It hurts."

"I'm sorry."

"That's okay."

Jackson looked at Nora and they exchanged a wink. They both felt they had witnessed the parting of the Red Sea.

Grandpa piped up, "Katherine girl, I need to find my knife. My whittling knife."

"Why Lloyd? You quit whittling. Remember, you can't see so good anymore."

"I want to show High Pockets how to do it. Then we can whittle when we talk."

"No. Absolutely not! High Pockets is too small. He will get cut. He is just a baby!"

"He told me he will be careful," Lloyd argued. "I asked him and he said yes."

"Clancy is way too young," Nora said. "We'll let you know when he is old enough. Please, don't do it before. Promise?"

"Will he be old enough tomorrow?"

"Maybe in a couple years," Katherine insisted. "You aren't to do that unless we say it is okay. Hear me?"

Lloyd scowled, "I'll wait until next week. He already knows about the war, right High Pockets?"

"War," Clancy smiled from his high chair. "Iwoooo Jima!"

"Yea gads," Andy groaned. "This place is a nut house. I'm glad that Zach's model shop is done. I guess we are moving the plane models over there tomorrow and then setting up our shop in our garage. Just think, we can start working next week Jackson!"

"I can't wait."

"Will you have time to finish your sketches for the clinic?" Marly asked.

"Yes, I'm all caught up. Nora helped me set up a calendar and it really helps."

Marly smiled, "How's the old leg doing?"

"Good. Zach said I have to take care of it, but it seems that the infection is finally giving in to the antibiotics. I might still get my artificial foot by June."

"I bet you are anxious, uh?"

"I am. I'd like to be able to stand up and walk without the crutches or leaning on someone."

"Katie will lose her job, huh?" Marly said.

Jackson got an odd look on his face, "No. I hope she will still be with me."

Marly grinned, "Oh, I think she will."

Clarence started to open his mouth, but he saw Jackson give him a look that meant no. He closed it again without saying anything. Jackson gave him a slight nod.

After their chocolate milk, Marly had to take off for her meeting.

Clarence followed Jackson back to his room and then closed the door, "I didn't know it was a secret what you said, Jackson. I won't tell anybody."

"I know I forgot to tell you it was private. It is just that it is a special thing that I want to keep very private until we get older, okay?"

Clarence suddenly felt very grownup, "You mean that you trust me with something very private?"

"Of course man, you're my brother!"

Clarence gave him a hug and Jackson said, "It was very nice what you said to Ginger. I hope it wasn't too hard to do."

"I didn't even think about it. When I saw her face, I just said it. She really got clobbered, didn't she?"

"Yes, she did. She took a real beating for you. Not many people would do that for someone."

"I would do it for her. I don't think that fat kid should go around kicking kids. He is trouble like Mr. Coot said."

45

After dinner, the family went to the musical. Danny and Jenny babysat Grandpa and Clancy. They were going to the musical the next night, so Nora was going to watch baby Matthew.

Diane was nervous and changed her clothes three times before Clarissa asked, "Are you going to wear all your clothes tonight?"

Diane giggled, "No. I just don't know what to wear. I want to look nice."

"You mostly look nice all the time, 'cept at the barn. But us girls don't wear our soft stuff to the barn, right?"

"Right," Diane agreed. "Which do you like best, this brown suit or the peach one?"

Clarissa looked them over studiously and then decreed, "The brown one. You should wear the peach blouse in it because it is more softer."

Diane looked at the suit and held the peach blouse next to it, "That is a fantastic idea! Why didn't I think of that?"

"Cause you're being worried about getting your leg broken. I don't think I'd like that. Do you think it'll hurt?" the little girl asked thoughtfully.

Diane sat down next to her on the bed, "Honey, when we say 'break a leg,' it is just a good luck thing. It's wishing the person good luck in a show. It doesn't mean they will really break their leg."

"That's pretty dumb."

"Yes, it is. I heard that it started because at the end of the play, the actors come out and bow or curtsy. They bend their legs to curtsy. Someone said that to tell someone to break their legs means you wish they have a lot a bows."

"A guy should just say that." Clarissa frowned, "Does that curtsy thing hurt?"

"Not at all. Let me show it to you. It is easy. You do it when you bow to a queen or a princess."

"Oh, I better learn that then, huh?"

Diane showed her how to do it and the two practiced a few times. "I think you have a great curtsy, little one. Very good."

Clarissa giggled, "I can't wait to see you curtsy tonight! I'll know you are breaking your bones, huh?"

"Yes, you will. I think I heard Matt drive in, so I better get a move on. Thank you for making me smile, Clarissa."

As the couple left the house for the school, Clarissa yelled, "Break your bones, Mr. Matt!"

He grinned, "Thanks Clarissa."

The family got to the auditorium a bit early, so the veterans could get to their places before the crowd came in. The little kids were excited, even though they didn't know why.

Ellisons arrived shortly after Schroeder's and Kate came out to talk to Jackson for a minute. He gave her a little kiss on the cheek and said he would talk to her after the show. "Don't be nervous."

"I'll try not to. Are you going over to Zach and Suzy's afterward? Mom said they invited us to their house for cookies after the show."

"Yes, we're going to stop for a little bit. I'll talk to you there."

Charlie and CJ sat between the GI's and were told if they caused trouble, they would get clobbered. The boys looked at each other as if they had no idea why the young men would say that.

Clarissa sat between Nora and Grandma and was very excited. She didn't know what was coming, but she was sure she would like it. She couldn't wait to see Diane curtsy.

Clarence and Ginger sat next to each other, between Elton and Byron. They only nodded their hellos to each other, but neither were talking much to anyone. Clarence was busy making sure that he was tucked obscurely under Elton's arm; while Ginger kept her head down struggling with a scarf over her head and dark sunglasses.

Elton asked Byron quietly how she was doing and he answered, "All she needs is a trench coat and she'd be giving Greta Garbo as run for her money. She is so afraid that someone will recognize her."

"It is too bad that she feels that way, when she is really a hero! It isn't everyone that would do that for someone else."

"Anyway, she is just keeping as low a profile as possible. She said she won't take off her sunglasses until the lights go out."

At eight o'clock, the lights dimmed and the spotlight shined on the closed stage curtain. The little Grey Hawks were mesmerized. Father Bart and Diane Waggoner appeared. Bart gave a brief welcome speech. Then they left the stage and the curtains opened.

The lights, music, dancing and singing was everything that Clarissa loved. She thoroughly enjoyed the whole thing. When Katie was in the scene *I Feel Pretty* and sang with three other girls, Clarissa almost flew off her seat! Between that and the Gym Mambo scene, there was nothing that could have been more exciting to the little girl. She whispered to Nora, "Missus, I just love this the mostest ever. I am so happiest!"

CJ and Charlie spent a lot of time crossing their eyes about love stuff or any slow song, but enjoyed the 'gang' part of it. Even Claudia could hear a little of it, and gave it her rapt attention. When she noticed Katie, she could hardly contain herself. She clapped the entire time she was on stage.

Clarence didn't think it was too big a deal, but was glad that Katie did a good job. He knew she didn't have to worry. He noticed that Jackson looked so proud of her.

Ginger took her sunglasses off when the lights dimmed and seemed to enjoy the show, but her face looked very painful. She couldn't smile.

As the show ended and everyone stood for a standing ovation, Ginger stood up and tried to put her sunglasses back on, but dropped them. Clarence could see that she was starting to panic, "Don't worry, Ginger. I'll get them."

He crawled under the seat ahead of them and reached her glasses. Then he handed them to her and patted her arm, "See, it's okay."

Then he went back to ignoring her. She put her glasses on and clapped as the actor's took their bows. She never acknowledged him.

Mr. Palmer came out after the actors left the stage and introduced Bart and Diane again. He shook Bart's hand and gave Diane a bouquet of roses. Then he introduced the faculty staff and they all took a bow.

Clarissa poked Nora's arm. "See, they are breaking their legs!" she squealed with delight. "This is so funnest."

After the show, the clan stopped by Zach and Suzy's for a small reception. They had cookies, punch and coffee. It was an opportunity to tell Bart, Diane, Matt and Josh about all the good work they had done with the production. Joallyn had helped paint the scenery and of course, Katie had worked on the costumes and was in the play. Jackson couldn't have been prouder of Kate. Clarissa extracted a promise from her to teach her the words to *I Feel Pretty*. She had already got Diane to promise to teach her *Tonight*.

Father Vicaro was there with Kincaids and proposed a toast, "May this get over so we can all get back to work!"

46

After breakfast, Zach and Ginger drove in. Zach brought in his microscope and set it up in the dining room. He was much more excited about the day than either of the kids. They were curious about the adventure, but still not particularly excited they were together.

Mo called to ask if Clarissa and Claudia wanted to come over with Diane. She, Ruthie and some of the Gophers were working on Marly's birthday present and she thought the girls would enjoy it. Maddie Lynn and Miriam were going to be there. Nora asked Clarissa, who went to get her coat before Nora even finished explaining it.

Andy and Jackson were helping the men move the model shop to Zach's new 'hangar' and then stayed home to start organizing their work area. They were very anxious to get started with their jobs on Monday. They already had about six items for repair!

Elton gave the Dynamic Duo instructions to clean out the brooder house and the coop that would be used for the turkeys. He wanted it all done in the morning and then after lunch, would help them get it set up for the chicks. They were excited, but thought it would be more fun to help move the model planes.

Zach got the microscope set up and adjusted. Then he laid out the slides he had brought to show the kids. He also had some blank slides, so he could show the kids how to prepare them. Then he helped them look at the dirt and germs.

Considering they barely said a word to each other, the kids did have a good time. They loved looking at the slides and seeing what germs looked like under magnification. Ginger was delighted to see the differences in some of her dirt collection when it was mounted on a slide. Even Clarence

311

was impressed how different it was. The highlight however, was when Zach had each of the kids cough on a slide, stain it and coverslip it. When they looked at the germs on the slide, they were shocked.

"I knew other people had germs, but I didn't think that I did," Ginger said. "I better remember to cover my mouth when I cough."

"Good idea," Zach agreed.

Clarence was very quiet and then finally said, "Most of those germs must not make us very sick, uh? Cause otherwise, we'd all be goners. There must be millions of them everywhere."

"There are," Zach agreed. "In fact, some of them are good for us. Some bacteria actually do things that we need and use. Well, what did you kids think? Was it awful, or did you like working with the microscope."

"I liked it. I liked to look at my dirt collection under a 'mikerscope'," Ginger said. "I can see the different stuff in it."

"I'm sorry I made fun of you liking dirt, Ginger. It is more interesting than I thought," Clarence nodded. "I still don't want a collection, but it is pretty fun to know about."

Ginger almost smiled, or as much as she could with her bruised face. "I think the germs are pretty interesting too. I didn't know some were round and some were skinny and stuff like that."

"Would you guys like working with microscopes when you grow up?"

"I might, if I could use it to see dirt. Otherwise, not so much," Ginger said.

Clarence shrugged, "It was okay, but I would rather milk cows."

Zach laughed, "Well, I guess I didn't talk you into being scientists, but at least you got to see how it works."

"It was good, but I like to run around," Clarence said.

After lunch at Schroeder's, Zach helped the men moving the hangar. Elton went out to get the brooder houses set up and Ian came to pick up Clarence. Harrington asked Clarence to bring his fishing book and promised they'd take good care of it.

The two went into the basement where Ian had set up a table. On it, he had all sorts of tackle and hooks. They spent the afternoon, learning about which tackle was used in what circumstances. They compared the book to the gear. It was a lot of fun and they both learned a lot.

Then over the snack Ruthie had left out before she went to work, the two looked over Harrington's fishing map. Clarence had a ball and learned to say, "And that's a blasted fact!"

"I can't wait for spring so we can go fishing, and that's a blasted fact," Clarence grinned.

"Me either. Maybe we can spend some time learning how to fly fish and cast. Okay? I can ask Elton if you can come over next weekend and we can practice. I have to learn how to do it with one hand."

"And I have to learn how to use both hands," Clarence teased.

"Well, we have our work cut out for us, huh? I'll talk to Elton about getting our fishing licenses."

"What is that?"

"A person has to pay for a license and then the state gives you a piece of paper that says it is okay for you to fish."

"I don't think we did that at Pine Ridge."

"Probably not, because the reservations have different rules. But here, we do. We need to follow the rules. I'll find out about them and then we can keep our licenses in our wallets."

Clarence's mouth fell open, "Did you know Mister got me a wallet?"

"No, I didn't, but that is cool. Do you have tons of money in your wallet?"

"No sir. I have my library card and the card that says I have an account at Carrie's bank. Do you have one of them?"

"Actually, I do. You are very grownup, you know."

"I know. I have to be, cause the kids need to play. Boy, CJ and Charlie are lunkheads!"

"Yah, but they are a lot of fun."

Clarence's face fell, "Harrington, do you think I'm not fun cause I don't play?"

"Not at all. Folks do different things for fun. You do fishing for fun! You are more serious."

"Is that good?"

"It is. We can't all be goof balls, like Charlie. Why that guy can get dirty walking ten feet!"

"Yah, CJ used to, but I made him quit doing that. One time before Auntie was there, CJ and Clarissa made a big pile of mud. Dad and Jackson's mom slept over at Spotted Calf's house. CJ and Clarissa got their clothes all messed up and I knew Dad would be mad. So I took the kids down to the creek to wash them off."

Then he face became very dark and he quit talking. Ian watched his expression and asked, "What is it, Clarence? You can tell me. If you want, I won't tell anyone."

"It is okay."

"No, nothing that makes you that sad is good to keep in. It will eat you alive! If you don't want to tell me, talk to Elton."

Clarence thought, "I pretty much don't want to tell Mister. I will tell you, okay?"

"Want me to keep it secret?"

"I don't know. Just don't be a blabber about it."

Harrington smiled, "You have my word."

"Well, I took all the kids down to the creek. I took Clarissa's top and washed it off in the creek. Then I put it on the grass to dry. I made CJ give me his jeans. I was washing them off and lost hold on them. They floated down the creek and it was too deep for me to get them. He got mad cause they were his only jeans and started to wail. The wind came up and Clarissa's top blew away and then she bawled. Claudia just cried because Clarissa did. I was trying to get them to shut up when I noticed Clancy was trying to eat ants from an anthill he had crawled into. It was awful! Dad had finally got some gas so they came home. They looked over the hill by the creek and saw everybody bawling, and CJ with no jeans. Boy, did I get walloped. Dad was so mad at me and told he couldn't trust me. I was in big trouble. Then I had to give CJ my jeans because he didn't have any. I was so glad that I found Clarissa's shirt. Jackson's mom whopped me when Clancy started upping the ants. It was bad. Finally in a couple days, Dad got CJ some jeans from the guy at the church. I was really glad, because then I got mine back. So when Dad went to Spotted Calf's the next time to sleepover, I told CJ and Clarissa to never ever get covered in mud again! They can only get their feet in it."

"That sure doesn't sound like it was a happy day for you. You are lucky it wasn't in the winter, uh? You would have got real cold with no jeans."

"Oh Harrington," Clarence giggled. "We don't get mud when it is real cold!"

Harrington shook his head, "Well, I guess that's a blasted fact!"

That evening, it was just the family at home. Clarence went down to the barn to help with chores again. Over dinner, the girls babbled about all the fun they had 'working' on Marly's gift, CJ regaled his adventures with Charlie while they got the brooder houses ready. Andy and Jackson were happy they got most of their shop ready to go, with the help of Darrell, Ken and Kevin. Clarence told them all that he had learned about fishing and what Ian had taught him.

Before dessert, Nora said, "I have a surprise for a certain somebody that came in the mail today. After our talk Clarence, I talked to Aunt Mabel. I asked her to send me something so I could give it to you."

Clarence couldn't figure out what it was. Nora went to the pantry and returned with a small flat box.

"What is it, Missus?"

"Open it and see!"

He did and saw a cedar flute! It was a flute carved from cedar that Lakota Sioux used and a fleece bag for storage. Auntie had included a couple of tapes of some of the Lakota artists. Clarence didn't' know what to do. He caressed the wooden flute with his hands and then said tearfully, "Wopila (many thanks), Missus. This is so wonderful. I love my Hokagapi. I forgot we talked about it. I still don't know how to play it, but I'll keep it forever."

Jackson explained, "Hokagapi means 'to make a voice' in Sioux, because each flute has like its own voice. We think that listening to the sound of the flute can mend your soul. We use it to play some of our most sacred music."

Diane smiled, "I'll talk to Mr. Larson. He teaches the band and knows about flutes. Maybe he can give you lessons. It will be my gift to you."

"You don't need to give me a gift."

"I know, but I want to, just like Nora did!"

Clarence got up and gave Nora a big hug and then gave Diane a hug too. Then he started to cry and ran off to his room.

Elton knocked on his door, "May I come in?"

Clarence was stretched out across his bed in tears, clutching onto his cedar flute. He said, "Okay."

Elton came over to the bed and gave the boy a hug. The little guy put his arms around him and had a good cry. "I don't know why I am crying, Mister. I'm so happy, it makes me sad!"

"I know. I've felt that way myself sometimes. Want to talk about it?"

Clarence shrugged, "Since we've been here, it is like magic! We have food and get to keep our clothes. The kids have friends and Kitten is going to get those ear things so she can hear. Nobody could ever get Clarissa to leave. She is so happy. And CJ is still goofy, but I know he is happy. Clancy hasn't been sick so much. He was always sick at home."

"How about you, Clarence? How is it going for you here?"

Clarence cried some more, "I didn't want to be here or to like it. Pine Ridge is my home and a guy should like his home the best."

"Sometimes things change. The home that you loved isn't there anymore. It was no one's fault, but it's the fact. You are making a new home. You can still keep the memory of your Pine Ridge home. But it's okay to like your new home, too. You're a part of our family and we only hope that you think that we are a part of yours."

Clarence squeezed Elton real hard, "But I'm afraid, Mister."

"Of what?"

"Maybe I like it more than I did my old home and my old family."

"That won't happen. Treasure your memories. They are an important part of your life. You know, someday you'll grow up and make your very own home. I hope that you will treasure the memories from this home, too!"

"I won't ever forget you. I even like being in my room alone sometimes. Sometime, I might move up here after CJ is better. I think he is getting less scared, huh?"

"I have noticed that too. Even Clarissa comes up to her room to play her record player and stuff."

"We go to Mister Pastor's church tomorrow, right?"

"Yes. Did you want to go to Sunday School first in the morning?"

"Not till my face is healed up. Ginger said she isn't going tomorrow unless she can wear her sunglasses. Her Mom told her that everyone would know who she was anyway, so she is going to visit with Grandpa instead."

"Her face really looks sore. How is your tummy where you got those bruises?"

"They are starting to turn green now and don't hurt too much."

"Good. I'm glad you are on the mend." Elton looked at him, "Are you worried about going back to school on Monday?"

"No. I'll go if Ginger goes. I should watch out for her if somebody pokes fun at her about her face. I know she is worried about that."

"Did she tell you?"

"No, I just know. She acts brave, but she gets nervous. Jackson says everybody does sometimes. Do you think that?"

"I know that's true. It's nice of you to keep an eye out for her. She'll appreciate that."

"Oh, I won't tell her! She would clobber me! Don't tell her, Mister!"

"I won't. You have my word," Elton chuckled. "You're very right. She wouldn't be happy to think you were keeping an eye on her. I'm taking the library book in when we take Kitten in to get her hearing aid. I'm sure that lady will let you borrow more."

"Oh Mister, that would be nice. I'll pay you for it from my piggy bank."

"Not necessary. You didn't wreck the book out of carelessness."

Sunday morning, after chores Ken brought Ginger over to Schroeders. Her eyes were beginning to turn a deep purple in some places, but the swelling was going down. Grandpa told her to stay out of the street so she didn't get run over by that truck again!

After church, everyone met for the clan dinner at Schroeders. They had a wonderful meal and Elsie and Lucy brought one of their fantastic decorated cakes for Marly's birthday. Then she opened her gifts. She loved the decorated basket from the Gophers. There were sugar cookies and bunnies made out of marshmallows. The kids had worked very hard and were glad she liked it; especially when Marly shared the bunnies with them.

She opened her other gifts and then finally Byron brought out the sketch that he had ordered from Jackson for her. When she pulled back the wrapping paper, she cried. It was a great sketch of her 'family.' All the kids, including Ruthie and Miriam. It was great.

Coot gave all the kids a talk about what to do if a bully started trouble with them. He and Mo had gone to town and he had something for each of his Gophers to help protect them. They had purchased several small whistles and put them on chains. The boys got silver-colored ones and the girls got gold ones. He even gave them to Katie and Becky. They were small enough to wear under their shirts or blouses. "If someone starts in

317

on you, you are scared or lost, blow on the whistle real hard. Someone should hear you!"

Becky Oxenfelter said, "Thank you Coot, but Katie and I are big enough to take care of ourselves."

"Not really. Young ladies should have a whistle! You never know what sort of creeps are around. This won't stop anything, but it will make noise so that someone can come help you."

Then Danny Schroeder had a plan. "I have a friend that works at the Coal Gasification plant. He teaches karate and judo in Minot. I will talk to him and see if he can do a weekly class for us. I've always wanted to learn it myself."

"Karate?" Father Vicaro asked. "Isn't that just causing trouble?"

"Not at all," Father Bart said. "If it's taught the correct way, it teaches respect and encourages only using enough force to stop someone from hurting you. I learned it when I was a kid. In fact, all my sisters know it. I could help the kids practice between lessons. Then I could keep in shape!"

Darrell laughed, "I can't wait to tell Sam and Joey!"

Bart chuckled, "They already know! In fact, Sam said that he was interested in learning it to protect himself from Bonnie!"

"Those two are getting pretty serious, huh? Just think Slick, you and I will be related!" Darrell crowed.

"Sometimes Darrell, I wake up at night in a cold sweat just thinking about it!" the young priest teased.

"Anyway, if you guys think we would have enough folks that are interested, I will talk to Jason about it. Marty and I have talked about it a couple times. I have room in my basement for the dojo." Danny continued. "I know baby Mattie is too young yet, but I know kids can start at about three or four."

Nora asked, "What is a dojo?"

"It is like the gym where you get self-defense classes. Jason teaches Korean Karate, not Japanese, but the term is the same."

"You mean all these little leprechauns?" Maureen gasped. "That seems like it would be dangerous."

"Well, if someone decided to use them for punching bags, they could stop them. That's all I want. You ladies could learn some self-defense too." Carl stated, "I had my brown belt in karate and was rather proficient in judo."

Joallyn, Jeannie's sister, piped in, "I would love it myself. There has been a couple times I would have loved to be able to just flip someone over my shoulder, so I could run away. Especially when I was living on the streets. Besides it is good exercise!"

Suzy giggled, "I will need it after the baby is born, to get back into shape."

"Have you decided on names yet?" Nora asked. "May isn't that far away."

"We've talked about it, but so far we don't know if I am going to be a real Heinrich and have twins. You know, we tend to do that."

"Twins! Begorrah!" Mo giggled, "Just think Coot, we could get two little elves at once! My, this is a prolific bunch of young folks!"

Suzy got serious, "Do you think that it will be too many for you to watch? I guess I could ask Mom to watch them."

"Not in the least, my girl. I wouldn't hear of it! If we need more help, I will call Gilda to come to our house to help out! We need an excuse to visit. I wouldn't miss out on some more Gophers! I just need to make an announcement. My birthday is creeping up in another month, so I will be expecting a few more dozen diapers and receiving blankets for the celebration!"

"When is your birthday?" Father Bart asked.

"May fourth," Coot answered. "Hey, by the way, guess who is having a birthday in April?"

Father Vicaro shot him a dirty look, "Keep your flap shut, Kincaid."

Coot laughed, "You got it. I need not say anymore."

"What day is it?" Ginger asked. "We can make a cake for you!"

"The seventeenth," the man groaned.

"Really?" Nora beamed. "Elton's is the nineteenth! That calls for a massive celebration!"

"Don't know about that! You can just celebrate his," Elton pronounced. "I don't need to celebrate."

"But Mister, are we going have a cake for Claudia?" Clarence asked. "Hers is like one of those days, right Jackson?"

"Yes, it is the eighteenth! That would be three cakes!"

"How about we just share one? I remember how sugared out we were with those weddings back to back!!" Jeannie giggled. "I'm just getting so I can eat cake again."

47

Monday morning was quiet and Clarence was quite somber. "Are you worried about going back to school?" Jackson asked.

"Sort of. I have to make sure to stay away from those big kids."

"You know, you might want to hang around with some other guys your age. Those big guys would bother you less if there were others around."

"Yah, Mr. Kevin said that, too. But what if I want to think? Why do I have to do something goofy, so I don't get kicked?"

"I don't think that Clark is as goofy as CJ, is he?"

"No, but those guys play sports stuff. I don't know how to do it."

"Ask them to show you how. You want to know a secret? If you ask somebody to show you how to do something, it makes them feel smart. And everyone likes to feel smart."

Clarence frowned, "But Jackson, that makes me feel dumb!"

"Why should it? You'll never learn if someone doesn't show you how, goony bird!"

The little boy thought and then grinned, "Okay. I'll tell Clark."

"Good man."

Elton walked the boys to the bus while Nora gave Clarissa a ride to Kindergarten. The little girl was very worried when they waved goodbye to the boys. "Missus, do you think Clarence will get beated up today?"

"No. The teachers will be watching very carefully and besides, now you all have Coot's whistles. Right?"

"I know. He said that we must never, never just blow them for fun. Cause of something about wolfs, right?"

Nora nodded, "He said you must not cry wolf. It is to be used for an emergency only. If you use it to goof off, folks won't pay attention when it is an emergency."

Clarissa watched her and then shook her head. "I think it is because it is too noisy. Wolfs don't use whistles."

Nora smiled, "You might be right about that."

Clarence sat next to Clark on the ride to school and asked him if he would teach him how to do that basketball stuff. Clark broke into a big smile, "That would be cool! The guys and I will teach you!"

Clarence thought to himself that Jackson might be right. He noticed that Ginger sat beside Katie today on the bus. She usually sat with some of her friends. She did have her sunglasses on, but not the scarf. She had pulled stocking cap way down over her head. She looked pretty silly, but he knew it was just because she was embarrassed. He sure hoped no one poked fun at her.

School went okay. The big boys weren't in school at all, or at least neither kid saw them. Clark and some of the other boys took Clarence as their 'recess project' and gave him all sorts of pointers on playing with the basketball at recess. By the afternoon recess, he was pretty good at dribbling. He couldn't wait to tell Mr. Darrell and Harrington.

At morning recess, Diane told Clarence that she had talked to Mr. Larson and he said he would be happy to work with the cedar flute. She told him to bring his cedar flute things the next day and they would go show them to Mr. Larson at noon after lunch. Clarence was happy about that. All in all, it was a not too bad day.

Ginger's day wasn't as good. Her eyes watered a lot, so she had trouble reading. Then she ran out of tissues in her desk, so she had to wipe her eyes on her dress sleeve. After she went out for recess, Clarence put his tissue box in her desk, but never said anything to anyone about it.

When she came back from recess, she opened her desk and saw the new box. She looked around and trying to figure out who gave them to her and then she saw Clarence. She nodded and whispered, "Thanks."

Clarence shrugged and went back looking at his math paper. It made him feel good that she figured out who did it, but they never talked about it.

Tuesday morning, there was a new box of tissues in his desk. He smiled at her and she nodded.

After lunch, Diane came over to where Clarence was sitting. "Are you finished with your lunch?"

"Yes, Miss Waggoner," he said as he closed his lunch bucket.

"Okay, let's go see Mr. Larson."

In the hall when there was no one around, Diane said, "I asked Mr. Larson and he was excited. He has heard cedar flutes and knows what they are, but he has never played one. After he looks it over, he will be able to tell if he can help you play it. Okay?"

"Okay. Is he a nice guy?"

"He is and Clarence, he doesn't yell at folks. So don't worry!" Diane assured him.

They met with the middle-aged man. He seemed to not smile very much, but he acted friendly. He looked over the flute and even learned how to say Hokagapi. That made Clarence feel very good.

They all three blew into the flute and Mr. Larson was able to make some nice sounds on it. Diane and Clarence just made noise, but they were pleased anyway. Mr. Larson looked over the materials and tapes that came with it and then said, "I know this is very special to you. If I give you my word I'll take very good care of it, may I take it home tonight? I'd like to I can take some time with it. I'll bring it back tomorrow."

Clarence caressed the flute and then asked Diane, "Do you think he is trusty?"

"Yes, I do."

"Okay. You can take it home, but please don't break it."

"I'll take extra care of it. Scouts honor."

Clarence asked Diane, "What is that?"

"It is like giving your word."

Clarence grinned and shook Mr. Larson's hand. The man smiled back and then said, "I appreciate the fact you trust me with it. See you at noon tomorrow?"

"Okay."

That afternoon, Elton, Nora and Claudia met Zach for lunch before they went to see the ear doctor. Claudia had enjoyed the previous visit and was all smiles when she went this time. When the doctor put the little headphones on her, she smiled.

The doctor played with her while he tested the sound levels for each ear. When the toddler could hear a sound in one ear, she would look to that side and smile slightly. She seemed very intent on listening.

When he took off the earphones, she teared up. It was obvious that she enjoyed hearing. She was very concerned when he came with the small behind-the-ear aids. She seemed quite worried about them.

Then the doctor adjusted the sound levels and showed the adults how to do it. Once the levels were up as high as the earphones, she started to smile again.

The doctor explained that the hearing level was still below normal range, but he wanted to leave it that way for a couple days so Claudia could adjust. Then they could raise the level. She was to wear them during the day, but not at night, or while she was taking a bath.

"It will take her a little while to get used to them, but it'll go faster than you think. Before long, she'll be reliant on them and will want to take care of them. When she is older, we can get her the inside-the-ear molds; but now she is growing so fast, we would have to get her new ones a couple times a year. This will last a lot longer. I'd like to see you next week, and call me if there are any issues."

While they were putting her coat on, Claudia took one off and gave it back to the doctor. He smiled and said, "You can keep these! Okay?"

He put it back on her and she beamed.

It was a wonderful afternoon. Claudia listened to everything, especially when Diane gave the piano lessons. She and Cotton sat at the end of the piano on the floor and played while the lessons went on. After her last student, Diane picked her up and put her on her lap. She put her hand over Claudia's and played a simple *Twinkle, Twinkle Little Star*. Then Clarissa came over, "We sang some of those words at school."

So, Diane and Clarissa sang the little song, while Claudia touched the keys with Diane. It was very exciting for Claudia.

When the boys got off the bus, Elton was waiting at the bus stop. The Dynamic Duo nonchalantly told him hi and raced to the house to see if Grandma had any brownies left. Clarence got off and gave Elton a big smile. "You don't need to worry Mister. Today was okay. The big kids weren't around and I learned about basketball at recess."

"That's great! I was worried. I have some news for you! I stopped at the library today and talked to the librarian. She said that she was sorry to hear that you had so much trouble and wanted to thank you for trying to protect the book. She said that she would trust you to take care of more books, so you shouldn't worry."

"What about her wrecked book?"

"I paid her for it. She will order a new one. She said that you could keep this one."

"I pretty much don't want to see it anymore. Can we give it to Mr. Coot? He can look at when he needs it."

"That'd be a great idea. We'll give it to Coot next time we see him."

"Mister, is it a lot of dollars? Will you have to trade stuff for it?"

"No, we'll be just fine."

After dinner, Darrell called and asked to speak to Clarence. When the boy answered, Darrell said, "Now, don't hang up!"

"I won't, Mr. Darrell," Clarence giggled.

"I was wondering if you could come over tomorrow after school and I can show you what I need you to help me with. Ask your parents."

"My parents were in a car wreck, but I can ask Mister and Missus."

"Okay."

Clarence asked them and they said that he could go home with Jeannie after school. He was excited, especially when Darrell said he would write down his first hours! He only needed eighteen to get the baby goat.

CJ was excited, too. Doug had told Elton that the chicks would be in any day. The coop was all disinfected and ready except for the feed and water. "Mister, will it be hard to take care of them? What if they get sick and die?"

"They won't. Don't worry, We'll help you guys. Just use your head."

CJ frowned, "What would I use my head for?"

"Thinking. If there is anything that concerns you, let one of us know. Okay?"

"I guess I get it." CJ squinted, "Sometimes you talk funny."

Elton burst out laughing, "I guess I do."

Grandpa and Clancy were spending a lot of time playing with blocks and talking about the wars. Everyone was hoping that Lloyd's idea to whittle was forgotten again. It seemed to be for now.

48

Life began to settle into a routine of sorts at the Schroeder farm. A couple more cows had their calves and Clarissa and Diane helped train them to drink from pails. They had finally decided on names for the calves; choosing the names of the Seven Dwarfs. The girls decided it didn't matter if they were boys or girls because anyone could be Sneezy or Dopey!

CJ brought home a picture book from school about rabbits. He was enthralled with them. He told Kevin about them while they were doing chores, and before long the two had decided to go into the rabbit business.

"If we're going to be partners, then you have to do your share. We can ask Dad if we can build a hutch and take care of them together. Do you think that would be a good idea?"

CJ thought, "I do, but I have to ask Clarence. If he says okay, we'll do it. Where will we get the bunnies from?"

"Don't get your cart before your horse," Kev pointed out. "We have to see if Dad says we can."

"Oh yah, huh? Dad will think it is okay, huh? I mean, he wouldn't get mad, would he?"

"No, he won't get mad unless we start this and then don't take care of them properly. He doesn't like that."

"We will do that, won't we?"

"We'll sure try. You know when you decide to raise animals, you must be ready to do a good job. It isn't just the fun stuff."

"That is what Agent Coot said about the ducks. But me and Charlie know about that because we are Chicken Men."

When they asked Clarence, he had to sleep on it. The next morning, he told them it would be okay, as long as CJ didn't be a lunk head. CJ took exception to that, "I'm not a lunk head all the time. I know some things are important. Kevin and me are going to do a good job. Aren't we?"

"You and Kevin are doing a good job about what?" Elton asked as he poured the pail of milk into the separator.

Kevin explained what they wanted to do, and Elton had a few questions. Then he said, "Okay. You have my blessing. You can set the cages south of the shop. I want you to learn what you can about raising rabbits and figure out what you need for it, write down how much you spend and all that. CJ needs to learn about keeping records, math and things like that."

Kev winked, "Way ahead of you Dad."

"Figured as much. Could we wait for a while before we build the cages? We're going to get the baby chicks any day now, and I would be happier if they were settled, before we do something else. We need to help Coot with his ducks. Would that be too late?"

"What do you think, CJ? Shall we get these other things finished first? Besides, we need to study up on what we need."

"Okay."

Kevin smiled, "Okay, Dad."

CJ grinned, "Okay, Dad."

When they got to the house for breakfast, there was a major fiasco. Grandpa had found a kitchen knife and decided to whittle on one of the wooden blocks. Andy saw him just as he cut himself and managed to get the knife away from him while the wound could be bandaged with a large bandaid. Nora was giving Clancy his bath at the time, so he wasn't a party to the situation; but Kitten saw it and was scared because Grandpa was bleeding.

Grandma got the maddest anyone had ever seen her! "You are to never touch a knife again, Lloyd! Do you hear me? You could have hurt the children! As it was, you cut yourself and scared them half to death. Do not ever do that again! If you do it again, I'll send you to the Retirement Home in Merton!"

Lloyd was shattered, "Don't send me away! I didn't mean to do that. I just wanted to show High Pockets how to whittle a horse."

"I know Lloyd, but don't you ever do that again. You can play with High Pockets, but no knives."

Lloyd sat down in his rocker and looked bewildered, "I know how to whittle. How am I going to teach High Pockets? He will never learn if I don't show him."

Andy had been listening, "Grandpa, would it be okay if I teach him when he gets older? Would that be okay?"

"Do you know how?"

"You taught me, remember?"

"I guess I do. I did that, right Katherine?"

"Yes, but Darrell and Andy were older when you taught them. Clancy is too little yet."

"Okay, I'll wait. I'll watch to see that you do it right," the elderly man said to Andy.

"Good."

As Katherine, Nora and Elton had their last cup of coffee after breakfast, Katherine said, "I decided. I'm calling the Retirement Home. We will move in there. I can't have him hurting the kids."

Nora burst into tears, "No. Katherine, please don't. Are the kids too much for you? Are we asking you to do too much?"

"Not at all. I love these little guys, and I know Lloyd enjoys them, too. But he is getting more and more difficult to care for and it is too demanding on everyone."

Elton set down his coffee cup, "Listen here. I'm saying this once. I would no more send you guys to the Retirement Home than send the kids back to Pine Ridge! This is our family and we are in this together. The next time you get that dumb idea, I'm going to send you off with Clarence to his thinking spot to talk it over. This is the end of the discussion."

"But . . . ."

"No buts. Don't even talk to me about this. We just need to keep an eagle eye on Lloyd and his whittling. You know, maybe if we got some of those plastic blocks, he wouldn't be as tempted. He and Clancy have been playing with those wooden blocks lately. That's what I'll do. I'm going to stop at the Dime Store today and pick some up. Besides, with the little rugrats around, we need to figure a way to make the knife drawer a little more difficult to access."

"Elton, it isn't that simple."

"I know, but it will help."

That week, the Harrington boys, Danny and Darrell dug and poured the footings for Kincaid's duck coops. It would take a while for it to set up in the cold, moist air. The lumber company delivered the materials for the coops and the fence. The group was going to assemble on Saturday to build the coops. They were all keeping their fingers crossed that the baby ducks wouldn't come before then.

Father Vicaro had his cast removed and everyone was a bit disappointed that his temperament hadn't improved. Bart laughed, "I know I am in the miracle business, but cheering up this old grump might even be a challenge for the good Lord!"

Matt teased, "Now they'll know that is just the way you are, Frank!"

"I'm worried Matt, the Diocese says they are keeping Landers out here. Do you think that they are about ready to send me to greener pastures?"

"No, I don't. I think they realize you guys have a big parish and they have Bart teaching full time. There is alot of work to get done. You aren't a spring chicken anymore, Frank. Maybe they think you need to have more help."

"Do you hear yourself? Those guys don't think like that! They are always afraid we don't have enough to do!"

Matt snickered, "Maybe you're suffering from a guilty conscience."

"I really don't like you very much. You might be right though. I wouldn't have given Landers such a bad time if I knew I'd be stuck with him."

"Yea gads, Frank. You are incorrigible."

The old priest grinned.

Plans were finalized for the upcoming travels. The Harrington/Kincaid crew and Diane would be going out east over Easter. Ian and Matt were going to be Godparents for their nephew Austin at his baptism. Diane was going to see her mom and brother while there.

Pepper and Chris would be home a few days over Easter and it would be the first time they would meet the Grey Hawks. Clarissa was really curious about 'her sister'. She and Diane had several long talks about if Pepper would like her, even if she didn't have sunshine hair. Diane assured her she would.

Nora and Elton had decided to go on their vacation in June, after school was out. Since they would be taking care of the Petunia Patch and the little Gophers while Coot and Mo were gone, Kincaids would return the favor while Schroeders took their vacation week to the Grand Caymans. Diane would be home from school and could help out.

Kevin and Carrie were going to take a trip to Banff in Canada right after the Fourth of July. When they returned, Darlene and Keith were going to Glacier National Park for a week. Andy and Annie were planning on going to Chicago with Horse right after that, to visit their Army friend, Chicago and his family. That would be their summer vacation.

Of course, Clarence was counting the days until they would go back to Pine Ridge for Memorial Day. He was very excited when he heard that Uncle Bear was going there for the week, too. They planned to all camp out at the cabin.

That Saturday morning, the crew all headed over to the Petunia Patch. The ladies came with Corned Beef and Cabbage, roasted potatoes and cupcakes with green frosting for dessert. They were going to celebrate St. Patrick's Day while they were there. The St. John's contingent showed up and were there as much as their schedules allowed; except for Vicaro, who was there all day. He had appointed himself the master architect of the duck pen project.

It was a blustery day, but the group was determined to get the work finished. It took the men the morning to get the coops built and after lunch, Clarence and Elton worked on the shingles with Matt and Joey Jessup; while the rest built the fences and finished the insides of the coops.

By chore time, the work was finished. The coops were ready to go, insulated, stocked with bedding and the feeders, waterers and heat lamps waiting to be put into use.

It was a long day, but fun. Sammy and Joey Jessup, Darrell's brothers, helped so Clarence got to meet them. He decided they would be 'trusty' and he liked Chatterbox Olson. He was married to Eve who was another of Darrell's sisters. Chatterbox was a carpenter and Clarence was impressed how fast he could put a building up. He told Elton that when he had enough money in his saving account, he wanted to buy a tool belt like Chatterbox wore. Elton thought that would be a good idea.

While helping at Jessups that weekend, Clarence got to know Joallyn. She lived with Jessups and was Jeannie's sister. She worked as a painter at Chatterbox's construction company and helped milk too; so they were coworkers.

Darrell and the two of them helped a momma goat deliver twins on Friday night. It was the first babies either one had delivered and Clarence knew she was as excited as he was. After he cleaned the mucus from the second kid's mouth so it could breathe, Joallyn gave him a big hug. It was one of the most exciting things he had ever done in his life. He held one of the little brown babies while Joallyn held the other and they posed for Polaroids. He told Darrell that he thought that he would probably want to buy the boy one, but he really liked the girl one. He loved the little white and black stripes on their faces. He couldn't decide which was prettier. He would have to sleep on it. Joallyn suggested that Darrell might be willing to sell him both of them.

Darrell grinned, "I might, if you can tell me how many hours two would cost. Remember one costs eighteen hours."

Clarence never said anything and changed the milker on another goat before he said, "I think it is thirty six?"

Darrell clapped him on the back, "I think you just bought yourself another goat! You are right!"

"Do you think Mister will let me keep two?"

"You have to ask him. That is the only way you will know."

Elton came over to pick him up after chores, and pulled up to the barn. Clarence ran out as soon as he heard the car and went to the driver's door. "Mister! Turn off the car quick and come! I gotta show you!! It is so cool! You gotta see what me and Joallyn did! Darrell told us what to do and we had twin babies! Come see!"

Elton grinned and turned off the car. Clarence grabbed his hand and nearly drug him to the barn where the nanny was nursing her little ones.

"Mister! I cleaned the goop off the baby's face so it could get air, but the mommy licked them all clean after! She gave them a bath with her tongue! Aren't you glad people don't have to do that? Look how big this one's eyes are! She is a girl and she looked right at me! I think she knows that I helped her breathe, so maybe she likes me! And the other one is a boy; Joallyn helped him breathe. We are good helpers, aren't we? And guess what? Mr. Darrell said if I could figure out how many hours, I could earn both of them if you think that would be okay. Otherwise, I will only get one. You know they are twins, so they might not want to be away from each other! Darrell says . . ."

Elton chuckled, "Take a deep breath Clarence! I think you are a little excited!"

"I'm so happy it makes my toes wiggle."

Elton gave him a hug, "Okay, you earn the hours and when they are weaned, you can keep them both. Now you have to think of what you are going to name them."

"I might have Mr. Darrell help me."

Elton stood up and shook his head, "That would be his first mistake."

All the way home, Clarence talked about the birth of the goats. He said, "I can't wait to tell Jackson, and Grandma, and Missus."

He suddenly became very quiet for a minute before he said, "Mister, do you think that my Dad would be happy about those baby goats? He never said much about that kind of stuff."

"Yes, sir. I think he would be happy and proud. Clarence, if you aren't being hurtful or dishonest, you can do anything. And maybe some of the things you will do, your Dad might not have known about. Don't let that stop you. There is a whole big world, and lots of things to do and learn. None of us can only do just what our Dads knew."

"I might have to sleep on that." The boy looked out the window for a ways, "I'm a pretty happy guy that I didn't go back to Pine Ridge right away! I think me and the kids are pretty lucky here. Of course, I'm only staying until I am old enough."

"Yes, I know Clarence."

Elton replaced the wooden blocks with the plastic ones and made the wooden ones disappear. It seemed to help. If Lloyd thought of the old blocks, he never made mention of them and Clancy didn't care. These could be stacked up and knocked over as well as the other ones.

Kevin put the new drawer stops in the knife drawer. In order to open the drawer, one had to open it about an inch and then reach a finger under it and move a lever. Grandma hated it and Clarissa figured it out in less than two seconds. Nora and Kevin explained to her to not show the little kids or Grandpa how to do it. She made a heart promise because she didn't want anyone to get cut.

She was very happy that Katie was starting to work on another wedding dress. Kate was doing three wedding dresses and had two at her house. For the other one, she used Grandma's dress form; so it was at Schroeders. Clarissa watched her put on some beads, and then Katie gave her a piece of cloth and some larger beads for her to practice. Clarissa was delighted. She told Katie she was going to make beaded dresses for Singer Fairies when she grew up.

The piano lessons were coming along well. CJ and Charlie had finally decided they would give the accordion a real effort, after Bill Heinrich promised them that if they practiced faithfully, they could play at the next dance that would be sometime after Easter. The invitation was given to Clark, Little Bill, CJ and Charlie, and only for one song. They were going to form a group, but hadn't come up with a name yet. All they could think of was the Beatles, but someone was already using that. Kevin suggested the Box Elder Bugs, but that idea was still under consideration.

The little girls were all doing well with their piano lessons, even Kitten who was rarely more than a foot away from the piano if someone was playing. She seemed to be adjusting to her hearing aids well, and only a couple times became frightened by a loud sound.

Mr. Larson talked to Diane and Clarence about the cedar flute. He was as excited about it as they were and ordered one for himself. He started lessons for Clarence. They would meet every Tuesday after lunch. During the week, Clarence would practice at home.

He also had to promise to learn to read music. Diane said she would teach him on the piano. He wasn't too excited about that until Mr. Larson told him that way he would help him find the right tones and keys. Clarence didn't know what that meant, but it didn't sound like playing the piano, so he could live with it.

Sunday, Clarence went to Sunday School for the first time. He knew most of the kids in the class and it was okay. Of course, he and Ginger still didn't acknowledge each other. They hadn't spoken since the day she said thanks for the tissues. However, if there was something that he was lost about, she always gave him a hint with her eyes or motions. When there was something she needed, he would discretely help her. Total strangers spoke to each other more passing on the street than these two. However, they both seemed to know the ground rules of their relationship and seemed very content with it.

Jackson and Andy had worked the entire week in their repair shop. They usually worked together, but spent time working alone, also. Andy decided that he would try to work more hours while Annie was working, so he could spend more time with her when she was home. Jackson worked at the church office Tuesday and Thursday mornings and had to keep up with his sketches. But they both managed to put in nearly forty hours a week. Elton, Byron and Zach reminded them they were supposed to work part-time and take it easy. Both guys were definite they were not overdoing it and in fact, felt better than that had in some time. Physically, Zach had to agree they were doing well. By the end of the week, they had completed several repairs and were getting more work coming in. They both felt like good about that.

49

School was back in routine. Clarence was doing well with his extra studies with Jeannie. Ian and Matt were both helping him with his math. He wasn't getting A's, but he was getting C's and B's. He had never received above a D ever before. With Denise Frandsen's help, CJ even managed one A and was very proud. Elton promised him that he would take him to get a wallet, bank card and library card on the next Saturday.

Clarence was helping at Jessups and was becoming familiar with the routine at their milk barn. Afterwards, he would work with Jeannie on his schoolwork. He took pride in being diligent. Every day he helped, he marked in his book how many hours he had worked and how long he had until he got his very own baby kids.

Wednesday, Coot called Elton at the shop. "Doug just called and said the ducklings are here. Are your chicks?"

"Not yet. You want me to bring them out to you?"

"Yah," Carl said. "Magpie, I'm really nervous about this!"

"You have nothing to be nervous about. I know you can handle it. Good grief man, you've handled more important things than this all those years in the FBI."

"I guess so, but I have no idea what I'm doing?"

"It has never bothered you before."

"I knew I shouldn't call you, you jackass!"

Elton laughed, "I'll pick up the ducklings and bring them out your way in about twenty minutes. Okay? I can help you get them set up."

"You just want to give me grief!"

"That too. Be there soon."

When Elton arrived at the Patch about ten-thirty, Marly and Nora were there with Gopher and Kitten. High Pockets was taking his nap, so he stayed home. Elton and Coot carried the boxes of ducklings out the coops.

"Why did you have three coops instead of just one?" Elton asked. "There aren't that many ducklings."

"It was a Gopher issue. Seems the little tykes had strong ideas about who was taking care of which and so on. Finally, Mo decreed we would do it this way. It was one of those things, you just had to be there. Trust me, this way is the best."

"Whatever you say. I guess it is a good idea to have more than one brooder, in case something would happen to one of them."

Carl panicked, "Like what? What could happen? Is it likely to happen? Oh no, what shall I do?"

Elton chuckled, "Good thing you and Mo are too old to have children. You would never make it to the hospital with her!"

"Oh be quiet. This isn't funny."

"I'm sorry. Here, help me with these little guys. Let's get the feed out and the waters filled. I see you turned the heat lamps on. They need to be 95 degrees for the first week and you can turn the temp down five degrees a week. The temp should be about 90 on the floor. Since it is pretty cold out today, you will need to check it to see if it is warm enough."

The men filled the feeders and the waterers. "Be careful not to set the water directly under the lamps. The water will get icky in the heat. Give the little guys room to wander around."

"Will they know the way to the food and stuff?"

"Oh yes. They're rather self-sufficient. Don't let them get wet, in a draft or cold. Check on them several times a day and you should be just fine. Okay, which breed goes in this coop?"

"Doesn't matter. Just need to keep them separate, at least until the Gophers get over their issues."

"I'm not going to ask. We have enough weirdness at our house. Thanks for the whistles, by the way. The kids really appreciated them and they all wore them to school today without a hassle."

"I feel bad those brats had to give Clarence a rough time. He is a good kid. He has had a tough row to hoe, but he's doing pretty well. I knew he would at your place, if anywhere."

"You must really be bent out of shape to be that nice!"

"I said at your place, not with you! There are enough good folks over there to help the kids and drown you out."

Elton reached into the box of white ducklings. "What kind are these?"

"The white are Pekin. Mo and I have been trying to teach the kids to call them by the right name. It might be easier now that they are more than just a picture. You just scoop them out?"

"Yah. They are nice little things. Here you go, little guys," Elton said as he scooped a couple ducks up and let them walk off his hand onto the chopped straw.

Carl held one and petted it, "Do they actually like people?"

"I guess some folks have pet ducks."

After the men saw that the ducklings were walking around, chirping happily and none were sick or injured, they moved onto the next coop. There they put the buff ducklings that were Golden Cascades and in the last coop, they put the black Cayuga ducks. When they were all finished, Carl stood up. "My first livestock! Just think, I own animals."

"You knot head, what about all the goats and cows over at Darrell's?"

"Yah, but they are mostly his, you know."

"You have the cat, Einstein."

"That is Charlie's cat. We are just boarding him."

Elton grinned and clapped Carl on the back, "Well, congratulations! You are now an official duckster! I need to get some food. I don't know about you, but I'm hungry."

"You're always hungry. How is your Whipple's?"

"Doing well. Doc says the germs are dying off and my electrolytes are getting back to normal. I only have to have IV's every other week now. That was a good scare, I must admit. I figured I was a goner."

"You would've been if you hadn't caught it in time."

"How is your ticker and those blood vessels that were all shot up?"

"Good. Doc says I may live to be a hundred plus."

"Gee, I thought you already had."

"Let's go in so I can talk to someone nice," Carl groaned. "Then we can bring the ladies out. Think the little ones will like to see the ducks?"

"They'll love them. Who all have you got here today?"

"Baby Matthew and Holly. Then Gopher and Kitten are here. The Olson Gophers will be over later."

The men were right, the kids loved the ducklings. Holly was the least interested, but Baby Matthew even held one. Then the Schroeder's headed home for lunch and Nora promised to bring Clancy over after lunch to see them.

After her luncheon meeting, Marly picked up Gopher and they went to Schroeder's for piano lessons. Gopher and Kitten went into the living room to play and decided to build a tent, using the afghan throws and the sofa. The cushions were stacked on the floor, and the afghans were draped over the sofa and onto the cushions. They worked and worked, and then crawled under their tent. There was a lot of giggling, until Clancy came through and dismantled the tent. Then the whole group decided to jump on the cushions.

When the ladies checked on the great squeals of laughter and ominous thumping, the whole plan was scrutinized. Nora explained that if they fell on the hard wood floor and not on the area rug, someone could be badly hurt. The plan was abandoned.

There were some long faces, but the little girls started to put the cushions back on the sofa. Clancy decided that was no fun and went to sit with Grandpa Lloyd in his big rocking chair. The ladies went back to the kitchen.

After a few minutes, Miriam came to the kitchen, crying. "Kitten bye-bye," she shrugged. "All gone."

"What do you mean, Miriam? She was just in there with you," Marly said.

"All gone. Kitten cry, go bye-bye."

Nora frowned and went in to check. Claudia was not to be found. The ladies searched the entire main floor and found no trace of the little girl.

The school bus stopped and when the other kids came in, they were put on search duty. Not a sign of her. Marly sent Katie down to the shop to get the GI's to come help. They came up as soon as they could and helped search. Every cupboard, crevice, closet and bed was checked.

When the teachers stopped in, they also joined the search. The upstairs and basement was checked thoroughly as was the main floor. Clarence, Charlie and CJ checked outside the house to see if there were any footprints in the snow. There were none.

Matt was near the basement steps and happened to notice that Cotton was sitting in the corner, next to an old door of a root cellar. It was rarely used anymore and hadn't been opened in years. He checked and saw the door was a bit ajar. He entered the dark, musty root cellar and saw nothing, even with the flashlight. He was about to leave when he heard a stifled sob.

He checked further and found an opening that held a large sauerkraut crock in earlier days. It was a cave-like area dug out that went back a few feet but was only a couple feet all. The two foot in diameter crock snugly filled the closet area, but had been moved a couple inches.

Matt knelt down and said softly, "Kitten? Are you there?"

There was no answer. It was quiet for a minute, "Claudia, it is Matt. Give me your hand. Please, Claudia?"

No response, save another stifled gasping sob. Matt couldn't reach her, so he moved the crock out and squished into the small space on the side of the little closet. He knew he was getting closer, because the sobs had turned into a cry.

He stretched as far as he could after getting himself jammed into the tiny space before he could reach her. Now she was wailing. He could only reach the waistband of her jeans and pulled her toward him. It took him almost five minutes to get the unwilling toddler and himself out into the room. The little girl was frantic by the time they got out of the root cellar.

Claudia covered both of her ears with her hands as tight as she could and was crying uncontrollably. Matt took her into her arms and tried his best to calm her down, but it wasn't working. He finally managed to carry her upstairs, however there was no way he could get her hands from her ears. If he pulled on one hand, she kept her head pressed to her hand, so he couldn't get it free.

Upstairs, he sat in the kitchen and tried to calm her down. She was nearly hysterical. Grandma, Nora and Jackson all tried, but nothing worked. She was impossible and determined not to remove her hands from her ears.

Clarence had been watching the whole thing for a couple minutes and then he lost it. He went over to her and started shouting something in Sioux. Then he raised her hand to smack her and she stopped crying. He said some more things in Sioux and she took one hand down. She uncovered her right ear and Matt checked it. It seemed fine.

Clarence was becoming more impatient and shouted something else in Sioux. The kids and Jackson knew what he said, but even the rest of the group knew it wasn't good. She would not remove her hand from covering her left ear.

Jackson said, "Clarence, calm down. Matt, you hold her head and I'll pull her hand away."

The little girl was stronger than anticipated, but they finally got her hand away. Her ear was fine, but the hearing aid was missing. She immediately crawled into Matt's shoulder and hid the left side of her head in his neck. She was trembling and still crying. He cuddled her and patted her back gently. "It's okay Claudia. We'll find your hearing aid. No one is mad at you. Shh, just relax."

Even Clarence assured her they would find the missing aid. Everyone except Matt and Claudia descended on the living room. They took the sofa cushions out and checked all the crevices, but no hearing aid.

Elton came home from work and asked Matt what was going on. Claudia had calmed considerably until Elton came in. His arrival prompted renewed wailing. Matt explained what happened and Elton took off his jacket.

"Come here, Kitten," he said as he almost had to peel her off Matt.

She was not at all happy with going to Elton. He held her close and talked to her calmly. "Kitten, if it is lost, we'll call the doctor and order a new one. Okay? You don't need to worry. It was an accident. With everyone looking, we will find it for sure."

Matt shook his head, "Yea gads, I don't think I'll have kids. Between Miriam and Claudia, I don't think I can handle it."

"Yah, and then they grow up! That is even more fun! Mark my words!"

"I guess, huh? Well, I better go help those folks before the living room is in shreds."

It must have taken a twenty full minutes to find the little hearing aid. It had become hooked on the yarns of an afghan and got tangled in it, making it almost invisible. Nora cleaned it and put it back in place on her ear. That was the first time that Claudia even vaguely smiled.

No one ever knew what Claudia was so upset about; losing the hearing aid or fear of being punished. Maybe it was both. Neither did anyone ask what Clarence said in Sioux. Whatever it was, they all knew it wasn't about butterflies but it got the point across. One thing they were all certain of was that Claudia would be very careful of her hearing aids.

50

Thursday, the baby chicks and turkey poults arrived. Elton took them home. He and Nora got them all settled in their coops and then brought Clancy and Kitten out to see them. The little kids loved them.

After lunch, they all went back to work and Nora checked on the chicks a few times until the Chicken Men got home. Their feet barely touched the ground once they heard the chicks had arrived. CJ and Charlie were in the house, changed into their Chicken Man hats and over to the coops in a flash!

It was a great day! CJ earned his 'promotion' and became the official Chicken Man; while Charlie was now the Turkey Man. Both boys went over to Coot's to take care of the ducks when they were finished with their chicken/turkey chores. While the other kids 'helped' with the ducks, the main responsibility fell to the Chicken Men. They took their duties seriously.

Elton and Carl had to keep an eye on the amount of feed going through the coops. Charlie had not been entirely convinced that feed did not spoil after it was in a feeder for an hour. He wanted to give them fresh food and throw out the other. Elton had finally conceded to let him to move the older feed to one feeder, but not throw it away! He had gone through a bag of chick feed in no time! Elton was convinced the kid owned stock in Purina Feeds.

With a lot of educating, talking and finally downright threatening, the boys relented. They decided when they had their own place, they would feed their chicks fresh feed all the time. Carl and Elton assured them they could do that; as soon as they grew up and had their own place.

For the most part, the boys did a good job. They cared for the babies and kept their coops clean. The other kids mostly just played with the chicks, or helped feed them a little scratch or greens.

CJ had asked Kev if Charlie could be a partner with the rabbits, too. Kev said he would have to get permission from his Dad and do his share of the work. Kevin pointed out to the boys, "Now I want you to know, this is not like the chickens. I am the Managing Partner with the rabbits. You guys have to follow my instructions or we can't do it. Got that?"

"But Kev, we can do lots of thinking," Charlie argued. "How come are you that Mangey guy?"

"It is going to cost money to get set up, which I'm lending it to the business. I don't want to waste the money with fooling around. When we start selling the rabbits and each get our share, you guys can start paying me back. Then you'll be bigger partners. Soon, we'll be equal; but until then, I'm the boss."

CJ listened, "Like Clarence is the boss of me, uh? That's okay, because you drive a car."

"Why is that, CJ?"

CJ looked at him like he was not quite functioning on all cylinders, "Because we can't reach the pedals."

Kevin shook his head and shrugged, "Whatever. This weekend, we need to have a meeting and decide on all the details. Okay? I'll talk to your parents about when we can get together."

Clarence was a busy fella. After school, he went with Matt to give Grandpa his ride and made sure the car was cleaned and polished. Some days, he rode to Jessups to help with chores. After chores, he sometimes stayed and did his homework at Jessups or he and Jeannie worked on his extra studies. He was doing very well with his reading.

He was looking forward to practicing casting his fishing pole with Harrington and practicing basketball. He and Mister practiced casting into old tractor tires in the yard. Mister and Kevin were going to put up their basketball hoop in front of the shop again. Kevin said they had one when he was a kid, but they wore it out.

Clarissa followed Elton around the barn one morning and then when they were alone, she asked, "Mister?"

"Yes Sweetheart, what is it?" He asked as he knelt down beside her.

"The big boys, they got stuff. Like live stuff."

Elton frowned, "I don't understand. What do you mean?"

"Clarence got baby goats and CJ is gonna have bunnies. I don't have nothing that's alive. Even Kitten has Cotton."

"Clancy doesn't have anything," Elton pointed out.

Clarissa hesitated a second and then said, "He has Grandpa."

Elton chuckled, "By crackie, you're right. What are we going to do about that? Would you like a dragon?"

Clarissa giggled, "I don't want one of them, like was in my book. They shoot fire out of their mouths!"

"No, that probably wouldn't be a good idea. What kind of an animal do you think you would like?"

The little girl shrugged, "I don't know. I don't take care of nothing butcept the calves. Miss Diane and I do that."

"Well then, what do you think? Would you like to have a calf of your very own?"

"I don't know. Will Diane get one?"

"I think that would be okay. I'll tell you what. You ladies talk it over and let me know which one of the calves you want. You each get one."

"Will we have to build a barn for our calves?"

"No, they can live in this one with their friends. They can play in the same pasture, because they like that. Let me know which one you want."

Clarissa watched him without expression, "You mean yes?"

"That is what I mean. Now you have to be responsible for your calf. You can't just goof off."

"I help take care of them now. Is that 'sponsible?"

"Yes, it is. You and Diane do a fine job."

The little girl threw her arms around his neck, "I love you, Mister! You are the best new Daddy I have!"

Elton grinned, "Thank you, Sweetheart. Now, you go talk to Diane and decide which ones you want. When we put the tags in their ears, we will put your names on them so everyone will know they are yours. Okay?"

"That is the mostest best goodest idea ever in the whole wide world!" She kissed his cheek and then ran off to find Diane.

Kevin chuckled as he shook his head, "That girl needs to get excited, huh? She is a little doll."

"Yes, she is."

At breakfast, Clarissa announced that she and Diane had decided on which calves they wanted. They both picked little girl calves. Diane picked the Guernsey named Sneezy and Clarissa picked Happy, a little Jersey. Clarissa talked non-stop for a full five minutes before Grandpa said, "You must be a cowgirl, huh?"

She looked at him inquisitively, "Why?"

"Cause you get so excited about cows! I never heard anybody talk so much about a cow in my life. You are sure a good talker!"

Clarissa giggled, "I learned it. I can show you how to talk a lot, if you want! Will that be fun?"

The old man shook his head, "If you say so."

The end of the following week, Clarence and Matt went into town on a blustery Saturday morning to deliver more of Jackson's sketches and stop at the library. This was his third trip to the library. He and Matt looked for more books and he sat quietly reading them, while Matt did some research for his class. After the library and grocery store, the two stopped at the Log House for lunch. Clarence was pleased that Matt showed him how to call in the order over the phone.

While they waited for their food, Clarence said, "Mr. Matt? I have been sleeping on something and I haven't been able to think it good yet."

"Do you need some help? I'd be glad to listen," Matt offered.

Clarence nodded seriously, "I think so. Mister said that sometimes we do stuff our dads never thought about. Do you think that is right?"

"Yes, I do. If everyone did only what their fathers did, nothing new would ever happen. We'd still be living in caves."

Clarence looked up in surprise, "Did you live in a cave?"

Matt grinned, "No, I didn't live in a cave. But the first men, way many years ago, did. Then someone got the idea to build a house. People used to have to walk everywhere. Now they can ride horse or drive a car. See what I mean?"

Clarence shook his head yes, then he said, "No. I don't need to know all that stuff. I just need to know if I can do stuff my Dad never thought about."

"Yes, you can Clarence." Matt smiled, "You know, I like having you for a friend."

"Yah, but I'm a kid."

"So? Aren't you going to get older?"

"I hope so."

Matt got some napkins out for the two when the food came. After he said grace, he said, "So how are things going with your cedar flute?"

"It is so cool! Mr. Larson says he really likes it! He ordered his own flute and said he can't wait for it to come. It should be here next week. Then we can both play. Miss Diane is teaching me to read notes. Some of the flute stuff is in your head, but some is written in those notes. What do you think of the Lunkhead's accordion band?"

Matt chuckled, "I don't know. What do you think?"

"They're wacky." Clarence rolled his eyes, "They even asked Katie to make them shirts with their names on them! They don't even know what their name is gonna be!"

"Maybe they should learn how to play before they worry about costumes."

"What is a barn dance, Mr. Matt? Everybody talks about them, but I have never seen one.

"Oh, you will like them. We go to Suzy's parent's farm, upstairs in their big barn. We play music, have good food and then dance and visit. It is great."

"Like a Pow-wow?"

"I don't know. People dance with their friends for fun. I can show you how to dance so you know how."

"Who would I dance with?"

"Girls or ladies."

Clarence grimaced and jerked his head back, "Like kissing stuff?"

"No kissing. Just dancing. You can dance with Nora, Grandma, Diane, Clarissa, anyone."

"Why would I want to dance with Clarissa?"

"Because she is a nice girl, your sister and she could be a good friend. Why wouldn't you dance with her?"

"Would you?"

"I plan on it. I dance with Katie, Ginger and Miriam."

"Does Mr. Darrell?"

"Yes, he does. So does Kevin and Mister. You'll like it. Trust me. Have I ever led you astray?"

"I don't know where astray is, but I did get whacked when you took me to that hair fixing place."

"Yah, that wasn't so good, was it? That is why you should ask Clarissa to dance. Otherwise, she might whack you."

"Maybe I won't go to the barn dance."

"Clarence, I wanted to ask you if you would do me a favor? While I'm in Boston, could you come in the cabin and check on the cats? They'll need their food and water checked and their kitty litter changed. If something is wrong, you could let Jeannie know. Would you do that for me?"

"Sure. I can do that when I help milk. Will you show me how?"

"I'll do that. I really appreciate you doing this for me. I know Lucky and Murphy will like it."

"Mr. Matt, can I ask you a secret?"

"Fire away," Matt grinned.

"Well, Clarissa calls Missus her new Mommy. I don't really care too much, because she called Jackson's Mommy that, too. But she told me that she might call Mister her new Daddy. Every so often, CJ calls him Dad. I think I should whack him, but he wants to be like everybody else. You know? He calls Andy Spud because Jackson does. Do you think it makes my Dad mad? I think he wants us to call him Dad, because he is our Dad."

"You know Clarence, Carl isn't my real Dad. My real Dad died many years ago. But Carl is like my Dad and he treats me like his son. He treats Ian like his son too; so we both call him Dad. I think my real Dad knows that we know who he is, but he also is probably very happy that we have someone that treats us like his sons. I'm pretty sure he doesn't mind one bit. In fact, I think it makes him happy."

Clarence swirled his French fry around in the ketchup, "I don't know. I think it would make my Dad sad. It is like we forgot him and he doesn't matter anymore. Clancy and Claudia probably have forgot already. But us bigger kids, we need to remember him."

"I remember my real Dad and I loved him; but I love Carl, too. Elton is not the real Dad of any of his kids. He adopted the kids."

Clarence ate the French fry and then took another, "Somebody told me that before. He hasn't adopted us kids, so maybe we shouldn't call him that."

"You know, I think that if the kids want to call them Mom or Dad, you shouldn't whack them. You don't need to call them that unless you want to and no one should whack you. It is a private thing and each person should be able to do what they want. Does that sound okay?"

The little boy frowned, "That is harder, huh?"

"Most questions are like that. You know, these folks have already made you part of their family."

"Tiyospaye," Clarence took more ketchup, "We have a big tiyospaye, don't we? I like it here. This is a good place for a home if you can't be at Pine Ridge."

"Yes, it is. I like it here. I used to live in Boston and it was nice. But I love it here now and I call this place home."

Clarence giggled, "You and me could call the Log House to be home. Then we could eat French fries all the time!"

"Who would milk the goats?"

"Yah, I bet my baby kids would miss me. Mr. Darrell said he had an idea for their names, Hansel and Gretel. I guess there is a fairy story about them."

"I know the story. It is about two little kids that get lost and an evil witch catches them and wants to cook them for dinner!"

Clarence made a horrible face and crossed his eyes, "I don't want to name my kids that!"

"They get away though; because they were very clever and left a trail of crumbs in the forest. Someone follows the crumb trail and rescues them."

Clarence let the story sink in and then observed, "They were lucky the squirrels didn't eat their crumbs."

51

When they arrived home, they noticed a car there with South Dakota license plates on it. Matt figured right away who it was, but Clarence didn't. Before they got out of the car, Matt told him. "Clarence, I think the folks from Social Services are here. It looks like their car. Do you want to talk to me about anything before you talk to them?"

Clarence started to panic, "Are they going to take us away?"

"I truly doubt it. When they ask you about things, just be as honest as you can."

The little boy nodded and then his face fell, "Can't I just run away?"

Matt was serious, "If you do, that will pretty much make certain they will put you in Foster Care. Just be your regular self."

Clarence picked up his library books and froze. It took him a minute before he said, "I really don't want to go away from here."

So they went, hand in hand, toward the old farmhouse. The steps seemed very hard to climb for Clarence and he became so slow, he could hardly continue his walk. Matt knelt down to him near the top of the steps before they went into the mudroom. "It'll be okay. I promise you. These folks just came out to make sure you guys are doing alright. They don't want to hurt you."

"But what if CJ is a lunk head and then he has to leave, or Kitten loses her hearing aid again and acts like a monster kid? I don't want any of us to have to go away from everybody else."

"That won't happen, almost for sure. Got it?"

Clarence gave Matt a big hug and Matt hugged him back. Then Matt said, "Ready to face it, Grey Hawk?"

The boy looked worried and then held his stomach, "I hope I don't up it."

"I hope you don't either. That'd waste the French fries!" Matt teased.

The snow was really coming down now, and the wind was coming up. A gust blew some snow off the roof and it fell in front of the mudroom door. "Wow, looks like it is drumming up a good one," Matt shivered. "Let's go in."

Clarence nodded in agreement, "Maybe those Rules people will have to leave early because it is storming, huh?"

"Nice try, Clarence," Matt chuckled.

Some of the family was gathered around the table, having coffee. Elton opened the door for the guys, "We thought we heard you."

Elton helped the little boy with his coat. "I see you got some more library books, huh? What are these about?"

"Goats and fishing with those fly things."

"Sounds interesting," Elton smiled. "Run put your books away and then come join us."

Clarence was more than happy to run upstairs. When he got into his room, he put the books on the desk. Then he looked around. There was a closet full of clothes for him and CJ, shelves with CJ's boats on them, CJ's bat leaned in the corner, sketches that Jackson had made of their parents and on his desk in a frame, the special one that Jackson had done of him and his Dad on the fishing trip they never had. Clarence picked up the picture and studied it for a minute.

He suddenly became so angry that he shook. He didn't know why, but he did. "Why didn't you take me fishing? You could have! You had time to go see Spotted Calf! You just didn't want to." Clarence frowned at the sketch. "That wasn't very nice."

He plunked on his bed and looked out the window. The snow was so thick and now the wind was coming up. He noticed the picture on the wall of that Jesus guy. He was sitting with a bunch of kids around him. Clarence shrugged and said to the picture, "You must sure like worrying. I wouldn't do it for all those kids."

Nora called from downstairs, "Clarence, could you bring your cedar flute down. Mr. Thunder would like to see it."

"Yes, Missus," Clarence answered.

He got his flute and went down the stairs. When he got to the kitchen, Nora smiled and motioned toward where Matt had saved a spot beside him at the table, "Thank you. I hear you two stopped at the Log House, huh?"

"We did! I love their ketchup and French fries."

"And their milk shakes?"

Clarence giggled back, "Yes."

"Do you remember Miss Thomas and Mr. Thunder?"

Clarence nodded to them, "Kinda. I was pretty crabby when I saw them before."

George Thunder was a short but well-built young man. He wore his black hair short and was rather nice looking. There was a long scar over his left eyebrow, but he had a huge smile and seemed very friendly. "I think you had every reason to be crabby that day."

"Here is my Hokagapi. Mr. Larson at school is helping me learn it. He ordered one for his own self, too. Then we can play together. He says he really likes the tones from—where was that?"

Diane answered, "Nature."

"Tones from nature, he says. He can play it pretty nice now. Miss Diane is teaching me to read the notes, so I can play some other stuff. If I learn it good, she wants me to play a special song on my flute when she and Mr. Matt get married."

"That's wonderful, Clarence. When are they getting married?" George asked.

The kid shrugged, "Don't know. Hope in a long time, cause I haven't learned it yet."

Matt grinned, "After school is out."

"Congratulations!" George said.

Elton poured Matt a cup of coffee, "These two just drove in a few minutes ago. They said the roads from South Dakota were a fright."

"They are and getting worse," Matt agreed.

Clarence looked at the social workers, "You guys should probably go now. It is snowing real hard, so you should leave right away!"

Miss Thomas's deep brown eyes twinkled, "Why I think you're trying to get rid of us?"

"You might get stuck in a snow bank," the little boy warned.

Elton handed Clarence a glass of milk, "We already told them if it gets too nasty out, they can sleep over."

Clarence looked at Elton like he had lost his mind and blurted out, "You mean you'd let them sleep in our house! With us?"

"They aren't exactly serial killers, Clarence," Andy laughed. "We have plenty of room and the weather is terrible."

Clarence looked to Matt for support, but he said, "You wouldn't want anything to happen to them, would you?"

Clarence dropped is head and mumbled, "No sir. They can sleep over. I hope it quits snowing."

George was stifling his laugh, "If we can possibly do it, we will go to Bismarck. Will that be okay?"

Clarence nodded, but just looked at his glass of milk. It had been a pretty good day, but it was getting lousy.

"We just have to see all the kids and your home. Then we will be on our way," Wendy assured him.

"Where is everyone?" Matt asked.

"Marly picked up Kitten to play with Miriam this morning. Clarissa went over to the Patch with Ginger and Maddie Lynn. They are helping Mo get Jeff's room ready. Jackson is working at the shop, Grandpa and Pockets are taking a nap and CJ and Charlie are over at Kevin's talking about the rabbit hutch. They were going to start building today, but because of the weather, Kevin is showing them what they need to write down in their ledger book to keep track of things."

George turned to the boy, "So Clarence, how are things going here?"

"Good. It is next good as Pine Ridge." Clarence squinted at the man, "We are coming back on that Memory Day. We are going to sleep over with Uncle Bear and plant flowers where we put my parents. I think we're going to plant some on Jackson's parents, too. Then, we are coming back here. The kids and me are going to live here. We like it here."

George said. "Could I ask you what you like about it?"

"We have lots of tiyospaye that are trusty. Besides, Clarissa has to take care of her calf, Happy. CJ is the Chicken Man. He and Mr. Kevin are going to raise rabbits. They got the wood for their rabbit cages. I think Mister and I are going to put the shingles on the roof. I have to earn my goats. I already got one, but I'm getting the other one. They are twins and want to be together. Mister is taking me fishing and he really wants me to go with him, so I can't leave. I promised him I would go with him. Then the next time, we are going with Harrington and his Dad. We are going to bring a dozen worms! Harrington already checked and I don't need a fishing license. Kitten has her ears and Clancy talks wars with Grandpa. So, no matter what you say, we're staying here. Even if you take us away, we'll come back. Our stuff is here and nobody has traded it away. We are staying."

George almost choked on his coffee, "I see you are very definite about that. I'm glad you like it here, but we have some other things to consider. How about school?"

"Clarissa loves her school, but don't ask her about it! She will talk until your ears break! CJ likes school because he hangs out with the guys. They are all weird, but they like each other. He was weird before, so it is good he can be weird here too."

"What about your school?" George asked.

"Mrs. Jessup is a really good teacher and I like her a lot. She is my friend too, and she is learning me how to read and help goat mommas with their babies. Mr. Matt is helping me get the library books. I'm going to read the whole library! Did you know that? I have already read nine books and have three more at home. Mr. Matt said that is a good start."

"That's great," the young man smiled. "Are things okay with the trouble you had when you got into a fight at school?"

"The principal told those guys not to do that again, and I hang out with Clark and some of the guys at recess. They are learning me basketball. I'm a good dribble guy, but I can't throw it in a basket yet. Harrington and Kevin are helping me practice. Those bad boys stay away from Ginger too, because we can blow our whistles if they kick at her."

"So you feel safe?"

"Oh yah, but I leave my library books at home. If I'm going to take them to Mrs. Jessup, I pick them up at home."

"Sounds like you have that all worked out. You seem to be real busy. What do you do all day?"

"I help with chores in the morning, ride the bus to school, sometimes take my cedar flute, come home and help Mr. Matt give Grandpa a ride in his car. Then we clean it up because Grandpa loves his Ford. And then I go over to Jessups for my job. I help milk the goats and cows. Miss Joallyn does too, if she gets home from working with Chatterbox in time. Did you know he has a great tool belt? And then somebody gives me a ride home for dinner. I practice my cedar flute and those notes with Miss Diane and sometimes we talk to Uncle Bear or Auntie Mable. Andy and Jackson are trying to learn me to play chest, but I don't do it so good. Then I take my bath. Did you know, these guys take baths all the time? I was worried my skin would wear out! But it's been okay, so far. Then some days I go to the library with Mr. Matt, or go to Harrington's to practice with our fishing poles, or I help Mr. Darrell with his saddles cause he is learning me how to take care of a horse for when Missus and I get our horse. She can't lift a saddle because a pig ate her arm, so we have to stay out of the pig pen; especially if they have babies. Did you know that I helped a momma goat have her babies? Miss Joallyn and I did it and Mr. Darrell helped us. That was so cool. Those are the babies I'm going to keep when I get enough money in my savings account. Miss Carrie got me my very own savings account. Do you have one?"

"Yes I do. I'm very glad that you do. Do you have a lot of money in it?"

"Not yet. I have a little bit and some in my piggy bank, but mostly I have been earning goats. Did you ever have a goat? I will have a boy and a girl. Clarissa's calf is a girl. Claudia has hearing aids. She sits by the piano when Miss Diane gives lessons. She gets lessons too! She likes that. Clancy has a wolf that Mister and me picked out. Next time we are getting him a fish because they don't howl!"

"So, if you are the quiet one, I can see why you don't think I should ask Clarissa about school!" George teased.

Clarence nodded, "She talks a bunch, so you should be careful. Mr. Matt said I should just tell you the truth; so that's what I did. I guess he forgot there was a lot of it."

"It sounds to me like everything is going rather well for you here," George smiled.

"Are you guys going now? Did I say enough stuff?"

Wendy giggled again, "Not yet. Sorry. We need to see the other kids."

"Oh. I guess that is okay, but I tell them what they want. So you only need to talk to me."

"Would it be okay if we talk to them too? We just want to see how they are doing."

"Yah, I s'pose."

Suddenly, there was an ear piercing howl from the other room and the social workers both jumped. Nora smiled, "That would be Clancy and his wolf howl."

Wendy raised her eyebrow, "I can see why you are considering giving him a fish!"

The little boy came toddling into the kitchen, carrying his afghan and his stuffed wolf. He went straight to Nora's lap, but never took his eyes off the visitors. Nora pulled him onto her lap, "Clancy, we have company. Can you say hi to Mr. Thunder and Miss Thomas?"

Clancy looked at them and then cuddled into Nora's lap. "That's okay, you can say hello later."

Grandma brought him some milk as Grandpa Lloyd came into the kitchen. He nodded at the group around the table and said, "Katherine, did you forget to tell me we had coffee?"

"I might have, Lloyd. Would you like some?"

"Does a duck swim?" he asked and then noticed the visitors. "So, I see you made it in from Duluth. Did you bring the seed corn? I ordered it last week. Keith can get it out of the truck."

"We came from South Dakota," George answered. "My name is George Thunder and this is my partner, Wendy Thomas. We came to see how the children are doing."

"Hm, you should keep your kids with you. It is not a good idea to let them walk so far away when they are little. They could get lost in the pasture. Elton, you tell them. They'll lose their kids! We keep our kids here. See, this is my little brother. Pockets sits in my chair with me so I don't lose him. Maybe you should get a bigger chair. Elton, tell them where you got that chair."

"I'll do that, Lloyd. Grandpa Lloyd and Clancy sit in their chair a lot and talk about the wars. Right?"

Lloyd nodded, "Smart kid. He gets a little mixed up about Eisenhower and Montgomery, but he is getting better. Do you know about them?"

George nodded, "Only a little. You're an expert, huh?"

"A guy shouldn't toot his own horn, but I know more than that encyclopedia," Lloyd answered modestly.

"Then Clancy has a good teacher."

"He can't whittle, though. I worry about that. Folks think better when they whittle."

Katherine interrupted, "Clancy is too little to whittle, Lloyd!"

Grandpa crossed his eyes and looked at George, "She can be such an old crank, but she is a good wife; even if she is short."

George chuckled, "She seems like a wonderful wife."

Grandpa frowned, "Get your own wife."

"I'll do that," George laughed.

The phone rang and it was Kevin. He called to say that he was picking up Kitten at Ellisons when he took Charlie home. Then they were coming over to the farmhouse. Carrie and Holly were coming too, and they were going to stay overnight since the forecast was bad for the night.

After he hung up, Matt looked out the window. "You know, I am going to go down and help Jackson come up to the house. Then I better head home too. It is going to be a fright doing chores tonight."

"I'll be ready to go when you come up with Jackson," Clarence said.

"You know, maybe tonight you shouldn't help. Joallyn and Josh are both at Darrell's, so we have help. You don't want to get snowed in there."

Clarence's face fell, "But I need some more hours to earn for Hansel."

"You can earn them tomorrow, but it is up to your Dad."

Clarence turned to Elton, "Mister, what do you think?"

"You could get snowed in there, you know? Would you mind being snowed in away from the other kids?"

Clarence thought, "They would probably get weird, huh? But I want to earn Hansel."

"You will soon enough," Elton assured him. "Besides, who is going to help me if Grandpa wanders?"

"Oh yah, huh?" Clarence nodded. "I should call Mr. Darrell and tell him. Okay?"

"I'll dial for you," Grandma offered.

"I'll go down and get Horse while you decide," Matt said.

It took almost half an hour for Matt and Jackson to manage the wheelchair through the snowdrifts. "Boy, there is a humungous drift piling up between here and the shop," Jackson explained as he came in the kitchen.

Grandma poured him some coffee and then they told Matt goodbye. Clarence hugged him and asked, "Will you tell Hansel and Gretel that I will be there soon? Tell Hansel I will get him earned as soon as I can."

"I'll let him know, Clarence." Matt assured the little guy.

Matt shook hands with the social workers and said, "If you want to talk to the boys' teachers, I'm certain that they would talk to you on the phone."

"We might do that, but we do have their school records. It seems they have been steadily improving," Wendy smiled at the boys. "I think we have a good idea how it is going. Mrs. Frandsen and Mrs. Jessup have sent us weekly updates. They have been very thorough. I wish other folks would give us half the information."

"Well, we are partial to those two," Matt smiled. "They are the best."

As Matt was leaving, Kevin drove in. Kev decided that before he put the car away, he would go over to the Patch and get the other kids.

George listened to their conversation and then suggested, "I'd like to come along, if you don't mind. It seems the children have a large extended family, and it would be nice to meet as many of them as I can. Would that be okay?"

"Of course," Elton grinned. "You are welcome too, Wendy. The Patch is like the day care for the entire clan. Carl and Mo do a fine job with the kids. You really should see it."

"Sounds interesting," Wendy said. "Will there be room?"

"We can pack in," Kevin said. "It's only across the road."

Everyone unloaded at Kincaid's house. Elton looked at the social workers, "You are staying until this storm lets up."

George nodded, "Sounds like we have little choice."

"It won't be that bad," Elton chuckled. "Now, I have to warn you. Carl Kincaid is a windbag, but he means well."

Mo opened the door, "Well Lordie be, look Coot! We have a pile of folks here! Come on in and we'll get some coffee for you!"

Elton introduced them all while CJ and Clarence decided to go take care of the ducks. Elton heard them, "Wait, boys. We'll go with you and get it done in no time. We need to get everyone in their proper nest while we can still travel."

Carl greeted the social workers, "Glad to meet you. I hope Elton hasn't bored you with all his jabber. He tends to do that."

Wendy giggled, "Not at all."

"We thought we'd go out and help you with the ducks. Did you put up guide lines to the coops?" Elton asked.

"Sure did, but you can help. Ian and Ruthie are coming down to stay here during the storm. Matt just called and said he made it home. Guess their yard is a mess. I can imagine," Carl said. "So, let's go do the ducks before you take your coats off."

With Kev, CJ, Clarence, Elton and George; it took about five minutes to get it all finished.

"They are looking pretty good," Elton acknowledged.

"I probably have my Little Ducksters to thank for that," Carl said as he tousled CJ's hair. "This crew has been definitely upgraded when the Grey Hawks came into the mix. Fine youngsters. They are a great addition to the Gopher Brigade."

George shook his head, "I'm sorry. I didn't follow."

Clarence took George's hand, "Don't worry, Mr. Thunder. These guys are nice, but they don't talk regular. Mrs. Coot talks about these lepperkahn things. You just smile. She is really nice even if you can't understand her."

"Thanks, Clarence," George smiled. "I'll keep that in mind."

In the house, Wendy was getting the grand tour of the Patch. She was fascinated by the cubes in the Gopher room and all the little cots, tables and even a special ordered flush potty chair toilet. "I've never seen one of these before. It is fantastic."

"Carl found one in a plumbing catalogue and just had to have it! He said it is ridiculous to expect a small child to learn to control his bladder while he is balanced over a pool of water!" Mo explained. "Wait 'til the men get in and Carl can show you our tornado shelter."

Clarissa had been listening to the whole conversation, "Miss Wendy, if there is a storm we can go whoosh! It is really cool, butcept there hasn't been a tornado yet!"

"Do you enjoy being here at the Patch?"

"It is almost the mostest funnest, butcept for Kindergarten. I like my house too, with my new Mommy and Daddy. They are pretty nice and I love Miss Diane. We are good buddies and she learned me how to curtsy for when I meet the queen."

Wendy smiled, "Are you going to meet the queen soon?"

The little girl didn't flinch, "When the weather is better. It is a long ways to drive to her house. If you learn to curtsy, maybe I can ask Miss Diane if you can come with."

"Not necessary, but you ask someone to take a picture to send to me. Okay?"

"Okay, Miss Diane has a new Instamatic camera. I will tell her to take a picture. She calls it a snapshot."

"That would be wonderful."

There was a knock at the door and Harrington and Ruthie came in without waiting for someone to answer the door. Mo introduced her son and daughter-in-law to Wendy. "So you are the Harrington that Clarence said is teaching him to fish?"

"Yes," Ian Harrington grinned, "That would be me. He is a good kid, and is picking up that casting very well. He is helping me practice with my lame arm. We have big plans. We are going to be fishing machines before the summer is over!"

"Will the other kids get to fish too?" Wendy asked.

"Sure, but his first trip is going to be special; just Elton and him. I guess his real dad never had time to take him, so that is their deal. The rest of us can wait, but that is important to both of them. CJ is going to come along on the next trips, if he wants."

"What about me? Nobody ever asked me to do fishing?" Clarissa pouted. "That is cause I'm a girl."

Harrington gave her a little frown, "I didn't know you wanted to go. If you do, you can sure come along."

"I don't want to see stinky fish or icky worms or sit in a boat and be quiet, but I might like to go fishing," Clarissa pointed out emphatically.

"We'll see what we can do," Harrington grinned. "Maybe you could be on the shore with Ruthie and have our picnic lunch ready when we get off the boat."

"Could we, Miss Ruthie? Wouldn't that be the coolest?"

"It sounds like fun, Clarissa. We'll have to plan a good lunch for them."

"I can't wait to tell Clarence!" Clarissa gloated, "He'll be huffy selfish about it!"

"Miss Clarissa, you little Leprachaun!" Mo interceded. "We don't condone any mischief here at the Patch. Trouble seems to come about easy enough. So, don't taunt your brother about it."

"Yes, Mrs. Coot. I won't be taunting," the little girl promised. Suddenly her eyes lit up, "Can I bug him a little?"

"Nope, but that was a good try," Mo chuckled. "I'm a-thinking he will get bent all by him own self. You don't need to help him."

Clarissa covered her mouth and laughed, "He'll have to sleep on it."

After a tour of the storm shelter and the slide to get to it, George announced he wanted to put one in his house. "That is a good idea. You could move a lot of kids fast. My only concern would be it they got the door opened to the slide when there was no storm."

CJ looked at George seriously, "We would get five to ten in the slammer without parole!"

George was shocked, "What?"

Mo chuckled, "That is just Coot's FBI talk. He is always telling the kids that stuff. My word, the little tykes were tattling on each other with 'grand theft auto' when they had a squabble over some toy cars! Pay him no mind."

"Kids need to learn the facts," Carl explained. "If they don't know the rules, how can they can figure out how to play? Right?"

George laughed, "I guess that makes sense."

52

The group returned to the Schroeder farmhouse about four. They decided to go out and get the chores done before the weather got any worse. It had been decided the social workers would spend the night, so their car was put in the garage. Zach called when he arrived home, and said the road was almost impassable north of Bismarck where it was closed. The officials were putting up the highway barricades right after Zach passed through. It took him almost two hours from Midway to Merton. It was a fright, but the forecast said the storm should be over by Sunday afternoon.

George went to the barn with the milkers, but Wendy decided to stay in. Clarissa and Diane could have stayed in, but went out to help with chores, because they always did. When Elton tried to convince Clarissa it was too stormy out there for her, she said, "But it isn't too stormy for the boys! If they can go, I can go."

"Honey, the wind will blow you away!"

"Not if you hold on to me, Daddy. Then I can see my Happy calf. You said I was 'sponsible for her. Please?"

Elton frowned, "Okay, but bundle up good, hold on tight and I'm tying you on to the guide line. It is awful out there."

Wendy visited with the ladies and spent time with Claudia and Clancy. They played together and Wendy looked over the medical records for both of them. She was pleased with how well they were doing.

Then she spent a great deal of time visiting with Jackson. She was very impressed with his sketches. "We were all so worried about you after the wake. You were so ill."

"A person couldn't have a better place than here to heal up," Jackson answered. "Zach, the doctor, lives right across the fence and stops over on his way to work. Then Andy's wife, Annie, and Marty are paramedics. They take care of us all the time. I know I would've been done for several times over, if it wasn't for these people. They are the best."

"There is something that I have a concern about. I think it is okay, but I need to check. Is there a lot of prejudice because you are Indian?"

"None. In fact, I've got into trouble for using being an Indian as an excuse. That doesn't fly around here. They know that there is prejudice, but Elton and Byron say you are what YOU are. You shouldn't let other people tell you what or who you are. They are supportive, but don't hesitate to tell you the facts if you get off kilter. Trust me. My dear little Grandma has grabbed me by the ear, more than once! That is scary!"

"Yes, the dainty lady seems very frightening," Wendy giggled.

"No one wants to be on her bad side! Self-pity leads to starched underwear pretty darned fast!"

"Seriously Jackson, how do you think the kids are doing? We were quite concerned because Schroeder's are older than most of our Foster Parents. But the kids all seem happy, but what is your assessment?"

"You might not understand our home. Nora and Elton are our parents and Grandma and Grandpa are our Grandparents. But we also have all sorts of family, of every age. We all do things for and with each other. The kids have little friends to play with and lots of other adults of every age. We all do things with everyone. And if something would happen to Schroeders, there isn't a clanner around that wouldn't step in and take the kids.

"I feel almost guilty saying this, but that car accident was almost the best thing that ever happened for them. I never knew they could be so happy. Of course, they act like boneheads sometimes and get bent out of shape; but for the most part, I've never seen them happier.

"Clarissa is like in a world she never knew existed before. She must have craved having a woman to look up to. She follows Diane everywhere and copies almost everything she does. She loves Nora and Kate, Pastor Byron's daughter, and wants to be like them. But, she also has friends her age at school and now thinks she wants to be a teacher when she grows up.

"Claudia is coming out of her shell. With the hearing aids, she is developing an interest in stuff. But even before she got them, her friendship with Miriam has made her laugh, play and giggle. I'd never seen that little girl do anything but watch before.

"Clancy. Well, I'm not sure about that. He really likes Annie, Andy's wife and he loves Grandpa. But those two, I worry about. Grandpa tells Clancy about some battle and Clancy shouts, "Iwo Jima!" Grandpa says, "Good, Pockets!" Then they pat each other on the back like they have found some great truth! They are both goofy."

Wendy smiled, "What about you, Jackson?"

"I love it here. I loved my parents, but this is my home. These people have accepted me and shown me more of the world than I ever imagined existed. What they have done for the kids is unbelievable; unless you know the clan. It is so them. We all are part of that . . . to be helped or to be the helper. It is all expected."

"Are you planning on going back to Pine Ridge?"

"I wouldn't even consider it until the kids are grown. But I doubt I will then. I know someday I'll get my artificial foot and get my own place, but this is my home. Andy is like having a brother. Matt and Diane have been great friends to me and Kate. They even took us to a piano concert! Can you imagine, a 'Skin' going to see a concert pianist? But they never flinched. Matt is the best. He helps me with my sketches and all that."

"Kate?"

Jackson blushed, "Ah, yes. She is Pastor Byron's teenaged daughter."

"Do I see traces of Cupid?"

"That would be too soon, but I really like her and she does me, too. She was at the wake. Matt and Diane brought her and Grandma down there."

"Oh, I remember her. The blonde girl? She is very pretty."

"Yes, she is and it would be hard to find a kinder person. I'll show you the bead work that she does. She is working on three wedding dresses right now and has one over here, so she can use Grandma's dress form. Come, let me show you."

Jackson took Wendy to the sewing room and with pride, showed her the dress Katie was working on.

"It is beautiful," Wendy smiled. "She is very talented. I hope I get to meet her."

They went to the dining room and helped the ladies set the table for dinner. "This is a magnificent dining room! I have never seen such a big one in a private home!" Wendy exclaimed.

Nora looked around the large room, "It has been a blessing. For years, our family got together for Sunday dinner after the last service at Trinity. We would either go to Ellisons or our place. As the clan got bigger, we sort of settled here, because we had more room to expand. The guys used to haul the folding tables and chairs up the basement steps! Finally, when Zach came to the clan, the kids decided that we should do this. There used to be an enormous, rarely used screened in porch here. They enclosed it and turned it all into dining room. Now, no more moving tables! It holds five tables of twelve each with room for one more. Then I suppose we will be hauling folding tables again."

"My goodness! Sixty people? What is this clan anyway?"

Grandma Katherine explained, "My husband and I always wanted a large family but we only had one son. When Frankie was killed in Korea, we thought we would be childless. But Lloyd never gave up. He said God would give us the family He wanted us to have. Honestly, I thought he was bats, but he was right. A few years later, Byron and Elton came into our world. Nothing has been the same since. They are our family and their friends are part of our family, too. The kids call themselves the Engelmann Clan, because this used to be our house and because Lloyd thinks they are all his relatives. We have truly been blessed because this is the best group of folks in the world. A little nutty, and not conventional, but our family just the same."

"That is fascinating. So, you all go to the Lutheran church?"

"No, we have Catholics and non-church goers, too. Several of the clan are Catholic. Some are relatives, some were friends and some just happened, but everyone has a special place in the clan. We are like the Three Musketeers: one for all and all for one."

Jackson laughed, "More like the Thirty Musketeers! Like I was telling you, Wendy, we're all in it together. Even though we are here for each other when things are bad, we have a lot of fun, too. Which reminds me, did we decide what we are going to do for Vicaro, Kitten and Elton's birthday?"

Carrie answered, "I talked to Aunt Gilda and we can have the barn. Uncle Bill and the Boys will play, so we can have a barn dance. She is just waiting for me to call back. It would have to be the 17th or 18th, since that is the Friday and Saturday. What do you all think? Then one birthday cake? I had thought we could talk about it tomorrow, but I doubt the clan will make it here tomorrow."

"No, it doesn't look like it. I imagine tomorrow everyone will be home polishing their snow shovels!" Andy stated as he put the plates around the table. "Does anyone have any ideas what to get these people for presents? We have Kitten's already, but those other two!!!"

Carrie laughed, "Kev and I are going to get Father Vicaro a Hercule Poirot mystery book by Agatha Christie. We thought we could get him started on them. He's read every Sherlock Holmes ever published. I talked to Sister Abigail. She kept a list and thinks he has them all. So, we are going to start on Poirot. Christie published thirty-three books about him, so we thought that would keep him going for a while."

Nora listened, "Good idea. Is Abigail keeping a list of them too?"

"Not that I know of. I guess we should though. We would hate to get them mixed up, huh?"

"Good job for you, Carrie," Andy chuckled.

"Or you! You can start with ours. We are getting him *Mystery of the Spanish Chest*."

"Okay, I'll do that. Spread the word, but I need suggestions for Dad. What are we going to get him? Any ideas, Mom?"

"You know your Dad. He wants his family to be happy."

"Oh good grief, of course he does! Who doesn't? You can't put that in a gift box! He is impossible!" Carrie frowned.

Nora laughed, "You're right, but that really is what he wants. He is very happy that Diane and Matt are on a good path now, and that the veterans are recovering. He is pleased that Kitten's hearing is improving and things seem well with the other kids. I guess there isn't much pending except to get the Grey Hawks adopted if that is what they want. So, other than that, June berry pie and a good polka will about cover it!"

"Yea gads," Andy groaned. "I am NOT doing a polka with him!"

"Nor would he want you to!" Jackson confirmed. "Does he really want to adopt the kids? He never said anything about it."

"I know. He figured they've had enough going on for right now. Oh my, Wendy! I'm so sorry." Nora stopped short. "We shouldn't have been talking about this in front of you. Please accept our apologies. We forgot ourselves. We don't even have custody yet and here we are jabbering like it is a done deal."

Wendy smiled, "Not a problem. It pretty much is. Of course, we have to go through all the channels, but everything looks excellent. In fact, George and I were rather certain about it before we even got here. Except for Clarence's problems at school, everything has been great. From what the school says, that situation has been resolved. I don't know how the kids would feel about adoption, but they all seem rather confident that they will be here for the foreseeable future."

"Matt confided to me that Clarence thinks that Elton doesn't want to adopt him because he never asked him." Jackson said, "You know, Clarence feels a strong loyalty to his real Dad. But between us, he is closer to Mister than he ever was to his Dad. His Dad was loyal to the bottle, and that makes it difficult to compete. I know Mom and I were a lot closer until she started drinking so much. A person can't even talk to them, let alone make any sense of what do they say."

"I know. It is a bearcat," Nora agreed. "I know we'd be pleased if the kids would get baptized into our faith; but that is our desire. I don't know how the kids feel about it."

"I do," Jackson said. "Except for Claudia and Clancy, they all like the church. They can still believe in the Sioux religion and be Lutheran, too. I have thought about getting baptized myself, but I would feel rather silly. I'm too old."

Nora shook her head, "Elton was fifty when he was baptized."

"You're kidding!" Jackson said. "I guess I'm not too old."

Carrie sat down, "I have an idea. How about, on Dad's birthday which is a Sunday, we get the whole shooting match baptized! I think Dad would love it, the kids would love it and we won't have to get him a present!"

Andy snorted a laugh, "I almost thought you were being nice there for a minute! You're such a jerk, but it is a good idea! Mom, can we plan this without Dad finding out?"

"Probably. I'll need your help, Jackson. Since you work over at the church, maybe you could help me. Besides, they're your Steps. You know them and what they want. What do you say?"

Jackson became very quiet and then answered, "I will talk to the kids and then Pastor Byron. I don't want to say for certain right now. Is that okay?"

Nora hugged him, "That is great. We don't want to rush you at all. It is far too important to do that. So, we all best be thinking of a contingency plan anyway. Some other gift . . . . like striped pajamas!"

Andy crossed his eyes, "You guys are just plain weird."

The Swiss steak, mashed potatoes and gravy dinner was delicious. Grandpa was in a good mood and kept trying to convince George that he should marry Wendy instead of Katherine. "She is a good wife, and I know you like her; but she is too old for you. You'll do better with a younger gal. This Wendy is just right, and she has a good smile. You can always tell, you know. She smiles at the right places!"

"Right places?"

"Yah, you know she doesn't smile when people are making fun of someone else, but when things are good and happy. That is important. She will be good for you."

"But we have never been on a date!" George chuckled.

"So? Better ask her. All you need to do is buy a cow and then ask her to marry you. That's all."

George busted out laughing, "What about her?"

"She doesn't have to buy a cow."

"That's good to know," Wendy giggled. "I wouldn't have a place to keep one."

"Elton might help you out. Right, Elton?"

"Lloyd, settle down," Katherine said. "Mind your own business."

Lloyd stared at her, and then turned to George, "I guess you can have her after all."

That evening was quiet, except for the wind outside. The weather got worse and everyone was feeling rather warm, comfy and secure in the house. Clarissa and Carrie showed Wendy how to bead and Diane played piano for them. Clarence played a little on his pipe and Grandpa really liked that.

"I don't think I know the words to that song, but I like it. You know, you're a pretty smart brother. It is good that you make music with your pipe and don't smoke it, like Elton. That's why he is so short."

Elton frowned, "You smoke pipe, too. What are you talking about?"

"I would have been way too tall, so I had to smoke. I wouldn't have been able to make it through the door!"

Kevin and CJ were looking through the book on rabbits and making plans for their rabbit business. Jackson and Andy were playing chess and High Pockets was having his bath. Afterwards, Nora brought him out to say goodnight to everyone. The little toddler gave everyone a hug and then told Grandpa, "Iwo Jima!"

Grandpa nodded, "That's my boy!"

Pockets grinned and then went off to his crib. Grandma suggested that Grandpa get his rest too, but he said he was hungry. "I didn't get a treat tonight. Where is my hot fudge sundae?"

"You know," Elton grinned, "That is a good idea. I'll get the ice cream."

So Nora made hot fudge, Carrie and Elton dished up the ice cream and they had their treat. Nora reminded the kids that they'd better brush their teeth very well before they went to bed. As they finished their sundaes, George said, "Well, we will discuss it tonight and should be able to give you a definite answer in the morning on if the kids can stay."

"Okay," Elton said. "Guess that's fair, but it would be nice if you could just tell us now."

That night, the wind blew, the shingles rattled and the temperature dropped. It was miserably cold out, well below zero, but still struggling to snow. They were no longer flakes, but more like ice pellets.

Wendy had the girl's room and George was in the boy's room. They had visited for a bit about the report they would turn in and then Wendy went to bed. George wasn't tired, so he decided to work on the report before he went to bed. He was about half way through writing it, when he realized that he needed a paper that he had left in his jacket pocket. He headed down to the mudroom to get it.

53

Elton felt someone patting his cheek frantically and opened his eyes. "What is it, CJ?" he asked as he sat up in bed.

"It's Clarence. I can't find him. I woke up to pull on the blankets, but he wasn't there. I started to go to the kitchen, but it was dark and I didn't like it. Should I go again?"

Elton reached for his bathrobe, "No CJ, I'll go. You did the very best thing. Don't you worry. You go back to bed, okay? I will get him. Did he say anything?"

"He said he was going to think and told me to go back to sleep. That's all. I know he was worried we'd be taken to that foster place. Now he is gone!"

"It will be okay, I'm pretty sure. Get your rest and I will let you know as soon as I find him. Shall I tuck you in?"

"No, I can. You go find him, Dad. He's a pretty good brother."

"Yah, he is at that," Elton kissed CJ's head.

Elton went down the hall and checked in Grandpa's room. He was in bed and asleep. That was a relief, but also a puzzle. Clarence rarely got up unless Grandpa was wandering.

He went into the kitchen and there was no sign of the little boy. The Pa Alarm was shut off and the light in the mudroom was on. Elton frowned and opened the door. There he found the mudroom door to the outside open and whipping back and forth wildly. There was no sign of the child, but his jacket was missing; as was his overshoes. Elton panicked.

He ran back into the house and called for Kevin. George was on the stairs and came down. Elton told the gathering people what he knew and ran to put his jeans on. CJ began crying in the hallway and was soon joined by Clarissa. Jackson was beside himself and was trying to console the Steps. Andy was consoling Jackson. "He will never survive outside in this weather. Oh my God, what happened? Why did he go outside?"

Diane, Carrie and Kevin dressed and were getting their coats on. "Why would he go outside?" Kevin asked.

"I know," Diane said. "He told Matt that he couldn't stand it that some of them might have to go away. It made him feel like upping it, so he wanted to just run away. Matt told him not to worry, but you know Clarence. He always has to think."

"I know where he went," Elton said.

Kevin caught his glance, "His thinking spot. At least it is under a yard light. Think he could find it?"

"Let's go look," Elton determined. "We need to tie ourselves together. I don't want anyone else getting lost."

"I'm coming along," Jackson said.

"Don't be stupid. You are on crutches! You and Andy stay here and keep an eye on the kids. You have a job and getting stranded out there is not one of them. Hear me?" Elton took charge. "Let's go."

"Me, too," Wendy said as she joined the group.

They all tied themselves together and went out into the black swirling night. George managed to fall down the bottom step, but Carrie helped him regain his footing. They headed off in the direction of Clarence's outhouse.

They spread out as far apart as they could and kept calling his name, but could see nothing. Their frantic cries were carried away in the wind. It was thankfully dark enough so that the yard light next to the outhouse served as a cloudy beacon, but the snow was caking on their faces making it nearly impossible to keep their eyes open.

They fell, stumbled and trudged toward the outhouse. It must have taken them forty minutes to find the building, and that was only because Kevin unwittingly bumped into it. It took him a few minutes to get the door open in the large drift that was accumulating in front of the door.

Inside the old outhouse, the small flashlight was on. Elton found the little boy curled up in the corner. He picked him up and said, "Clarence? Clarence! Say something! Are you okay? Please say you're okay?"

There was nothing. Elton sat on the bench of the outhouse with the boy while Kevin and George started rubbing on his arms and legs. Elton was talking to him steady, "Come on son, just be okay! Please God, let him be okay! Clarence! Clarence, say something."

Finally, there was a groan. Only a groan, but it was the most beautiful sound those folks have ever heard. Kevin said, "Thank God, he is still alive! Let's get him in the house."

The group bundled him into Kevin's jacket and then helped Kevin walk. Together they trudged back toward the house, slipping and falling all the way.

When the exhausted rescuers finally made it to the mudroom, the folks in the kitchen opened the door anxiously. Nora fearfully looked at Elton, "Is he alive?"

"Yes, Mom. Our boy is alive. Let's get him warmed up."

Jackson helped unwrap his brother and then held his limp body in his arms. "Come on Clarence, don't give up. Hear me?"

CJ was rubbing on his back and crying. Then Grandma instructed them to lay him down and she and Nora wrapped warm towels around him. Everyone stood there mesmerized and speechless. While Andy and Jackson helped warm him, Kevin began to recite the Lord's Prayer. Soon, they were all saying it.

It took a few minutes, but the child began to move. Then he opened his eyes, "Mister, I just went to think."

Elton held him tight, "I know, son. I'm so glad you are okay. You really scared us. Don't ever go out into a storm again. Hear me?"

"I hear," the boy mumbled.

Elton cried and Kevin held his father. "It is okay now, Dad. Just relax. Okay? Grandma has some coffee."

Elton sat down, "I should have taken more time to talk to him, but I thought he was doing okay. I felt everything was okay. Why didn't I know he was so worried?"

"Dad," a little voice said as CJ came up beside him, "Clarence didn't want anybody to know. He told me to keep it a secret, but he was going to talk to that sheep guy about letting us kids stay here. I should have tattled, but I didn't think he'd go outside."

Elton gathered him up into his lap, "You didn't know that he was going to do that, CJ. It wasn't your fault."

CJ put his arms around Elton and gave him a big hug. The embrace was the best thing for both of them. Then Clarissa said, "Mommy, will Clarence be fun again or are we going to have to put him in the ground?"

Nora gave her a hug while she held Kitten on her lap, "I think he'll be okay, Sweetheart. He is warming up now. Don't worry."

"Dad?" the little boy asked, "Is my Dad here?"

Jackson looked worried, "Do you think he is delirious?"

Kevin shrugged and Elton said to CJ, "Mind if I put you down now? I want to check on your brother."

CJ nodded and Kevin scooped him up. Elton moved over to the boy who was beginning to be in pain, "Clarence, I'm here for you. What do you need? I'm here."

Clarence looked at Elton and asked, "Can you hold me on your lap?"

Elton said, "Of course."

"I just went out for a minute, but I couldn't get the door open again after I talked to the sheep. Then I got scareder and really cold."

"I understand, Clarence. Promise me that you'll never go out into a storm again unless someone knows where you are. Have I got your word?"

"Yes, you have my forever word."

After a bit, Elton was able to rock the boy who was wrapped up in a blanket. Everyone else had gone to bed again, although Clarissa had decided to sleep with Diane and Claudia had crawled in with Nora. Andy said that CJ could sleep with him and Clancy, of course, slept with his wolf.

Grandma picked up the kitchen and stopped by the living room on the way back to bed. "And we are always so worried about Lloyd walking off. Little did we think our Clarence would."

She reached down and kissed his forehead, "I love you, Clarence."

"I love you too, Grandma," he replied.

George came into the living room behind Grandma and said, "Thank God, it all ended well. It could have been a disaster."

Elton looked at him with worry, "Will this mess up your approval? I mean, do you think we are careful enough take care of the children?"

George smiled and put his arm on Elton's shoulder, "This was as much our fault as anyone else's. We shouldn't have scared you folks so, especially the little ones. He wouldn't have had to worry, if he knew he would be able to stay. I see no reason that we'd move them from here."

"That's a relief," Grandma said. Then she gave George a hug, and went off to bed.

George watched until she left the room and then sat on the sofa next to the rocker, "Elton, may I ask a question?"

"Sure."

"Who is this sheep guy you guys are talking about?"

Elton smiled, "Jesus. You know, the 'Lamb of God'. Clarence calls Him a sheep."

George chuckled, "I hope he figures it out we can talk to Jesus in the house."

"I think he has now," Elton agreed. Then he held out his hand to the man, "Thanks George. I have to admit, I was very worried too."

"No need to be. This is a good family and I'm sure the children will do well here."

"You mean, we get to stay?" a weak little voice asked as Clarence moved his head so he could see the man.

"Yes Clarence. You get to stay. I think you found a good home."

"I do, too. We are glad we gave Mister a chance."

"I'm glad too. Goodnight now."

As George went up the stairs, he looked back at the man rocking the boy. This was one placement he had no doubts about.